"You're probably going to think I'm crazy."

She took a deep breath. "Her husband told me that she killed herself on Christmas Eve."

"Oh, God. I'm sorry," said Grant.

Isabelle pulled herself together before any tears fell, which made Grant want to hug her.

"After finding out about Linda's suicide, it took me a while to find the courage to look up Sam to see why his card also came back. He's dead, too. Gunshot to the head." Tears sparkled in her eyes, making them glow a vibrant green. "Then a few weeks ago, my friend Beverly slit her wrists. I found her body, Grant."

Grant pried her hands from her empty mug and held her chilly fingers in his. He feared the worst—that those deaths had put the idea of suicide in her head, too.

He modulated his voice so it was calm and even. "Tell me what's going on. I can help."

Hope brightened her eyes. "You believe me? No one else does."

"Believe what?"

"I don't think they killed themselves, Grant. I think they were murdered."

Please turn this page for raves for Shannon K. Butcher's previous novels.

Also by Shannon K. Butcher

No Regrets

No Control

No Escape

Shannon K. Butcher

FOREVER

NEW YORK   BOSTON

Cover design by Dale Fiorillo
Cover photo by Gabriel Moisa

Forever
Hachette Book Group USA
237 Park Avenue
New York, NY 10017
Visit our Web site at www.HachetteBookGroupUSA.com

Forever is an imprint of Grand Central Publishing. The Forever name and logo is a trademark of Hachette Book Group USA, Inc.

Printed in the United States of America

First Printing: October 2008

10 9 8 7 6 5 4 3 2 1

For my son, who will probably never read any of my girlie books. If you weren't so awesomely supportive and independent, I never would have had the time or energy to pursue writing. Mom loves you, Monkey.

ACKNOWLEDGMENTS

I'd like to thank all of the people who helped make this book better than I ever could have alone: Nephele Tempest, Michele Bidelspach, Sara Attebury, Dyann Barr, Julie Fedynich, Sherry Foley, and Liz Lafferty. Thanks, ladies. I know this was a tough one.

And, as always, I want to thank my husband, Jim Butcher, for his boundless support and his putting up with all my yammering about my stories.

No
Escape

PROLOGUE

❖

Beverly Sinclair had finally done it. After years of working to get her life on track, she finally had a decent job, a great husband, and the smartest, most beautiful baby boy ever born. He was only three weeks old, but she was certain he was destined for great things.

She could hardly wait to show Cory off to her friend Isabelle.

The doorbell rang five minutes early, but that was just like Isabelle. She was never late a day in her life.

Beverly rushed to the door, filled with a proud, maternal excitement she'd never known existed before Cory was born. Isabelle was going to love him.

She swung the heavy wooden door open, wearing a welcoming smile.

A masked man rushed forward, pushing her inside before she had time to react. His weight slammed into her, knocking her against the wall.

Shock jolted through her, making it hard to breathe. A scream formed in her mind, but that was as far as it got. Her lungs heaved, filling with air scented by a faint hint of men's cologne.

He kicked the door shut behind him with a final, sickening thud.

From the nursery, Beverly heard the squeaky beginnings of her baby's cry.

She had to get Cory out of the house. Run away.

Panic flooded her body with strength, and she shoved hard against her attacker. She let out a cry of outrage that made her throat burn with its ferocity.

The man rocked back on his heels enough that Beverly was able to slip out of his reach, but her freedom didn't last long. He grabbed a fistful of her hair and yanked her back, catching her before she fell.

She saw a flash of silver out of the corner of her eye and turned toward it, praying it wasn't a knife even as she brought her arms up to protect herself from a slashing blade. But the man held a small aerosol can in his gloved hand. Something wet and cold hit her face as a sharp medicinal stench filled her nose. Her body crumpled like rag doll, and her captor's arms tightened around her, keeping her from hitting the hard tile floor.

Beverly tried to move, but her body didn't respond. She could see and hear perfectly, but nothing else worked. Her arms and legs buzzed for a moment, then went numb. She couldn't move. She couldn't even twitch.

The man settled her gently to the floor. "We can't have you bruised," he said in a clinical tone. "That would ruin everything."

A thick, suffocating fear settled over Beverly. She had no idea what he meant by that, but it couldn't be good. Not for her. Not for her baby.

Cory let out an angry wail, giving away his presence in the next room.

Beverly struggled to move something—her arm, her finger—anything.

A hoarse moan floated up from her chest, but it was all she could manage, and even that wasn't loud enough to be heard in the next room, much less by her neighbors.

The man smoothed her hair away from her face and leaned over her so she could see right into his bright blue eyes. "Everything's going to be okay. You'll see. I'm going to take good care of you."

Helplessness made it hard to breathe, impossible to think.

He left her there, lying on the floor, struggling to make a movement or sound. Only the knowledge that Isabelle would be here at any minute kept her sane. Isabelle would save her.

She heard water running in the bathroom. The antique clock on the wall bonged, telling her it was two. Isabelle would be stepping through the door at any second.

Cory's cries got louder. Maybe the neighbors would hear him.

Please, let them hear him.

The man came out of the bathroom and hovered over her. It made him look huge. Monstrous. He was a giant black shadow ready to devour her.

"We don't have much time. Let's get you out of those clothes."

Beverly's heart gave a hard, fearful kick. She struggled not to panic. She had to stay calm for her baby and get him out of this any way she could.

The man picked her up as if she weighed nothing and carried her into the bathroom. The air felt warm and humid, and she heard a drip of water landing in the tub.

A tingling sensation began along the bottom of her feet, and hopeful excitement made her break out in a cold sweat. Maybe whatever he'd done to paralyze her was wearing off.

The man unbuttoned her blouse. "This would be faster without the gloves, but we wouldn't want to leave any fingerprints behind, would we?"

He stripped the shirt off her body and reached around her to unfasten her bra. A new kind of panic found its way to the surface as Beverly realized that he might be here to rape her.

Then again, if that was all he wanted and he left Cory alone, she'd count herself fortunate.

He continued stripping her clothes away, talking to her in a calm voice. "I have too much work to do. Too many people to help."

A warm, buzzing sensation worked its way up her legs, and she began to get the feeling back in her hands, too. As much as she wanted to fight him, she remained still, not letting him know that she could move. Surprise was the only advantage she might have, and she didn't want to give it up.

She still wore her stretchy maternity pants because they were more comfortable, and he slid them and her panties down and off her legs without any trouble. He didn't even look at her naked body. There was no hint of lust in his eyes, only clinical detachment as he lifted her into the bathtub.

Warm water sloshed around her as he arranged her limp arms along the sides to hold her head up.

Beverly lay there, naked. Helpless. She cringed every

time he touched her, barely restraining the urge to jerk away from him.

Cory was screaming his little head off in the next room, and she silently willed him to quiet down. To not draw attention to himself.

Where the hell was Isabelle? She was never late, unlike Beverly, who was late so often her husband had set every clock in the house fifteen minutes fast.

Oh, God.

Isabelle wasn't due for another ten minutes, at least. A lot could happen in ten minutes. Too much.

The man left the bathroom. His heavy footsteps moved down the hall toward her son's room.

Cory stopped crying. What had he done to her baby?

Beverly panicked and tried to crawl out of the tub. Her limbs thrashed around clumsily, making water spill over the side. She lost her precarious balance and slipped under the water. A scream tore out of her throat and water rushed up her nose, choking her.

She was not going to drown. Not while her son was out there with that maniac.

Her lungs burned as she tried to push her head above water on weak arms. She slipped twice more before she was finally strong enough to break the water and draw in a desperate breath.

She coughed violently, spewing water out of her airway. Her arms shook, but they held her weight, barely. Her body was stronger now, though still wobbly. Whatever he'd sprayed on her was wearing off almost as fast as it had started working. Thank God.

Water ran into her eyes, but she didn't dare wipe it away and risk falling into the water again. She blinked several times to clear her vision, and when she could see, the sight that greeted her made her blood run cold.

The man was holding her baby, cradling her son in one burly arm while he held a gloved hand around the boy's throat. The threat was clear. He would kill Cory.

"Stop," was all he said. It was all he had to say.

Beverly froze, afraid to even blink. "Please don't hurt him." Her words came out slurred, but he seemed to understand.

"I don't want to hurt him. But I will."

"Just tell me what you want me to do."

The man reached into his pocket and pulled out a bright orange box knife. He set it on the edge of the tub. "You're going to use this."

Beverly had no clue what he meant. What did he want her to cut? "Use it on what?"

"Yourself."

Her stomach lurched even as her mind tried to grasp onto some sane part of what he was saying. "You're crazy."

She couldn't be certain, but behind the mask, she thought she saw his mouth tighten in anger. His hand went back to her son's neck. When he spoke, his voice was clipped and harsh. "You will end your suffering before you can inflict any on your child."

"I'd never hurt my baby."

"You wouldn't mean to. Parents never mean to."

"Please. I don't understand. Who are you talking about?"

The man's fingers tightened around Cory's fragile neck. "Your life or your son's. Which will it be?"

This made no sense, but as crazy as this man was, he

was deadly serious. She had no doubt he'd do what he said and hurt her baby. If she could stall for time . . .

"Can't we talk about this? Tell me why you're doing this."

"No more talk. We don't have much time. Isabelle is coming."

How did he know that? "You can give her my baby. She'll take good care of him."

"Enough talk! Do it and I'll let the child live. Fight me and I'll end his suffering before it can start. I swear I will." He gave Cory a small shake and Beverly's chest squeezed with panic.

Cory's face turned red and scrunched up as he wound up to let out a cry. He was so beautiful. Tiny and perfect. Beverly loved her husband, but she'd never known love like she had the moment they placed Cory in her arms. It had been overwhelming. Consuming. She would do anything for her baby.

Anything.

Tears streamed down her face as she picked up the knife. Her weak, wet fingers slipped on the plastic, but she managed to slide the blade open. Sunlight from the window shone along the razor edge.

"Nice and deep," said the man. "You'll just float away. Free after all these years."

Not free. Dead. But her son would live. She had to believe that.

Beverly positioned the blade on her wrist, looked at her baby one more time, and held that image in her mind as she made the first cut.

CHAPTER ONE

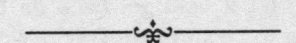

*T*hings have been a little . . . weird here lately. Watch your back, okay?"

Grant Kent always did—it's how he'd survived nearly a decade in Delta Force—but in the week since hearing Isabelle's odd message, he hadn't been able to get those words out of his head. Nor had he been able to forget the way her voice shook when she spoke them.

It was the first time she'd ever called him, and it hadn't been to catch up on old times. Something was wrong, and Grant had driven three hundred miles out of his way to find out what it was.

His Mustang slid through the quiet residential streets as he searched for the right house. He only hoped that the return address on the Christmas card she'd sent him last year was still good.

It didn't matter that he was starting a new job tomorrow and had to be in Denver by morning. Nor did it matter that he hadn't seen Isabelle in fourteen years. What mattered was Isabelle had called him, and although she hadn't asked him to come, there was something about the slight vibration of fear in her voice that made everything else seem unimportant.

So, here he was, in Springfield, Missouri—the home of bad memories—where he promised himself he'd never go again. All because little Isabelle Carson was afraid and Grant couldn't let that stand.

He figured he had about two hours to find out what was freaking her out, fix it, and get back on the highway if he was still going to be sitting at David Wolfe's breakfast table by morning.

Anticipation rolled through him and settled in his chest, making him grin like a fool. After fourteen years in the military, he was out for good now. He could hardly wait to see his friends again and start his new life.

Grant Kent, security consultant. It had a nice ring.

He turned the corner onto Isabelle's street and found the right house number. The place was old, but well maintained and way too big for one person. Even in the dark, he could see the bright white paint glowing under the porch light. The landscape was tidy, the trees pruned, and even the winter-dead grass managed to look manicured.

Grant pulled into the driveway, hoping this was the right place. She hadn't left an address in her message, and he was afraid that if he'd called to ask for one, he would have regretted it.

They hadn't exactly parted under the best of circumstances, and Grant wasn't going to make it easy on her to push him away, not while there was any chance she was in trouble.

He got out of his car and stretched to ease the tightness in his back. As much as he loved his Mustang, it wasn't really made for his tall frame, and he hadn't taken much time to stop and stretch along the drive. He'd been too anxious to get here and have this over with.

Of course, now that he was here, he was seriously reconsidering the wisdom of his decision. He had no idea what he was getting into here, or even if she'd want to see him after so many years.

A cold March wind whipped around his body as he headed for the front door on reluctant feet.

The last time he'd seen Isabelle, she'd been sixteen, sitting in the back of an ambulance hugging her knees. Tears had been streaming down her face as she'd watched the police drive away, with him handcuffed in the back seat of the patrol car.

He wasn't exactly looking forward to their reunion, but he was man enough to reach out and push the lighted doorbell.

Pleasant chimes filtered through the leaded glass at the top of the door, and a moment later he saw a shadowy movement behind the window. The door opened, and it took Grant a full ten seconds to recognize her as Isabelle Carson. He'd been expecting a larger version of the sixteen-year-old, sickly child he'd last seen, with stringy hair and sallow skin stretched too tightly over frail bones. In fact, if it hadn't been for the exotic Japanese heritage accenting her American girl-next-door features, he might never have recognized her at all.

Grant had seen a lot of beautiful women, but Isabelle was simply . . . stunning.

The shock of it silenced him for a moment as he drank her in. She was tall now—easily five-nine—when before she'd only come up to his chest. Beneath her casual clothes were slim, tempting curves made to fit just right in a man's palm. Her glossy black hair hung straight down her back, but a fringe of bangs drew his attention to her eyes. They were a deep, rich green, like a forest in twilight, canted slightly at an exotic angle.

Those eyes widened, and she stood there in shocked silence, staring at him.

Grant stilled, giving her a moment to adjust to the surprise. He wasn't sure how much he'd changed since she'd last seen him at seventeen, and he found himself holding his breath, hoping she wouldn't slam the door in his face.

Grant's knuckles ached from clenching his fists too tightly. Not a good sign at all for the man who was used to controlling his body rather than the other way around.

On more than one occasion, he'd spent days peering through the scope on his sniper rifle, gathering intel or waiting for a shot, knowing that an enemy patrol could stumble upon his location at any moment, but he'd never been as nervous as he was right now, facing Isabelle again after so many years.

What if she didn't like him? What if she saw only that angry, belligerent kid he used to be? Or worse, what if she hated him because he was the boy who'd killed their foster father?

Grant stifled the urge to run, to protect himself from whatever bad opinion of him she might have. He wasn't sure he was man enough to live through her disappointment. But instead of running, he squared his shoulders and stood his ground.

Isabelle blinked several times as if she wasn't sure she believed what she was seeing. She stood frozen, holding the door open, and he could feel the heat from her brightly lit home sliding over his face as it leaked out into the night sky.

"It's really great to see you, Isabelle."

She stood there, just far enough away that she didn't invade his personal space, but close enough that he could reach out and touch her.

He didn't. He was too worried how she might react.

Grant tried to smile—normally such an easy thing for a man like him to do with a woman—but no smile would come.

"Grant?" she asked in a confused tone, like maybe she wasn't sure it was him.

"Hi, Isabelle. Been a long time." He sounded casual, almost careless.

"What . . . what are you doing here?"

Not exactly a warm reception, but then again, he hadn't expected one. Too bad that didn't make it sting any less. "I got your message. Thought I'd come find out what was going on."

She glanced past him, looking up and down the street. After years of covert operations, Grant knew that look well. She was expecting trouble.

"You shouldn't be here," she told him.

"I probably should have called first before dropping by."

Again, she didn't look at him but kept her eyes on the street. "No. I mean you should go. Now."

If it had been anger or resentment brightening her eyes, Grant would have turned on his heel and marched out of here. But it wasn't. He saw the faintest flicker of fear cross her face, heard it waver in her voice.

If she expected trouble, then Grant was going to be right here when it showed up.

"Will you please let me in?"

"No. Just go, Grant. Before someone sees you. Please."

Grant turned and looked at their surroundings. He saw nothing out of place, no signs of anyone watching from the deep shadows surrounding her home. "Who's going to see me?"

A car turned the corner at the end of the block, its headlights splashing bright swaths of light against the house across the street.

"Get inside." Isabelle grabbed the front of his shirt and gave him a hard tug.

Grant barely stopped himself from stumbling into her as she pulled him into the house and slammed the door shut. "Get down." She yanked on his shirt again, tugging it toward the floor.

He ducked even though he had no idea why. He figured he must just be too used to doing whatever the ladies asked. Usually, when they asked him to do odd things, it ended in both him and them having a really good time.

He was pretty sure this was not going to be one of those times.

Through the window, he saw the car drive by without stopping or slowing.

"What the hell is going on?" he demanded.

She let go of him and turned to peek out the window. Grant tried not to look at her ass, but he couldn't help it. She was right there, he was ducking as she'd asked, and everything just aligned so that he had no choice.

Her tight jeans molded to her perfectly, showing off the kind of curves a man never forgot. Her black hair fell to her waist, and it shimmered an instant before she turned back around.

"Why are you here?"

"That message you left worried me. I was on my way to Denver to start a new job, so I thought I'd stop by and make sure you were okay."

Her slim shoulders sagged a bit in relief. "Denver. That's hours away. You'll be safe there."

Safe? As in, he wouldn't be safe here? What kind of mess was she in?

Frustration was swiftly eroding Grant's patience, so he took a deep breath and tried again. "Will you please tell me what's going on?"

"It's best if you just leave. There's no need for you to get involved."

Grant crossed his arms over his chest and planted his feet. "I'm not going anywhere until you tell me what the hell is going on."

Her full lips tightened and her eyes narrowed, glowing with a hint of anger. "I didn't invite you here. You have no business being here. If you don't leave, I'll call the police."

He shrugged. "Fine. Call them. Maybe they'll know what's got you so spooked."

"I'm not spooked. I'm just being cautious."

"Why?"

Her mouth clamped shut and she looked away.

Grant had never touched Isabelle before. She'd always seemed so frail, and he was afraid of hurting her, maybe even breaking her.

But she wasn't breakable anymore. He'd felt the strength of her body as she'd tugged at his shirt. He could see for himself that she was whole and healthy.

No reason not to touch her now.

He put one finger under her chin and forced her to look at him. The pad of his finger grazed her soft flesh, and when her eyes finally met his, they were such a stunning deep green he nearly forgot what he was going to ask her. But that spark of fear was still there, and it helped his brain keep spinning rather than stall out under the power of those eyes of hers. "Why, Isabelle? Why should I leave town? Why are you so afraid?"

She swallowed nervously, and a subtle vibration made her chin wobble for a second before she controlled it by gritting her teeth. "Because people are dying, and I don't want you to be next."

Isabelle never should have let the truth slip out, but she'd never been able to resist Grant Kent. Not when she was sixteen, and certainly not now when he was standing right in front of her, so beautiful and big and unexpected. And he was touching her. She'd spent years dreaming about him touching her, and now that he was, she could hardly think straight. Sure, it was just the tip of one finger, but with Grant, that was enough to make any woman's body heat up.

Like she needed any more excitement in her life right now. She had more than enough without adding both ancient history and a years-old crush to the mix.

Grant was bigger than life. Confident, self-assured, gorgeous. He was tall, lean, and graceful, with eyes that glittered gold when he looked at her. His hair was shorter now than it had been during his rebellious youth, and even though winter was only now fading away, there were still sun-bleached streaks running through his hair that caught the light whenever he moved. He had the kind of magnetic appeal that made women flock around him, and Isabelle wasn't immune to the gravitational pull of his good looks and charm. She never had been.

Isabelle hadn't understood everything she'd felt for him when she was a girl, but now she knew exactly what those goose bumps meant, as well as the little shiver that ran along her spine when his finger grazed her skin. She was no longer innocent, which also meant that she knew what she had to lose by letting herself become charmed by the potent effect he'd always had on her.

His glittering eyes caught her gaze and held on. There was a fierceness there, a kind of unyielding determination lurking just below that charming exterior. Whatever the army had had him doing for the past fourteen years, she was pretty sure it hadn't been behind a desk. He had the air of utter competence, complete control.

His eyes moved over her face, and though the finger under her chin hadn't moved, she still felt as if she'd been caressed by him. "What do you mean, people are dying? Who's dying?"

No denying it now. Time to switch tactics. "I'm being melodramatic. I was just shocked to see you. That's all."

Grant's jaw hardened, his eyes narrowed in warning. "Bullshit. Tell me everything, and tell me now."

No. She wasn't going to cave just because he wanted her to.

She pushed his hand away, breaking the contact between them.

The best way to protect him was to get him out of town, as far away from this place as possible. If she pulled him into this mess, he'd stay, and she couldn't have his death on her hands. Not after what he'd done to save her fourteen years ago, what he'd risked.

He'd given up his life for her, gone to jail for her. She wouldn't repay him for his kindness by pulling him into danger—assuming she wasn't just imagining the whole thing.

Which was entirely possible. No one else believed her.

"I'm sure it's nothing," she said, plastering a bright smile on her face.

"Let me be the judge of that." His tone came out too demanding, so he softened it with a "please."

Maybe she should tell him everything. He was former military. If anyone could see a threat, it would be Grant. And if he looked over the evidence she'd gathered and didn't think there was anything odd, she would at least be able to relax.

"You're probably going to think I'm crazy."

"Crazy chicks are hot."

Isabelle felt the blush warm her cheeks. She hadn't been a girl for a long time, but one minute with Grant and she was already feeling like a teenager again, insecure and uncertain. The only difference was that back then she hadn't been able to gain his attention, and now she had every bit of it aimed right at her.

It was more than enough to make any woman squirm.

"Spill it, Isabelle, or I'll have to show you just how much I learned about interrogation techniques in the military."

"You don't scare me."

A slow, lazy grin lifted his mouth. "That's only because

I'm being very careful not to, honey. I'm still playing nice here. Want me to move on to plan B?"

Yes, a crazy part of her mind screamed—the part that was still sixteen and so infatuated with Grant she couldn't think straight. Anything he wanted to do to her had to be better than letting him walk away. Again.

But the rest of her, the sane, rational, adult part of her, knew better. She had moved on to bigger and better things in her life. She didn't need anything from Grant. Not anymore.

"No. That won't be necessary. Just get in your car and drive off, and I swear I'll tell you anything you want to know on your cell phone on your way out of town."

"Not good enough. Start talking."

Grant had had a powerful presence even as a teen, yet it was nothing compared to the force of will she saw blazing in the man he'd become. He was harder than he had been. More formidable. More irresistible.

"I never should have called you." Too bad she hadn't realized it before she'd picked up the phone. All she'd been thinking about was warning him so he'd be safe. She'd never once thought that call would bring him to her doorstep.

"But you did."

It wasn't the first mistake she'd made, and she knew it wouldn't be the last. The only thing she could do now was damage control. "Fine. You might as well sit down."

Grant held out his hand for her to lead the way. She left the foyer and went into the living room. A brightly lit fish tank

sat against one wall, its colorful occupants gliding grace-
fully through the water. A few pieces of art hung here and
there, mostly paintings of flowers. The furniture looked
comfortable, but it was piled with mountains of superflu-
ous, girly pillows covered in beads and tassels and other
shiny bits of fluff he couldn't name.

Isabelle perched at the far end of the couch, well out
of range of any more touching, which was truly a pity.
Grant took the hint and cleared away enough pillows that
he could sit on the love seat, positioned between her and
the front door.

If there really was something outside to be afraid of, it
was going to have to get through him first.

Isabelle fidgeted with a pillow, and Grant could see the
faintest tremor running through her fingers.

Whatever was scaring her, Grant wanted to find it and
kill it. He'd never been sure what it was about Isabelle
that brought out these fierce protective instincts in him, but
he'd always thought it was simply the fact that she'd been
so small and frail.

Apparently, he'd been wrong, because she was neither
of those things anymore, yet his irrational urges hadn't
died down over the years.

The knowledge was more than a little unsettling.

She took a deep breath, closed her eyes, and blurted,
"In January, I got two of the Christmas cards I sent re-
turned unopened."

Grant sat there waiting for the rest of her dark confession. It didn't come. "Okay. I can tell that it bothered you,
but I'm dense, so you're going to have to fill in the why
part for me."

"I've been sending birthday and Christmas cards to

every one of the kids that shared a foster home with me since the night you . . . left."

Grant felt a little blush creep up his neck at the knowledge that every one of the cards she'd sent him was tucked away safely in a weatherproof bag with all of his other precious belongings. He'd never been able to throw them away. He wasn't sappy enough to pull them out and reread them or anything. At least not very often.

"In case I haven't said it before, thank you for that. I always look forward to hearing from you."

"Thanks. Everyone seemed to enjoy getting my cards, which is why it was odd when those two came back."

Grant shrugged. "People relocate."

"That's what I tried to tell myself, but . . ."

"But what?"

She shook her head, and some slippery strands of hair slid over her shoulder to graze her smooth cheek. Grant shoved his hands under his thighs to keep from reaching out to brush her hair back into place just so he could feel the slippery weight of it running through his fingers.

He knew what women's hair felt like. He didn't need to feel hers, too.

"It just bothered me," she said. "The cards were to Sam and Linda. Remember them?"

Grant shook his head. He tried not to remember too much about the years in between the time his mom wrapped her car around a tree because she was too drunk to drive, and the time he joined the army. It was best that way. "I was only there a few days. And a lot happened in those few days."

Sadness tilted the corners of Isabelle's full mouth. "But

if it weren't for those few days, who knows where I'd be now? You saved me from Lavine."

Edgar Lavine. It had been years since he'd heard that man's name, but not a day went by he didn't think about him—about how much he wished he could kill him all over again for what he'd done to so many children. Slower this time.

Grant didn't let his anger toward the man show, worried Isabelle might think it was directed at her. Instead, he lifted a shoulder in a casual shrug. "Anyone would have done the same thing."

"No, they wouldn't have. There were a lot of anyones around at the time, and no one did a thing to stop what was going on. You did."

He really didn't want to talk about Lavine. Not now, not ever. "I guess I don't remember them. Sorry."

"I think Sam might have already left Lavine's place when you came to live with us. Linda was there, though. She would have been about eight at the time."

A memory sparked in his head from his first day living at Lavine's. A little blond girl crying in her closet, hugging herself and unwilling to come out.

A lump of revulsion in his throat. No way could he go back to that page in his life. He hadn't realized it at the time, but as an adult, he was pretty sure that Linda's behavior had been the first sign he'd had that Edgar Lavine was a sadistic, child molesting bastard.

Finally, after a too-long struggle, Grant was able to speak, though his voice shook. "I remember her."

"She grew up to be a happy woman. You need to know that. What happened to her was horrible, but she overcame it. She even got married about a year ago."

"Good for her. I'm glad she's doing well."

Isabelle's gaze fell to the pillow she cradled, but not before Grant saw the sheen of tears she hurriedly blinked away. "She's not doing well . . . anymore."

"What happened?" he asked her, not really wanting to know, and feeling like a coward because of it.

"When her card came back, I called her to make sure she was okay. Her husband told me that she killed herself on Christmas Eve. Overdose."

Shock slid through Grant, tightening his muscles against the need to reach for her, offering her comfort he wasn't sure she'd welcome. "Oh, God. I'm sorry, Isabelle."

She sniffed and straightened her shoulders, though Grant could still see a shadow of grief haunting her eyes. "I'm fine. Really. She and I ended up in different homes after Lavine's. We weren't that close. It's just sad, you know? She was so young. Only twenty-two."

Grant could barely remember what he was doing ten years ago when he was twenty-two. Raising hell and chasing women whenever he was on leave, no doubt. Same old, same old. He probably still believed he was immortal at that point.

"After finding out about Linda, it took me a while to gather the courage to look up Sam to see why his card also came back. And then when I did start looking, it took me a while to actually find him."

"So you did find him?"

Isabelle gave a tight nod.

"Where?"

"He's dead, too," she said.

This was beginning to sound bad. Like more-than-two-hours-to-fix bad. "How?"

Isabelle pressed her lips together as if willing herself not to speak. Her hands shook harder, but she said nothing.

"How did he die, Isabelle?"

"He killed himself. Gunshot to the head." Tears sparkled in her eyes again, making them glow a vibrant green. "Then a few weeks ago, my friend Beverly slit her wrists." She swallowed hard, twice, then cleared her throat. "I found her body. Her baby was in the next room, crying. She was lying in a tub full of blood. The tears on her face were still wet. She was still . . . warm."

She pulled in a long breath and let it out slowly. "If I'd been five minutes earlier, maybe I could have saved her. But I wasn't, and now she's gone, too."

Grant couldn't sit still any longer, not when she was shaking like that, on the verge of tears. He knelt in front of her, took her hands in his, and modulated his voice so it was calm and even. "Tell me what's going on, honey. I can help you."

He feared the worst—that those deaths had put the idea of suicide in her head, too. He couldn't let that happen.

"If you really want to help, then you'll leave. Right now. I don't know what's going on, and I can't risk you, too."

"Risk me how?"

She squeezed his hands, though Grant didn't think she realized she was doing so. "It's not safe here for you."

"Why not? You've got to help me understand."

She was silent for a long moment, and then finally, her shoulders slumped in defeat. Her voice was a quiet whisper of sound, but he heard her clearly enough. "I don't think those people killed themselves. I think they were murdered."

That news shook Grant to the core, leaving him floundering. He kept his voice and expression carefully neutral, reserving judgment until he had more information. "If you think people are being killed, why didn't you call me and tell me about this sooner?"

She tried to pull her hands away, but he wouldn't let her. He held firm, keeping her right there with him, demanding that she give him an answer.

"I called once to warn you. You weren't available, and I felt weird leaving a message. I figured you'd think I was crazy."

Grant's jaw clenched in frustration. How many other times had she tried to contact him when he couldn't be reached? He should have been there for her—for all of those kids. After all, he was the one who had put them all back out on the street. He should have done a better job of looking out for their welfare, even if he had been just a kid himself.

At least he'd gotten to her now, before it was too late.

"Well, I'm available now. And I'm not going anywhere until I know you're safe."

David, his new job, and his new life were just going to have to wait.

CHAPTER TWO

Isabelle couldn't let Grant stay. It wasn't safe for him, and it certainly wasn't safe for her and all of the plans she'd made for her life.

"I'm a big girl. I haven't needed a protector since I was sixteen."

Grant's jaw muscles bunched as his gaze slid away, and she immediately regretted bringing up the past.

He'd killed a man to save her. Sure, he'd saved a lot of other kids, too, but Lavine had come for her for the first time that night. Grant had pulled Lavine off of her, protecting her from that hellish fate so many of his other foster kids had suffered. Because of Grant, Isabelle had to deal with only attempted rape rather than the horror the rest of those children had faced.

"I'm staying. You might as well fill me in on everything." His voice was hard and unyielding.

"I just told you everything."

"There's got to be a reason you think these people were murdered. Tell me what it is."

She swallowed hard to ease the lump of relief tightening her throat. He didn't assume she was crazy, as she'd feared. He didn't assume she was lying or making things up just to get attention.

He hadn't seen her for years, yet he gave her more benefit of the doubt than her closest friends.

"You do have a reason, don't you, Isabelle?"

"I do."

Muscles along her spine unclenched, and until now, she hadn't even realized just how tense she'd been, just how relieved she was that someone wanted to listen to her.

She'd show Grant her files, and he'd tell her she was reading too much into what she'd found, and she'd be able to let it go and get on with her life. "Follow me."

Isabelle went down the hall that led to the small bedroom she used as her office. Every few steps, she glanced back to make sure he was still there. She should have known that Grant wouldn't ditch her, but life had given her enough nasty surprises that she wasn't entirely trusting. She'd been left behind one too many times to be that foolish.

She flipped on the office lights. The secondhand desk was a little the worse for wear but big enough to grade homework as well as house her PC.

Using a key she kept with her, she opened the locked file cabinet. She didn't want her foster son to accidentally stumble on her findings and worry himself. Dale had enough to deal with on his own without fear for her safety adding to the mix.

She pulled the drawer all the way open and reached into the back for an expandable file where she kept everything she'd found.

"Here you go. Look at these and tell me what you think."

She moved aside her ungraded homework and the *Consumer Reports* article on swing sets and laid everything out on the desk. She let him see the newspaper clippings and medical examiners' reports without saying anything that might sway his opinion one way or another.

She watched him as he picked up each paper and read over it. His jaw tightened more with every page he read. The glittering interest in his eyes darkened to lethal menace.

Light from the desk lamp washed over his features, casting deep shadows on his face. She could see a couple of small scars—one on his cheek and another over his left eyebrow. The split lip Lavine had given him hadn't left a mark, which relieved her. She didn't like the idea of him carrying a reminder of that night where he'd have to see it every time he shaved.

Grant set down the first stack of pages and reached for the next. Isabelle stayed silent, watching him.

She knew exactly what he read. Page after page revealed the facts around the deaths of six people. Carrie was the first. She left her car running with the garage door shut and the car doors open. Then Henry. He hanged himself from a beam in his basement after his wife left him—his wife who had been missing for weeks. Jamal jumped from the tenth floor of his apartment building. Linda overdosed.

She hadn't really known any of those people well, but she'd known Sam and Beverly, who had also reportedly killed themselves.

Isabelle knew in her gut that was a lie.

Grant set the last paper down on the desk very carefully and turned that menacing gaze to her.

"Who are all of these people, and exactly how are

you connected to them?" he demanded. His voice was hard and cold, and Isabelle had to stifle a little shiver of apprehension.

"You're connected to them, too. Every one of them was Edgar Lavine's foster child at one time."

His mouth tightened in a disgusted grimace at the mention of that man's name. "How did you find that out? Aren't those records private?"

Isabelle felt the heat of a blush crawl up her neck. "I'm not going to tell you how I got that information. It would get someone else in trouble, someone who was trying to help me."

He accepted that and moved on without hounding her like the police had. "Are you sure all of them lived with Lavine?" he asked.

"Positive. What I'm not sure of is that any of them committed suicide."

"Lavine did a lot of terrible things to the kids in his care, Isabelle. Maybe these people never got over it."

Even though Grant had saved Isabelle from being raped, the fact that she'd come so close to being another of Lavine's victims still haunted her sometimes. She'd see a man who resembled Lavine at the grocery store and stop dead in her tracks. Once, a student's father had reached out to shake her hand and those blunt, gnarled fingers—so much like Lavine's—had flung her back to that horrid night. She'd run to the bathroom to throw up and never could bring herself to go back to face the baffled father.

If she still dealt with what had nearly happened to her, how much worse was it for the kids Grant hadn't been around to save? Bad enough to commit suicide?

"I'm not sure anyone ever gets over something like

that," she told Grant, "but I still don't think they killed themselves."

"Why not?"

"I just don't," she stated with every ounce of belief she possessed.

"Give me something to go on here. I'm trying to understand."

"Sam and Beverly were not suicidal. I *knew* them. I'd bet my life on it."

Grant's mouth flattened at her choice of words. "Okay, let's say that's true and they weren't suicidal. What about the rest of them? Did you know them, too?"

"No. And as sick as it sounds, I really want to believe they killed themselves. It's much easier to think that they took their own lives to be at peace than to believe they were murdered, made victims yet again. The problem is, everything in me is screaming that's what happened."

"Why?" Not judgment, just curiosity.

Isabelle shrugged. "Women's intuition? Instincts? I don't know. All I know is that if I'm right, then there are others out there in danger. Including you."

That news didn't even rate a shocked flicker of his eyelid. "I can take care of myself. It's you I'm worried about. If you are right, then we've got to talk to the police about this. Get you some protection, especially since you're digging up all of this stuff. If someone is killing people and disguising murder as suicide, they aren't going to want you figuring it out. If they find out you're investigating, they'll try to stop you."

Isabelle stuffed everything back into the file, feeling a familiar rise of frustration. No one believed her. Maybe she *was* wrong. "I've already been to the police. They don't have any proof that a crime has been committed, and some of these apparent suicides are way out of their jurisdiction."

"Let me guess, they want to help but say they can't."

"Exactly."

"What about the missing woman?"

"Trina. She's Henry's wife. They looked for her for a few days, but I doubt they're putting much manpower into it. Henry had a note from her in his hand when he died, saying she'd run off with another man."

"But you don't think she did?"

Isabelle shrugged. "I didn't really know her or Henry well enough to say one way or another. They both had left Lavine's before I arrived."

"This is a hell of a mess, isn't it?"

"I really didn't want to dump this on you."

"I didn't give you a choice."

"And now that you know, what do you think we should do?"

Grant was silent for a moment as if waging an internal debate, then straightened his shoulders and pushed away from the desk. "I know exactly what to do."

"Does that mean you believe me?" She held her breath, waiting for his answer.

"I believe you believe it. For now, that's enough. We'll figure this thing out. Don't worry."

Don't worry. Right. Easier said than done. At least he didn't automatically jump to the conclusion that she was crazy to even consider looking into the possibility of murder, the way her friend Keith had.

Grant held out his big hand and waited expectantly for her to give him the file. Isabelle wasn't ready to give it over so easily. Not until she knew what he planned to do with it. Gathering this information had taken weeks and used up about every favor she'd ever earned.

She flattened it against her chest and crossed her arms over it, ensuring that he wouldn't snatch it away. She wanted his help with this, but she didn't want him to take any risks without her there to watch his back. No way was she letting him take over and go all macho on her.

"So what are we going to do?" she asked.

He ignored the fact that she was holding the file against her breasts and slid it away from her. She was sure he hadn't meant to make her nipples bead up with the inadvertent caress, but they did anyway. It was enough to make a girl wonder how her body would react if he actually touched her—the teenage girl lurking inside her with the bad case of hero worship.

Thank goodness that girl wasn't behind the wheel anymore.

Isabelle shifted her arms to cover the shameless effect he had on her body. He didn't need any more advantages over her than he already had.

"*We're* not going to do anything. You're going to go about your life," he told her, "and I'm going to look into this. Talk to the police again and see what I can figure out."

So much for him not going all macho. "I never intended for you to swoop in and take over."

"No one's swooping. Besides, you've already done all the hard work researching everything. Let me take a turn."

"I don't think that's a good idea."

"I thought you already said the police couldn't help you."

"And you think they'll help you?" she asked, her voice rising up an octave in irritation.

Grant shrugged. "Maybe. It's worth a shot. If you're not the only one coming to them with the concern that there's something going on, maybe they'll be convinced to look into it more thoroughly."

As much as she hated to admit it, that made sense. In fact, it would probably strengthen her case if he went to the police on his own instead of with her.

A slow, languid smile curved his mouth. "Besides, we don't want them to think I'm being swayed by a pretty face, now, do we?"

Isabelle suppressed the shiver his compliment caused and forced herself to focus. It didn't matter if he thought she was pretty. Not one bit. And if she kept repeating it to herself long enough, she'd believe it.

"If we do it your way, you have to promise to come back and tell me what they say."

"Coming back is not a problem," said Grant. "Until this is settled, I'm staying here with you."

She stood there silent from shock, able only to blink and stare at him like a fool.

Grant sleeping under her roof only a few feet away, so very accessible? Grant at her table, sharing meals and conversation? Grant in her shower all naked and slick with no one to wash his back? She'd never survive it. Even if she managed to stay strong enough not to seduce him while he was here, her house would never be the same again. She'd see him everywhere she looked. "You can't."

He actually had the audacity to look hurt, giving her

a sad little pout that made her feel like she'd pinched a puppy. "What? I'm not invited?"

No. He absolutely was not. Not if she wanted to stay sane. "You're not good with rejection, are you?"

"Not enough practice, I guess."

"It's nice to know I can help you learn this valuable life lesson, then. I am a teacher, after all."

"Maybe, but I'm sure as hell no second grader."

Isabelle was stunned silent again. How had he known she'd moved to teaching second grade? She'd never told him. "Have you been checking up on me?"

He pointed to the stack of ungraded homework, to where her student's name was. Right under that was *Miss Carson, 2nd grade*.

Grant lifted his blond brows and shot her a charming grin. "See? I'm not too shabby at this whole investigative stuff. You should let me stay."

"I thought you said you were starting a new job. I don't want you to get fired."

"Let me worry about that. I've got it covered."

"What will Dale think?" she asked.

"Dale?" His eyes shot to her left hand, and she knew he was looking for a ring. The smile slid from his face and his eyes went flat. "I didn't know you had a boyfriend."

No way was that jealousy she was hearing. Not from Grant I-can-get-any-woman-I-want Kent. Was it?

"Dale is my foster son."

His smile came back, so bright she could hear it warm his voice. "Seriously? That's great."

She hadn't realized until that moment how important his opinion of her decision to become a foster mom was. A satisfied glow filled her up, making her steps a little lighter. "He hasn't been here long, just since August. It's working out well, though. He's a great kid. Well, nearly a man, I guess. I only wish I'd found him sooner." For too many reasons.

"Why's that?"

"He's had a rough time. His mother is dead. His biological father was released from prison a few months ago and wants him back, which I'm not going to let happen. The man was locked up for assaulting his wife, for heaven's sake. He says he's rehabilitated."

"Rehabilitated my ass," ground out Grant. "Once an asshole, always an asshole."

Isabelle grunted her agreement. She couldn't have said it better herself. "I'd love to adopt him, but I don't see that working out."

"Why not?"

"Even if there wasn't an issue of Dale still having a father who wants custody, I don't know if the adoption paperwork would go through before he turns eighteen in a few months."

"Eighteen is still young enough to wish you had a family," said Grant.

Isabelle's heart squeezed hard for a moment. Grant would know all about how it felt to be a young man with no family of his own.

She kept her tone light rather than let him think she felt sorry for him. "Dale will always be part of my family, whether or not we have the paperwork to prove it."

"You've grown into one hell of a generous woman, Isabelle."

His praise made her face warm. If he kept acting like this, she wasn't going to stand a chance of keeping her distance. He'd walk away again with her half in love with him, and she wouldn't be able to do a thing about it.

Only this time, it wouldn't be puppy love.

That thought scared her straight. She had to be careful with Grant. He was her weakness. Her childhood hero. She needed him to talk to the police, but that didn't mean she needed to fall for him in the few hours it would take him to do so. It was best if they just kept their distance and dealt with this as quickly as possible, with all of her body parts still her own and him well on his way to his new life.

"Does your son know what's going on?"

"No. And I don't want him to, either. He's got the SATs coming up, and he's working his butt off studying for them. I don't want anything to distract him."

"If you let me stay, I promise he'll hardly notice I'm here."

Isabelle snorted at that. "You couldn't go unnoticed if you wanted to."

He lifted a brow in challenge. "Wanna bet? I could tell you some stories that would make you change your mind." He gave her a smile that made her legs tremble. "Though I do have to admit that the idea of you noticing me has its appeal."

"Don't you dare flirt with me," she warned him.

He took a step closer so that his body nearly touched hers. He lifted up a few strands of her slippery hair to his nose and breathed in. His low hum of approval vibrated the air between them. "Why not, Isabelle? A little flirting never hurt anyone."

Isabelle felt frozen, unable to move away from him. "Maybe it never hurt you, but then, you're not the one left behind wondering what went wrong."

God, he was so beautiful. Age had been good to him, honing his features to sharp, masculine edges. He looked harder, stronger, like the kind of man a woman could count on to stick around. She had no idea how he pulled off the illusion, but she couldn't let herself fall for it.

"Is that what happened, Isabelle? Is that why you're alone? Someone left you behind?"

Too many someones. Her mother had given her away at birth, more than a dozen foster parents had decided not to keep her, countless friends had walked away over the years, along with two men she thought had loved her. Even Dale would be leaving for college next fall.

People left. That's just what they did.

"I'm not alone. I have Dale."

"You know what I mean. Why aren't you married yet? Why hasn't some man snatched you up so the rest of us can't get to you?"

An old ache throbbed inside her, but she was so used to it she hardly noticed. She wanted too much from the men in her life, and she'd never found any who loved her enough to give it to her. And she wasn't willing to settle. Her future was too important to too many special people.

"I guess no one has been good enough for me yet," she told him.

He slid his long finger over her brow and along her cheekbone. Isabelle had to work hard not to shiver at his touch and give away the effect he had on her.

"Now, that I can believe," he said.

"Don't do this," she begged.

"Do what?"

"Touch me like this." Even as she said it, she leaned closer to him, unable to stop herself.

"Like what?"

"Like I'm a woman."

Grant laughed and cupped her cheek in his wide palm. "Honey, you're all woman, but if you want me to keep my hands off, I swear I'll try."

His hand fell to his side so he was no longer touching her, but she still couldn't pull out of that gravitational well that surrounded him. She stood there, unable to move or even blink. She'd had too many girlish daydreams about this man over the years, and here he was, only inches away, coming on to her. It was too surreal.

He kept staring at her with that wicked light glittering in his eyes. "I have to admit, you surprised me. I was expecting some tiny little frail thing. You're all grown up and did a great job of it, too. And I don't just mean your killer body, either. Taking in Dale couldn't have been an easy decision for you."

Killer body? That kind of praise was nice from anyone, but coming from Grant it was practically a narcotic.

"You're wrong," she told him, struggling to focus on the rest of what he said. "It was the easiest thing I've ever done."

Grant shook his head, giving her a crooked grin. "Like I said. All grown up."

She wasn't sure exactly what he meant by that, but she let it slide. There was still the matter of him staying here for her to deal with. "All things considered, I don't think you should stay here. What will Dale think?"

"It's not like I'm asking to sleep in your bed. The couch will work fine. I'm just an old friend in for a visit."

"An old friend who can't keep his hands to himself or stop flirting long enough to have a conversation?"

He gave her a dashing, almost apologetic grin and shoved his hands deep into his pockets. "I'll be good. I swear it."

Isabelle never had a doubt that he'd be good. She had fantasized about just how good more nights than she cared to remember over the years. Maybe it was because he'd been her first real crush. Maybe it was simply chemistry. Whatever it was, a piece of him had lived inside her for fourteen years, sparking thoughts and memories of him when she least expected it. "You're not going to take no for an answer, are you?"

"Not a chance. At least not until I know you and Dale are safe. Sorry. You're the one who put the worry in my head, so you're just going to have to deal."

"Fine." The only thing she could do now was put him as far out of reach as possible. "You can sleep upstairs. Next to Dale's room."

The smile of victory curving his mouth was only going to add fuel to her fiery fantasies of him. The ones that left her sweating and aching for relief that never came no matter how hard she reached for it.

Isabelle let out a heavy sigh of defeat. "Go get your stuff and I'll show you your room."

Grant sauntered off in a long-legged stride that made her mouth water. Everything about him was appealing to her—his graceful stride, the way his jeans clung to his tight butt, his carelessly tousled hair, and that confident glint in his eyes that said he knew just how to please a woman. Over and over.

But all of that by itself wouldn't have affected her. As handsome as he was, she could resist him if it weren't for that noble streak a mile wide—the one she'd witnessed firsthand.

He hadn't just hopped in his car and driven away with a thanks for the warning. Not Grant Kent. He was staying to help. Staying in her house, right within reach, after fourteen years of being nothing more than a long-distance fantasy.

Isabelle sat down and laid her head on the cool desk. She was doomed. A bad case of childish infatuation was one thing. Add to it the instinctive knowledge of just how good she knew she and Grant would be together, mixed in with a case of it's-been-way-too-long-since-I-got-laid, and she was simply doomed. In way over her head, fated to suffer, doomed.

"Isabelle?" came Dale's worried voice from down the hall. "There's some guy outside."

Isabelle took a deep breath and forced her head off the desk. By the time Dale came into the office, she was pretty sure her face was still flushed with thoughts of Grant and the kind of lover he'd be.

So much for being a good mom dedicated only to what was best for her son.

Dale's dark hair was ruffled from the wind, and his letterman's jacket made his shoulders look as wide as a grown man's. Of course, that's what he nearly was at seventeen, and it still shocked her sometimes. Right now, his bright blue eyes were filled with worry and a hint of fear. Dale wasn't the most trusting of boys—it had taken him six months after he'd moved in to learn to trust her—and he wouldn't enjoy having a stranger in the house. Especially not a man.

"It's okay, Dale. That's Grant. He's an old friend of

mine who's going to stay for a day or two. Are you okay with that?"

Dale shrugged. "Sure. Whatever."

Isabelle stood and looped her arm over Dale's shoulders as they walked to the kitchen. He was taller than her now, though she wasn't sure exactly when during the past seven months that had happened. "Come on, I'll introduce you. Are you hungry?"

"Starved," answered Dale, as she knew he would.

"You're going to like Grant."

Dale stiffened. "You got something going with him?"

"No. We're just friends," she said, though her body was clamoring for more. She was going to have to keep it under control.

"Uh-huh."

"Really," she insisted.

"You know, you haven't dated since I came to live here. I don't want to cramp your style or anything. I like it here too much."

As if she'd send him away because he got in the way of her dating. Dale had no idea how much she loved him, but she knew better than to go all mushy. He hated that, so she settled for giving him a one-armed hug and said, "You're not cramping my style."

"You're allowed to have sex if you want."

He sounded like the thought grossed him out, which made her grin. "Thanks for your permission."

"I mean, don't go doing the nun thing on my account."

Isabelle laughed. "Is that what you think is going on?"

"Must be. You never even date, and I know you've been asked out."

"Not by anyone I was interested in."

"But this Grant guy? He interest you?"

Way too much. Maybe Dale sensed it somehow. Through the window, Isabelle could see Grant heft a duffel bag onto his wide shoulder and head toward the house, muscles bulging in a mouth-watering display. Even with the heavy load, his stride was smooth and effortless.

She still couldn't believe he was staying here, still wasn't convinced that it wasn't a huge mistake for her to let him.

"He's only passing through," she told Dale, forcing herself to recognize the truth.

Dale's eyes brightened as if he was relieved Grant wouldn't stay. "Oh. Well. If you want to hit that while he's here, or whatever, I'll go study at the library."

Isabelle's cheeks heated with embarrassment. "'Hit that?' How charming. Can we please discuss something other than my love life? Like how your practice test went today?"

Dale pulled away from her and shoved his head into the refrigerator. He mumbled something grumpy and incoherent as Grant came back in the house, keeping Isabelle from asking him what he'd said. If the practice SAT hadn't gone well, she didn't want to embarrass him by making him talk about it in front of a total stranger.

The files Grant had taken from her office were nowhere in sight, thank goodness. Then again, in his line of work, she figured he knew a thing or two about keeping information to himself.

Dale backed out of the refrigerator with an armload of sandwich fixings and a gallon of milk.

Isabelle pulled a plate out of the cabinet to encourage Dale to actually use it, instead of eating over the sink.

"Dale, this is my friend Grant Kent."

Rather than stick out his hand, Grant took the milk that was dangling precariously from one of Dale's fingers. "Good to meet you. Is there enough there for two?"

Dale laid the huge quantity of food on the counter. "Guess so."

Isabelle pulled out another plate and watched as a pile of sandwiches started to disappear.

She hoped they figured out this mess soon, because at this rate, she wasn't going to be able to afford to feed both Grant and Dale for very long.

Wyatt Townsend watched Dale go into the big brick house of the goody-two-shoes bitch who was nothing more than a glorified babysitter. Dale was *his* son, and no one was going to keep them apart. No one. The boy had some serious learning to do, and Wyatt was going to see that he did it before it was too late.

The first thing he was going to do was make the boy burn that fucking jacket. No son of his was going to proudly display the fact that he'd lettered in debate. Wyatt wasn't going to have his only son acting like some kind of nerd. The boy needed some backbone—a little toughening up. He'd turned into a pussy since Wyatt had been in prison, and he couldn't stand by and let that happen.

Wyatt was ready to be a father now, though it had taken him a while to realize that. He didn't have much time left with the boy before he grew up, and if social services didn't hurry the hell up and pull their heads out of their bureaucratic asses, Wyatt was going to have to take matters into his own hands.

He put his piece-of-shit car into gear and eased away from the curb. Mr. Pruitt, his caseworker, said he'd have to find a decent job if he was going to have any hope of getting custody of Dale again.

Yeah, right. It wasn't like good jobs for ex-cons were as common as dog turds. It was easy for Mr. Pruitt to say. He got to boss around parents for a living and tell them all the ways they weren't good enough to raise their own children.

What a prick.

Maybe it would be better if he just took Dale and left town. He'd be violating parole, but he didn't care. Life might be better on the run, anyway. At least then it would just be him and Dale, without anyone sticking their nose into family business.

He'd go to the job interview for the bouncer position he'd applied for and see how it went. If he got it, maybe he'd stick around and play by the rules for once.

If not, he knew exactly how to play outside of the rules. And he was damn good at it. He'd been watching the goody-two-shoes bitch long enough to know her patterns, her friends, and her vulnerabilities. Taking back what was his was going to be easy.

CHAPTER THREE

❧

Grant forced down another bite of his sandwich, stifling a groan. He couldn't eat like a kid anymore, and there was no way he was keeping up with Dale's appetite. Still, he remembered how much he'd hated it when people watched him eat when he was Dale's age—how self-conscious it had made him feel, like he was some sort of freak show. The Amazing Bottomless Boy. Watch him eat more than he's worth in a single sitting.

If they were both eating, then at least Dale wasn't the only spectacle.

There was so much about Isabelle's foster son that reminded him of himself. Not the physical stuff, like hair and eyes and build, but the attitude was there—the constant worry that tonight might be your last night in a warm, clean bed. He'd been through more foster homes than most because of his bad attitude, and although Dale didn't seem to have the same consuming anger that Grant had had, there was still that wild animal skittishness about him that told Grant there was more to him than what showed on the surface.

Dale wasn't going to like having Grant here, because

it threatened the status quo—and when things were going well, anything that did that was dangerous.

Grant pretended to be consumed with interest in his food as he listened to Dale and Isabelle chat. Technically, Isabelle chatted and Dale would occasionally grunt in response, but it was as close to a conversation as she was going to get with a teenage boy in the middle of a feeding.

"Do you have any homework tonight?" she asked him.

Dale gave an affirmative grunt.

"A lot?"

He shook his head and washed a mouthful down with a swig of milk.

"Need any help?"

"Nope. Got it covered."

If Isabelle was disappointed that he didn't need her help, she did a good job of covering it. "You always do. You're a good kid, Dale."

The boy blushed, shoved the last quarter of his third sandwich into his mouth, and got up from the table in a clumsy rush.

"I'll clean this stuff up," offered Grant, giving him an easy escape route. "Thanks for sharing."

Dale gave a quick nod, grabbed his bulging backpack, and fled the kitchen. The heavy tread of his footsteps running upstairs nearly rattled the dishes.

Isabelle winced. "I keep forgetting he's not into compliments."

"He'll survive," said Grant, giving her a wink. "Besides, they're good for him. Make him tough."

"If he was any tougher, he'd be shoe leather."

"He seems like a good kid."

"The best. He never gives me any trouble. I think he's afraid I'll send him away if he does."

Grant gathered up what little was left of the sliced turkey and mayo and stowed them back in the fridge. "He doesn't know you very well, then."

"And you do? After fourteen years and a few letters?"

It was more than a few letters. It was little bits and pieces of her life she'd chosen to share with him, and that was of more value than she'd ever know. She'd remembered him, and she cared enough about him to keep on remembering him even when he wasn't very good about writing back.

What was he going to write? He couldn't talk about his job beyond the surface stuff, like promotions, and there really wasn't a whole lot else in his life. Eventually, he got tired of thinking up stuff to say and stopped writing. Even so, Isabelle kept writing to him.

"I know enough about you to know that you'd never throw a kid out for screwing up a little. I also know that any woman who cares about whether or not a kid has homework is certainly going to care about whether or not he has a warm place to sleep at night. You can't fool me. You're still as soft as ever."

And not just her heart. He could still feel the slippery weight of her hair gliding over his hand, the silky smoothness of her cheek beneath his fingertips. He wanted more. A lot more.

Part of him stalled out every time a thought like that went through his head, like he was invading on forbidden territory. She wasn't some woman in a bar who was expecting to hook up with him for a night of debauchery. And Grant couldn't give her more than that. At least not right now. He had plans. A new job waiting for him in

Denver. He had a schedule to keep that would hopefully lead him to a woman like Isabelle in a few years, but not yet. He wasn't ready yet.

He had to be sure he'd burned every shred of his father out of his makeup before he committed himself to a woman. Until then, he'd never take the chance that he'd abandon a family and do what his father had done. Anything less would be unforgivable.

Isabelle cleared the dishes from the table. "Do you think I'm too soft on him? I mean, maybe he'd be better off in a home with a father figure. That's something I can never be for him."

The insecurity in her voice made Grant want to kick himself. He went to where she was rinsing off dishes in the sink and pulled her around by the arm until she looked at him. "You misunderstood me. Soft is a good thing. Dale doesn't need anyone to teach him the harder lessons of life. Life has a way of taking care of that without any help, and probably already has in his case." He knew he shouldn't be touching her so much, but he couldn't seem to help it. He slid his hand down her arm and took her wet fingers in his hand, giving her a little squeeze. "What he needs is to know he's safe, that he has a home where he'll always be welcome, and someone to lean on when things get hard. You're doing all of that, so give yourself some credit. He's lucky to have you."

Isabelle's eyes went shiny, and she blinked several times to clear them. "Don't you dare make me cry, Grant Kent. You're here to help, not make me all sappy."

He gave her a wink, when what he really wanted to do was see if her mouth was as soft as the rest of her. "Fine.

No sap here. I'm all about the help. How about I start by taking out the trash?"

She stared at him with a strange look that he couldn't decipher but said, "It goes in a bin around back."

Grant took care of the chore, but when he came back inside, Isabelle was no longer in the kitchen. He heard her voice float in from the living room, along with that of another man. Not Dale. He said something to her, and when she spoke, her tone was tight with anger. "I won't do it."

"You have to," said the man. "Wyatt will do anything to get his son back. You're not safe with Dale in the house."

"If you didn't think I'd be safe, then why did you bring Dale to my attention? We both know he needs to be here right now. I'm not kicking him out."

Grant ignored the fact that he was not invited into their conversation and stepped into the living room. Isabelle looked stricken, almost like she was going to be sick. Grant went to her side so she'd know he was here for her. And to let the man in her living room know it, too.

He turned to the man standing there and demanded, "Who the hell are you?"

The man had short, dark hair and wore a well-fitted suit. He was average height with a slightly stocky build that told Grant he had some muscle under his jacket.

He frowned and tilted his head up at Grant as if he recognized him. "Grant Kent?" he asked. "Is that you?"

Grant tried to place him but couldn't.

"Grant, this is Keith Elders," said Isabelle.

She'd recovered some of her composure, but he could still see a slight tremor of tension running through her slim frame.

"Do you remember him?" asked Isabelle.

The man's name struck a chord in Grant's head, but he couldn't quite place him.

"I lived with Lavine, too," said Keith. "I was a few years younger than you at the time, so you probably don't recognize me."

Grant spent a lot of time trying not to think about the short time he'd lived with Lavine. Unfortunately, he remembered the face of every one of the children he'd put out on the streets the night he killed his foster father. Two of those faces could have matched the man standing before him, but Grant didn't know which one it was. "Sorry, man. It's been a long time."

"Too long," said Keith as he extended his hand in greeting. "It's really great to see you again. Isabelle didn't tell me you were coming for a visit."

Grant shook the man's hand. "She didn't know I was coming. It was kind of a last-minute thing."

"I told him what's going on," said Isabelle. "He's going to talk to the police tomorrow."

Keith's mouth flattened on a frown. "You need to stop worrying about those poor souls and worry more about what's going to happen to you if Wyatt decides to come take his son by force."

A stab of fear for her made Grant's body tighten, and he took a half step closer to Isabelle.

"Is that a risk?" Grant asked her. "You didn't mention it."

"It's an irrational worry. Wyatt doesn't have any idea where I live."

"It's not irrational," insisted Keith. "The man has a record for assaulting women. He wants his son back. It doesn't take a genius to do the math."

"No. It doesn't," agreed Grant, giving Isabelle a hard stare. "You should have said something."

Isabelle gave him a back-the-hell-off glare. "Why? Because it's somehow your business?" She pushed out a harsh breath. "Listen. Wyatt wants Dale back, and he's not going to do anything to mess up his one and only chance of making that happen by hurting me. He'd go back to prison if he did, so it doesn't make any sense. He's got to work inside the system, and he knows it."

Keith shook his head. "Men like Wyatt spend their lives working around the system. I've defended enough men like him to know. Don't trust that he's suddenly developed some moral code since getting out of prison. I don't want to see you hurt. Or worse."

The whole notion that someone was killing Lavine's former foster children was bad enough, but knowing that there was some ex-con out there who might want to hurt Isabelle made Grant want to find him and remove the threat. Permanently.

Down, boy. Isabelle was right. It really wasn't his business.

Of course, that wasn't going to stop him from getting involved, either. Not if there was some kind of threat to her and the kid.

"I'll be fine," said Isabelle. "Besides, Grant is staying here tonight, so you can stop worrying."

"Maybe longer," offered Grant. As much as he hated the thought of telling David he was going to have to come later than planned, he hated the idea of leaving Isabelle even more. David could take care of himself. Isabelle and Dale, on the other hand, needed him.

The news that Grant was staying seemed to relax Keith

somewhat. "Good. Wyatt probably won't try anything with Grant here. He's too much of a coward to risk anything unless he's sure he can get away with it. But what are you going to do when Grant leaves?"

"I won't leave until I'm sure there's no threat. I can promise you that, Keith."

She poked a finger at Grant's chest. Hard. He resisted the urge to rub away the sting. "You'll leave when I say you'll leave. This is my house."

Wow. Isabelle was hot when she was being pushy. Bright chips of gold lit her green eyes, and a pretty flush brightened her cheeks. Grant almost wanted to push back to see what would happen, but not with an audience. Maybe he'd push later, when they were alone.

There was no way he'd agree to leave her and Dale on their own to face this Wyatt asshole. "It's your house," agreed Grant without lying. "I won't forget."

That seemed to appease her for now. Later he'd set the record straight and make sure she had some decent security set up. If he had to, he'd pay for it himself. David's company had some cutting-edge toys that would go a long way toward making him feel better when he left.

"See that you don't." She turned to Keith. "If you'll stop being all doom and gloom, I'll invite you in for a cup of tea."

"I'd love to stay, but I have a hearing in the morning and I really need to prepare a little more. Rain check?"

"Anytime. Good luck with your hearing." She left Grant's side and kissed Keith on the cheek. In a quiet voice that Grant could barely hear, she said, "Thank you for worrying about me. It's nice to know someone cares."

Grant felt an unreasonable flash of jealousy. *He* worried about her. *He* cared. Where the hell was *his* kiss?

It took him several seconds to calm down enough to remember that he hadn't been in Isabelle's life for years. Keith was close enough to her that he dropped by without notice and got invited in for tea. Grant was just some guy from her past—not a friend who was there for her on a daily basis. He had no right to be jealous.

Too bad that didn't make it go away.

Isabelle shut and locked the door. Before she'd had time to turn all the way around, Grant asked, "You two seeing each other?"

Isabelle's black eyebrows rose nearly an inch. "Keith? Heavens, no. We're just friends."

"Does he feel the same way?"

"Why do you care?"

She was taunting him. Maybe she didn't mean to do it, but she had, and Grant found himself unable to resist. He liked touching her and wanted to do it more, enough that she'd forget all about Keith and how close a friend he was.

He moved toward her, which backed her against the front door. From here, he could smell her skin and the sweet-scented lotion she'd smoothed over it. He lowered his head so that his mouth was right by her temple and breathed in deep.

His world spun for a moment, and he had to force himself to remember where he was and why he was here. "I care because I want you to be happy."

Her voice was thin, almost breathless. "And you don't think Keith could make me happy?"

"Maybe. I bet he'd like to try." Grant knew he sure as

hell could make her happy. At least for a few hours. He'd love to make her so happy she'd howl for him.

Just the thought of getting the chance made him sweat.

Isabelle pressed her hands against his chest and gave him a push so slight he wasn't really sure it had happened. Her eyes were wide, her pupils dilated, and a sexy hint of color warmed her skin. "This isn't right," she told him. "You and I."

"Why not?"

"Because you're leaving tomorrow and I'm not into hit-and-run sex, no matter how good it might be."

Right. Grant knew that. She was a nice girl. A freaking elementary school teacher. He had no business pursuing her like this.

So why the hell couldn't he stop?

"And even if I was into it," she said, "Dale is right upstairs."

Dale. A kid. One who didn't need to see his foster mom sprawled out on the living room floor, next to his fish tank, naked with a total stranger.

That was enough to get Grant thinking straight again.

He nodded slowly and backed away from her. His blood was pounding hot and hard through his limbs, but he'd spent too many years controlling his body's reactions to let them get the better of him now. "Sorry."

Isabelle swallowed. "How about some tea? That will keep your hands busy."

"No thanks. I've been on the road since two a.m., so I'm ready to hit the sack. I'll go see the police first thing tomorrow and see what they have to say." And he'd be sure to tell them about Dale's father, in the hopes that they might have a patrolman drive by her house a few times every day. If Wyatt was a coward, as Keith suggested, then he'd be less likely to mess with Isabelle if the police were always around. If not . . . Grant would just have to stick around a while and find out.

Dale was deep into the futile effort of studying for the SATs when he heard the click of a small rock hitting his window.

For a second he thought it might be Angela and his heart kicked in, pounding hard. Her image filled his head, knocking out everything else that had once occupied the space. He saw her sweet smile, her long blond hair that always looked too perfect to touch. In his mind, she was still wearing that tight pink sweater she had on last Thursday that showed off her perfect breasts—the sweater that had him staying up until well after midnight to learn the history lesson he'd missed in class because he couldn't quit staring at her. She was so pretty he had no idea why all the other guys in his class hadn't fallen on their knees at her feet for just the chance to talk to her.

Maybe they were as gutless as he was, too afraid she'd turn him down to actually ask her out. As long as she hadn't said no, there was still a chance she might say yes, and that was the thing that got him out of bed every morning. A chance with Angela.

God knew he needed something to get up for.

Another rock hit the glass, and Dale scrambled off the bed to see who it was. In his head, it was Angela and she'd come to confess her undying love for him. He'd climb down to her and she'd throw herself into his arms. They'd find a nice, quiet place where they could make out, which would, of course, turn into a wild night of endless sex that would ruin her for all other men forever. They'd run off together to a place where SAT scores didn't matter, and he'd buy her a pink sweater for every day of the week.

When he looked down into the yard, all his hopeful thoughts that Angela had fallen in love with him shattered. It was dark outside, but the neighborhood was well lit enough for him to recognize his dad's prison build and the expectant stance he'd used with Mom until the day he'd beat her unconscious and gone to jail for it.

Cold, bitter pain slammed into him, making it hard to breathe. He missed Mom so much. Isabelle was nice, but it wasn't the same. It never would be.

Dale stared for a moment, choking on his anger and hatred for the man below. He knew that killing his old man wouldn't bring Mom back, but some days, it still sounded like a good idea. Wyatt should have been charged with murder, not just assault. He'd beaten his wife so often she felt the need to escape with a hefty does of heroin as often as she could get it. If it hadn't been for that, his mom might still be alive.

As far as Dale was concerned, that was murder.

Wyatt motioned for Dale to open the window. For a long moment, Dale considered ignoring him. Let the bastard freeze down there while he was safe and warm up in his room.

But if he did that, chances were Wyatt would get angry. And when he got angry, he hurt people. Isabelle didn't deserve to have that kind of shit come down on her just because she was nice enough to open her home to him. Dale owed her more than that.

He opened the window and stood there with his arms crossed over his chest. He'd been hitting the weights pretty hard for the past year, but he was no match for the strength of a fully grown man—especially one who'd spent the past eight years with little else to do in prison but lift weights, getting stronger and meaner.

"I need to talk to you," Wyatt whispered.

"Fuck off," Dale whispered back, adding in a hand gesture to ensure that his dad didn't misunderstand.

"Get your ass out here, boy."

"You're not even supposed to be here. Supervised visits only, remember?"

"I'd be happy to come in and let the little lady supervise."

Shit. Dale had heard Grant go to bed about an hour ago. Wyatt would never mess with a man like Grant, one who radiated confidence with every breath he took, but if Isabelle was alone . . . Shit.

"Hold on," said Dale. He grabbed his new letterman's jacket—the one that made him feel like he was part of something for the first time in his life—and crawled out the window.

The trip down wasn't too hard, but the trip back up would be interesting. Maybe he'd wait until Isabelle went to sleep and sneak back in the back door. Assuming he didn't get caught first.

Dale reached the ground and stood eye to eye with his father. "Whatever it is you want, make it quick. I have homework to do."

"Well," sneered Wyatt, "wouldn't want to get in the way of such important stuff, now, would I?"

Dale kept a tight hold on his temper. What the hell did

he care whether or not his murdering-son-of-a-bitch dad approved of his life?

"What do you want?" he demanded.

Wyatt pointed over his shoulder. "My car's down the street. We'll talk in there, where it's warmer."

For half a second, Dale wondered if his dad didn't intend to kidnap him rather than go through the messy process of regaining custody. Part of Dale hoped he'd try. He could kill the man and it would be self-defense. He'd get rid of his asshole father and avenge Mom's death all at the same time. Two birds. One stone.

"Okay," said Dale. "We'll talk in the car."

CHAPTER FOUR

After two hours of grading papers and doing next week's lesson planning, Isabelle went upstairs to check on Dale. He hadn't come down for a snack before bed, which was unusual. He could hardly go two hours without eating.

She knocked on his door, but he didn't answer. Panic flared inside her, but she tamped it down. She would not overreact. He was probably just listening to music on his headphones.

"Dale?" Isabelle knocked again, and still there was no answer.

She opened door open, hoping she wouldn't walk in on him changing but willing to risk it to get rid of this seething fear that something was wrong. His room was empty and cold thanks to a wide-open window. His bed was rumpled where he'd been lying on it, and his SAT prep book lay open as if he'd just vanished in the middle of studying.

"Dale?" she called. She checked his closet and under his bed, though why he'd be in those places she had no idea, but she looked anyway. He wasn't there. She raced down the hall to the bathroom, which was open and empty.

"Dale!" She shouted louder.

Grant burst from his bedroom wearing only a pair of

tight boxers. A sleek black gun was in his grip, and though his messy hair and creased cheek said he'd been soundly asleep, there was nothing sleepy about his gaze or movements. His eyes were clear, bright amber. "What's wrong?" he asked in a calm, sleep-roughened voice.

"Dale's gone."

Grant didn't waste time asking if she was sure. Her panicked tone made that much obvious. "Is his car still here?"

Isabelle hadn't checked, so she hurried back into Dale's bedroom, which faced the front of the house, poked her head out the window, and looked down into the driveway. "Yes. It's there."

Grant's tall body was right behind her, peeking out over her shoulder. "Do you recognize that car down the street?" he asked.

Isabelle hadn't seen it until he pointed it out. It was an old beat-up Tempo that had probably been manufactured the year she started high school. "No."

"Turn out the lights."

So they could see better. Right. Isabelle rushed to the switch and flipped it down. The light from the streetlamps was bright enough to see by, but the car was too far away for her to tell if there was anyone inside.

"He's in the car," said Grant.

"You sure?"

"I have good eyesight. From the looks of it, there's a man in there with him."

"Oh, no. It's got to be his father."

"The one Keith warned you would stop at nothing to get his son back?"

Isabelle nodded in numb horror.

"Call the police," ordered Grant. "I'll deal with this until they get here." He shoved his gun in the elastic waistband of his boxer briefs, opened the window wider, and stepped through.

Isabelle watched Grant glide down the side of the house, using the porch roof and support beams to climb down to the ground as easily as he would have used the stairs. Muscles rippled over his torso as he moved effortlessly, making no sound. A few feet from the ground, he jumped down and landed in a crouch. A moment later, he disappeared into the shadows.

For half a second, she was too stunned to act. Then she pulled herself together, found Dale's phone sitting on his desk, and called the police.

Grant used the deep shadows cast by the well-aged landscape to cover his progress toward the Tempo. The air slid over his skin, sucking heat as it went, but he ignored the chill the same way he ignored the sharp bits of rocks and sticks that poked the bottoms of his bare feet.

It didn't take long to close in on the car. The question was how to handle this.

His first instinct was to shoot the man and ask questions later, but he knew that wasn't the best way to proceed. Killing Dale's father, assuming that's who this was, wasn't going to help the boy become a well-adjusted adult. Even if it would ensure Isabelle's safety.

As far as he could see, they were just sitting in the front seat, chatting. No one was angry. No fists were flying.

Caution was probably best, though not necessarily the most fun or most satisfying.

Grant appeared by the driver's window and tapped on the glass.

The shocked look that crossed Wyatt's face—and it had to be Dale's father, because the family resemblance was uncanny—pleased Grant. Wyatt hadn't seen him coming, which would make the man wonder when he might pop up again.

"Out of the car, Dale," said Grant, knowing the boy could hear him through the glass.

Dale moved to open the door, but Wyatt stopped him by grabbing his arm. "We're not done talking yet," he told Grant.

The temptation to escalate things was getting harder and harder to resist, but Grant was man enough to control himself. He crossed his arms over his naked chest and stuck a patient, carefree pose. "Fine. I'm sure the cops will sort it all out."

"You called the fucking cops!"

As if orchestrated by a master conductor, the wail of sirens split the night air. "What do you think?"

"Shit! Get out of the car, boy."

Dale did as he was ordered while the Tempo rattled to life. Dale had barely cleared the car before it took off in a screech of tires.

Isabelle ran across the lawn and down the street with her glossy hair flying out behind her. She didn't stop until she'd caught Dale in a nearly smothering embrace. "Are you okay? Did he hurt you?"

Dale stood stiff in her arms, and Grant had no choice but to save the boy from being humiliated in front of the cops, who were sure to pull up at any moment. Motherly hugs were one thing. Motherly hugs in front of a bunch of grown men were another.

Grant tugged at the fluffy bathrobe Isabelle had brought out with her. "That for me?" he asked Isabelle.

She pulled away from Dale just as the flashing lights started glittering off the windows down the street. Grant made quick work of pulling on the robe and tucked his weapon into one of the deep pockets.

Lights in the neighboring houses started flipping on one after another, and anxious faces peered out. And he was freezing his ass off.

"I suggest we move this inside," he said, taking both Isabelle and Dale by the arm to get them moving toward the house.

They made it as far as the front door when a pair of police officers caught up with them.

Grant wanted to speak to them, but he preferred not to do it in a pink bathrobe that barely stretched over his shoulders. Especially not one with a weapon in the pocket that would raise all kinds of unnecessary questions.

He said loud enough for the cops to hear, "I'm going to put some pants on. I'll be right back," before running up the stairs two at a time.

Isabelle couldn't think straight. All she could think about were the things that could have happened to Dale if Grant hadn't found him.

Thank God Grant had been here and Dale was safe.

Her hands shook with relief as she rummaged through the cabinets, looking for the coffee can she was sure had to be in here somewhere. She always drank tea, but she kept coffee on hand for guests. Where the heck was it?

Tears blurred her vision, making the search harder. She wiped her eyes carefully, hoping they wouldn't be red and puffy when she went back in the living room where the police were currently questioning Dale. She didn't want him to know how much Wyatt's presence and the danger it posed had upset her.

Or how much it had hurt her that Dale had gone out without even letting her know. She'd thought he trusted her more than that, but apparently, she'd been wrong.

Maybe she'd been wrong about a lot of things, including making the decision to become a foster parent.

What the heck was she thinking? She didn't know anything about raising kids. She hadn't even had a normal childhood herself to serve as a good example. Who was she to think that she could help someone else when she was just as lost and confused as they were?

Isabelle stifled a sob and tried to pull herself together. Dale was safe. That's what really mattered here, not her hurt feelings.

Where the hell was that blasted coffee?

Isabelle was in the process of emptying the third cabinet onto the counter when Grant came into the kitchen. He was dressed again, for which she was grateful. Nearly-naked Grant was too much stimulus for any red-blooded woman, and she had enough to deal with without adding to it a pile of useless hormones.

"What are you looking for?"

"The coffee. I know there's some in here somewhere." She slammed a cabinet shut and started emptying another one.

Grant came up behind her and looped his fingers around her wrists, stilling her frantic motions. He wrapped his arms, as well as her own, around her body in a hug. Or maybe he was playing human straitjacket.

Either way, his touch felt good, so solid and reassuring she couldn't help but lean into him just a little.

The hard curves of his chest pressing against her back and the living warmth of his body sinking into her made it easier to breathe. She wasn't used to being comforted, and it shook her to the core.

He leaned down so his mouth was right by her ear. "It's going to be okay," he told her in a voice so soothing and confident she almost believed him.

Too bad it was all a gentle lie her body was willing to accept in an effort to find solace. The truth was, no matter how long he held her, or what pretty words he whispered, her problems would all still be waiting for her when he walked away.

She was a big girl and needed to learn to deal with this kind of crisis on her own. "I need to find the coffee."

Isabelle moved against him to let him know she wanted him to let go, but he ignored her and held her tight. "To hell with the coffee. I'll go buy you some when this is all over."

"But I'm supposed to make coffee for the police." She knew she sounded frantic, but she couldn't stop the words from coming out.

Grant loosened his hold and turned her around to face him, but he didn't let go completely. His big hands slid up and down her arms, helping to soothe her rattled nerves. "Says who?"

"The TV."

His mouth lifted in amusement. "You're a teacher. You're supposed to know better than to do everything you see on TV. I've already told them what I saw and gave them Wyatt's license plate number. They want to speak to you."

"Why? I didn't do anything to help Dale."

"He needs you."

The crushing weight of what could have happened to him nearly drove Isabelle to her knees. He was her responsibility, and she'd failed him. "You're the one who saved him. You should go out there."

"I didn't save him, Isabelle. I just ran his dad off."

"What if you hadn't been here tonight?"

He frowned at her as if he didn't understand what she meant. "You would have dealt with the situation yourself."

"How? I don't have a gun. I don't even know how to use one."

He was still rubbing her arms in a slow, soothing sweep. "We can take care of that if you want, but you don't need one. Hell, I didn't need one, either, I just didn't know that when I woke up to you yelling for Dale."

"I could never have climbed out that window like you did."

"The stairs would have worked fine. I was just showing off for you."

The grim, determined look he'd worn on his face at the time was proof enough for her that he would have walked naked into a burning building if it would have saved him a few seconds in getting to Dale. "Liar."

"Maybe a little," he admitted.

"I didn't even see Wyatt's car. He could have hurt Dale in the time it took me to even figure out where he'd gone."

"That wasn't going to happen. I'm glad I was here for

you tonight, but that doesn't mean that you wouldn't have taken care of it on your own."

Her real fear billowed up inside her, and she couldn't stop a fresh flow of tears from sliding down her cheeks, no matter how much she hated the idea of letting Grant see her cry. She didn't want to admit the truth, but she knew she had to. There were few people in her life who would understand, but she was sure Grant was one of them. "As much as I want to, I'm not sure I should be a parent."

"Why not?"

"I never had a real family. I have no clue how one is supposed to work. My teenage mother put me up for adoption at birth. I was passed from one home to another, and although most of them were good, I always knew it would be temporary." *She* was temporary, like a Christmas tree. Everyone made a fuss over having her in their home, but only for a short while. Then she was simply in the way, taking up space, making a mess, and a pain to dispose of. "What right do I have to inflict my messed-up childhood and lack of experience on Dale? He deserves better than I'll ever be able to give."

Grant hugged her tight, cupping her head in his big hand. "Shhh, now. Don't talk like that or make more of this than it is. This was not a failure on your part as a parent."

She could hear the strong, steady beat of his heart and feel the low rumble of his voice. It had been a long time since she'd been this close to a man, and part of her wanted to curl into him and pretend that all of this was going to go away. "That's easy for you to say."

"Because it's the truth. Kids sneak out all the time to do stupid stuff. Dale made a bad decision. That's all that happened here tonight. He might have even made it for a good reason. You won't know until you talk to him."

Isabelle wanted Grant to be right. She wanted to believe that she hadn't failed at such a fundamental thing as keeping Dale safe. Still, that fear crouched inside her, turning her stomach and making her palms sweat.

She'd never had a mother. She was afraid she didn't know how to be one.

Isabelle took a deep breath and pulled herself back together. She'd be afraid later. Right now she had to deal with this mess. Kids messed up. Parents corrected them. If she wanted to be a parent, that was her job.

She eased away from the comfort of Grant's embrace and looked up at him. "He's never going to make that same bad decision again. I promise you that."

Grant gave her an approving nod. "I'm sure he won't once he realizes he made you cry. There's nothing worse on a young man than making a woman cry."

"Yeah, right."

"Between the two of us, who has more experience at being a young man?"

Isabelle let her head fall to Grant's chest in frustration. "I don't know if I'm the right person to do this."

"Do you know someone better for the job?"

"No, but I'm sure there's someone."

"Right. Because there are so many good foster homes open and available for a teenage boy with an ex-convict father. You know what a load of crap that is. He's lucky to have found you."

"I'm the lucky one. He's such a great kid. This is the first time he's ever given me any trouble."

"I doubt trouble is what he set out to cause tonight. Why

don't you talk to him? Talk to the police. I'm sure that you can all sort this out and find a way to get Wyatt back in jail for breaking parole or something."

"Do you think?"

"You won't know until you try."

Isabelle nodded. "I'll talk to them."

She stepped out of Grant's embrace and went to wipe the tears off her face, but he grabbed her hand, stopping her. "Let him see the consequences of his actions. He needs to know that what he does affects you."

"I don't want him to see me cry."

"Better that than letting him do something like this again. Trust me."

Isabelle stared into Grant's amber eyes for a long moment. "I do trust you." And because she did, she left her face wet and went to join her son.

Trina didn't know how long she'd have before her kidnapper came back, so she had to hurry. The drugs he'd given her had finally worn off enough that she could get off the cot without falling down. Hitting her head on that hard cement floor once had been enough of an incentive for her to be more careful this time.

She had no idea where she was, but she felt like it had to be a basement. Every once in a while, she could hear the faint creak of floorboards overhead and what she thought might be the sound of water running in the pipes.

Wherever she was, it was dark. There were no windows, no lamps. The light switch for the single bulb overhead was on the outside of the door. Only a thin ribbon of light from under the door allowed her to see anything at all.

At least he'd left her that much. Trina was sure that if he hadn't, she would have panicked weeks ago.

Or was it months? She couldn't be sure anymore. Her life was now a series of drug-fogged memories and terrifying nightmares where Henry was killed over and over again.

Every time she closed her eyes, she saw his body hanging from the ceiling, swinging slightly, that motion the only remnant of the life that had burned so bright within him.

Trina's eyes welled up, and she bit her lip to keep from crying. It was hard enough to see in here without the added hindrance of tears. If she was going to have any chance of getting out of here, she needed to find a plan soon, before her husband's killer came back and drugged her into unconsciousness again.

She looked around the tiny space. It was about eight feet square, with a cot along one wall and a toilet and sink tucked in the corner. The floor was bare concrete. There was no mattress or blankets. The only thing in here that wasn't permanently attached was the light bulb in the ceiling, a bar of soap, a washcloth, and a single roll of toilet paper.

Trina had already tried to open the door the last time she'd woken, and it hadn't budged. She wasn't going to waste whatever little time she had now trying it again. She needed a new idea.

Maybe if she moved the cot, she could reach the light bulb, break it, and use the pieces as a weapon.

Of course, as soon as the killer came back and saw the light didn't go on, he'd know something was wrong.

He'd warned her that he'd punish her if she gave him any trouble.

He seemed to know how long the drugs he gave her lasted, and she was never awake for more than a few minutes before he knocked her out again.

Trina figured she had maybe twenty minutes before he came back to drug her again.

A sick sense of panic swelled inside her veins. She didn't know how much longer she was going to last in here. She'd spent most of her imprisonment sleeping, and already she was starting to feel her mind fraying around the edges.

Not to mention her body was getting weaker by the day. With little use, her muscles were wasting away, and even though the killer fed her, she didn't eat much. She couldn't, no matter how hard she tried.

Trina scanned the dank space, searching for something she'd missed before. Something she could use as a weapon or a tool.

The toilet. It had bits of metal in it, didn't it?

Trina stumbled across the small space and lifted the lid off the back of the tank. It was dark inside. None of the ribbon of light from under the door found its way in here.

She stuck her hands in the frigid water, feeling around for something she could use. The first thing she found was a metal rod that connected the lever on the outside of the toilet to a chain.

Hope speared through her as her shaking fingers moved over the rod, trying to figure out how to free it.

The next time her husband's killer came at her with that needle, she was going to ram this thing right into his eye.

CHAPTER FIVE

❖

Isabelle had to sit on her hands to keep from reaching out to Dale to reassure herself he was okay. She knew he wouldn't like her coddling him in front of the two officers sitting on the couch.

"Let's go over this one more time," said the younger of the two policemen, Officer Reynolds. He was rope thin and held his pencil poised over his notepad in anxious anticipation. "You were in your room studying at what time?"

Dale's jaw tightened with frustration. "It was about ten, I guess."

"And then what?"

"I already told you," Dale nearly shouted.

Isabelle had never seen him so agitated, and it worried her. Maybe something more had happened than the simple talk he claimed he'd had with his father. Then again, maybe that was enough.

Reynolds opened his mouth, but the older officer who'd introduced himself as Officer Brooks held out a warning hand to his partner. He had a calm patience about him that spoke to his obvious experience in dealing with children. He was a little on the heavy side, but it only made him look more rock solid.

"Tell us again, son," said Officer Brooks in a calm, steady voice. "It helps make sure we didn't mess up any details the first time 'round."

Dale sighed and rubbed his eyes with the heels of his hands. It was nearly midnight, and he looked exhausted. Isabelle barely stifled the urge to run the police off and send Dale to get some much-needed rest.

"He threw rocks at my window," said Dale. "I thought it was one of my friends, so I went over, but it was Da—Wyatt."

He'd almost said "Dad," and the fact that he had to stop himself and call his father by his first name to distance himself from him broke Isabelle's heart.

"Had you already opened the window at that time?" asked the older officer.

"No, but he wanted me to, so I did."

The younger policeman's pencil raced across the page, writing down who knew what vital information.

"What did he say to you then?" asked Brooks.

"I already told you!" shouted Dale.

Isabelle couldn't hold back any longer. She put her hand on his shoulder, hoping she was offering more comfort than embarrassment.

Dale stiffened at her touch, but at least he didn't shrug her off.

"Tell us again," came the calm reply of the seasoned cop.

"Coffee, anyone?" Grant came into the living room with a fistful of coffee mugs and a full carafe. Apparently he'd found the secret hiding place that she couldn't.

The young cop perked up, nodding at the offer, but Brooks kept his attention steady on Dale, not letting the interruption bother him. "Go ahead, son. Tell us what he said."

Dale let out a gusty, dramatic sigh. "He wanted me to come out and talk to him."

"So you did."

"Yes. I did."

"Why?"

Dale looked at Isabelle, then down at the carpet.

Brooks looked at Isabelle, too, then nodded as if he'd found the answer. "You didn't want him to come in the house, did you?"

Dale shot to his feet, knocking Isabelle's arm away from him, and threw his hands up in exasperation. "I don't know why you all are making such a big deal about this. He didn't hurt me. All we did was talk."

"What about?" asked Brooks, unfazed by Dale's explosion.

Dale's mouth tightened, and he remained silent.

"Dale?" said Isabelle. "What did he want?"

"Nothing," said Dale.

Grant handed both officers a cup of coffee, then propped himself against the wall, listening.

The younger policeman stopped writing long enough to shoot Dale a disbelieving look. "He came all the way out here late at night to talk to you about *nothing?* You don't think we're going to believe that, do you?"

Isabelle fought an uncharacteristic surge of anger but lost the battle. They were not going to treat her son like a felon. "Hey! Don't you call Dale a liar in his own home. If he said they talked about nothing, I'm sure that's what happened."

"Well, Dale?" asked Brooks. "Was it really nothing?"

Dale gave Isabelle a guilty grimace. "Well, it wasn't exactly nothing. Just stuff, you know. He asked if I liked it here. And he wanted to know who Amanda and Rachel were. If they were close friends of yours, Isabelle."

The hair on the back of Isabelle's neck rose. If he knew about them, he'd been watching the house since last week, when she'd babysat Rachel.

"Who are they?" asked Brooks.

Her voice came out faint. "Amanda's a friend of mine. Rachel is her daughter and my student. She's seven."

The officer's mouth flattened. "Did he threaten them, Dale?"

"No. He said he thought Amanda was hot and wanted to ask her out. I didn't tell him who they were. I swear."

"Good. That's good." Brooks looked to Isabelle. "Do you have Amanda's address and phone number?"

"In my address book." She fetched it from the kitchen and gave it to the younger officer, who wrote the information down. "Can you drive by her place and check on her?"

"Yes, ma'am. We'll see to it."

Isabelle wished that relieved her, but it wasn't enough. She was going to have to warn Amanda, let her know to keep an eye out for Wyatt.

"Did Wyatt ask you to leave with him, Dale?" asked Brooks.

"No."

"Did he threaten you in any way?"

"No."

"Did he threaten anyone else?"

Dale paled a little and glanced Isabelle's way. "Not exactly."

"What do you mean by that?" asked Brooks.

Dale shrugged. "I just know him, you know."

And he'd seen Wyatt hurt his mother over and over.

Isabelle laced her fingers together tight to keep them to herself. "You don't need to worry about me, Dale. I'll be careful."

Dale flushed a guilty red, but didn't look at her. Instead he asked Brooks, "Are you worried that he might hurt Isabelle or Amanda?"

"I'm just trying to sort this out, son. Did he say he was going to come back, or ask you to meet him again?"

"No. I think he was going to, but then Grant came along and he ran off."

The younger man was still scribbling when his partner stood and slugged back the last of the coffee, signaling they were done here. "If he tries to contact you again, you need to let Isabelle or one of us know, okay?"

"He's not going to hurt me," said Dale.

"I'm sure you're right," soothed the older man. "But he's not supposed to see you without supervision. If he tries anything, we won't have any choice but to charge him with breaking a court order. Maybe even parental kidnapping."

Dale snarled, "Good. I want him to go back to jail."

"Keep your distance, son. It's the safest thing for both of you and your friends." He turned to Isabelle. "We'll file a report in case you need any official documentation that he came by tonight. His caseworker can call for a copy in the morning."

"Thank you."

He handed both her and Dale a business card. "If you

need anything else, don't hesitate to call. Custody battles can turn ugly fast."

"I understand."

He gave her a sympathetic nod. "Thanks for the coffee."

The police left, and Isabelle shut and locked the door. Dale stood there with his feet braced apart and his face grim. He looked like he was expecting a punch, and Isabelle felt the sting of tears. Again. He'd been through so much. All she wanted was for him to be safe and happy and healthy. He had so much potential that that's all he needed to bloom. It wasn't much to ask.

When she said nothing, Dale started to fidget like he was nervous. "I'm sorry."

"You should be. You really scared me tonight." It came out as a whisper, soggy with tears even though she'd tried to stay strong.

"I didn't mean to."

"I know you didn't. I also know you'll never sneak out like that again, right?"

"I promise."

"Good. Go on to bed and make sure that window is locked. We'll talk more after you've had some sleep."

Dale scrambled away as if he couldn't get away fast enough. He was halfway up the stairs when he stopped but didn't turn around. Isabelle knew he wanted to say something, so she waited silently.

"I'm sorry I made you cry," he said and hurried up the stairs, two at a time.

❧

Grant moved quietly from window to window, checking each to make sure it was locked. Isabelle's house was old, and the only secure windows were the ones painted shut. Not that that would keep anyone from breaking the glass.

She needed a security system installed before he left. And maybe a big dog. That way he wouldn't have to worry about her when he was gone.

Yeah, right. Hardly a week had gone by since he'd joined the military that he hadn't thought about the sickly little girl he'd left behind and wondered how she was. Her cards and letters had helped ease his mind, but not entirely. And now his fears were no longer all in his head. The danger to her and Dale was real, and he had to do something to fix it.

Grant finished his security check downstairs and went to the second floor.

He heard the soft thrum of music coming from Dale's room, and without knocking and waking him up, Grant crept inside.

Dale was asleep, his body flung out across the bed, covers twisted around his restless body, barely keeping him warm. Poor kid had been through the wringer tonight, and it wasn't over yet. Not until Wyatt went back to jail or gave up any hope of reuniting with his son.

Grant grabbed the blanket off his own bed and covered Dale up. After a quick window check, he left the boy in peace, hoping he'd found some solace in sleep.

The light of day was only going to highlight last night's ugliness. Grant knew that from experience.

He shut Dale's door and went back to his own room. The bright yellow walls hurt his tired eyes, even though he was sure the color was meant to be cheerful. Isabelle's touch, no doubt.

He sat on the wide bottom bunk bed, careful not to smack his head on the narrower twin bed above him. He unlaced his boots and toed them off. He'd been so exhausted when he'd crashed earlier that he hadn't noticed anything about the room other than the fact that it had a bed and he wanted to be in it.

Two small chests of drawers flanked the window. The drawer pulls were molded into the shapes of different animals. On the closet door was a growth chart, void of any markings. A child-sized art center sat in the corner, waiting for the touch of little hands to give it life.

It was a kid's room, freshly decorated, waiting to be filled.

Was Isabelle expecting another foster child? If so, then maybe Grant was in the way. Maybe he shouldn't have been so insistent that he stay here.

Then again, people were dying, and Dale's father was a complete asshole who clearly could not be trusted. Until those problems were removed, she had no business bringing a child here.

Not that it was any of his business. He had no say in her life.

That fact shouldn't have bothered him nearly as much as it did.

Grant stripped out of his clothes and settled back in bed. He couldn't let himself get sucked into her problems. He'd talk to the police and see if her suspicions about the deaths were valid, beef up her security, and be on his way.

The thought made him uneasy. Isabelle had no idea how

to protect herself. And she had a child. He had to be sure it was safe to leave them. There could be no mistakes.

And once he was sure, he'd hit the road and never come back. This place was full of bad memories, and more were piling up by the day.

If he never saw Isabelle cry again, it would suit him just fine.

Trina was breathing so hard she almost didn't hear the faint squeak of floorboards overhead.

The killer was back.

She jerked at the metal rod inside the toilet tank, but it didn't come free. All she managed to do was bend it so that the water started rushing out of the tank in a deafening hiss.

Now she couldn't hear anything. He could be coming down the stairs right now and she couldn't hear it.

Panic flooded her body, making her hands shake. A quiet sob of panic tore from her chest. She had to stop before he caught her.

Trina let go of the rod, but the tank was refilling and she still couldn't hear over the noise of water.

Inside her prison, the light bulb blazed to life, searing her eyes.

The lid to the tank was still off. He was going to catch her.

He slid a key into the lock. Metal scraped metal as it turned.

Trina grabbed the lid and set it in place. Her hands were soaked, and water dripped off the edge of the lid.

He was going to know what she'd been doing. He was going to see the water and know. And then he'd punish her. He'd kill her like he had Henry.

Terror gripped her and squeezed hard.

The doorknob rattled as he turned it.

Trina grabbed the washcloth with one hand while she turned on the sink with the other. She swiped away the telltale wetness with the cloth.

He opened the door.

She plunged the cloth into the streaming water and covered her terrified face with the cloth to hide any signs of guilt.

He husband's killer walked in. She could hear his heavy footsteps on the concrete floor.

Trina spun around and held the dripping cloth to her chest, praying it would hide any water spots she might have gotten on her while fiddling in the tank.

"You're awake," he said, giving her a smile that made his blue eyes sparkle. "Did you sleep well?"

Trina refused to answer such a ludicrous question.

He set a tray of food on the foot of her cot. Her stomach turned at the sight of it, but she needed to eat and retain what little strength she had left.

"Eat," he ordered.

Trina stared into his face, loathing everything about him. His neatly combed hair, the wide bulk of his shoulders. But most of all, she hated his blue eyes. They were eerily bright, clear, and they missed nothing.

"Why are you keeping me here?" she asked him for the hundredth time.

And for the hundredth time, he replied, "It's not your turn yet."

Trina didn't know what he meant, but her instincts told her it wasn't good. "My turn to die?"

"Eat," he told her again, and this time there was an edge of steel in his voice. "Now, or I'll take away the food and put you back to sleep hungry."

Put her back to sleep. A chill of revulsion raced over her skin, making her stomach turn even more. Chocking down the sandwich he'd made her wasn't going to be easy, but Trina was going to find a way.

The next time she woke up, she was going to get that metal rod out of the toilet and kill the fucker.

CHAPTER SIX

Late the next morning while Isabelle was at school, Grant used the key she'd loaned him to let himself back into her house.

She was right. The police weren't going to be jumping to help them without more evidence. Three of the people who'd died had done so in other states, so it was well out of their jurisdiction. And they weren't about to bring in the feds unless they had some solid proof. The best they were willing to offer was to give Grant the phone numbers for the right people to contact about the out-of-state deaths so he could ask them questions.

From the tone of the detective he'd talked to, they weren't likely to be of any more aid than the local police were. Which meant Grant had to figure out whether or not he believed Isabelle's theory. If he didn't, then he'd go on his way, after making sure Wyatt was back behind bars where he belonged. If he did believe her, then that changed his course of action dramatically.

Neither Isabelle nor Dale was due home anytime soon, so Grant fixed himself a pot of coffee and laid all of the information Isabelle had given him out on the kitchen table.

He'd purchased a map of the United States along with a notebook to help him organize the details.

He marked the map with the location of each death, then he assigned to it the name of the victim and date it had happened. He drew a line across the map, linking the dots in chronological order, but it didn't show any sort of pattern. No straight line, no circle or partial circle, there was no single highway connecting the cities. They jumped all over. That was a dead end.

Grant recorded other details in his notebook, hoping it would help him see some kind of pattern that would prove someone was acting alone. The times of day for each death differed, as well as the method of death. The victims had nothing in common other than the fact that they had all lived at Edgar Lavine's foster home at one time, which wasn't enough for the police to get involved.

Isabelle had included a small amount of personal information about each of the victims, but it looked to be only the kind of facts that the state would have on file for any foster child. There was a list of foster homes where each child had lived, and again, the only intersection was Lavine.

Grant compared the dates of the deaths to any significant date he could find in each file, hoping for a match. Birthdays were a bust, as was the date that each child came to live with Lavine. There was nothing he could see significant about the dates that each one died, though it would have been handy toward proving murder if they'd each happened to be killed on the anniversary of the day they entered Lavine's home or something similar. Maybe that would have been enough proof to get the police on the case.

He was out of ideas, mostly doodling on the paper, drawing lines between dates, when he noticed something. They'd died in the same order that they'd arrived at Lavine's home. That couldn't be a coincidence, could it?

He knew one person who would know the answer to that for sure, so he pulled out his cell phone and called Noelle, David's wife. She was freakishly smart and had a knack for seeing patterns, which is why she was now one of the foremost cryptologists in the nation.

"This had better be important," she answered after about ten rings.

"It's good to talk to you, too," said Grant.

"Grant! Sorry. I was rude, wasn't I?"

Grant couldn't help but smile. Noelle was easily distracted by her work, but she was the biggest egghead he could find. "Working on something important?"

"I hope so. Otherwise I'm being terribly overpaid."

"Good to hear it. I just need a quick favor. Can you tell me what the odds are that six people would die in a specific order?"

"What?" she asked, and he could hear in her tone that he now had her full attention, which was a truly rare thing for anyone but David or their new son. "What have you gotten yourself into now?"

"I don't know. It kinda depends on the answer to that question."

"You mean six specific people, right?"

"Right."

"Out of how large a group?"

"Does it really matter?"

"Absolutely."

Grant stifled the urge to rub his temples. "Out of a group of twelve."

"Can I assume they're each equally likely to die? Or is someone sick or significantly older?" She uttered the macabre questions with clinical detachment.

"Assume they're all equally likely to die. Just give me a ballpark, Noelle. That's all I need."

"Okay. Your ballpark is less than a percent. Would you like me to be more specific?"

"Uh, no." Less than one percent? That was a pretty tiny ballpark.

"Are you sure?" she asked, her tone telling him she thought he was making a gross error in judgment.

"Positive. Thanks, Noelle. I owe you one."

"Then get here as soon as you can. David could really use the help. He's swamped and it's making him grumpy."

"I thought Caleb was coming to help."

"He was, but Lana came down with that flu that's been going around, and Caleb refuses to leave her until she's better."

Guilt gnawed at Grant. He really needed to step this thing up and go do his job. His buddies needed him, and they were as close to real family as he was going to get. He couldn't let them down. "I'll hurry. I promise. Kiss the baby for me?"

"Twice."

"Thanks, Noelle." Grant hung up and looked down at the notebook. It was looking more and more like Isabelle's instincts where right. Those people were murdered.

Which begged the question, who was next?

CHAPTER SEVEN

❧

Grant had just finished making dinner reservations when Dale got home from school.

He came in through the kitchen door and slammed his backpack down so hard it rattled the windows.

"Bad day?" asked Grant.

Dale jumped, clearly not expecting anyone to be home, and a bright flush of embarrassment stained his cheeks. "I'm fine."

"Your backpack would beg to differ."

Dale ignored the comment and headed straight for the refrigerator.

"I ordered a pizza earlier. Feel free to eat the leftovers."

Dale's voice perked up a notch. "Pizza?"

"With the works."

"Thanks, man." Dale loaded a plate and slid it into the microwave.

Silence reigned, but it wasn't that comfortable guy silence where there's just nothing that needs to be said. It was that awkward silence where Grant wanted to ask a teenage boy he hardly knew to tell him what made him throw his stuff around in anger and frustration.

It was possible that Dale had another run-in with his father, and if that was the case, Grant wanted to know about it and deal with it before Isabelle got home.

He found a pair of sodas in the fridge and set them on the table. "Would you mind keeping me company for a few minutes? It's been too quiet around here today. I almost invited the pizza guy in to share lunch with me."

"I was just going to go study, but I guess I can hang for a minute."

"That'd be great."

Dale sat down with his steaming pizza and started shoving the slices down, one after another. Grant was careful not to stare and sipped his soda slowly. "You look a little tired. Did you get any sleep last night?"

"Enough."

More thick silence filled the kitchen, making Grant squirm. He was no good at this tiptoe-around-the-teenager stuff. "Did something happen today?"

Dale lifted his eyes from his pizza and gave Grant a look that told him to back the hell off. "No."

"Because if Wyatt came around again bothering you, I'd really like to know about it."

"He didn't."

"Would you tell me if he did?" asked Grant, deciding that blunt might be a better approach.

"Why should I? I don't even know you, man. Just back the hell out of my business."

"I wish I could, Dale, but I know Isabelle worries about you, and she's a friend of mine, so—"

"You're only here because you want to fuck her," accused Dale.

Shock rocked Grant back in his chair. "Whoa. Hold on

a minute. First, that's not the reason I'm here. Second, if I were, we're both adults and it's none of your business."

"But it's your business whether or not I talk to Wyatt?"

"I'm only trying to help keep you safe."

Dale's lip lifted in a sneer. "I don't need or want your help."

"So you want Wyatt to keep coming around until something happens? Maybe even to Isabelle?"

"Of course not."

"Then tell me what's going on. You saw him again today, didn't you? That's why you're angry."

"No. I told you that it has nothing to do with him."

"Then what's got you so upset?"

"I failed a test!"

Grant fell into stunned silence. He'd expected some bigger problem and was totally unprepared for such mundane news. He knew that it was of monumental importance to Dale, but at least it wasn't life-or-death important. Grant stumbled to shift gears. "What class?"

"It wasn't for a class, moron. It was a practice test for the SATs. I've taken it twice now and fucked it up both times."

Grant ignored Dale's foul language and focused on the problem. "You can take the SATs more than once, right?"

"Yeah."

"Is there still time?"

"Yeah. Some."

"So take it again. I'll even help you study." Grant wasn't sure how much help he'd be, but he was willing to try. Now that he believed the deaths weren't suicides, he was going to be here for a few days until he could make sure the problem was dealt with.

"Why bother to take it again? I'll just fail again."

"You don't know that. If you study harder this time—"

"I study every free second I have, and it doesn't help. I know all the stuff on the test, but it just doesn't come out right when I'm sitting there. I get all nervous and know I'm going to suck, then that makes me more nervous, and pretty soon, they call time and I haven't even answered ten questions."

Grant had no idea how to help the kid, though he wished he could. He'd never been very good in school himself, so he wasn't going to be able to give him any pointers on testing. "Is there someone at school who can help?"

"I'm already working with a study group three nights a week and Saturday mornings. If I do any more than that, my grades will start to slip. I can't let that happen. I *need* to get into college." The desperation in Dale's voice was hauntingly familiar to Grant. He'd chosen to join the military as his escape route. Dale must have chosen college.

"You'll make it. You want it bad enough to do what it takes. I can tell."

Dale shoved away from the table, put his plate in the sink, and grabbed his backpack. On his way out of the kitchen, he said, "Sometimes it doesn't matter how bad you want something. You still don't get it."

There wasn't a doubt in Grant's mind that he was speaking with the voice of experience. Poor kid. He had a lot to deal with. Grant knew it would make him tougher in the end, but getting there was hard as hell.

He wanted to figure out some way to help Dale get through this, but he had no idea how. He didn't have any good fatherly advice for him, or any tricks on how to ace his test. He didn't even know what to say to make Dale feel better, which made him about a half a step away from useless.

Just like his old man.

It was best if Grant just didn't get involved. Dale wasn't his kid, so as long as he kept his mouth shut, he couldn't screw up the boy's life. He wasn't going to be here long, anyway, and when he left, he didn't want Dale to even think twice about it. Grant wasn't important to him, and it was going to stay that way. He wasn't going to get close to some kid, then walk away and leave them hanging, hoping he'd come back.

Grant would *not* repeat his father's mistakes.

CHAPTER EIGHT

Isabelle shifted nervously in the front seat of Grant's Mustang. Dinner tonight was not going to be pleasant. Not by a long shot.

"Relax," he said in a soothing tone as he eased the car onto the crowded highway. "Everything is going to be fine."

Grant settled a warm hand on her sleeve. She was sure he'd done it to soothe her, but the feel of his wide palm on her arm sent a little thrill careening through her. Her body started to heat up for him, and she was sure that if he hadn't been paying attention to traffic, he would have seen the flush of excitement warming her cheeks.

She hated it that she reacted to him so easily when she knew there could be nothing between them. He'd leave in a day or two. He had a life of his own to lead, and after the years of service he'd put in, he deserved it.

Besides, even if he'd decided to settle down here instead of Denver, it wouldn't be with her. There was something about her that drove people away. She didn't know what it was, because she'd always tried to be a good person, but she knew it was there. It had to be. Too many people had walked away from her during her life for her to believe it was a coincidence.

At least she wasn't alone now, left to stumble around trying to figure out how to protect those she cared about from a murderer. Even though she had some issues with the way Grant was choosing to proceed, she was glad he was here.

"I'm pretty sure that meeting publicly to talk about murder is a bad idea," she told him.

"I checked all the records you had listing the kids who'd lived with Lavine. The five of us are the only ones left alive. Six if you count Trina. Although it's likely that the killer is some social worker gone loony or something, it's possible the killer is one of them, so meeting in public is much better than meeting in private."

One of her friends the killer? A new rush of panic flittered through her system, chilling her skin.

She'd never considered that. Why would she after knowing these people for so long? It didn't seem possible that any of them would want to hurt others.

They could be dining with a murderer tonight. And if they were, how could they even tell?

Isabelle's hands started to shake, and her pulse pounded hard in her limbs. It was too frightening to consider. Even with Grant at her side.

She laced her fingers over her purse to keep Grant from seeing her tremble. She didn't want him to hold back information simply because he thought she wasn't strong enough to handle it. She'd find a way to handle whatever bad news he threw at her.

"I can't believe that any of them are capable of murder. I know these people. I've known them for years."

"The killer is probably someone else tied to Lavine, but either way, we have to warn the others. If the killer continues in order of when they arrived at Lavine's, then Everett is next. That's not the kind of news you give over the phone. And we're sure as hell not going to meet with him at his home, on the off chance that he's our guy and he pulls a gun."

Isabelle stifled a shiver of fear and revulsion. She still couldn't believe she hadn't seen what Grant had—that they were being killed in a certain order. At least that got the police to pay attention.

"What was the name of the detective assigned to our case?" she asked.

Grant exited the highway. "Clayton Mathews. I'll meet with him first thing in the morning and fill him in on the details while you're at work—unless you want to come along. In the meantime, he asked that we don't tell anyone that we know about the order of deaths. If the killer knows we know, he might change his pattern, which will make it a lot harder to keep people safe."

"I won't say anything, but they might not believe us without that little bit of news. The police didn't."

"It'll be our job to convince them," said Grant.

"And if we can't?"

He pulled into the parking lot of the Italian restaurant where they'd chosen to meet and parked the car on the outskirts of the lot, away from the other cars. Security lights cast deep shadows inside the Mustang and over Grant's lean face. He unfastened his seat belt and turned toward her, shifting his long body beneath the wheel. His golden eyes seemed to catch and hold the light, glittering in the dimness as he looked at her.

He was so beautiful it nearly made her forget all about their dinner plans. It would have been nice to sit here in the quiet with him and look her fill—soak him up as fantasy fuel for after he was gone.

His hand captured hers, and he cradled her fingers in his warm grip. His thumb stroked over her palm, sending a dancing riot of sensation careening toward her heart. He was such a gentle man when he touched her, and for a moment, she let herself imagine what it would be like to have him for a lover.

She could almost feel his wide hands sliding over her skin, grazing her stomach and ribs, cupping her breasts. He was always so warm, she was sure the heat of his touch would make her melt. She could only imagine how hot his mouth would be as it moved over her body.

The potent image made her tremble and drove all the oxygen from her lungs.

"Don't worry," said Grant. "We'll find a way to convince them. And if we can't do that, then we'll make sure they're protected."

"How?"

"The police will help now. Detective Mathews has ordered extra patrols on all of your homes."

"It's not enough. The police are overworked and understaffed."

"My buddy David can probably offer some help. He owns a private security company."

"You mean the man who you're going to work for? Isn't he going to be mad that you're not already there to help him?"

Grant shrugged and gave her that charming smile that made her feel hot all over—the one that no woman anywhere was strong enough to resist, the one that made her feel like she was the only woman alive and there was nowhere else on earth he'd rather be than here with her.

What a beautiful lie.

"He'll get over it," said Grant.

"For your sake, I hope so. I never meant to interfere with your new life."

"You're not interfering. I'm choosing to stay."

No matter the personal cost to his own life. That was the part he didn't say.

A rush of emotion tightened her throat, and she had to fight the urge to cry out of sheer gratitude. She'd felt the same way the night he'd pulled Lavine off of her and ended up handcuffed in the back of a police car with blood running down his chin.

"Thank you. It means the world to me that I'm not alone in this."

Isabelle laced her fingers through his. He was so easy to touch, never making her feel like she'd invaded his space, and the more she touched him the easier it got. In truth, she hardly knew him at all, but he'd been in her thoughts for so many years, her body couldn't tell the difference.

She loved the way his hand felt so solid and strong and how the work-roughened patches of his skin stroked over her softer flesh. He was all man, completely beautiful, and she was finding it more and more difficult concentrating on their job rather than what it would feel like to have those hands glide over her body in a lover's caress.

"You'll never be alone, Isabelle. Not so long as I'm only a phone call away."

She had nothing to say to equal the power of those words, and she tried hard not to tear up. She didn't want to scare him away or make him think he'd said something wrong when he'd given her such a priceless gift. "I'm lucky to have you in my life." Even if it was only for a few days every fourteen years.

He gave her a grin and a wink. "You haven't seen anything yet, honey."

Isabelle laughed and her tension dissipated. She was pretty sure Grant had planned for that to happen—his teasing calculated to take her mind off what was at stake.

"Let's go before we start steaming up the windows."

Grant waggled his eyebrows. "I don't know. Steaming up the windows sounds like a fun time to me."

She grinned at him and unfastened her seat belt. "Maybe after dinner."

"Is that a promise?"

"I see you're still the same insatiable flirt."

"Are you kidding? I'm much better at it now than when you last knew me."

They got out of the car and headed across the parking lot.

"Practice makes perfect. Is that it?" she asked.

Grant looped an arm over her shoulders and pulled her tight against his side. "I've only been practicing because I wanted to make sure I was good enough for you."

She shook her head at his ridiculous statement. "I bet you say that to all the women."

"Maybe, but it's always been a lie before now," he teased.

Isabelle laughed. "If some woman ever does manage to pin you down, she's going to have her hands full, isn't she?"

Grant grin widened. "You were peeking when I showered this morning, weren't you?"

Against her will, her eyes traveled down his body until she was looking at the front of his jeans.

Grant tipped her chin back up with his hand. "No staring," he chided. "When you look it makes me hot, and I am not walking into a packed restaurant to face a potential killer with a raging boner."

"You were the one who brought it up," she reminded him with a grin.

"No, honey. You're the one who brought it up. I promise."

The idea she could turn him on made her feel a wicked sense of power. She was itching to see whether he was simply teasing her or he really meant that she could turn him on, but they were at the restaurant doors and her time to experiment was up.

It wasn't until he was speaking with the hostess that she realized all of her worry and fear had faded away. She no longer felt brittle with tension. He'd distracted her on purpose, she was sure, and once again, she owed him a debt of gratitude.

The hostess showed them to their table.

Isabelle's feet slowed as they got closer, and her stomach started to churn.

"You can do this," whispered Grant. "I'll be right beside you."

She had no choice but to do this. Her friends needed her.

Isabelle plastered a fake smile on her face and went to the table.

Amanda was already there, waiting for them. Smudges

of fatigue darkened her cocoa brown eyes, and her blond hair fell limp around her pretty face. She looked out of place here, wearing the uniform from one of her two waitressing jobs.

Isabelle greeted her with a hug. "Long day?" she asked.

"Not as long as it will be when I'm finally done. I've got another shift in an hour, so I can't stay long."

"We'll try to be quick, then." Isabelle turned and motioned toward Grant. "Do you remember Grant Kent?"

Amanda took the hand Grant offered. "How could I forget? You were my first crush."

Grant gave her the same charming smile that had probably caused the crush to begin with. It certainly had caused Isabelle's. "I'm flattered."

Amanda chuckled. "I'm sure you are. I look so glamorous in my uniform."

Grant winked at her. "Absolutely fetching."

Isabelle's little stab of jealousy shocked her. Grant was a die-hard flirt, and she had no reason to mind that he was doing it with Amanda. But she did.

"Where's Rachel?" Isabelle asked Amanda, interrupting their banter.

"The teenage girl next door watches her for me on my late nights, which are almost all of them lately. I don't know what I'll do when my babysitter goes off to college next year."

"Rachel can always come stay with me when you're working. I'd enjoy having the company, especially since Dale will be leaving next year, too." Isabelle kept the sadness from her voice so Amanda wouldn't think it had anything to do with her little girl. Rachel was a joy to be around and would help ease Isabelle's sense of loss when Dale went to college. She knew it was the way it was supposed to be, and that she'd be proud of him when he left, but she wasn't looking forward to him leaving.

Amanda's look of relief made Isabelle ache for her friend. The poor woman was barely holding her life together. She'd just come out of a bad marriage, had to work two jobs to make ends meet, and, on top of it all, her daughter was a constant worry. Rachel was one of Isabelle's students and shy to the point of being nearly crippled by it. Isabelle had been working on pulling her out of her shell for two years now, but she hadn't made much progress.

"She loves staying with you," said Amanda. "That's all she could talk about last week after you watched her."

"I'm not sure if that's a good idea," said Grant. "At least not until Wyatt is back behind bars."

Amanda looked from Grant to Isabelle. "Wyatt?"

"Dale's father. He came to my house last night. He told Dale he'd seen you and Rachel there."

Grant's mouth flattened. "He said you were hot, which means he's taken some interest in you. You need to be careful. He's a dangerous man."

Amanda's brown eyes closed in weariness. "Don't worry. I'm used to watching out for dangerous men."

Ricky kept his eyes fixed on the wad of cash dangling in front of him in a clear plastic bag. The muscle-bound man holding it creeped him out, but for that much cash, Ricky could stand a little creepy.

Ricky squared his shoulders and tried to pretend he

wasn't aching to reach out and snatch that bag away. "That's not enough for anything permanent, pops, but it's enough to rough the guy up a little. Send him a message."

The man's face was shadowed by his deep hood, but his eyes still glowed bright blue. "A broken leg would be my first choice. That way, he won't be able to run away."

From what, Ricky didn't dare ask. He so did not want to know.

"Broken leg. Got it." Ricky stared at the money and had to shove his hands deep in his pockets to keep from snatching it away. He needed a fix bad, and that much dough would keep him hooked up for a month.

"He'll be with a woman. Do not touch her."

"Sure. Whatever you want."

Ricky pulled his gaze away from the money long enough to check out the guy's face. He had a creepy-serious look in his eyes that said he meant business. Those eerie blue eyes would haunt Ricky's dreams for a year, he was sure.

"If you hurt the woman, I'll find you and kill you in your sleep. Slowly. Are we clear?"

Even with his body burning for a fix, Ricky still felt the shudder of fear that slid through him. "We're clear. Can I call in my crew?"

"I don't care how you get the job done, just do it tonight. They'll be coming out of the restaurant soon. He drives a flashy silver Mustang. Be waiting for him."

The guy offered him the bag of cash, and Ricky grabbed it and stuffed it down the front of his jeans for safekeeping. "I won't be late, man."

And he wouldn't. No way was he going to give creep-o here a reason to come back and find him.

Grant hadn't actually expected any of tonight's dinner companions to stand up and announce they were a killer, but it would have been nice.

David had called today and was breathing down his neck about getting his ass out to Denver, pronto. And if that wasn't enough to light a fire under his ass to get out of town, his inconvenient attraction to Isabelle would have done the job.

On the way into the restaurant, he'd only meant to tease her to get her mind off of all the doom and gloom, but it had backfired in a serious way. As soon as her exotic green eyes had slid down his body, looking like he was something good to eat, he knew he was in over his head.

She wasn't a kid anymore. She wasn't married or attached in any way. She was fair game. And Grant really wanted to play.

He stared across the table to where she spoke quietly to Amanda. The flickering candle on the table cast a soft light over her skin, making it glow. The flame was reflected by her glossy hair, making it shimmer every time she moved.

It was the kind of sight a man never got tired of seeing, and right then, Grant knew he was headed for trouble. He wasn't good at keeping his hands to himself. Especially not when he knew he wasn't the only one wanting to touch.

He'd just reached out his hand to stroke hers when their next dinner companion arrived. Grant pulled his hand back and rose to his feet.

"Everett," greeted Isabelle. "I'm so glad you could make it. Do you remember Grant?"

Everett was on the short side, with mousy brown hair that was combed to exacting standards. His glasses were too large for his face and thick enough that they'd worn grooves in the side of his nose from years of being perched in the same spot. He gave Grant a limp, sweaty handshake, which sent a stack of papers under his own arm fluttering to the floor.

"Sorry," he squeaked out and dropped to the floor to frantically recover his papers.

Grant bent down to help, using the opportunity to see what Everett was toting around. Without looking like he was, Grant scanned the pages as he picked them up. They were financial documents of some kind, along with tax forms. Isabelle's tax forms.

What the hell was he doing with those?

"I'm sorry, Isabelle," said Everett. "I was going to give these to you tonight, but now I'll have to take them home and reorganize them."

"It's fine," soothed Isabelle as she helped gather papers. "Tax day isn't for a while yet. I'm just glad you were able to fit me in. I know how busy you are this time of year."

Everett blushed. "It was no problem. Your forms are simple."

She gave him a wide smile. "Then why can't I figure it out myself? I don't know what I'd do without you."

Everett's blush darkened, and he tugged at his tie as if he had a hard time swallowing.

Grant handed Everett the folder that had housed all of the papers and watched as he carefully righted the chaotic stack of tax forms.

"You're an accountant now?" asked Grant as he helped Everett to his feet.

"Yes." He set the folder on the table and brushed off his knees, though Grant could see no dirt.

"That's great."

"I suppose. It pays the bills."

Everett sat down across the table from Isabelle but barely raised his eyes from his lap. The way he could hardly look at Isabelle without blushing made Grant think that the guy had a bad case of the hots for her.

Not that Grant blamed him.

Keith showed up right on Everett's heels. He smiled at Grant and shook his hand, while offering hugs to the ladies and a hearty slap on the back to Everett. The smaller man nearly landed on the floor, but Grant steadied him.

"Good to see you all again," said Keith. "We should get together like this more often, though under better circumstances if I read Isabelle's expression right."

"That would be nice," said Isabelle, "but we'll have to do it without Grant. He's on his way out of town in a couple of days, so enjoy him while he's here."

Grant raised a brow at her comment and said in a low voice to her, "I do so like to be enjoyed."

Isabelle shot him a warning look, but it was softened by the feminine smile that warmed her mouth.

"Amanda doesn't have much time, so I'm going to get right to it." Isabelle cleared her throat and glanced nervously at Grant.

He nodded in encouragement. "Go ahead, honey."

Keith gave him a narrow, disapproving look at his endearment, but Grant ignored him. He sat back and let Isabelle explain to the group what was going on while he kept an eye on their reactions. He was hoping that something about one of them would jump out at him and proclaim their guilt as the killer.

She took a deep breath. "I think we're all in danger. I have reason to believe that someone is killing people who used to live with Lavine and staging their deaths as suicides."

Amanda's weary eyes widened. "Please tell me this is a joke."

Isabelle reached for her hand. "I'm sorry, but it's not."

Everett sat silently.

Keith leaned forward, his handsome face furrowed with concern. "I looked into those deaths when you told me about them, Isabelle. There was nothing to support your claim. You talked to the police, and so did I."

"The police were wrong not to believe me," said Isabelle.

Keith shook his head at her. "Those poor people were suffering and chose to end it. They'd never want their actions to make the rest of us afraid. I can't believe you're doing this."

Isabelle frowned at Keith, then pinned the others with a pleading look. "I wouldn't worry you all with this if I didn't think it was real."

Amanda gulped down some water, and Grant noticed her hand shake. "I can't deal with this right now. I have to go to work." She stood and slung her purse over her arm.

Isabelle shot to her feet. "Amanda, wait. We need to figure out what to do."

"What to do?" Amanda nearly shouted.

People at neighboring tables glanced over, but Grant gave them a hard stare, telling them to mind their own damn business. They went back to eating with only curious, fleeting glances toward the women.

Amanda lowered her voice. "What I have to do is go to work and pray my tips are good enough tonight that I can make my rent payment tomorrow. Then when I get home, I have to do laundry so Rachel has something to wear to school tomorrow and so that I can get to my next job by six in the morning wearing a clean uniform so I don't get fired. I'm already doing everything I can. I can't *do* any more."

"But you could be in danger," said Isabelle.

"I'm already in danger of not being able to put a roof to put over my daughter's head, or food on her plate. For a mom, it doesn't get more dangerous than that."

Isabelle took hold of Amanda's arm, keeping her from fleeing. "Please, let us find a way to help you. I have some friends you could go stay with where no one could find you or Rachel."

"And what about my jobs? Rachel's school? We can't walk away from our lives."

"You could stay with me. I'll get Rachel to school."

"She's been through enough already. If you want to help, then you all figure out what I can do that doesn't cost me my paychecks or uproot my daughter's life and I'll listen. But right now, I've got to go to work."

Isabelle followed after Amanda for a few steps, then came to a halt. The look of failure on her face made Grant want to gather her in his arms.

He stepped in front of Isabelle, who was still watching Amanda leave and tilted her chin up until she looked him in the eye. He kept his voice low enough that it wouldn't carry to the rest of the group. "Let her go. She's dealing with the news in her own way. I'll check out her place tomorrow and see how safe she and Rachel are."

Isabelle gave him a small nod. "Thank you."

"For now, let's figure out what the other two want to do, okay?" He guided her back to her seat. Everett gave her a quick glance before his gaze scuttled away.

"This is why I didn't want you to worry the others," said Keith. "Now Amanda is going to be scared for no reason."

Isabelle's eyes narrowed. "There *is* a reason, Keith. You just don't want to believe it because it makes you vulnerable."

"I've tried cases involving some of the most useless pieces of filth on the planet, and more than one of them has threatened to kill me. Those were real threats. Those made me feel vulnerable. This is just a string of bad coincidences affecting a bunch of wounded children."

"They weren't children any longer," insisted Isabelle. "They were adults who'd made something of their lives. They'd moved on."

"And so should you."

"I *am* moving on. I'm trying to help the people I care about."

"You're not helping. You're only scaring them," said Keith.

"I think Isabelle is right," said Everett. "I, for one, am not going to risk my life staying here. I'm going to get out of town until this all goes away."

Isabelle gave Everett a relieved smile. "Thank you for believing me, but thank you more for protecting yourself. I don't want anything to happen to you."

Everett blushed.

Keith let out a rude, scoffing sound. "This is ridiculous. I can't believe you're going to send people running for the hills. How are any of us going to find peace if you keep disrupting our lives?"

"I'd rather disrupt your lives than see you dead."

Keith looked at Grant. "What do you have to say about all this? Do you believe her?"

"Yes. I do."

"Why? Because it will get you into her bed quicker?"

"Keith!" scolded Isabelle.

Grant refused to let the man ruffle him. "I believe her because she's right. I believe her because the evidence supports her."

"I know you. You're a womanizing bastard who'll screw anything with legs."

"You have legs, Keith. I haven't screwed you yet."

"I've lost my appetite," said Keith and pushed away from the table. He threw a bill down to cover his drink and stomped away.

Everett looked around nervously at the emptying table and said, "I should probably go start packing. Sorry to leave so soon."

"Best of luck," said Grant.

"You'll call me when you get there safe, right?" asked Isabelle.

Everett nodded and scurried away.

"Guess it's just the two of us now," said Grant.

Isabelle sighed. "Guess so."

CHAPTER NINE

The night wind was cold on Isabelle's face as they left the restaurant. Ravioli sat in her belly like a pile of wet cement. Even the smell of the takeout she was bringing home for Dale's evening snack turned her stomach. All she wanted to do was go home, spend some time with Dale as soon as he got back from his study group, and go to bed. Maybe things would look better in the morning.

Then again, maybe she'd lie awake all night trying to figure out what to do now. She'd done what she could to help her friends, and she'd continue to do whatever else she could, but it wasn't enough.

At least Everett would be safe. She could count that as a win.

"You look cold," said Grant. He put his arm around her and pulled her close as they walked side by side to the car.

It felt good to have him near, and not just because of the warmth spilling from him or way his fine body fit hers so well. It was more than that—the support of another person who didn't think she was crazy was a precious gift.

"Try not to worry," he said. "I'll find a way to convince the police to keep an eye on Amanda's house and places of work. Keith, too."

Isabelle feared that wouldn't be enough. "Maybe after they have some time to think about it, to be afraid tonight, they'll come around."

"I hope you're right."

As they neared Grant's Mustang, Isabelle felt him slow. Three young men stepped out from where they were crouched behind his car. One of them opened his long coat and took out a baseball bat.

Isabelle was staring in shock when Grant stepped in front of her and held her behind him with one firm hand on her arm.

"Evening, guys. Admiring my car?" asked Grant.

"It's a fine ride. Toss over the keys and no one will get hurt," said the man with the bat. He couldn't have been more than twenty, and he had to have at least one piercing for each of those years. His hair was shaved close to his scalp, and an angry glint of violence lit his dark gaze.

"Here you go." Grant tossed his keys near the feet of the closest man. "Isabelle, go inside."

"No, Isabelle," said another young man. "Stay and play with us. We'd love to take you for a ride."

"Go." Grant's order was harsh and unyielding.

Isabelle backed away, fumbling for her cell phone, which was buried somewhere in her purse.

Before she'd moved five feet, all three men charged Grant.

Isabelle let out a terrified squeak and tripped over a concrete divider. She sprawled to the ground and a sharp bite of pain tore at her back.

The first man reached Grant, who stood in a loose-limbed stance, ready for him. Grant went through a smooth series of motions that were nearly too fast for Isabelle to see, and the man was left in a moaning heap on the asphalt. She had no idea how he'd moved like that, but he was beautiful in his violence, as if he'd been born for it.

For a moment, Isabelle was too shocked to do anthing. She'd never seen anything like this before, not even in the movies. Grant was incredible. Deadly grace personified.

This couldn't be real.

The next two guys saw what had happened to their buddy, so they came in at the same time, one wielding that heavy wooden bat. He took a swing at Grant's head. Grant ducked to the side as if he'd known for a month the blow had been coming. He used his momentum to knock the second guy down with a hard jab of his elbow, but not before the other guy managed to slam his fist into Grant's head.

Grant stumbled and shook his head as if trying to clear it.

Isabelle's hands were clumsy with fear and cold, but they found her cell phone. When she pulled it out, the battery was missing. It must have been jarred loose when she fell on it.

Sirens blasting through the night, getting louder. Someone's hands closed around her arm and she screamed and batted them away.

"Easy," said an older woman. "I'm just trying to help you up."

Isabelle looked over her shoulder at the three women who had just walked out of the restaurant. Two of them were talking into cell phones, hopefully calling 911. "Someone needs to help him!" she shouted.

No one moved. Then again, they were all women at least twice her age. What were they going to do?

"Go inside and get help," Isabelle ordered the woman at her side.

She pushed herself up, though something along her spine protested the movement. She grabbed a fistful of landscaping stones and shoved them into her purse. No way was she going to sit by and watch as Grant got hurt.

She knew he was tough, but three against one? Those were really bad odds, even for a tough guy.

Grant was holding his own, keeping his distance from that wicked bat, but he didn't see the man he'd knocked down first rising to his feet behind him.

Isabelle took hold of the strap of her purse and started swinging it like a sling. She didn't have to get close enough to reach him—or more importantly, for him to reach her—only close enough for him to worry she might and distract him. If he was forced to deal with her, it would give Grant a few more seconds to take care of the two men he was facing.

"Behind you!" she shouted the warning to Grant as she neared her target.

Grant shifted to cover his flank but didn't look away from the guy with the bat.

The man who was about to go for Grant turned and saw Isabelle coming for him and, behind her, the crowd of onlookers.

"Shit!" he cursed and lunged for her.

She swung her purse at his arm, but she missed. Her blow glanced off his shoulder and he turned toward her. He was pissed. She could see it in the vicious sneer twisting his mouth and the promise of violence in his eyes.

He grabbed her arms hard enough that Isabelle thought he might have broken one of them, then he slammed her against the hood of a car. Her head bounced off the hood, stunning her.

Security lights floated around overhead, blinding her for a moment. Then she saw the man scramble away, running toward the drycleaner's.

The next thing she knew, Grant's furious face filled her vision. His eyes were too bright, and a trickle of blood dripped from a cut on his cheek. "Don't move," he ordered.

Isabelle's back ached and her arms throbbed, but there was no serious damage. If she kept lying in this awkward position of being bent backward over the car, that might change. "Let me up."

Was that her voice? It sounded faint and raspy and desperate, not at all like it should have.

Grant's fury faded to concern, but his mouth was tight with anger. "Are you hurt?"

"Lying like this hurts. I need to sit up." She pushed against his hold, but all it did was make her back hurt worse.

"All right. Let me help you up. Slowly." He helped her sit up slowly, doing most of the work for her.

Moving hurt, but the pain was already easing. The same could not be said of two of the men who'd attacked. They were lying facedown in the parking lot. Neither one of them moved.

Flashing blue lights and sirens filled the night as several patrol cars pulled in, blocking off the exits. Policemen swarmed the scene. While the first responders checked out the men on the ground, Officer Brooks and Reynolds arrived and headed straight for Grant and Isabelle, while still more officers began to question the crowd of onlookers.

"You two are magnets for trouble," Brooks stated. "Wanna tell me what happened here tonight?"

Reynolds held his pencil at the ready.

Grant's voice was hard and cold. "Three men were waiting by my car when we came out. They attacked first. I fought back."

"I only see two, and there's not much of them left."

"The third one ran off that way," said Isabelle. She pointed in the direction of the drycleaner's, but her arm felt so heavy and weak, she could barely hold it up for two seconds.

She was shaking. Cold. Grant held her tight, but it didn't help.

Grant could have been killed tonight. So could she. Who would take care of Dale if she was gone?

"Were they armed?" asked Reynolds.

"Just a bat," said Grant.

Brooks nodded his head in the direction Isabelle had indicated. "Check it out, Reynolds. See if he's still hanging around."

"I'm on it," said Reynolds as he jogged off to coordinate with other officers.

"You all right, ma'am?" asked Officer Brooks.

"Fine," she said, as Grant answered, "She needs to be checked out."

"So do you. That cut on your face will need a stitch or two, most likely."

"It'll wait."

Brooks radioed in that they were going to need an additional ambulance, then asked them, "Any idea why they attacked you?"

"No clue," clipped out Grant. "They said they wanted the car, but it was a cover story."

"What makes you say that?" asked Brooks, narrowing his eyes.

"I gave them my keys and they didn't leave."

Brooks looked unconvinced but said nothing.

"They might be friends of Wyatt," offered Isabelle. "If he thought he could get Dale back by taking us out of the picture, he would."

"Did you see Wyatt tonight?" asked Brooks.

"No."

"Have you seen him since last night?"

"No."

"Has Dale?"

"If he has, he said nothing."

Brooks nodded. "Okay, you folks sit tight and we'll have a paramedic look you over. I'll be back in a few minutes."

Cold wind blew over them, but it wasn't nearly as cold as Grant's silence. He was stiff, brittle with tension.

They watched as the two attackers were loaded into ambulances. They still hadn't regained consciousness.

A paramedic came over to them and said to Grant, "I'd like to check you out."

"Her first."

The young woman balked at his hard, cold tone but didn't offer any resistance. "Okay. Ma'am, if you'd come with me."

Isabelle didn't want to leave Grant, but he urged her forward with the arm around her body, so she went.

Maybe he just wanted to be alone.

The paramedic sat her in the back of the ambulance. She was a pretty girl, maybe twenty-five, with a pair of deep dimples that never seemed to go away, even when she wasn't smiling.

"Are you hurt anywhere?"

"I scraped my back when I fell, but it's fine."

"Can I look?"

Isabelle lifted the back of her jacket and shirt and showed the woman. There were a few dots of blood on her shirt, but no more than she'd have from a skinned knee.

The paramedic gave a sympathetic, "Ouch. That's gotta sting. I should probably take you to the hospital for some x-rays, just to be sure nothing's broken."

"Nothing's broken. I'd know."

"Not always. Adrenaline can mask pain."

A sharp sting radiated out from the small of her back where the concrete had scraped away a patch of skin, but it wasn't that bad. "I'm not even really bleeding. I'll patch it up when I get home, and if I start to hurt, I'll go see my doctor."

"Are you refusing to let me take you in?"

"Yes."

Her dimples disappeared with her frown of disappointment. "Guess I'll check out your boyfriend, then."

"He's not my boyfriend."

"Oh yeah? Then why is he looking at me like he'd kill me with his bare hands if I so much as make you wince?" asked the paramedic.

Isabelle glanced over at Grant and her breath stilled in her lungs. He was staring at her, his jaw hard, his eyes narrow and glittering with anger. His body was tense, and his fists were balled up tight as he stared across the parking lot, giving the paramedic a warning glare.

"That's just his way. He's protective."

"Well, hon, I'd suggest you hold on to him with both hands, then, 'cause guys as hot as that that care as much about you as he clearly does are few and far between."

The paramedic was clearly too young to know the truth. It didn't really matter how much a man cared. They always walked away in the end.

Everett packed quickly, taking only a few changes of clothes with him, a few pictures of Isabelle. He'd always been a neat person, so gathering his things hadn't taken long. He called his boss's work phone and left a message, claiming he had to leave town for a family emergency.

No one at work knew he didn't have a family, so the lie would work fine. He'd learned a long time ago that people saw him differently—as an outsider—when they knew he was an orphan. As it was, they thought it was odd that he hadn't married, but Everett wasn't interested in anyone but Isabelle, and she wasn't interested in him.

He accepted it and went on with his life, loving her from a distance, which might not have seemed like much of a life to others, but it was important to him. There was no way he was going to stay here in town with the possibility of a murderer on the loose. If only he'd had the courage to ask Isabelle to come with him. He wouldn't have minded leaving town at all with her by his side.

Everett had just zipped his suitcase shut when he saw a movement on the far side of his bedroom. He looked up and, reflected in the mirror, he saw a large man covered from head to toe in black, standing in his hallway, right outside the bedroom door.

Panic struck Everett statue still, and a pathetic squeak squeezed past his tight vocal cords.

"Don't fight me and this will be a lot easier on you," said the man.

Somewhere in the back of his brain Everett found the voice familiar, but a detail like that didn't matter right now. He had to run. Get away.

The only way out was past the masked intruder, so Everett made a run for it, hoping his momentum would carry him through.

The man stepped aside as if to let him pass, but just as Everett got near him, he lifted something that looked like a small can of Mace and sprayed it in Everett's face.

The medicinal smell assaulted his nose and burned his eyes. Almost instantly, his legs went numb and he started to fall. The man caught him before he could slam into the doorframe. "Easy," he said in a mockery of concern. "I don't want you to hurt yourself."

Everett tried to move but couldn't. He couldn't even speak. Nothing worked, though his brain screamed at his body to obey.

The man picked him up easily, which scared Everett more than not being able to move. Even if he could move, there was no way he'd be able to defend himself against a man so strong.

A sick feeling of helplessness crawled around inside him, taunting him to give up and let go as he'd learned to do as a child. He couldn't do anything to save himself. Whatever the man wanted to do to him was going to happen. Better to accept it like a wounded animal than make things worse by fighting. Prolonging the inevitable.

At least that's what he tried to tell himself so the panic wouldn't eat him alive.

"That's better," said the man as he settled him on the bed, arranging his limbs to a comfortable position.

Recognition sparked again at the sound of his voice, but who he was wasn't nearly as important as what he was going to do.

When he had Everett arranged to his liking, he went about unpacking his suitcase, item by item, putting everything back in its place as if he'd lived here for years.

Maybe he'd been watching Everett. Maybe he'd been in the house before. Both of those thoughts sent new waves of terror streaking through him. A sour sweat broke out over Everett's body.

Slowly, feeling started to return in some of Everett's extremities, but he still couldn't move. "Please," he managed to slur out.

The man stopped unpacking and came to the bedside. "It's wearing off already, huh? Well, I guess I'll have to finish straightening up after."

Everett didn't have to ask after what. He already knew the man intended to kill him, just as he had the others who had lived with Lavine. "Please don't." It was hard to understand the garbled words, but the man seemed to hear him clearly.

Then again, he'd done this before.

The man leaned down so he was only inches from Everett. Blue eyes. His killer had blue eyes. Familiar, bright blue eyes.

Dear God. He did know the man.

It was Keith Elders.

Everett's brain ground to a halt as he tried to assimilate

this new data. It didn't make any sense. They'd known each other for years. They'd played together as children. Cried together, too. How could he do this?

"Why?" managed Everett.

Keith gently stroked Everett's hair with a gloved hand. "Because you need my help to escape. We're brothers. I won't let you suffer anymore."

Suffer? Everett had no idea he was talking about. He tried to say it, but his mouth barely worked. He was too panicked, and his throat just clamped down, refusing to let out any air.

Everett told himself to be calm. Relax so he could speak. He could figure a way out of this, maybe convince Keith to let him go. "Not suffering."

Keith frowned. Everett saw his cheekbones shift under the thin black mask—not a ski mask—something else that was smooth and lightweight, covering everything but his eyes. "You've been suffering so long you don't even realize it anymore. But I know. I was there." He leaned down close enough that Everett could see tears welling in Keith's eyes. "I should have helped you escape before. I'm sorry about that, but I was too afraid. I didn't want to get caught before I could finish helping all of you." He swallowed and blinked back tears. "I'm not a coward anymore, Everett. I've learned a lot from the criminals I defend. I know how to not get caught now, and I'm going to take care of you."

Keith was insane. Everett had no idea what he meant by all of that except for the fact that it made him certifiable. He stopped wasting valuable energy trying to talk and screamed instead, hoping a neighbor would hear him.

Keith clamped his hand over Everett's mouth, but not hard. "Shhh. Be still. There can't be any bruises. I'll spray you again if I have to," he warned. "I can stay as long as it takes."

As long as it takes. That was possibly the most frightening thing Everett ever heard. No one would look for him for days. Weeks, maybe. The thought of dying was horrible, but not nearly as bad as dying slowly, painfully.

He couldn't let that happen.

Everett screamed until he was out of breath, and Keith's hand over his face made it even harder to breathe. Soon he was dizzy and on the verge of passing out. He was panting when Keith moved his hand from Everett's face. "Are you done now? Or should I get the spray?"

Everett said nothing but stayed quiet. He didn't want another dose of that stuff, not when the first one was finally wearing off. If he couldn't move, he had no chance of getting out of this.

"Good," said the man. "You lie still and I'll be back in a minute."

He disappeared into the bathroom, and Everett heard him going through the medicine cabinet. From the bathroom, he said, "I would have taken you for the antidepressants type, Everett. You surprise me." He came out and stood in the doorway with the belt to Everett's robe hanging from his gloved hands. "Don't worry. I know how to improvise. You won't suffer much longer. I know how hard it is to wake up to the nightmares every night. To feel the weight of his body holding you down again. Hurting you. To smell his excited sweat and feel his breath hot on your skin as he pants like a dog."

Everett knew what he was talking about now. The images Keith painted were all too familiar. Edgar Lavine must have molested Keith, too, only it had apparently driven Keith over the edge.

Everett's mouth was starting to cooperate, though his speech was slurred. "I got help, Keith. The nightmares are gone. I'm better now. You can be, too. Let me help you."

Keith's eyes welled with tears. "There is no help for me yet. Not until all the others are free."

Everett struggled to move. If he could just push Keith away, he might be able to make a run for it. "Please. You don't have to do this."

His arm twitched, but that was all he could coax from it.

"Yes, I do. If you were sane, you'd see that."

"You're the one who's insane."

A bright, cold light spilled from Keith's eyes. "I'm saving you, and you thank me by insulting me? How dare you?"

Keith looped the fabric belt around Everett's neck and tied it. "You're ungrateful. Just like the rest."

Tears slid down Everett's face. "I want to live."

Keith jerked the belt tight, cutting off Everett's air. Through the thin mask, he could see the determination harden Keith's features. "No, you don't. You're just afraid to die. You're a coward."

Keith lifted his hand and sprayed another dose of that stuff in Everett's face. His body went limp. Numb. He couldn't seem to pull in enough air.

"But don't worry. I'll help you. You're my brother. I love you too much not to."

CHAPTER TEN

———— ❧ ————

Isabelle shifted uncomfortably in the bucket seat, trying not to abrade her raw back. It had taken two hours for the police to finish their questions and let them go, and she was barely holding herself upright against the heavy fatigue that weighed down on her.

Since he'd gotten in the car, Grant had been silent. He gripped the steering wheel until his knuckles turned bone white. Tension radiated from his body until she was sure the air around him was vibrating with it.

He wasn't just angry. He was furious.

Isabelle had seen him like this only once before. On the night he'd killed Edgar Lavine.

He navigated the nearly empty highway, putting all his focus on the road.

Grant pulled in behind Dale's car. The light in his room was off, so he was probably already asleep. At least he wouldn't miss the takeout that was now splattered somewhere on the restaurant's parking lot.

Isabelle stifled a sigh. Dale had been working too hard lately, but until his SATs were conquered, she didn't see any hope of him relaxing. Then again, until the police

caught whoever was killing people in her life, she wasn't
going to find much downtime, either.

Grant got out of the car without a word.

Isabelle rubbed her eyes with the heels of her hands.
Things were getting too big and heavy, and something was
going to have to give. What she wouldn't have given for
the time to take a vacation—get her and Dale away from
everything for a while.

Grant opened her car door and stared down at her with
a hard, almost fierce frown. He reached out and offered
her his hand up.

Isabelle took it, not because she needed the help, but
because she thought it might make him feel better to
give it.

As she moved, the skin on her back stretched and she
barely hid a wince of pain.

They went in through the back door, and Isabelle tossed
her purse on the counter. Grant didn't seem to be in the
mood for company or conversation, so she told him, "I'm
going to check on Dale and hit the sack."

He gave her a silent nod and watched as she went up
the stairs. She knocked lightly on Dale's door, and when
he didn't answer, she peeked in. He was sprawled in bed,
asleep with one long arm hanging off the side.

She had a sudden flashback to last night when she found
him missing and stood there for a moment, watching him,
thankful he was safe and sound.

His radio switched songs and started playing a new
alternative rock song quietly in the background. A deep
bass rhythm thrummed out of the speakers, but Dale didn't
even shift.

Isabelle never would have been able to sleep with the

noise, but Dale said it helped him sleep, so she let it go. She figured he'd probably used the sound to mask the noise of his parents fighting when he was younger.

When she came back downstairs, Grant was waiting for her in the living room. The cut on his cheek had been taped closed by the paramedic, and a bruise was already starting to form around it. His feet were braced apart and he had the strangest look on his face—like he was preparing to do battle with her.

A sliver of worry wormed its way into her, because this was not right. This was not the Grant she knew.

Grant watched as fear made Isabelle's face go pale.

Guilt twisted inside him at the thought that he was scaring her, and he tried to say something reassuring, something light, but nothing came out. The frenetic rage that had threatened to engulf him since the moment he'd heard her pained cry tonight was still rampaging through him. It took every ounce of concentration he had just to appear civilized.

Not killing the bastard who'd touched her had burned off all of his reserves of willpower and goodwill, and there was simply none left in him.

He hadn't felt this way since the night he'd caught Lavine in her bed, holding her down as she fought against him. She'd been small for her age, weak. If Grant hadn't been trying to sneak out of the house that night, he never would have passed by her door and heard her muffled, panicked cries. He never would have seen Lavine on top of her and gone into a blinding rage that ended only when the last breath had been choked from that bastard's lungs.

Grant had always hoped the uncontrollable need for violence that had led him to kill Lavine that night had simply been a case of excess teenage hormones flooding his system. He'd killed since then out of duty or self-defense, but it had never once felt the same. It had never felt quite as personal. Or satisfying.

But after tonight, he knew teenage hormones weren't to blame. The sound of Isabelle crying out in pain had brought all of that rage back, though he had no idea why.

He couldn't let anything happen to her. Not then, and certainly not now.

"Grant?" she said with more than a hint of worry in her voice.

He took a step forward, then jerked to a halt, knowing he couldn't touch her now, not while his instincts were running the show.

"Are you okay?" she asked.

He stood rigid, nearly shaking with the force of keeping himself away from her. He wanted to hold her, reassure himself she was okay, but he didn't dare touch her until he was calmer. And he wouldn't be calmer until he saw for himself that she was safe.

"You're going to let me see," he told her in a thick, ragged voice.

Isabelle's exotic eyes narrowed in confusion. "See what?"

"You." He swallowed hard, and his breathing sped as he struggled to hold himself back. He wanted to strip her naked and check every smooth patch of skin for injury, and if he moved so much as an inch, his instincts would take over and that's exactly what he'd do. "I need to see you're safe," he tried to explain.

She closed the distance between them, apparently not realizing how close he was to the edge. She reached up and put her hand on his chest as if to calm him. "I'm perfectly safe."

Grant shuddered at her touch and closed his eyes in an effort to regain control.

"Show me." His voice shook, cracking with tension that made his whole body feel brittle.

"Are you talking about my back?"

Grant nodded.

"Okay." She slipped off her jacket and turned around, lifting up the hem of her shirt. "See. It's just a scrape."

Grant bent to look at her back. It was a hell of a lot worse than just a scrape. The skin was rubbed bloody over a patch the size of his hand, and she was already bruising.

That killing rage bubbled up inside him, and he had to take several deep breaths to keep from losing control. He'd already done that once tonight, and two young men were going to be hospitalized for a long time because of it.

Too bad he couldn't have made it three.

Grant reached out with trembling hands and lifted the back of her shirt higher. Slight bruises marred her skin all the way up to her bra. With a light tough, he ran his fingertip over the marks.

Isabelle tensed and froze in place.

"Did I hurt you?"

"Uh, no." Her voice held a strange, thready quality that Grant had never heard before.

The scrapes disappeared below the waistband of her jeans, so without thinking how she'd react, only needing to see the damage for himself, Grant reached around her and unfastened her jeans.

"Grant?" she squeaked. "I don't really think you should—"

"I won't hurt you," he reassured her as he eased the top of her jeans down two inches, where her injury stopped.

"I know you're not going to hurt me."

The way she'd said it simply, as if stating a fact, helped ease the tension that stretched his control thin. If she could trust him, then he couldn't be some kind of monster.

Grant ran his finger along her smooth skin, being careful to avoid the abraded area. She was so soft and warm, so smooth and sweetly curved. He hadn't intended to turn himself on by inspecting her injuries, but a low hum of arousal buzzed along his spine as his fingers soaked up her heat.

He leaned forward and pressed a gentle kiss over one of the bruises.

Isabelle let out a soft whoosh of air. Grant wasn't sure if the noise was due to shock, dismay, or pleasure, but he couldn't stop himself from finding another spot he needed to kiss.

Beneath the warm woman scent of her skin was the faint smell of flowers. He wasn't sure what kind, but it hardly mattered. She didn't need any additional perfume to entice him. Everything about her tugged at his senses, making him want more.

He wanted to see the smooth curve of her shoulder, the gentle swell of her hips, and the sleek length of her legs. He wanted to run his hands over her skin, learn where she liked to be touched. But most of all, he was dying to know what she tasted like and how she'd sound if he was ever given the chance to make her come.

Grant closed his eyes and breathed her in, trying to memorize her scent. His lips slid away from her wound, down to where her lovely bottom started to flare into maddening curves.

Isabelle swayed a little, but Grant held her steady as his mouth opened and his tongue met her skin. Salt and woman, such an intoxicating flavor, but never before had it gone to his head quite like it did with Isabelle.

Feeling her under his hands, tasting her on his tongue, helped to calm his anger, but it was replaced by something just as intense. He wanted her. Needed her.

His dick hardened, straining uncomfortably against the front of his jeans, but he ignored it. He didn't want anything distracting him from this moment, from this chance to touch and taste Isabelle and know for a fact that she was going to be okay.

He allowed himself one more kiss, one more taste, before letting her go.

Grant cleared his throat and stood, but couldn't find the strength to step back. He peered down at her glossy black hair, trying to pull himself together. Against his will, his hands reached around her and found the zipper of her jeans. Leaving them open was too much of a temptation.

Isabelle sucked in a breath and covered his hands with hers. "I can do it."

Grant slid his hands up to her bare waist. They fit perfectly in the womanly hollow above her hips, and felt even better. He rubbed his thumbs over her skin, just under the hem of her shirt.

Isabelle hadn't moved to refasten her jeans, but her breathing had sped. He could feel the quick expansion of her ribs under his thumbs and itched to slide his hands up to see if her heart was pounding faster, as well.

He knew women. Well. He knew the signs of arousal, and Isabelle was showing too many for him to ignore.

Even though the air was cool, a fine sweat had broken out over her skin, or maybe that was his own palms going hot at the chance to touch her. He was careful not to press his body against her sore back, but he was close enough to feel the heat coming from her.

She still hadn't moved, and he wasn't sure if it was because she wanted him to make the next move, or because she didn't. He didn't want to push her, but he also didn't want to miss an opportunity see how far she'd let things go, either. If she wanted him, he was more than happy to oblige. To hell with the consequences.

Maybe it made him an ass, but he was dying to touch more of her. Taste more of her. He wanted to feel her body moving under his hands, make her feel good to make up for the injury he'd allowed to happen to her tonight.

"Would you like me to help you clean up that scrape?" he asked, testing the waters.

"I think I can get it. I'll jump in the shower."

Grant rubbed his cheek against her silky hair. A short growth of stubble caught and held the fine strands. "You sure?"

She stood there for so long, he almost wondered if she'd heard his question. "Yeah."

Disappointment made him sluggish, but he took the hint and released her.

Isabelle turned around, still holding the front of her jeans closed. Her eyes were dark, and her cheeks were stained with the blush of arousal.

She wanted him. Grant was certain. What he didn't understand was why she turned him down.

Of course, women were complicated. He loved that about them when he wasn't cursing the trait. And he didn't have to understand a refusal to respect it.

"You'll call if you change your mind?" he asked.

Isabelle nodded but stood there as if she wanted to say something else.

Grant waited, hoping she'd change her mind and invite him to her room, but when she looked down at the carpet, he knew it wasn't to be.

"Thanks for being there tonight," she said.

"It's why I'm here."

"Will I see you in the morning before I leave for work?"

"We'll have breakfast together, you, me, and Dale," he promised.

"Sounds nice." She left, and Grant watched her walk away a little unsteadily.

Nice. Breakfast would be nice, but getting there was not going to be any fun at all, not with the erection he had now.

Grant briefly considered hopping in his car and finding some willing woman in a bar. It would have been easy enough to do, but it wasn't what he wanted. He wanted Isabelle.

The knowledge shocked him. One willing and eager woman was always as good as another, as far as he was concerned. What was different now?

Maybe he just didn't want to leave Isabelle and Dale vulnerable. That was probably it. Nothing else made any sense.

CHAPTER ELEVEN

❧

Isabelle couldn't sleep. She could still feel Grant's big hands on her body, his thumbs stroking her skin. That simple touch had made her shake with need, and even though he was no longer touching her, she hadn't stopped shaking. None of her past lovers had come close to making her feel like this, but a few strokes from Grant's hands and she was halfway to meltdown. It was almost enough to make her give up her good intentions and go climb into bed with him. Almost.

Only the knowledge that Dale was in the room next door kept her in her own bed. She wasn't going to set a bad example for her son by sleeping with a man who'd been back in her life for only two days. What a lousy role model she'd be if she did that.

Isabelle squirmed in her bed for what felt like half the night. She couldn't sleep comfortably on her back, so whenever she would doze off and roll over, it woke her up. By the time her alarm went off, she felt nearly sick with fatigue. Her joints ached, and her eyes were hot and dry.

No amount of caffeine was ever going to fix this, but she wasn't going to wimp out and call in a sub. She wanted to see Rachel and make sure the girl was holding up okay.

If Amanda came home upset last night, Rachel was sensitive enough to pick up on her mom's tension. A sub would never know how to deal with that.

Isabelle pushed out of bed, stifling a wince of pain. Her back and neck muscles were stiff, and there were new bruises on her forearms where that guy had grabbed her.

By the time she was dressed, some of the stiffness was gone, but it was going to be a long day.

Grant and Dale were already at the breakfast table when she came into the kitchen. They were shoveling down a pile of scrambled eggs and toast. "Wow. Someone cooked on a weekday?"

"Don't look at me," said Dale around a bite of toast.

She looked at Grant, enjoying the view. His hair was still damp from his shower, making it look darker than usual. He wore a tight gray T-shirt that showed off his muscular chest and made her question the sanity of her decision to sleep alone last night.

He gave her one of his patented smiles that sent her stomach for a loop and said, "We saved you some."

Isabelle sat, noticing that she already had a cup of steaming tea waiting for her. "Thanks."

"No problem. I wanted you all agreeable when I asked you for a favor."

Doing favors for Grant sounded like a nice time. Especially naked favors. She could get into something like that. "What favor?"

"My buddy David wants to test out this new security system he designed. I was hoping you'd let me install one here to help him out and give me some practice putting one into an older home. They can be tough."

Isabelle was sure that asking for her agreement in front

of Dale was not a coincidence. It sounded like a cover story to her—one that would keep Dale from worrying about why she'd need a security system.

"I really can't afford something like that."

"Not a problem. David said he'd comp it for the chance to test it out."

"If I agreed, he'd have to let me pay something."

Grant shook his head. "David would never go for that. Sorry. You should still do it, though. With Wyatt sniffing around, I'd feel better if you had some protection once I'm gone."

Isabelle's lungs tightened at the thought of him leaving. She didn't feel vulnerable when he was in the house. He made her feel safe, and she was going to miss that. She was going to miss him.

Still, he was right about Wyatt. She would feel better knowing she had some measure of security. Who knew what the future might hold and what she might be facing with the other foster children she'd take in. Dale was nearly a man, better equipped to take care of himself than the younger children she might care for. She owed it to them to do what she could to protect them.

Isabelle nodded. She'd find a way to pay for it. "I suppose we can work something out."

"Great. I'll have to drill some holes in your walls. Not too many, but a few."

"Need any help?" asked Dale, his eyes lighting up over the possibility of getting to use power tools.

"Sure. That'd be great. Assuming Isabelle will let us." Grant and Dale both looked at her expectantly.

"How can I refuse?" she said.

"Don't worry," Grant assured her. "I'll patch everything up once I run the wires, and the place will be as good as new."

"Better," said Dale. "It will have a security system. Keep thugs like Wyatt from nosing around."

"Has Wyatt bothered you again?" asked Grant before Isabelle got the chance.

"No. But that doesn't mean he won't. Better safe than sorry, right?"

"Absolutely," agreed Grant. "What are you doing after school? Do you have another study group?"

"Not tonight."

"Do you want to help me when you get home?"

"Sure, if I don't have any homework."

"Sounds good."

She reached for the salt, and Dale's face drained of color.

"What happened to your arm?" he asked, pointing to her forearm with his fork.

Isabelle saw the bruise and pulled her sleeves down to cover it. "I fell last night."

"Fell?" asked Dale in a flat voice. He looked between her and Grant, wearing the strangest look, like her bruise was somehow Grant's fault.

"You sound like you don't believe me."

"My mom used to 'fall' a lot, too," he said to Grant, his accusation blatant in his harsh tone.

Grant sat there looking guilty, though Isabelle had no idea why. Her injuries were not his fault.

"I really did fall, Dale. In the restaurant parking lot. That's why there's no takeout in the fridge for you. It got smooshed all over the pavement."

"Did you accidentally hit Grant in the face on the way down? Is that how he got hurt, too?"

Isabelle opened her mouth to respond, but Grant beat her to it. "I already told you what happened," he said. "Some guys wanted my car. They jumped me, I got hit. Isabelle fell trying to get me help."

"I should have watched where I was going," said Isabelle.

"I should have gotten you out of harm's way," argued Grant.

"You were a little busy dealing with the carjackers." If that's, indeed, what they were. She still wasn't convinced they weren't friends of Wyatt's sent to get rid of Grant so it would be easier to get to Dale. It was just one more reason to get that security system installed before he left.

"I should have handled it better," said Grant, his voice tight.

Dale looked back and forth between them. Finally, he seemed satisfied that they were telling the truth. "You're okay, right?" Dale asked her.

"I'm fine."

He frowned for a moment, thinking, then said, "I'll take care of the laundry and vacuuming this week—just until you feel better."

His sweet offer made her want to hug him, but she resisted embarrassing him. "I feel fine, Dale. It's no big deal, and you do plenty of chores around here already."

"I'm still doing the laundry," he told her as if daring her to stop him.

Isabelle couldn't help but smile. He was such a sweet kid to want to take care of her instead of the other way around. "Be my guest if it'll make you feel better."

"It will," he said. "You can wash your own underwear, though, 'cause that's just gross."

"Gee, thanks," she said, secretly pleased because that comment somehow made her feel like a real mom.

He checked the clock on the wall. "I gotta run."

"Have a good day," said Isabelle.

"We'll start that project as soon as you get home," said Grant.

"Cool." Dale slipped his jacket on and grabbed his backpack on the way out the door.

Once it closed behind him, Grant smiled at Isabelle, a slow, lazy smile. "I happen to like your underwear."

She lifted an eyebrow at him. "And how would you know? You've never seen my underwear."

"I'm pretty sure I got a tiny peek last night. Purple, I believe."

A little shiver raced over her arms as she remembered the way he touched her, kissed her, last night. "Lavender."

His eyes slid over her face and stopped at her mouth. "My mistake. Guess I was a little distracted."

He wasn't the only one. She'd spent most of the night distracted, and thinking about it wasn't helping. She swore she could still feel the heat of his palms gripping her waist, the stroke of his tongue along her back, the soft sweep of his breath over her spine. A few touches from him was enough to spoil a woman for all other men.

She could only imagine what it would be like to actually make love with him. And it would be love, at least for her. Isabelle didn't doubt that for a moment. She'd cared for him for too long not to fall for him if she let her guard down enough to sleep with him.

Grant would be an easy man to love, and it scared her to

death. She'd already fallen for two men who couldn't love her enough to share her dreams. Her college boyfriend simply hadn't wanted children, but Phil had been the one who'd really broken her heart. He wanted kids but refused to take in someone else's "unwanted problems."

He said it as easily, as if she hadn't *been* one of those unwanted problems.

Isabelle had cried when he left two years ago, taking her dreams of a future together with him. But she'd gotten over it and moved on. Men left. That's just what they did. She knew that now and accepted it.

Grant would do the same. She couldn't let his kindness toward Dale fool her. It was one thing to include a kid in your plans for the evening, but totally another to include them for life.

She'd be smart and keep her distance, even though smart didn't sound like a good plan at the moment. Not when she was sitting across the table from his teasing smile and glittering, hungry eyes.

"You're a bad, bad man, Grant Kent. You know that, right?"

"And here I was, all proud of how good I was being by not trying to seduce you." He slid the tip of his finger over the back of her hand, tracing each of the bones that led to her wrist.

"If you're not trying now, I think I'd combust if you do."

His smile melted into a hot, dark grin, and he was staring at her mouth. "Wanna give it a try and see?"

"I don't think so. I've got about three minutes before I have to leave for work."

"Three minutes is plenty of time."

"To do what?"

He stood and walked around the table until he was behind her. She should have stopped him, but she couldn't. She was too excited to see what he'd do.

He lifted her hair away from her neck and leaned down until she could feel his breath just behind her left ear. "I'd only need two of those minutes to make you want me so bad you'll agree to take a long lunch."

She wasn't sure he even needed two. Part of her was willing to skip work and let him show her what he could do with a whole day, just not the part that was in charge.

"Arrogant man."

"Only if it's not true. Otherwise, it's just confidence. Knowing my strengths." His lips glided beneath her ear, then down her neck until he reached the sensitive skin where her shoulder started.

Isabelle tried and failed to stifle a shiver.

Grant's teeth grazed her skin, and she let out a faint moan.

"I'm barely touching you," he whispered.

With him, that's all it took. "You're not playing fair."

"Who says I'm playing?" His teeth pressed harder against her skin, giving her a delicate bite that sent ribbons of pleasure flying down her spine.

Isabelle hissed and tried to concentrate. She had to keep their relationship honest. She couldn't let him make her forget who she was and what was important to her. She couldn't forget that he wasn't here to stay.

"You're a player," she said in a faint, dry voice. "It's what you do."

His tongue soothed the marks she was sure he'd left on her. "You know me so well?" he asked. "How can that be when we've hardly shared more than a few letters every year?"

"I know you. I know what you want."

"And what, lovely Isabelle, do I want?"

"Sex. With me."

"Absolutely. What sane man wouldn't want that?" He placed more soft, wet kisses over the nape of her neck, and Isabelle nearly agreed to sleep with him right then and there. Screw work. She'd call in just this once.

But what about Rachel?

Isabelle strengthened her resolve. No one was going to cause her to neglect a child.

She forced her tone to come out lighthearted, teasing. "No. I mean that's all you want. You're a love-'em-and-leave-'em kind of guy."

Grant's mouth stilled in its path over her skin, and he pulled away. Isabelle's cool, slippery hair slid into place over her shoulders.

"What did you call me?" he asked her in a deceptively gentle voice.

She turned around to look at him. He was more than just angry, he was enraged. His face was red, and a snarl curled his mouth. All the humor was gone from his eyes, leaving behind only a glittering, feral glow.

Isabelle stood up in shock and took a small step back. She knew he'd never hurt her, but she couldn't help her instinctive reaction to back away from such anger. It was so unexpected coming from Grant.

He kept his distance, breathing deeply as if trying to calm himself. "Don't ever call me that again," he demanded.

"Call you what?"

"Love-'em-and-leave-'em Kent. I'm nothing like him."

"Him who?"

"Don't tell me you didn't know."

Isabelle struggled to make sense of his words. She'd hurt him somehow—hurt him badly enough to make him mad—but she had no idea what he meant. "I don't know, Grant. Whatever it was I said, I didn't mean for it to make you angry."

He loosened his fisted hands and took a deep breath. He crossed the room and stood in front of her. Isabelle refused to cower or back away. He wouldn't put his hands on her in anger, no matter how badly she might have hurt him. She knew it deep down, the same way she knew the feel of her own heartbeat.

"Help me understand, Grant. What did I say wrong?"

He stared down at her, his eyes blazing with banked fury and pain. "Love-'em-and-leave-'em Kent. That's what they called my father—all his loser buddies," he told her.

"And you don't want to be compared to him?"

"The fucker abandoned Mom and me when I was twelve. He walked out because things were tough and sent Mom spiraling into a drunken depression. When she finally drove her car into a tree and killed herself, he couldn't even be bothered to come back and make sure I was okay." He pulled in a harsh breath. "That's why I was in the foster-care system. Not because my dad was dead, but because he didn't want to stop fucking around long enough to be a father."

Pain for him swept over her, making tears burn her eyes. She'd never seen him hurt like this before, never seen the bone-deep, gaping wound his father had left on him. She would have given anything to take back her careless words, but it was too late.

"Grant, I'm so sorry. I didn't know. I never would have said that if I had."

"Forget it." He closed his eyes and turned his head away as if not wanting her to see his pain.

Too late. She saw it all too clearly and couldn't stand to let him suffer.

Isabelle slid her hands over his wide shoulders and pressed her body against his in a tight hug. She didn't know what else to do to comfort him.

He stood statue still but didn't fight her. She stroked his hair and back, telling him without words how much she regretted her accidental insult. "Clearly, you're nothing like him."

"Mom always said I was just like him." It was a confession given in a bare whisper of sound, as if he could hardly stand to say the words.

"Maybe you look like him, but you don't act like him."

"How can you know that? You never met him." His words were sharp-edged. Biting.

Isabelle refused to let his anger push her away. She cupped his face in her hands and forced him to look at her. "Maybe not, but I know that any man who would abandon his son when he was needed most is selfish. You're not."

"No? I think you're wrong." His gaze slid down to her mouth, and his hands found her hips. He tugged her forward until their bodies met from chest to knees. She could feel his heart pounding hard against her breast. Or maybe that was her heart. She wasn't sure.

"If I wasn't selfish, then I wouldn't be thinking about seducing you. I'd find a way to keep my hands off you."

His hands tightened on her hips.

"If I wasn't selfish, then I wouldn't be looking for reasons to justify sleeping with you when I know casual sex isn't your thing. You've got good girl written all over you, and for some reason, it makes me want you that much more."

Isabelle's body shuddered at the thought, and she was sure he could feel it.

"And if I wasn't selfish, I wouldn't have forced my way into your home where I could more easily seduce you. I can pretend that I stayed to keep you safe, but the truth is I want you and have from the moment I saw you again. I want you in my bed. In yours. On the kitchen floor. Wherever and however I can get you."

The potent images his words conjured made her head swim. If she'd had some time and space to let herself calm down, she might have been able to think straight. But as it was, that powerful pull he had on her was at work, dragging her toward him until there was no escape.

Right now, she didn't even care that she might be making a mistake. Dale was gone, and the only person she could hurt was herself. Grant was definitely worth that.

He lowered his head to kiss her, and Isabelle did nothing to stop him. She'd wanted this for too long. Needed it.

His lips brushed hers in a barely-there kiss. It wasn't enough, and she pulled him back for more, earning the rough sound of his pleasure against her mouth.

Isabelle's body hummed with excitement, and the skin along her spine grew hot and damp. She could smell his aftershave—feel the smooth skin of his face beneath her palms. His breathing sped, along with her own, and his hands tightened on her body.

Yes. This was what she'd wanted for so long it almost didn't seem real. Then he parted his lips, coaxing hers to open, as well, and she didn't care if it was real or not. As long as it didn't end.

Isabelle didn't hesitate to let him into her mouth. She wanted to taste him, to feel the rasping heat of his tongue over hers. She couldn't hold back, not when she had her chance to kiss Grant the way she'd always wanted. Not when it might be the only chance she ever had.

His tongue glided over her bottom lip, and she slid her hands into his damp hair, making sure he wouldn't pull away again. Against her belly, she felt him grow hard, and it thrilled her to know she could do that to him.

She kissed him deep, sighing into his mouth. His big hands slid down to cup her butt and fit them more closely together. His erection jerked against her, hot and hard, and just like that, she was wet and ready for him, dying to feel him push inside her.

"The kitchen floor works for me," she told him as she reached for the top button on his jeans. She kissed her way over his wide jaw and down his neck, where it was easier for her to reach. Her hands shook, making the job of undoing his jeans much harder than it should have been.

"Wait," Grant rasped out, covering her hands with his to stop her. "We can't."

His hands shook with restraint, but they held firm.

No way was she going to let him stop her now. Not when her body was hot and ready and she knew he wanted her just as much as she did him. "Yes, we can. I won't cling or cry when you go. I swear it."

He gathered her wrists in his hand, holding her tight. His chest worked hard as he tried to catch his breath, and a fine sweat dampened his brow. "We can't. It wouldn't be fair to you."

"What wouldn't be fair is to leave me hanging on the edge like this."

He closed his eyes and dragged in a ragged breath. "I'd do just about anything to have the chance to make you come, honey, but not like this. Not unless you've had time to make sure it's what you want."

"I'm sure."

He stroked the back of her hand with one thumb as if trying to soothe her. It didn't work. She was aching inside, almost frantic to force him to keep going. "You and me have the kind of chemistry that could set a house on fire, but that doesn't mean you wouldn't be sorry later. I want you, but I care about you too much to hurt you."

"It's just sex."

He lifted a blond brow. "So you do this with men all the time?"

"You are not all men."

"That's my point. Who was the last man you slept with?"

"My last boyfriend."

"Did you love him?" he asked with a blunt directness that made her believe he already knew the answer.

"I don't see how that matt—"

"Did you love him?" he asked again.

Isabelle forced herself to look him in the eye. "Yes."

"And that's why we can't do this. I don't have enough friends to risk losing you, Isabelle. Not you."

"But you wouldn't lose me. I'm a grown woman, perfectly capable of making rational decisions about who to sleep with."

"And when you were rational, you told me no."

"I changed my mind."

"Fine. If that's still the way you feel about it after you cool off, then we'll talk. But for now you need to get to work. And so do I. The sooner we find the killer, the sooner we can stop tempting each other with a fantasy we both know would never work."

He was right. Isabelle hated it, but she knew he was right.

Detective Mathews stared at the man hanging lifelessly from his own ceiling fan and felt nothing. A couple of years ago, he would have cared that some mild-mannered accountant had been murdered, but a lot could happen in a couple of years.

"Another suicide?" asked the photographer as he captured yet another angle of the scene. "Is there something in the water?"

"It's not a suicide," said Mathews, his voice harsh and rough from too much worry and not enough sleep.

"What makes you so sure?"

"Forced entry. There were signs the lock on the back door lock had been tampered with." That, and the fact that the man hanging by his neck was the next person on the list some special forces hotshot had given the police.

Mathews had checked out Grant Kent and found plenty of interesting reading material. Kent had already murdered one man before he went into the military. Chances were he'd done it again now that he was out and back in his old hometown, free to do whatever he pleased.

Mathews didn't care how clean his military record was. Once a killer, always a killer. He had Kent's prints on file, both from his juvenile record and his military one. Maybe the guy was cocky enough not to have worn gloves. And even if he had, all Mathews needed to bring the bastard in was a scrap of evidence, just one sign that Kent had been here.

As spotless as the accountant's home was, Mathews didn't think they'd have any trouble finding something out of place.

CHAPTER TWELVE

❧

Isabelle was already late for work when Grant pushed her out the door. He felt like a pansy for getting all sappy at her like that. He never should have told her how he felt about his dad. He'd never told anyone else, so why her? It was only going to make her think he was weak when she needed to be able to depend on him to be strong.

What Grant needed to do was suck it up, keep his dick in his pants, and do his job.

Easier said than done.

He never should have kissed her, though he couldn't bring himself to regret it. Not something as good as that. How could he regret a kiss that was so hot it made him hard, yet so sweet it made him ache that it had to end?

Grant shook his head and tried not to think about it.

He rinsed off the dishes and loaded them into the dishwasher, then straightened up the kitchen so she wouldn't have to come home to a mess.

He'd told her that if she still wanted him, they could talk about it. Maybe she'd come home and do just that. Sex didn't have to be about love—he knew that without a doubt. Maybe Isabelle could learn the same thing. They could enjoy each other while he was here, then part ways. No problem.

Hell, he'd even consider doing a long-distance relationship with her if she wanted. Nothing serious or binding, since he was sure she'd still want to be on the lookout for husband material, but he could live with that if it meant they could be together some of the time.

Couldn't he?

His stomach started to burn at the notion of sharing her, and he knew then that it wouldn't work. They were both better off if he learned not to think of her as a woman. He could do that. He'd done it with Noelle as soon as he'd found out she was David's woman.

In fact, it had proved surprisingly easy. David loved her, and that was enough to make Grant keep his distance. All he had to do was find a way to feel the same with Isabelle.

No problem. He could do it. He wasn't sure how, but he'd figure out something, for Isabelle's sake.

After five minutes of scrambling for ideas and coming up blank, a sick sense of panic settled in his chest. He needed advice from someone whose head wasn't quite so fucked up.

He checked his watch. It was still early, but Caleb would be up. He'd know what to do. Caleb always knew what to do.

Grant dialed his friend's cell phone.

It took four rings for Caleb to answer, and when he did, it was in a whisper. "Hey, Grant."

"Did I wake you?"

He heard the sound of a door clicking shut, then Caleb

cleared his throat. He sounded awful, like he was sick. "I was up late, taking care of Lana."

That didn't sound good. "What's wrong?"

"She's got the flu, bad."

"Oh, man. That sucks. Is there anything I can do?"

"Get David off my back. He needs an extra pair of hands, but I can't leave Lana until she's over this crap."

"I wish I could do that, but there's some serious shit going down here and I can't leave, either."

"I thought you were just going to visit an old friend on the way to Colorado."

"I was, but it got complicated."

"Let me guess. Lady trouble?"

"Is there any other kind?"

"Then why are *you* calling *me?* Hell, Grant, you've got more experience with the ladies than three of me put together."

"She's special."

"Oh. I see. How special?"

"Special enough that I can't fuck it up."

Caleb's rough laugh vibrated the phone. "About damn time you settled down."

"It's not like that. She's just a friend."

"Yeah, right. You don't have female friends, just fuck buddies."

Grant winced at the crude term, though it had never bothered him before. "That's the problem. I don't know how to deal with this."

"Sorry, man. Wish I could help. The only advice I can give you is that if you want her to continue to be your friend, lock your dick in a drawer until you leave."

That's pretty much what Grant figured he'd say. At least

his instincts were right. Now all he had to do was follow through on them. "I'd better figure this shit out fast, then. I'm not sure how long I'll be able to hold out."

"Something other than women troubles?"

Grant wasn't going to pull Caleb away from his sick wife. Lana was tough, and if she needed him, she really was in bad shape. "Nothing I can't handle."

Caleb let out a long, wheezing sigh. "Good. I got my hands full here."

"I hope you're not coming down with what Lana's got. You sound like hell."

"I'll survive."

"Kiss Lana for me."

"Hell, no. You want to kiss a woman vicariously, find someone else's wife."

Grant smiled at the possessive growl in Caleb's tone. If he wasn't too sick for that, he'd be fine. "Take care of yourself, man."

"You, too," said Caleb and hung up.

So much for an easy answer, and there wasn't time to look for more advice. He had a meeting with Detective Mathews in half an hour, and he needed to be clear-headed enough to make his case. If he could get the good guys to back him, then they could find the asshole who was killing people, and both he and his grounded dick could be on their way before he did something with Isabelle they'd both regret.

Wyatt had no trouble finding Isabelle's car in the teachers' lot. She was nice enough to show up late, and he was already there, watching to see where she parked. Lucky for him, she was on the last row of the lot, farthest away from the building, right between a minivan and an SUV.

He couldn't have asked for a better setup. No one was going to see a thing, and he'd have plenty of room to work.

It had been a long time since he'd tinkered with a car, but he was pretty sure they hadn't changed so much he couldn't do what needed to be done to get his son back.

Detective Mathews greeted Grant with a firm shake and a suspicious glint in his eyes. He had the build of a man who could take a hit and come up swinging so fast you wouldn't know what hit you back. His shirt was a bit rumpled, as if he'd slept in it, and his tie was already loose around his throat. The red rims of fatigue around his eyes told Grant that he'd either worked or played too hard last night.

From the looks of the stacks of files littering his desk, Grant figured it was the former.

He led Grant down a hall and opened a door for him to proceed.

"It'll be quieter in here," said Mathews. "Go ahead and have a seat."

Grant looked around the dank little interrogation room, already hating its dreary paint and two-way mirror. It reeked of fear, desperation, and stale coffee in here, but from Mathews's neutral expression, he apparently didn't notice the stink.

"I've read the police reports," he told Grant without

preamble. "Gotta say this whole thing looks like a hell of a mess."

"I couldn't agree more," said Grant.

"We've got patrols going by the residences and businesses you listed, but I don't think that's going to be enough. We need to catch this son of a bitch."

Right down to business. Grant liked the man already. "What can I do to help?"

"Why don't we start with you telling me where you were last night between eight and midnight?"

Warning bells gonged in Grant's head, making him frown at Mathews. He could see that frown in the mirror and wondered if there was anyone on the other side. "Is this an interrogation?" he asked.

"You know a reason it should be?" Mathews shot back. "Just answer the question."

"I was with Isabelle. If you read the police reports, you know we didn't get away from that restaurant until nearly ten. We went home."

"Just the two of you? Anyone see you at home?"

"No. Dale was asleep." Grant stood up, letting his body language tell the detective how pissed he was getting without words that could later be used against him. "What the hell is going on here?"

"We found Everett's body this morning."

Shock rolled through Grant, making him sway. He gripped the table to steady himself, bracing for the impact of the grief he knew would come next. He'd seen a lot of good men die, and even if he didn't know them, he always felt a sense of loss for what could have been. Everett would never have a wife and kids. He'd never even get the chance to grow enough of a backbone to let Isabelle know how much he was crushing on her.

"He was getting out of town," said Grant. "He was supposed to be safe."

"Is that why you hurried up and killed him? Or was it all the photos he had of Isabelle that set you off?"

What the hell? Mathews thought he was the killer? "Whoa," said Grant, holding up his hands. "You can't believe I did this."

"Have you ever been in his house?"

"No. I don't even know where he lives."

Mathews's eyes brightened with excitement, which could not mean anything good for Grant. "Are you sure about that?" asked Mathews.

He couldn't believe that he was a suspect. He'd put his life on hold to come out here and help. How could this guy actually believe he'd kill anyone?

Grant held his anger in check, but only barely. He really wanted to slam his fist into this guy's smug grin. "Yes, I'm pretty fucking sure I've never been in the man's house."

"We found your prints there."

"Bullshit you did."

"You know I'm not lying. You were there, just like you were there for all of the others who you killed. Tell me, Grant, how did you make it look so convincingly like suicide?"

Grant turned his back on the guy to keep from punching him. "This is unbefuckinglievable. We come to you for help and this is the shit you think up?" He whirled around, his fists tight and longing for something to pummel.

"Was it really self-defense when you killed Lavine?

Are these other killings some kind of way for you to finish what you started?"

Grant shook with the force of his anger. "Get your ass out there and check on Amanda. She was next on the list."

Mathews nearly smiled. "Did you already get to her, too? Anxious for us to find the body so you can get your little thrill?"

"That's it. If you won't go check on Amanda and her daughter, I will."

Grant started for the door, but Detective Mathews blocked his path. "You're staying here until I say we're done."

"Are you charging me with something?" asked Grant.

"Is that a confession?"

"Fuck you," ground out Grant.

Mathews leaned close, getting right into Grant's face. He kept his voice so low that Grant was sure that if this was being recorded, the mic wouldn't pick up his words. "It's no wonder no one wanted you as a kid. You're a murdering prick, and I'm going to see you fry."

CHAPTER THIRTEEN

———— ❖ ————

Isabelle checked her cell phone messages after the last kid left for the day. Thirty seconds later, after listening to Grant's message, she felt numb with shock.

Everett was dead. Grant was a suspect.

Grief for Everett welled up inside her, but she couldn't deal with that now. Not when Grant was in trouble. She had to hold herself together long enough to do what needed to be done.

Then she could grieve for poor, sweet Everett.

Isabelle pulled in a shuddering breath and tried to concentrate on what to do. Her mind whirled at a million miles an hour, and nothing good came of it.

How could the police be so stupid? How could they ever think a man like Grant would hurt innocent people?

There was only one person she knew who might be able to help Grant.

Her hands were shaking when she dialed Keith's number. He was the only defense lawyer she knew, and she didn't know where else to turn.

"Isabelle," he greeted her. She could hear the smile in his voice, and it helped calm her nerves a bit to know he was still safe and sound. "How are you?"

Isabelle skipped the pleasantries. "Grant's being held by the police for questioning. They think he had something to do with the murders. Can you help him?"

There was silence on the other end of the line for so long Isabelle thought she might have lost the call. "Keith? Are you there?"

"Yes. Just thinking how best to handle this. I'll go to him and see what I can do." His voice was emotionlessly even.

"You think he did it, don't you?" asked Isabelle, unable to believe Keith could turn on Grant like that. What the heck was wrong with the world?

"No. I still don't think any of those deaths were murder, and that's exactly what I'll tell the police when I get there. It may not do any good, but I can try."

"It gets worse, Keith." Isabelle clutched the phone, fighting off the crushing weight of grief. She could barely bring herself to think about it, much less say it, and when she did, her voice trembled. "Everett is dead. He was murdered . . . strangled to death . . . it looked like a suicide, but I know it wasn't."

Again, silence filled the line.

"Keith?"

All warmth was gone from his voice. "I'll meet you at the station, Isabelle."

"You're going to be able to fix this, right?" she asked.

"Let's just see what evidence they have against him and go from there."

Isabelle hung up the phone and rushed out of the school, stopping only long enough to let the office know she was leaving for a personal emergency. The cold March wind beat against her face as she raced to her car, helping to clear her head.

She had to keep it together for Grant. And check on Amanda. She was next on the list after Everett.

His shy smile filled her mind and tears welled in her eyes. She tried to shove the grief away again, but it broke through her resolve. Hot tears cooled on her face as she unlocked her car and slid inside. She wiped at her tears and dried her hands on her pants, trying to pull herself together.

She could do this. She could hold it together long enough to get Grant out of this mess. After all, it was her fault he was in it at all. He'd never have come here if she hadn't left that message. She'd only meant to warn him, not get him into this kind of trouble.

When she started her car, it sounded odd, but she didn't have time to worry about it now. It ran, and that was all that mattered.

Isabelle had just merged onto the highway when her cell rang. She fumbled to answer it, hoping it was Grant or Keith with some good news. "Hello?"

"Hey, Isabelle," said Dale. "Grant was supposed to meet me at home to work on the security system, but he's not here. And he's not answering his cell. Know where he is?"

Isabelle didn't want Dale to know about any of this mess, especially not now that Grant was a suspect. "Sorry. I can't help you."

"Are you okay? You don't sound good."

A catch jerked her voice. "I'm fine."

She gripped the wheel hard, hoping Dale hadn't heard the lie in her tone. Just as he started to speak again, the steering wheel locked up and Isabelle couldn't move it. The car's dashboard lights winked out and in front of her, the highway was clogged with stopping cars. Brake lights loomed ahead of her as traffic slowed for construction.

She dropped the phone as she eased off the accelerator and pressed the brake.

Nothing happened. Her car barreled down the highway toward all the stopped cars, and she couldn't slow down or steer clear of any of them.

All she could do was brace herself as her car slammed into the back of another with a sickening crunch of metal and breaking glass.

Keith tried not to panic. His hands trembled as he drove to the police station, searching to find some sense of calm.

They'd found Everett too early. It was supposed to have taken days for anyone to find his body. Maybe weeks. Keith had been hiding in Everett's house while he packed and heard him make the call telling his boss he was leaving town.

How had this happened? Who would have gone looking for him?

Even worse was the fact that if Grant was being held for questioning in Everett's death, then there was a chance the police suspected that Everett hadn't committed suicide. His death could be listed as homicide instead of suicide. Keith couldn't let that happen. It would mess up everything. It would put the police on alert and make everyone more cautious.

It was hard enough waiting his turn without all the

delays this would undoubtedly cause. He wasn't sure how much longer he could keep going, not when Lavine kept haunting him night after night.

Keith was going to have to step things up and move faster, even if it meant being less gentle with his brothers and sisters. The important thing was helping them escape their pain, even if doing so hurt a little.

He turned into the parking lot outside the police station and parked his car. He wasn't sure what he was going to find when he went inside, and that bothered him more than a little. He was queasy, shaking—not at all as cool and collected as he needed to appear when facing the police.

Too bad Isabelle hadn't been earlier on his list. Things would be a lot simpler if she hadn't started nosing around. Then again, if she hadn't suspected something, she never would have asked Grant to come here, making the task of freeing him much easier.

Keith had always worried about how he was going to gain access to Grant with him overseas so much of the time. He kept hoping that Grant would be killed in the line of duty, but he hadn't, and now that he was here, Keith was sure that God or fate or whoever controlled the universe was on his side, because there was no way it was just dumb luck that he'd chosen to leave the military when he did.

Of course, if Grant hadn't come back, Keith would have found another way to help him. He'd spent months learning about poisons. Which ones left a signature behind for a medical examiner to find and which ones didn't. He loved the long-distance lethality they offered. Some of them were even supposed to feel good.

That appealed to Keith. He didn't like hurting his siblings, but sometimes it was necessary. Like with Everett.

Keith's stomach twisted at the memory of Everett's bulging eyes and tongue.

At least he was free now. He'd escaped his pain. Four more and it would finally be Keith's turn to escape, as well. No more nightmares.

That thought lightened his step and calmed his shaking hands as he entered the police station. Because he was a public defender, the police knew him and allowed him access to Grant with hardly any trouble. He entered the interrogation room and shut the door behind him.

Grant looked tired but unhurt, other than a small cut. The thug Keith had hired hadn't done his job and slowed Grant down enough to give Keith a shot at subduing him.

Maybe Grant was going to be even harder to deal with than Keith thought.

He studied the man sitting at the table, thinking of which way would be best to help him. If it weren't for the fact that Keith would certainly be caught, it would be an easy thing to paralyze him with the spray Keith kept in his briefcase and shove one of the poison capsules he'd made down Grant's throat. By the time the paralytic wore off, Grant would already be gone.

But it wasn't Grant's turn. He'd lived with Lavine for only a heartbeat of time compared to the others. It wasn't fair that he would get to go first. Amanda was next. Then Trina. They'd both earned their place in line.

Grant looked up in surprise. "Keith? What are you doing here?"

"Isabelle called me and told me the police were holding

you for questioning," said Keith. "Have you been charged with anything yet?"

"No, but I'm pretty sure that won't last much longer if Mathews has anything to say about it."

"Do you know if they have any evidence against you?" asked Keith.

"Mathews said something about finding my fingerprints in Everett's house."

Keith tried to hide his surprise that the police had even bothered to check for fingerprints. Everett's death should have been more convincing than that. What had he missed? He needed to find out before he went to help Amanda.

"Maybe they were just bluffing, thinking they'd get a confession out of you."

Grant shoved his fingers through his hair in frustration. "I don't know what else it would be. I've never been in his place, so my fingerprints can't be there."

Even though Keith knew the answer, he was playing a role and needed to ask the right questions to be convincing. "Did you kill him?" he asked, feigning sincerity. Using that word—*kill*—nearly made him choke with rage and disgust. It was such an ugly word for the gift Keith had given Everett.

"Hell, no!" shouted Grant.

Keith held up his hands. "Okay, I believe you. Our job now is to convince the police. Do you have an alibi?"

"I was with Isabelle."

Of course he was. Isabelle still hadn't gotten over her crush on Grant and likely never would. But that was okay. Keith would free her from that unrequited love, too, soon enough.

The door opened and Mathews entered. He looked like

he hadn't slept in days, or if he had, it was in the same clothes he was wearing now. Keith wondered if his wife's illness had taken a turn for the worse, though he knew better than to ask the man about her. Mathews didn't like answering questions about his personal life.

He set a short stack of folders on the table and said to Grant, "I need to know where you were on the following dates: January eleven, seventeen, thirty, February six, nineteen, and March three."

Those were the dates Keith had freed each of the others. Somehow, the police had made the connection, and Keith was pretty sure it was Grant's or Isabelle's fault.

Now that the police knew the deaths were connected, they were going to investigate them. Keith's time was running out.

He struggled to remain calm and tried to channel his panic into what would appear like anger. "What is this about?" he asked Mathews.

"Murder. We're looking into the deaths of six more people that might have been tied to Everett."

Murder? The word made Keith's mouth twist in disgust. What he'd done hadn't been murder, and he wanted to scream at Mathews until he took back the ugly insult. If only Keith could explain what they'd been through—if only Mathews could know for himself what it was like to suffer the way Lavine's children had—he wouldn't ever use such a disgusting word to describe the sacrifice Keith had made to save them.

Grant picked up the files and leafed through them. He didn't look surprised at what he saw, which meant he'd seen it before. That lack of surprise also made him look guilty.

Keith's mind scrambled to find a way to make the most of this turn of events. If Grant was charged with the murders and put behind bars, then he'd be difficult to access when it was his turn. And Keith didn't need Grant to take the blame. He already had someone else in mind for that on the off chance that he needed to remove any suspicion that would fall on him.

Keith didn't mind going to jail for helping his siblings, but what he did mind was the possibility he'd be put on suicide watch, unable to escape the memory of what Lavine had done to him—what he still did to him in his dreams every night. He'd be stuck in this world, suffering indefinitely with no means of escape.

He'd always known that getting caught was a possibility, so, to protect himself from that ever happening, he'd found another man to take the blame. Months ago. He'd brought Dale to Isabelle's attention, knowing she'd never be able to turn him away. Once Dale was part of her life, so was Wyatt—a man who looked enough like Keith to pass as him, with a history of violence.

And if a grudge against Isabelle for keeping his son away from him wasn't enough proof of motive, there was one as yet undiscovered fact about Wyatt that would be.

Wyatt would go back to jail, and Keith would be free to take care of whoever was left.

It was a solid plan, but something had gone wrong. Something had caused Mathews to suspect Everett hadn't committed suicide. What was it?

He leafed through the files as Grant finished with them, pretending that he'd never seen the images of death before. Thankfully, the paralytic he used metabolized quickly and was hard to trace even if one knew what to look for. So far, no one had, and there was no mention of it in the tox screen. "These are all suicides. You can't charge Grant with a suicide."

"We're working on getting the deaths reclassified," said Mathews.

"Why?" asked Keith.

"Because of the timeline. The deaths happened in order of when these people came to live at a certain foster home. That's not a coincidence."

Keith's body stiffened with shock. He hadn't expected anyone to see that pattern, though maybe he should have. All he'd been thinking was that it made sense to free the ones who'd suffered the longest first.

Now he was going to have to change how he did things. Amanda was supposed to be next, but maybe Isabelle or Trina was a better choice. He would have preferred to get Grant out of the way to make it easier to get to Isabelle, but he was probably going to have trouble with Grant. The man was too strong not to put up a fight. And he was well trained. Grant had to remain last on his list because the chances of making his death look accidental were slim. It would have to be a surprise attack. Nothing else would work.

A bullet in Grant's head, followed by another in his own. That was what he needed to do. They'd die together as brothers so neither would have to go alone.

"That can't be right," said Keith. "I was the first one to go live with Lavine, and I'm still alive."

Mathews's eyes narrowed in suspicion. "Then maybe you should tell me where you were on those dates, too."

"I was traveling some of them." And he had proof. He'd paid well for it, hiring a man who looked like him to fly in his place and use his credit cards so there were nice, solid records.

"Traveling where?"

Keith looked at the list of dates again as if he hadn't committed them to memory. "I was in Mexico on vacation for three of those weeks."

"Can you prove it?"

"Absolutely. Call the airlines for their passenger records if you don't believe me."

"I want your flight information on my desk today."

"Fine. Whatever. If you're done throwing out baseless suspicion, give me a few minutes with my client," ordered Keith in his professional tone.

Mathews glared at both of them. "I'll be back in ten. While I'm gone, have your client explain to you how his fingerprints were all over the papers on Everett's desk."

Once the detective was gone, Keith turned to Grant. "Can you explain that?"

"Either he's lying to try to get me to confess to something I didn't do, or those were the papers I helped Everett pick up off the restaurant floor. Isabelle helped, too, so her prints are likely there, as well."

No way was Keith going to let Isabelle spend even one hour in jail. "Okay. I'm sure there were witnesses there who can verify that's what happened if it comes to that."

Grant gave him a hard, glittering stare. "If you went to Lavine's first, why aren't you dead?"

"Assuming there is someone killing these people, perhaps they got the wrong date for me. Lavine adopted me days before you came. Maybe that's the date he's using for me."

"It's possible."

Keith waved off Grant's suspicion with a negligent flip of his hand. "Listen, Mathews will know soon enough that I wasn't around and he'll clear my name. I suggest you focus on your problem. Do you remember where you were on those days?"

Grant nodded. "Oh, yeah. I remember. Trouble is, it's classified, so I can't say."

"Is there anyone who can?"

Grant let out a deep sigh as if even trying was futile. "Maybe. I can give you the number for Colonel Monroe. He might be able to help."

"And if not?"

He met Keith's gaze, and for a moment, Keith wanted to free Grant right now. The poor man was suffering so much. He probably didn't even realize why.

Grant said, "If Monroe can't help, then I'm completely fucked, 'cause I won't give out classified information."

CHAPTER FOURTEEN

———❦———

Dale heard Isabelle scream, the tortured squeal of crushing metal and glass, followed by her silence.

Panic made his voice crackle. "Isabelle?" he shouted into the phone. "Isabelle? Are you okay?"

There was no answer, but he could hear the sound of screeching tires and realized she'd been in a car accident.

Fear congealed in his stomach as he screamed her name again. He had no idea where she was, but he was already on his way to his car to go find her, keeping the phone pressed to his ear for any signs she was okay.

Dear God, please let her be okay.

Dale had just shut the car door when he heard voices on the other end of the line. "Ma'am?" said a man in a concerned tone.

Someone groaned, and he prayed it was Isabelle. At least if it was her, she was still alive.

"An ambulance is on the way," said the man. "Don't try to move."

Dale's tires squealed as he sped down the street toward her school. Maybe she was on her way home and he'd see the accident along the way.

"Can you hear me?" he shouted into the phone.

"Dale?" came Isabelle's voice from far away.

A loud scratching noise filled the phone before the man spoke into it. "You know this woman?" he asked.

"Her name is Isabelle Carson. Where are you?"

"Highway sixty-five, just south of forty-four. Don't try to come here, though. Highway's jammed."

There was no way Dale was just going to sit around and wait to see if she was okay.

"Dale?" It was Isabelle, though she sounded groggy.

"I'm here."

"I'm fine. Just a little shaken up."

Relief made him shake hard enough that he had to pull his car over or risk having his own wreck. "You don't sound fine."

"I am."

Dale heard sirens in the background.

"I think I'm going to need you to come get me as soon as we're finished with the accident report. My car is . . . totaled."

But she was still alive. That's all that mattered. She was safe.

"Sure. Just tell me where."

"I'll call soon," she said loud enough to be heard over the wail of sirens. "Don't worry."

The line went dead and Dale didn't move. He couldn't. He'd almost lost the best thing in his life, and all it took was a split second. Isabelle would be gone and he'd be on his own again. No mom. No Isabelle. Nothing.

He couldn't let that happen. Not again.

A tap on his car window made him jump. He looked up, and Angela was standing there with the sun lighting her blond hair.

Dale blinked, sure it was just another trick of his over-active imagination. When she didn't go away, Dale rolled the window down.

"Heya, Dale," she greeted with a smile so sweet it made his chest ache beneath the hammering of his heart.

"What are you doing here?" he asked because nothing suave or cool leapt to mind.

"I live in that house." She pointed to the beautifully landscaped two-story house across the street from where his car sat. "I saw you pull up and just sit here. Are you okay?"

He wasn't, but he also wasn't about to admit it to the girl of his dreams. He wiped his face, checking for any traces of tears. When they came away wet, he knew his humiliation was complete. There was one girl in the world he wanted, and she had to be the one who saw him cry like a baby. Just his fucking luck.

"Dale?" she said, sounding more concerned by the moment. "What happened?"

Might as well tell her and get it over with. "My foster mom was in a wreck."

"Oh, God! Is she okay?"

"I don't know. I mean, I talked to her for a minute, but she sounded bad. She asked me to pick her up." He ran his hands through his hair, not able to look Angela in the eye. He didn't want to see her disgust for his weakness, or worse yet, her pity.

"You shouldn't drive right now. You're shaking. Let me do it for you, okay?"

Dale looked up in shock. She was offering to help him? After she'd seen him cry? "Why?" he asked, sounding distrustful even to his own ears.

She smiled a little, and Dale was such a bastard he forgot all about Isabelle for a moment. All there was in the world was Angela's smile and his pounding heart.

"Why not?" she asked. "Move over while I run and get my purse and leave a note for Mom."

Dale's brain still hadn't quite wrapped itself around the idea that he was about to be in the same car with Angela. It seemed too good to be true, especially on the heels of the day he'd had. "I don't even know where we're going yet."

"That's okay," she assured him. "We can just drive around for a while until we do."

"Don't you have more important things to do?"

"More important than making sure you don't crash your car, too? I don't think so."

Grant's patience was at an end. After three hours, he was just about to do something drastic, and likely regrettable, to get out of the fucking police station, when Keith came back into the interrogation room.

"Colonel Monroe vouched for you. Mathews is satisfied that you had nothing do to with those previous deaths," said Keith.

"Thank God," said Grant, nearly wilting with relief. He was going crazy trapped in here with Isabelle and Amanda out there in danger.

"Since all of the deaths were connected to Lavine, I suggested that Mathews create a list of his family members. He had a big family and some of them were a bit . . . odd. There are a lot of possible suspects there."

"At least that's something. Is he going to let us know if any of those people lead anywhere?"

"You need to let him do his job and keep out of it. In fact, you should just leave town and be on your way. The police can handle this."

"I'm not leaving or letting my guard down until the killer is behind bars and I know Isabelle and Dale are safe."

Keith's phone rang and he checked the caller ID. "Speak of the devil," he said to Grant, then into the phone, "Hi, Isabelle. I thought you were coming down here. Where are you?"

Grant watched as Keith's face lost all its color. "Okay. Grant is with me. We're on our way." He listened for a moment and replied, "I don't care. We're coming anyway."

"What?" demanded Grant as Keith hung up.

"Isabelle was in a car accident. She's in the hospital."

A bellow of denial erupted from Grant's chest as fear and rage swept through him. "Where?"

"I know the way. You can follow me in your car."

Grant was already heading down the hallway before Keith finished speaking.

CHAPTER FIFTEEN

———◆———

Grant raced into the emergency room, ignoring the attempts by the staff to stop him from finding Isabelle. He found her behind a partially closed curtain, sitting on a hospital bed. Standing nearby were Dale and a girl Grant didn't know.

"Grant?" said Isabelle as if surprised to see him.

Isabelle's face was swollen and she had a black eye. Her shiny hair was a wreck of tangles, and part of one sleeve had been cut away from her shirt. She was awake and alert and, although banged up, she seemed to be fine.

Grant stood there for a long moment, shaking with relief. His knuckles ached from gripping the steering wheel too hard on the way over here. He didn't think his heart rate would ever drop back to normal.

He went to her, dying to touch her but scared as hell he'd hurt her. So, instead of actually touching her, his hands hovered over her hair and face as he fought back the urge to let them land.

"I'm fine," she told him. "Didn't Keith tell you?"

"You're not fine. You're in a fucking hospital bed."

She pinned him with a stern stare. "I'm fine, Grant.

Really. You can stop worrying." She captured his hands in hers, stilling his erratic movements.

Her fingers were cold, and he pressed them against his chest to warm them. He wasn't sure he was ever going to let her out of his sight again. Not if it meant her getting hurt. Or worse. He'd never survive it. Just hearing the word *hospital* near Isabelle's name had stolen years from his life.

"Where's Keith?" she asked.

"He's parking his car. I'm sure he'll be in in a minute."

"What happened?" Grant asked in a voice that trembled as much as the rest of him. He was sure she could feel the tremors running through his body, and he hated it that he couldn't be stronger for her right now, when she needed it most.

"My car just . . . stopped working. The steering and brakes went out. I couldn't stop or avoid traffic, so I ran right into it. It was all my fault."

"The airbag kept her from being hurt a lot worse," added Dale.

Grant glanced at him and saw the girl he was with take hold of his hand. "Was anyone else hurt?" he asked Isabelle.

She nodded, and tears welled up in her eyes.

As gently as he knew how, Grant pulled her head against his chest and hugged her, stroking her hair. "It wasn't your fault," he whispered to her.

"It was. The car sounded funny when I started it. I shouldn't have driven it."

Something about that scenario sparked a memory in Grant's head. He'd nearly started a truck rigged with explosives once. If Caleb hadn't stopped him, they'd both be dead.

What if her car trouble wasn't a coincidence? What if it was the killer's way of taking her out and, instead of making it look like a suicide, making it look like an accident?

The idea made rage boil up in his throat. He should have thought of something like that before. He should have planned for the killer to change his strategy now that the cops were involved.

Dale knew nothing about this and, out of respect for Isabelle, he wasn't about to tell him.

Keith came through the door, glaring at Grant for leaving him behind. "They're going to tow your car. You're in a red zone."

"Let them tow it," said Grant, refusing to take his eyes off of Isabelle long enough to move it. Not until he got this sense of helpless panic out of his system.

"I'll move it," offered Dale.

"Are they keeping you here tonight?" Grant wanted to know where he'd be sleeping tonight—at her home or here in the hospital with her. No way was he leaving her unguarded.

"No. They're finishing up the paperwork so I can go home."

Grant nodded and pulled some cash out of his wallet. He gave it to Dale, along with the keys to the Mustang. "After you move my car, why don't the two of you pick up some food—something we can reheat easily—and go home. I'll bring Isabelle back as soon as they're done with her here."

"What do you want, Isabelle?" asked Dale.

"Anything's fine. I'm not sure I'm going to be able to eat, anyway."

Dale looked down at his pretty friend and his eyes sparkled with the serious crush he had on the girl. "I can drop you off on the way back."

She gave Dale a shy smile. "Or I could go with you and help you carry the food," she offered.

Dale didn't appear to know how to respond to her offer, and his throat was moving like he couldn't get it to work, so Grant stepped in. "That would be great," he told her.

Her smile brightened. "No problem." She laced her fingers through Dale's as they left.

Keith sat down next to Isabelle's bed and put his hand on her shoulder. The kick of jealousy Grant felt made him grit his teeth.

"I'm not sure you should leave," said Keith. "You'd be safer here."

"I'll rest better at home."

"And I'll be there to make sure you do," said Grant.

Keith's mouth tightened with irritation as his gaze shifted from Isabelle to Grant. "She'd be safer here."

Isabelle gave Keith a warning look. "I know you mean well, but I'm going home. Feel free to come by the house tonight if you're worried. In fact, maybe you should come stay with us until the whole thing is over."

Grant barely stomped on the urge to demand he be the only one to take care of her, but he managed to clamp his lips over the words that would have surely gotten him in trouble. Keith was her friend and, like it or not, Grant had to respect that.

"Three's a crowd, don't you think?" asked Keith as he

stood to leave. "Is there anything I can get you before you leave?"

"Will you check on Amanda?" asked Isabelle.

"Sure. She's at work, right?"

"I think so."

"I'll take care of it. Call me if you need anything else."

Keith left, and Grant couldn't stop touching Isabelle. He tried to reassure himself she was fine, but parts of him were still shaking with panic, unconvinced. He stroked her hair, relishing the feel of the slippery strands under his palm.

"Keith is threatened by you," said Isabelle.

Good. At least he'd done that right. "He'll live. I'm more worried about you. You could have been killed."

She gave him a slight nod, her mouth drawn tight with fear. "You don't think my accident was accidental, do you?"

God, he hated seeing her afraid. Still, he wasn't going to lie to her. "I'm sure you had to have considered the possibility."

"I thought it was just my way of finding someone else to blame for my mistake so I wouldn't feel so guilty, you know?"

"This wasn't your fault."

"Tell that to the man whose wrist I broke today by slamming my car into his. I doubt he'd agree."

Grant took her face in his hands, holding her gently. "You can't do this to yourself. I've seen what guilt can do to a person, and I won't let that happen to you."

Isabelle blinked back tears. Her green eyes, normally so bright, were dimmed by shame. "I've never hurt anyone before."

"And you didn't this time, either. And to prove it, I'll have Mathews check out your car and see if it's been tampered with."

"I don't know where it went," she said. "They must have had a truck tow it away."

Grant smoothed her hair away from her face. "Don't worry about it. I'll find it and take care of everything."

She nodded and leaned her head against his chest. "Everett's dead," she whispered in a bleak tone.

Grant climbed up onto the edge of the bed and held her close, wishing he could make her grief disappear. "I know, honey. I know."

"He doesn't have anyone to plan his funeral."

"We'll do it together," he assured her.

She was quiet for a long time and then, in a faint voice, said, "Amanda's next. I can't lose her, too."

"You won't lose her. I promise. It's going to be okay." Grant wanted to hold her until this whole mess went away, but it wasn't in the cards.

The nurse came into the curtained area, interrupting her reply. "You're all set to go home now, Isabelle. Call or come back if you have any problems, okay?"

"I will," said Isabelle.

The nurse looked at Grant. "Are you going to be with her tonight?"

"Yes." Right by her side. He'd seen men who'd been hit in the head take a turn for the worse in the blink of an eye. Her bump didn't look so bad, but he wasn't taking any chances. Isabelle was too precious.

"Good. Keep an eye on her, just in case, but she should be fine."

"I won't let her out of my sight."

❧

Grant wrapped his long fingers around Isabelle's upper arms in a gentle grip to help ease her from the hospital bed.

"I'm fine, Grant. Really. You don't need to hover."

His jaw was hard and his mouth tight with anger. She could see him vibrating with it, all his muscles drawn tight. "I almost lost you today."

Isabelle slid her arms around his muscled body and pressed herself against him in a hug meant to comfort both of them. She laid her head on his shoulder and breathed in the warm scent of his skin, ignoring how he stood stiff in her arms like he didn't really want to be here. Whether or not he admitted it, he needed this. He needed to know she was safe and whole and that she cared about him.

Maybe too much.

"See, I'm perfectly fine."

He pulled in a deep breath, which shifted her head more closely to his neck. She could see his pulse pounding in his throat, fast and hard.

Her hands stroked down his back over and over, and slowly, he started to relax. One by one, the corded muscles along his spine became less rigid. The coiled strength of his body yielded to her touch and she felt him soften, heard a nearly inaudible sigh of relief slide out of his lungs.

After a few moments, his arms closed around her, then tightened as if he'd never let her go.

That was a really nice thought, even if it was pure fantasy.

His mouth moved over her hair. His words were quiet and clipped. "I should have known this could happen."

"How could you predict a car accident?"

"I'm not sure it was an accident. And if it wasn't, not only did the killer go after you when it wasn't your turn, he also changed his tactics from making it look like suicide to making it look like an accident."

A cold, oily fear settled low in her stomach. Had she been fooling herself thinking she was safe for now? That Grant was, as well? She'd held herself together by focusing on the others—trying to keep them safe. If she had to worry about Grant and what would happen to Dale if she was murdered, she didn't think she could survive.

"Call Detective Mathews and tell him," said Isabelle.

His body went tense, and it wasn't just anger. It was more than that. Isabelle pulled away so she could look into his face. His expression was tight, his lips pressed into a hard, flat line. But it was his eyes that shocked her. They were cold and glittering with disgust, not warm and bright.

"I'm not sure I'm the best person to be dealing with Mathews right now," said Grant.

"He didn't really think you were the killer, did he?"

He let out a harsh bark of laughter. "Are you kidding? He was sure I was his guy. A fucking *murderer.* It's like my fourteen years of service meant nothing and I'm right back to where I started with everyone seeing me as a punk kid who killed his foster father."

"I don't see you that way."

He gave her a sad smile. "Yeah, but you were there. You knew what would have happened to you if I hadn't stopped Lavine that night, what would have continued happening to all those defenseless kids."

Isabelle barely controlled a shiver of revulsion. She'd dealt with the terror of nearly being raped, but that didn't mean she didn't remember what it had been like to be victimized, or to hear the other children cry at night, afraid to go to sleep.

"I'm sorry," he said on a sigh. "I shouldn't be talking to you about this. Digging up the past won't make things better."

"I don't see any way around it. This whole situation stems from our past. We can't simply ignore it because it's unpleasant."

"Unpleasant? Is that what you call nearly being raped? Living in a home of a child molester?"

"I was only there a few weeks, and I didn't really understand what was going on around me. I mean, I knew that some of the kids were afraid and sad, but I didn't understand why."

"Didn't that make it even more frightening?"

Isabelle shrugged. "I'd been moving around between homes and hospitals my entire life. Everything was always different at each new place. I learned to adapt, to accept the differences, and try to make the most of it until it was time to move on again."

"No kid should have to grow up like that."

"It wasn't that bad, or if it was, I didn't know any better. I'm happy with the way my life is turning out, and I feel blessed to be given the chance to make the lives of kids better than mine was."

"And I'm going to make sure you're able. I'm not going to let anything happen to you again."

"What happened today wasn't your fault."

He tightened his hold on her, fisting his hands in her shirt like he couldn't stand the thought of letting go. Fooling her like that was such a dangerous temptation. She wanted to believe it so badly.

Isabelle closed her eyes to block out the beautiful lines of his face, but it did nothing to stop his smooth, deep voice from sliding into her. "I should have realized the threat to you, rather than assuming the killer would continue the same pattern."

"Why? I didn't."

"I'm not going to make the same mistake again." Grant rubbed his cheek over her hair, and she could feel strands of it clinging to his evening stubble, connecting them. The slight tug on her hair made her shiver. "Too many people need you."

His flattery swept over her like a warm caress.

She looked up at him, expecting to see a teasing grin lighting his amber eyes. Instead, his face was hard and serious. "I don't think I could live with myself if anything happened to you. I need you to stay safe. To be happy."

"Why?" she asked.

His thumb traced a gentle arc over her eyebrow, careful not to hurt her bruised skin. That touch slid along her temple, over her cheekbone, and down to her mouth. "I just do. Promise me you won't take any chances, Isabelle."

Her lips parted under his touch, and she longed to let her tongue reach out and taste his skin. Just once. Just to see what it was like to share the intimacy with him.

She was shaking with the force it took to hold herself back, and the tremor came out in her voice, dark and soft and nothing at all like fear. She sounded sexy and sultry, even to her own ears. "I'll be careful. I have too much to live for not to."

CHAPTER SIXTEEN

Isabelle was shaking with fatigue by the time Grant drove her home, but she had one more thing to do before she could go out and join the others for dinner.

She shut the door to her bedroom, sat on the edge of the bed, and dialed Amanda's cell phone. It was the middle of the dinner rush, but Isabelle knew Amanda always kept her cell phone handy in case Rachel needed her.

Amanda picked up on the fifth ring. "I can't talk right now."

"It's important," said Isabelle.

Amanda sighed. "Hold on."

The clank of dishes in the background faded, a door squeaked, and when Amanda spoke, her voice had a hollow echo. "Okay. I'm in the bathroom, so make it quick."

Isabelle gripped the phone hard and kept her tone even, calm, and steady out of a sheer force of will. "Everett's dead."

"Oh, God. Isabelle, I'm so sorry. I know you and he were friends."

Isabelle blinked back tears and swallowed to loosen up her throat. "He was a sweet man. I'm going to miss him."

"What can I do?" asked Amanda. "Do you need anything?"

"I need to know you're safe. Come stay with me for a few days. We'll be safer together, and you'll have built-in babysitting anytime you want it."

"I can't uproot Rachel like that. You know I can't. She's too fragile right now."

"I know it would be hard on her, but she'd be a lot safer here with me than with your neighbor's kid."

"How am I supposed to get around? You don't have any bus stops in your neighborhood, and my car only works about half the time."

"I'll drive you to work." Isabelle still had to deal with her insurance company and get her car replaced, but she'd get a rental or something in the meantime.

"You have to work, too."

"I'm sure Grant would help," offered Isabelle out of desperation. "We'll make it work somehow."

Amanda was quiet for a moment. "What's going on? What aren't you telling me?"

Isabelle knew she wasn't supposed to say anything; she just didn't care. Amanda and Rachel's safety was more important than police secrets. "The killer has been murdering people in the same order they went to live with Lavine. You're next after Everett. And now he's gone."

"Holy shit! You're serious about all this, aren't you?"

"Completely. Please come stay with me. Grant's setting up a security system here. He'll make sure we're safe until they find the killer."

"Are you kidding me? Putting all of us in one spot is like baiting the water to draw a shark. No matter who he wants to come after next, it's one-stop shopping."

Isabelle hadn't thought about it like that, but maybe Amanda was right. "If we're all together, we can protect each other. The police can concentrate their manpower on fewer places."

"Screw that. I'm taking my baby and getting out of town."

Isabelle sagged with relief and felt the sting of grateful tears prick at her eyes. Amanda and Rachel would be out of harm's way. "Where are you going?"

Amanda was quiet for a long minute. "I have a friend who's been asking me to visit for a while. I'll go see her."

"Are you sure it'll be safe there?"

"Safer than here. I'll lose my jobs, but I suppose there are always more crappy waitressing jobs where these came from."

"If you need money, I can help. I don't have a lot, but I'll do what I can."

"I may have to take you up on that, but not yet."

"When will you leave?"

"I'm punching out right now. We'll be on our way out of town within an hour. Assuming my car starts."

"Don't tell anyone where you're going, but call me when you get there so I know you're safe."

"I will. Gotta run."

Amanda hung up, and Isabelle sagged on the headboard, barely able to move against the sluggish feeling of relief that pulled at her. They were leaving town. They'd be safe.

Of course, Everett had been on his way out of town when he'd been killed.

Isabelle wasn't taking any chances. She found Officer Brooks's card and dialed the number he'd written. It took a little convincing, but she managed to get him to agree to keep an eye on Amanda as she headed out of town with Rachel.

Now all she could do was wait and pray they'd be safe while she figured out how to do the same for Keith.

She was pretty sure that if she begged enough, Keith would give in and come stay with her for a few days, just until this was all over.

Keith entered Amanda's house through the back door. The lock took him all of thirty seconds to bypass and he slipped in quietly, unheard.

The TV was droning on in the living room, and the faint glow of bluish light flickered over the worn tile floor. The place was a mess, with dishes piled in the sink and laundry spilling out of the baskets in front of the washer. Mail sat unopened on the kitchen table in sloppy stacks.

Amanda worked long, hard hours. He knew that, but it didn't excuse the mess she forced her daughter to live in.

Keith shook his head. Such horrible living conditions were a sign of just how much Amanda was suffering. She couldn't even get her life together enough to keep the dishes done.

Of all the people Keith had helped, he was certain that Amanda was going to be the most grateful one. She would understand what he was trying to do. She would welcome the freedom he offered.

A quick glance at the teenager lying on the couch told him that Rachel's babysitter was still here, sound asleep.

He slipped by silently and went up the stairs to Rachel's

bedroom. The door was cracked open, and he saw that she'd kicked the covers off. She was curled into a tight ball, as if cold, so Keith eased the door open and went inside.

Her walls were plastered with crayon drawings depicting a life that didn't exist. Her house was drawn as a bright, happy yellow instead of the dingy gray it really was, and overhead, a sun shone, wearing a smiley face.

Poor, deluded child.

Keith shook his head over the sadness of it all. Maybe Rachel needed his help, too. He knew her home life had been bad before Amanda split up with her husband, but he didn't know how bad.

Moving slowly, Keith reached down and lifted the thin, torn blanket from the floor. He tucked it around her small body and slid his finger over her cheek.

She was such a pretty thing. He couldn't let her suffer anymore. She needed his help, and he couldn't turn his back on an innocent.

Keith was going to save Rachel, too.

CHAPTER SEVENTEEN

Isabelle had only meant to close her eyes for a minute before going to eat dinner, but when she opened them again, the light from outside had faded and the shadows in her bedroom had deepened. A glance at the alarm clock told her it was almost eight and she'd been asleep for an hour.

Grant sat across the room in a kitchen chair, watching her. He was completely still, unblinking. She couldn't even see his chest moving as he breathed. For a moment, she thought she'd imagined him, but as her head cleared of sleep, he didn't disappear.

The lean lines of his face were tight with worry, and his golden eyes glittered in the soft glow of the night-light she kept in the bathroom.

"What are you doing?" she asked him as she pushed the mussed hair from her eyes.

"Watching you sleep."

"Why?"

"You hit your head," he said as if that explained it. "How are you feeling?"

"I'm a little stiff, but it's not bad. How's Dale? Is he okay?"

"I made sure he knew you were okay so he wouldn't

worry. He went to help Angela with her trig homework for a couple of hours. He'll be back by ten."

Which left her alone in the house with Grant. Just the thought was enough to make her blood heat.

"Do you want something for the pain?" he asked. "Or maybe some dinner?"

She shook her head, trying to figure out what in the world was going through his. He still hadn't moved, and his glittering gaze was starting to make her squirm.

"You don't have to watch me. I'm fine."

Grant didn't move. "Go back to sleep, Isabelle. You need your rest."

"So do you."

"I'll sleep tomorrow."

"You can't sit there and watch me sleep all night."

His long fingers tightened around the arms of the chair until his knuckles turned white. "It's either that or I'm climbing into bed with you, close enough I can feel you breathe. Take your pick."

A slow, honeyed warmth slid through her limbs, making her shiver. Her heart rate picked up and her breathing sped as he stared at her, waiting for her response. Her body was soft and relaxed from sleep, her mind still hovering in that languid state where life's problems had yet to intrude. All there was in her world was the pounding of her heart and Grant's intent stare glittering in the darkness.

Before she could stop herself, Isabelle patted the mattress next to her.

Isabelle felt it then, his shift from protective Grant to something more. She saw it in the way his pupils dilated and the way his throat worked as he swallowed. An easy sort of grace fell over him, as if he was stepping into a comfortable pair of jeans.

A bare hint of a smile tilted his mouth, and his eyes slid over her face, taking in the desire she was sure was as plain as day.

Conquest. Victory. That was the look he wore now—the one that told her he knew he was getting what he wanted and liked it that way.

He rose from the chair and stalked across the carpet, his every move a study in grace. She saw the muscles in his abdomen ripple under his tight T-shirt as he neared her, saw the flex of his thighs as he came toward her.

A shiver raced over her skin, making it tingle with a bubbling hiss of pleasure. She felt a rush of sensation slide through her until it wound around her insides and tightened until it was hard to breathe.

He moved onto the bed, pressing his body close to hers.

"This is good," he said, staring at her mouth. "This is the way it should be."

Isabelle couldn't speak. There wasn't enough air in her lungs for speech.

Grant's thumb stroked her mouth carefully, and the need to taste his skin swelled up inside her, taking over. No amount of common sense was going to change that blazing need.

Just one taste. That's all she needed to prove to herself that Grant held no magic. She could walk away from him whenever she liked.

"Does your mouth hurt?" he asked.

"No," she whispered.

Grant's thumb slid over her bottom lip as if testing to be sure.

Before she could stop herself, she licked the salty pad of his thumb and watched as his eyes darkened to hammered bronze.

"Good," he whispered as he tilted her head back and placed a gentle kiss on her lips.

It wasn't enough to quench her desire, not even close. It was way too soft for that, but even so, that one little kiss made Isabelle's toes curl. She let out a sigh of need, no longer caring about whatever had bothered her so much a moment ago. After all the pain she'd suffered today, both physically and mentally, the pleasure of Grant's kiss felt almost too good. She clenched her hands in his hair to make sure he didn't go away. She needed this too much to let it end.

His lips coaxed hers wider, and she complied without hesitation. He flicked his tongue along her mouth, teasing her, making her want more. Her fists tightened in his hair, and she let out a low growl of desire that she'd never made before. Grant made her hungry. Needy.

Her body heated beneath her clothes until she was sure she'd combust. No way was she letting him go. She needed this, needed this pleasure.

Isabelle tugged his shirt free of his jeans and slid her hands underneath, over his back. The muscles along his spine were tight, and a fine layer of sweat dampened his skin. So much power was packed into his long, lean body, and she wanted to feel every inch of it.

Grant's tongue thrust into her mouth to play with hers, and he let out a deep growl of his own. His hands roamed over her back, questing lower until his long fingers cupped her butt. The feel of his hands on her bottom made her breathing spiral out of control and her stomach quiver.

She knew she was rushing things, and that there was some reason why she shouldn't, but just didn't care. She'd deal with the consequences later, because she wasn't going to be able to wait much longer to feel Grant slide inside her. Not if she wanted to stay sane.

It had been way too long since she'd been with a man, and she needed this—needed to be more than a teacher and a mom and a target. She needed to be a woman, desired and wanted by a man made to give pleasure.

Isabelle wedged her hands between their bodies and fumbled for the button on his jeans, letting him know exactly what she wanted.

Grant groaned, low and hungry, then pulled his mouth away from hers and covered her hands.

She took a deep breath, forcing herself to be blunt. "I want you."

He gave her a slow, bone-melting smile. "I love hearing that, honey. I want you, too."

She started shaking. She couldn't help it. She'd fantasized about him saying that on more occasions than she cared to count. None of them came close to the real thing. "That's good. We're in agreement."

"But we're friends. I can't stand the thought of fucking that up. Not with you."

"I'd never let that happen."

"Are you sure? It happens to people all the time. Things turn awkward or ugly even though no one wants that."

"Are you saying it's not worth the risk?"

He took her hands and pressed them to the pillow on either side of her head. He held them there while he looked down into her eyes. "What I'm saying is that we don't have to do this. But if we do, I won't let you push me away later. I don't have enough friends in my life to let one as special as you go."

He thought she was special, and that knowledge swelled up inside her, filling her with warmth. "I could never push you away."

Belatedly, she realized she sounded like some kind of schoolgirl with a crush. She felt her cheeks flame and started blabbering. "I mean, I know you're a free man and can do what you want. I swear I won't get clingy or needy or anything. You don't have to worr—"

He grazed her mouth with a finger to stop her. "I just want you to be sure. That's all."

"Oh, I'm sure," she told him. She felt like she'd been waiting for this for years.

CHAPTER EIGHTEEN

Grant could barely keep his hands from ripping the clothes from Isabelle's body. He told himself to slow down, but it didn't work. He'd never wanted a woman like he wanted Isabelle, and it scared him almost as much as it thrilled him.

Using a large chunk of reserve willpower, Grant kept his pace slow, giving her time to change her mind, though he wasn't sure he'd survive it if she did. His dick had been hard and aching for her since the moment her lips touched his thumb, and there was nothing he could to do convince it to settle down. Normally, he had more control, but apparently not where Isabelle was concerned.

She was stretched out under him, her long body fitting perfectly under his.

She looped her hands around his neck and pulled him down hard. Her mouth crashed against his in a ferocious kiss full of blatant need. Her tongue demanded entry into his mouth, and Grant's body heated another notch as he let her in.

Isabelle clung to him. Her grip around his neck was unbreakable, and one thigh rubbed against the outside of his leg. She was panting as she kissed him, giving him desperate little noises of need that thrilled him like nothing else ever had.

There was no question that she wanted him, and that was enough to allow Grant to let go and give her what she wanted. No more reservation. No more holding back. Isabelle was his.

He straddled her hips, being careful to keep his weight from hurting her. "How's your back?" he asked.

She frowned for a second as if she didn't understand what he was talking about, which was good enough to convince him it wasn't really bothering her. "It's good."

"If it hurts, tell me."

"So you can stop? I don't think so. I'd rather suffer."

Grant gave her a wicked smile. "I wouldn't stop, but I would roll you over and take you that way. I'd make sure you enjoyed it."

Her green eyes darkened, and Grant made a mental note to put that on his list of things to do to her.

Her quick hands had already found their way under his shirt and roamed over his bare skin. When they slid over his chest, she closed her eyes and groaned. "Take it off," she ordered him.

Always willing to please a lady, Grant stripped out of his shirt.

Isabelle sucked in a breath and went totally still. "Wow. I didn't think men like you actually existed outside of Hollywood."

"I'm glad you like what you see."

He let her touch him for another few moments until the feel of her slender fingers on his skin made him shake. If she didn't stop, he was going to come before he'd even had a chance to get her naked.

Just the thought was enough to push him closer to the edge, and he had to take several deep breaths to ease away from the point of no return. He captured her hands and pressed hot, open-mouthed kisses against her palms.

Isabelle shivered and her eyes slid shut. "You like that?" he asked, knowing the answer already.

"Like your mouth on me."

Oh, yeah. That was good. He planned on getting his mouth on a lot more of her. Right now. "My turn," he told her as he started to undo the row of buttons down the front of her shirt.

He peeled back the shirt slowly, teasing her as much as he was himself. He could see her dark nipples through the thin fabric of her bra as they puckered and tightened for him. Like her hips, her breasts fit her slender frame perfectly, giving her graceful female curves that made his mouth water.

He made quick work of her bra and found smooth, hot skin beneath.

Grant traced a finger from her throat, down the center of her body, and back again. Isabelle squirmed beneath him, and a pretty pink flush bloomed over her chest.

"Stop teasing and touch me," she said in a breathless voice.

"I am touching you, honey."

"You know what I mean."

Of course he did, but he also knew how much better for her it would be if he made her really want it. Like he did.

"Like this?" He drew his finger along the underside of her breast, closing in on but not quite reaching her nipple.

Isabelle twisted, but Grant's weight kept her pinned in place. "Payback is hell, Grant."

His smiled widened. "I can hardly wait."

Rather than touch her like she wanted, he leaned down and pressed his torso to hers, letting his chest hair tickle her skin. She groaned and arched her back to complete the contact.

The feel of her tight little nipples against his chest should not have affected him quite so violently, but it did. He was mostly naked. With Isabelle. Touching her. He gritted his teeth to stave off his impending orgasm and took several deep, sucking breaths.

What the hell was wrong with him? He could normally tease a woman for hours without getting so worked up. Something about Isabelle was different, and if he didn't want to embarrass himself, he was going to have to change his usual tactics.

Her mouth was on level with his throat, and she flicked her tongue out over his skin in a hot, wet caress. Her hands slid over his back as if soaking up the heat of his skin.

If she wanted heat, he'd give her an inferno.

Grant pushed up off of her enough to maneuver his body down so he could finally kiss her breasts. He licked and nipped his way down her neck and over her collarbone, leaving a trail of damp skin in his wake. Her lungs were working overtime, and that was all the proof Grant needed that she was right there with him.

He closed his mouth over the tip of her breast and felt her nipple harden further against his tongue. Isabelle let out a soft whoosh of air and grabbed a double fistful of his hair. He suckled gently, keeping his teeth away until she was ready for that kind of intense sensation.

And at this rate, she would be soon.

He'd never been with a woman who got so hot so fast.

It was enough to make a man's head swell, as well as his dick. His heart was pounding, shoving blood through his veins, but it did little to cool him down. He didn't know how much longer he'd be able to last as turned on as he was, but he was going to find out.

Grant switched his attention to her other breast and looped his thumbs in the waistband of her pants. He needed to get his hands on her luscious ass.

The pants and stretchy panties went down without a fight. Grant followed suit, kissing his way down over her ribs and stomach. He looked up to see if she was still with him but was distracted by her still-wet, distended nipples. He'd done that to her—made her body show him just how much she liked his mouth. And he wanted to do it again. Lower this time.

He made quick work of stripping her legs bare the rest of the way and urged her thighs to open for him. She gave in, melting beneath his touch, and when he kissed his way up along the inside of her thigh, she quivered and dug her fingers into his hair.

Grant let her guide him and kept careful track of the things that made her suck in her breath or let it out in a blissful moan. He knew he'd never get enough of her, never get tired of having her spread out before him like an offering, making her feel good.

Sweet, lovely Isabelle was all his.

Her body tensed, drawing tighter as Grant used his mouth, tongue, and fingers to pleasure her. The woman taste of her, the smell of her arousal made him ache with the need for release, but he wasn't ready to give in to the urge just yet.

But Isabelle had other ideas. She tugged at his hair, trying to pull him up to cover her body.

Grant grudgingly gave in and lay down beside her where he could kiss her. He loved her mouth, all soft and supple against his. A man could live for years on fantasies about her mouth alone.

Her fingers found his waistband, and she tugged in an effort to free the button of his jeans. When it didn't work, she resorted to rubbing his erection through his jeans.

Pleasure rocketed up his spine, and he let out a hiss of surprise. It must have just been too long since he'd gotten laid or something. It was the only reason he could think of that it felt so good this time. Better than it should have.

Grant didn't need any more encouragement to convince him to get naked. He wanted to feel her fingers stroke naked flesh before he had to don a condom. He'd love to feel her mouth, too, but he'd take whatever she wanted to give and count himself the luckiest man alive.

It took him longer than normal to get his pants off, even though he sat on the edge of the bed to make it easier. Isabelle was kneeling on the bed behind him, rubbing her breasts against his bare back as she kissed his neck and stroked his shoulders and chest. For some reason, his jeans were stuck, and there wasn't enough blood left in his brain for him to figure out how to fix the problem for a few seconds. Finally, the brain cells sputtered enough for him to remember he was still wearing boots. He fumbled to unlace them, and finally, he was home free.

Isabelle reached around him and wrapped her hands around his jutting penis. "Do you have a condom?" she asked.

Grant's head was about to blow off from the force of

sensation that shot through him at her touch. It took a moment for her words to make sense though the buzz of pleasure filling his ears. "We're not going to need one if you keep touching me like this. I'll come in your hands instead."

He pulled on her wrists and she let him go. When he turned around, she reached for him, smiling.

She didn't try to hide her body. In fact, she didn't appear shy at all with him. Not that she had any reason to be. She was beautiful. Tall, slim, but not skinny, and curved like a woman should be in all the right places. The way her nipples stood out made his mouth water for another taste, and those long legs of hers were going to feel so good wrapped around his waist. He was sure of it.

Grant had no idea what he'd done to deserve this time with her, but he hoped he figured it out fast enough that he could do it some more before he left.

He went into her outstretched arms and kissed her. She purred her pleasure into his mouth, and he eased her back down to the mattress.

The feel of her naked body stretched out next to his was exquisite. She was all smooth and soft everywhere he looked. Everywhere he touched.

His hands roamed over her hip, down into the indentation of her waist, and back up over her ribs. He traced the delicate bones with his fingertip until he worked his way up high enough to cup her breast. Gently, he pinched her nipple between two fingers. She leaned into his touch and shivered, so he knew he was doing it just like she liked.

A satisfied smile curved Grant's mouth as he kissed his way over her jaw and down her neck. He wanted to feel her nipples against his tongue again and make her writhe with need. He latched on to her other breast and she nearly came off the bed.

"Grant." His name was a breathless sigh of need, a sound he'd never forget.

"Let me feel you," he said, barely pressing his fingertips against her mound. "Open your legs, honey."

Isabelle did, and Grant let his hand slide down over slick, hot skin. She was wet for him, scalding hot.

Grant groaned, and his hips bucked against her once before he got himself back under control. He couldn't stop his fingers from parting her soft folds to feel her more completely, nor could he stop himself from pressing one finger inside her. She was snug but relaxed, and he slid in easy.

Isabelle sucked in a breath and stiffened. Her legs clamped closed on his arm, locking his hand against her.

"Give me the condom," she told him.

"In a minute. There's no hurry."

"That's not what you said a minute ago."

"A minute ago, you had your hands wrapped around my cock. I'm more in control now."

"Oh, yeah?" She reached down and stroked his erection from tip to base and back again. "How about now?" she taunted.

Grant's voice shook when he ordered her, "Let go of my hand."

Isabelle relaxed her legs, freeing his hand. Grant fetched a condom from his jeans and ripped it open with his teeth and covered himself.

"Spread your legs for me," he said as he moved over her. Isabelle complied, but not enough to make room for his body. He nudged her knees farther apart and settled between them. His penis throbbed, begging for him to shove himself inside her, but that was the caveman side of his brain talking. Instead, he rubbed against her slick folds without penetrating her.

Isabelle shifted restlessly beneath him, gripping his hips as if she could actually control where they went. She spread her legs wider and lifted her bottom. "If you don't stop teasing me, I'm going to—"

Before she could finish her threat, Grant eased his erection a few inches into her slippery body. She stiffened and dug her fingers into his flesh.

He was pretty sure he wasn't going to make it more than two minutes, and he'd be damned if he came before she did. He had his pride.

"You good?" he squeaked out.

She hummed her approval and grabbed his ass, pulling him closer.

Grant could take a hint with the best of them, so he pressed forward, sliding in a couple more inches.

Isabelle started panting, which was either a really good sign, or a really bad one.

"You still with me?" he asked.

"Oh, yeah. Right here all the way."

Grant kissed her and began a slow, steady pace. He tried not to think about how good she felt so tight and slippery around his cock. Instead, he focused on her reactions. Gauged her breathing and all the little hitches he caused when he drove deep. He found the spot she liked and angled his hips to hit it just right. It didn't take long before she was digging her fingernails into his back, arching up to meet his thrusts.

Grant felt the crushing weight of his climax bearing down on him. Sweat beaded on his skin, and he recognized he was nearing the point where all rational thought vanished. Where all that existed was his own body and the pleasure he could wring from it. He didn't want to do that to Isabelle—didn't want to use her like that.

He eased an arm under her hips to raise her slightly and pushed into her until he was seated to the hilt. She tensed and clutched his biceps, making desperate little panting noises that made Grant feel like the biggest stud on the planet. Her eyes were dark, with only thin rings of green around the pupils. Her hips undulated, grinding her clitoris against his pubic bone, pushing her closer to the edge.

"That's right," he whispered to her. "Almost there, honey." He pinched her nipple and gave it a slight tug.

Isabelle sucked in a breath and held it. Her hips bucked harder and Grant shifted, giving her the extra friction she needed in short, hard thrusts.

He felt her climax ripple through her belly and tighten the muscles gripping his penis. Isabelle let out a long, low cry of release, and he couldn't hold back any longer. Not with her sweet voice filling his ears and the scent of her arousal filling the air.

He let go of his control as she came, moving in long, frantic thrusts that sent him over the edge in seconds. Raw pleasure spiraled up his spine and coursed out over his limbs. His cock throbbed as he came, shoved as deep into Isabelle's tight body as he could go. His vision went a little gray around the edges, but he didn't care. Nothing mattered but the soft cushion of her sated body beneath his and the aftershocks of pleasure ricocheting through his system.

His heart was pounding hard, and the ragged sound of his breathing filled the room.

Grant had had a lot of sex in his life, but he'd never had an orgasm as intense as that. In fact, he still wasn't sure he was going to live through it.

A man could get used to sex like that. If it didn't kill him outright.

Isabelle's hands stroked his back in clumsy sweeps. She wasn't any better off than he was if the way her heart was racing like a rabbit's was any indication. And he was crushing her, which couldn't be comfortable.

Grant lifted himself off of her, hating the feeling of separating his body from hers. He would have loved to stay joined with her, as close as a man could get, but he didn't dare risk it.

He pulled away from her and sprawled on the bed until he could find the strength to get rid of the spent condom.

"That was . . . wow," she said, her voice as unsteady as his pulse.

"Amen."

"I'm just going to rest here for a minute, okay?"

Grant leaned over her and kissed her eyelids, her nose, her bruised cheek. Even with the bruises, she was the most precious, beautiful thing he'd ever seen. Generous and kind. He was a lucky man to have her in his life, if only for a short time now and then.

She grabbed his head so she could get a proper kiss. Her lips were soft, a little puffy from all the attention he'd been giving them. He'd never get enough of her mouth, not if he married her and he lived to be a hundred.

The thought jolted him, scaring him to death. He wanted to settle down someday, but not until he was sure he could be a decent husband and father. He would not do to Isabelle, or any other woman, what his father did to him and his mom. Until he was sure that he wasn't wired the same as his old man, he had no right to think about marriage or family, no matter how much he wanted it.

Wanting something and being able to have it were two different things. He had to remember that so no one got hurt.

"I'll be back in a minute. Gotta clean up."

Isabelle gave a sleepy nod, and Grant used the excuse to escape to the bathroom. He needed a moment alone to clear his head and get his priorities straight. Sex with Isabelle was fantastic, and he was already aching to do it again, but he had a job to do. He had to keep her, Dale, Amanda, Rachel, and Keith safe, and he wasn't going to do that if he kept thinking with his dick.

There was work he needed to do, and it was about damn time he got to it.

Amanda's home was dark when she pulled in to the cracked driveway that was now closer to gravel than concrete. The scent of old cooking oil clung to her uniform and hair, making her stomach turn.

She'd lost too much weight since she'd left Bobby, but too much worry and not enough time to eat had taken its toll. She'd thought the worst was over—that she was finally getting back on her feet.

And now this.

If she left town—assuming her car would even get her that far—all her hard work and meager savings would be gone in days. There was no friend she could stay with. She'd lied to Isabelle because the truth was too humiliating.

Bobby had torn her away from every friend she'd ever had in an effort to isolate and control her. And God help her, she'd let him, thinking it might bring them closer, might make him happy.

Amanda's head dropped to the steering wheel with a thud. She was so tired. Worn too thin. A sad, secret part of her almost wished for it all to end so she could finally rest.

If it weren't for Rachel, Amanda was pretty sure she would have saved the killer the trouble by now and taken care of the job herself.

But she did have Rachel, so she kept going even though she was numb with fatigue, struggling for every breath while simultaneously wondering why she bothered.

Amanda locked her car out of habit, even though no one would want it, and went inside.

Her babysitter, Nicole, was asleep on the couch. The goth clothes and overdone makeup looked ridiculous on her, but she was a good kid, and Amanda didn't exactly have a lot of choices for child care in her neighborhood.

She gave Nicole's shoulder a gentle shake. "Wake up. I'm home."

The teen's brown eyes opened and she shoved her purple hair out of her face. "You're home early."

"Yeah. I wasn't feeling well." At least it wasn't a lie. "Go on home, and thanks for watching Rachel for me."

Nicole grabbed her backpack and shambled out the door. "Why is there a cop car out here?"

Amanda looked past Nicole, and sure enough, a police car was parked out in front of her house. The officers inside saw her and nodded.

Isabelle's doing, no doubt. Amanda was sure of it.

"I don't know," lied Amanda. "Guess the police are just patrolling the area."

Amanda stood on the porch and watched Nicole, making sure she got home safe and sound. The neighborhood wasn't horrible, but it got worse each year. A lot like her life.

When Nicole disappeared behind her front door, Amanda went back inside, stifling a sigh of defeat. Her house was a wreck. Bills and junk mail littered every horizontal surface. Laundry was piled in one corner, waiting for her to find time to get to it. There was a sinkful of dishes and a nearly empty pantry she didn't have the money to fill.

If she left, it wasn't as if she'd be leaving much behind. A few belongings. A lot of bad memories.

She found herself standing in Rachel's doorway, watching her sleep. She seemed to gravitate there when things were bad. Rachel was the one bright spot in her life, and even though she was a sad, broken child, at least they were together. A pair of sad, broken people trying to find their way to happiness.

Amanda's one wish was that Rachel would succeed.

She shifted in her sleep, whimpering and curling into a tighter ball under the threadbare blanket. Amanda's heart twisted as she went to hold her daughter.

Bobby had been gone almost a year now, but he still managed to ruin their lives. She prayed every night he'd burn in hell for it, and if that made her a bad person, then so be it.

"Momma?" said Rachel in a tiny, frightened voice. She'd learned to be quiet at Bobby's hand and had never lost the habit.

"I'm here, baby. Momma's here."

Rachel clung to her, her thin body surprisingly strong. Maybe the rest of her was strong, too. Isabelle seemed to think so. Amanda could only hope.

"I was dreaming again."

"It's just a dream. It's not real." Anymore.

"Can I sleep with you tonight?"

"I was thinking we could take a little trip. Go somewhere fun, like a vacation."

Rachel rubbed her eyes. "Now?"

"Sure. Why not?"

"It's night."

"I know. We can see the stars better this way."

Her bottom lip started to wobble. "I don't want to go."

"Why not?"

Rachel's grip tightened, and Amanda could feel her trembling. "Please don't make me go."

Amanda had no idea what had upset Rachel, but she pulled her into a tight hug and rocked her. "It'll be fun. You'll see."

Rachel pushed away and scrambled against the far wall, clutching the covers tight against her chest. "I don't want to go back. I'll be good. I promise."

"Go back where, baby? I don't know what you mean."

"To live with Daddy. Please don't make me. I'll be good, Momma."

Amanda captured her daughter's face gently in her hands, making sure she was looking right into her eyes. The fear she saw there nearly tore her apart, and she'd do anything to take away the pain Rachel had suffered. "I'd never send you away, baby. Not ever. You and I are a team, and I'd never be able to get along without you."

"You wouldn't?"

"Not a chance. What made you think I'd ever send you away?"

"Christopher told me. His mom sent him to live with his dad so she could have a boyfriend."

"Baby, the last thing I want is a boyfriend. And even if I did, I'd never want one who didn't want you."

"You sure?"

"Positive."

"Then I don't have to go?"

Rachel was on the verge of another breakdown. Amanda could see it in the desperate gleam brightening her eyes. She couldn't survive that again. Neither of them could.

Of course, they wouldn't survive a killer, either.

"I'm sorry, baby. We have to go. But don't worry, we're not going anywhere near Daddy."

"Promise?" asked Rachel as her chin started to tremble and her eyes filled with tears.

"I swear it. We'll go see Vicky. Remember her?" Vicky had been Amanda's closest friend for years before Bobby had slept with her and shoved a wedge between them. Vicky had moved to Tulsa for work, and even though they hadn't spoken since, maybe she'd open her door to them for a few days. It was worth a shot.

Rachel nodded. "She had orange hair."

A small smile tugged at Amanda's mouth. "It's called red, but you're right. That's her."

"I liked her."

"Good. That makes two of us. Put on some clothes while I pack, and I'll meet you downstairs."

Amanda didn't own a suitcase, so she threw the few

good outfits she and Rachel had into a trash sack and
hauled it out to her trunk.

Ten minutes later, they were on the road in a car that
barely started. Amanda had fifty bucks in her pocket and a
credit card that was nearly maxed out. Beside her, Rachel
sat in silence, clutching her pillow as she stared out at the
road ahead.

Behind them, a police cruiser followed at a discreet distance as they hit the highway and headed to Tulsa.

Keith stayed hidden in Amanda's closet until his legs
started to go numb. He'd heard the front door close and
the engine of Amanda's car rattle to life about ten minutes
ago, but he wasn't sure if it was safe to come out yet.

The police were here. He'd heard Amanda talking about
it with her babysitter.

Keith couldn't be caught now. Not yet. So he stayed
hidden and waited until he was sure they'd left.

In her haste to leave, Amanda had left the bedroom
light on, and the dingy lace curtains would do nothing to
obscure his movement from the police if they were still
there.

Why they'd be watching an empty house he had no
idea, but he was sure they were still out there. He could
hear them breathing, panting like a dog, like Lavine always did.

No. Keith shook his head to clear it. Lavine was dead,
and those cops were too far away for him to hear them
breathe. It was just his imagination.

He was rattled, that was all. His nerves were getting

the better of him. The stress of everyone knowing what he was doing was too much. He'd liked it a lot better when it was his secret—one he shared with his brothers and sisters one at a time. Now he felt like everyone was watching. Judging him.

None of them understood. They all thought he was hurting people.

Isabelle had actually called them murders, as if it was some kind of crime he committed, as if he was no better than the scum he defended. Drug dealers and pimps and armed robbers. He wasn't like them. What he was doing was good, and if the dead could speak, Isabelle would know he'd saved them. She'd look at him with that bright glow of adoration in her eyes like she did when she looked at Grant.

Just the thought was enough to make him want to find her and show her what he was doing. She might not understand now, but once all that fear was gone, once she was free and happy, she'd see he'd been right all along.

CHAPTER NINETEEN

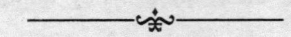

Isabelle watched Grant slip into the bathroom, and she knew by the way he moved so furtively that he wasn't coming back to bed with her.

Her chest tightened as her bathroom door clicked shut, but she refused to give in to the urge to cry. Or run after him.

She'd always known he would leave, and no matter how good the sex had been, it changed nothing. It was best if she got used to the idea of him going sooner rather than later.

Besides, if he'd stayed, she'd want him again. And if he was here, she might just take what she wanted and wake her son up with noises he should never have to associate with her.

So, even though her body felt sated and heavy, she dragged her butt out of bed and put on some pajamas before Grant could come back, see her naked, and change her mind.

And he could. She had no doubt about that. The man could read the nutritional label on a cereal box and make her hot. He'd nearly killed her with pleasure, and she was already considering the possibility of convincing him to do it again.

She slid her shirt over her head, and when she looked up, he was in her bathroom doorway, leaning against the opening. He was shirtless, and she stopped dead in her tracks, unable to do anything but stare and soak in the sight of his body. He had a sprinkling of dark blond hair across his pecs that narrowed and led her eyes down to where it disappeared under the waistband of his jeans.

At least he was wearing pants. That should have given her some advantage in resisting him, but instead, she found herself wondering how long it would take her to get him naked again—just like she wanted.

"You look tired," he said.

"I am." But she'd find the energy to stay awake if it meant she got to touch him again.

"You should go back to sleep." Without him. She saw that truth glittering in his eyes.

"I will. What about you?" she asked.

"It's still early. I'm going to work on the security system and hang out until Dale is back from Angela's. I'll be careful not to wake you."

"Are you sure you don't want to sleep a bit?" she asked. It would have felt good to curl up with him for a while and soak up his heat.

"Maybe later." He walked past her and pulled down the blankets on her bed. "Want me to climb in and warm it up for you?" he asked.

"I might not ever let you get out if you do," she teased.

Grant looked away before she could see his reaction, but he was silent, which made her wonder if she'd said something wrong. She knew he wasn't the type to be tied down to one woman, but he'd always been able to take a joke. She wasn't sure what to think.

Isabelle slid under the blankets and accepted Grant's good-night kiss to her forehead. She felt insecure now, like she'd made some irreparable mistake. He started to walk away, and she knew she'd never be able to sleep if she was worried about what he was thinking.

She grabbed his hand before he could get away. "Grant, I didn't mean anything by that."

He looked at her and his eyes were bright topaz, almost glowing. "I know you didn't."

"Then why do you look so freaked out?"

His jaw bulged as if he was angry. "As much as I wish it was different, I can't be the kind of man you need. You want stability for a family, for the children you plan to bring into your home."

"How did you know that's what I planned?"

"Bunk beds and kid-sized furniture in the guest room. Ads for swing sets and toys cut out of the paper. Brand-new child locks on all the cabinets and drawers with dangerous stuff in them. You're preparing for a family."

Isabelle nodded. "As soon as I know it's safe, I want to bring two more foster children into my home."

He was silent for a long moment, and when he spoke, his tone was one of bleak acceptance. "I can't be a father."

"I'm not asking you to be. I didn't ask you to come here, and I certainly know better than to depend on you or cling to you. I'm a big girl, Grant. I knew the score the moment you stepped through my door."

"I wish I was so certain. A part of me is tempted to stick around and see where this goes."

Whoa. That sounded suspiciously like he meant he wanted to try having a relationship with her. That didn't sound like the carefree Grant she thought she knew.

His thumb stroked the back of her hand. "But it's different when kids are involved. I'm not ready for that kind of commitment."

That little bubble of joy at the thought she and Grant could try to stay together burst. He was just like all the other men she knew. None of them wanted to be saddled with someone else's kids. None of them wanted to stay.

Anger sharpened her words. "No one's asking you for any kind of commitment. We had sex. It was great sex, but I'm not some little girl who can't separate a romp in the sheets from a real relationship. You don't have to be worried."

"I've never once worried that you would try to hold on to me. In fact, it's just the opposite. We share a past, and you know what a rare and valuable thing that is for us. Maybe I'm the one who wants to cling a little."

Isabelle blinked twice before she could speak. "You do?"

Grant gave a casual shrug, but his tight jaw told her just how tense he really felt. "Maybe."

"I'm sorry, Grant. I won't change my life plans for a maybe. Heck, I wouldn't even change my plans if you were on your knees with a diamond ring in your hands. I know what I want to do with my life, and I'll find a man who shares my dreams or I'll do it alone."

Grant's eyes went wide, and he looked a little sick. "God, Isabelle. Is that what you thought I meant? I'd never ask you to change for me. What you're doing is too important. That's not what I meant at all."

"Then what did you mean?"

"I just wanted you to know that this thing between us can't go any farther. It would never work out. I wanted you to know that I knew it, too. That way, if I do cling a little, at least we'll both know where we stand."

She knew exactly where she stood. Alone.

No. Not alone. She'd have her kids, and that would be more than enough for her. If she found a man someday, it would be a blessing, but if not, she'd be fine. Better than fine.

Sex with Grant had taken the edge off her inconvenient hormones, and all she needed now was a good night's sleep. After that, she'd be good as new, ready to face her life and figure out how she was going to manage to hold on to her career and keep the people she loved safe.

No problem.

Grant had just sat down to eat reheated takeout when Dale came home. There was pep in Dale's step that hadn't been there before and the flush of infatuation on his cheeks. He tossed his backpack on the floor and went straight for the refrigerator.

"How'd the tutoring go?" asked Grant.

"Great. She's smarter than she thinks she is. She just needed someone to explain it to her so she'd understand."

"And that someone was you, huh?"

"Yep."

Isabelle's untouched plate was still sitting on the table. "If you're hungry, you can eat Isabelle's dinner. She went to bed."

Dale's head popped up over the refrigerator door and his eyes were bright with concern. "She okay?"

"Yeah. Just tired."

Dale grabbed the plate and slid it into the microwave. "No kidding. I was only listening when her car crashed, and I'll probably sleep until noon tomorrow."

Grant grunted. "If you're like most young men, sleeping until noon is the norm."

Dale sat down across the table and started shoveling food into his mouth. "Not for me," he said around a bite of eggroll. "Saturday morning study group."

Grant gave him a sympathetic wince. "You really are putting in the hours. Is it helping?"

Dale shrugged as if he didn't care, but the tension flowing through his body told Grant his nonchalance was a lie.

"You said you already know the answers to the test, they just don't come out when you get nervous."

"Yeah. So?"

"So, if you already know the answers, then why do you keep going over them again? That's not your problem."

"And you know what my problem is?"

"Sure do. Performance anxiety."

Dale scowled. "Isn't that what guys call it when they can't get it up?"

Grant held back his laugh, but he was sure he'd damaged something internally in the effort. "Yeah, I've heard it called that, too, but that's not what I'm talking about."

"Good. 'Cause my dick works fine, and even if it didn't, it's none of your business."

"I couldn't agree more. Can we focus on something other than sex for a minute here?"

Dale lifted a dark brow. "I'm seventeen. What do you think?"

Grant did laugh then. He couldn't help it. "Right. I'll make this quick. I think I know how to help you."

Dale looked skeptical, but interest lighted his eyes and Grant had his full attention.

"Have you ever done practice questions outside of the actual test?"

"Yeah. Sure."

"How did you do?"

"Fine. I aced them."

"But during the actual test, you get nervous, right?"

"Yeah. So what?" He was getting defensive, and that wasn't going to do either of them any good.

"Everyone gets nervous, man. It's just one of those normal body reactions. The trick is to keep it from messing you up."

"How do you do that?"

"You learn to control your body better. You keep your breathing slow and steady, which helps keep your pulse down. If you don't have a ton of adrenaline pumping into your system, you can concentrate better."

Dale shook his head, giving Grant a disgusted sneer. "Yeah, right. That woo-woo shit doesn't work."

"Sure it does. It's how I became a sniper."

Dale's eyes flew wide. "You were a sniper?"

"Sure was."

"That's so cool. Do you have your gun here with you?"

He did, but there was no way Grant was going to let on. His rifle was tucked away in his trunk, inside a locked box only his fingerprints or a diamond-tipped saw blade could open. That box was bolted to the frame of his Mustang, and, God willing, it was going to stay there.

"Focus, Dale. This isn't about weapons. It's about you passing your test so you can get into a good college and make something out of your life."

Dale put his fork down, even though the plate was only half-empty. "I'm listening."

And he was. Grant could see him listening with every part of his body, poised on the edge of his chair, ready to do whatever it took. Doing well on this test was important to him, and Grant was going to see to it that he did everything he could to help Dale succeed.

Maybe he did have something to offer Dale, after all. It wasn't much, but it was something.

A strange feeling swelled inside Grant as he quickly determined the best way to help Dale with what he knew. He wasn't sure what this feeling was, but he liked it. Later, maybe he'd try to figure it out, but for now, it was enough to know that he could help Isabelle's son.

"What do I do?" asked Dale.

"First, you need to learn how to breathe."

"Breathe? I kinda got that one down."

Grant shook his head. "Not really. You'll see what I mean in a minute. Just hang in there, okay?"

"If it will help me nail the SATs, I'll stand on my head and gargle peanut butter."

"Don't get ahead of yourself," said Grant. "That's lesson two."

❧

Trina felt the rush of victory course through her system. She'd done it. She'd figured out how to get that metal rod out of the toilet, and now it was clutched in her hand, hidden under her body, waiting for her husband's killer to come back.

She lay on the bed, forcing herself to stay still and feign sleep. The squeak of floorboards overhead warned her that he was back. He'd be coming for her soon, and when he did, she'd ram her hard-won weapon into his eye and shove it into his brain until the fucker died twitching.

Her hand sweated around the lever attached to the rod, making her grip slippery. She wished she could have wrapped the washcloth around it, but she needed that to hide the hole left in the toilet tank. If he saw that, he'd know what she was doing.

Trina's fingers tightened, and she swore to herself she would not let the thing slip. She was only going to have one chance at killing him. She was pretty sure he'd never give her another. If she failed, he'd kill her just as he'd killed Henry.

Gentle Henry. He was gone. She'd never again feel the warmth of his touch or hear his deep, booming laugh. How was she going to live without him?

Trina scrubbed the tears from her eyes and gritted her teeth. She wasn't going to think about that now. For now, it was enough that she needed to kill this man for what he'd done to Henry. After he was dead, then she'd let herself fall apart, but not now.

The light switched on in her prison cell and Trina's body tensed. She tried to keep her breathing slow and even, praying he'd believe she was sleeping. He'd woken her before so she could eat. She was sure he'd reach down and shake her shoulder again.

Only this time, she'd plunge that rod into his eye.

The lock grated open, the knob turned, the door swung out, and his heavy footsteps landed on the concrete floor, getting closer.

"Time to eat," he said. "Wake up."

She stayed still and breathed. Through a tiny crack between her eyelids, she saw his shadow fall over her body.

Revulsion coursed through her that even that much of him had touched her. And yet she waited for his hand to shake her shoulder, knowing she had no choice but to let him touch her even more.

When he did, when Trina felt his beefy hand make contact, she lunged with her hidden weapon, crying out with every bit of anger and fear and grief she could find. Her aim was good, and that rod was headed right for his eye. Then a split second later, she flew across the room and slammed hard against the wall.

"Bitch!" he shouted.

Trina's head spun, and it was hard to keep her eyes open. Pain pounded against her skull, making it hard to think.

Lying on the floor at his feet, the metal rod gleamed. There was no blood. She hadn't even grazed him.

His blue eyes blazed with anger, and he reached down, grabbing her around the throat. He lifted her up the wall, choking off her air.

Trina kicked and flailed, but it did no good. He didn't let go. She tried to pry his fingers away, but he was too strong.

His blue eyes bulged with rage, and spittle leaked out

from between his clenched teeth. "I try to help you and this is what you do?" His grip tightened. "Ungrateful bitch!"

Thick gray fog closed around her vision, and she knew this was the end. He was going to kill her. Right here, right now.

Keith let Trina go and she crumpled to the floor in a sprawling heap.

Anger sliced through his veins with every heartbeat, making his body throb.

She'd tried to kill him. He'd kept her alive, cozy and warm in her very own special place, and she'd tried to kill him in return.

Ungrateful bitch, just like all the rest.

Her chest rose and fell as she breathed. He hadn't killed her in his rage, though it had been a close thing. Another few seconds and it would have been over. She would have pushed him over the edge and made him kill her too soon.

He had special plans for her. A job only she could do.

Keith picked up Trina's fragile body and laid her on the cot. She'd lost weight since she'd been here, but it was her own fault. He had to keep her quiet. Asleep.

If he hadn't been sure of that before, he was now.

Keith measured out a bigger dose of tranquilizer than he'd been giving her and shoved the needle into her arm. She wasn't going to be giving him any more trouble. Not for a long time.

Her uneaten food was strewn across the room, though she could scarcely afford to miss another meal.

Keith didn't care. He was past caring anymore. All he really wanted to do was put a gun to his head and end it now. He was tired of working so hard not to get caught and then still worrying that it wasn't enough. He knew it was selfish to want to end his nightmare without helping his brothers and sisters first, but God help him, some days, it hardly seemed worth the effort. None of the people he'd freed seemed thankful for his aid. They hadn't wanted to die, but then again, neither did Keith. He wanted to live free of his nightmares. He wanted to sleep without feeling the sickly weight of Lavine's body pressing him into a musty mattress. He wanted to remember a childhood without fear and pain. But he couldn't have any of those things, and he wasn't strong enough to continue living with the weight of so much sickness hanging around his neck.

It had to end. Soon. He wasn't going to make it much longer.

Grant held out until just after midnight before he finally gave up the fight. He needed to be with Isabelle. Needed to hold her in his arms and watch her sleep. Needed to know she was safe.

Dale had turned the music down about an hour ago, just like he did every night before he went to sleep. Out of respect for Isabelle, Grant waited until he was sure Dale wouldn't know before he crept downstairs and into her room.

The room was dark, but a soft glow from a night-light in the bathroom made it possible for him to see his way to her bed.

She slept on one side of the double bed, as if she'd gotten used to sharing it with someone. That notion grated against him, turning his stomach. He wasn't normally a possessive man, but he didn't like picturing Isabelle with another man. It made him a selfish bastard, because he should care only that she was happy, but he couldn't help it.

Her breathing was deep and even, and none of the faint noises he made opening and closing her bedroom door caused her to stir.

Slowly, he eased himself onto her bed, trying to shift her as little as possible. She let out a sleepy sigh but settled again without waking.

Grant was fully clothed and forced himself to stay on top of the covers rather than snuggling under them with her. He didn't trust himself not to take advantage, so he'd also left all the condoms in his room, ensuring he wouldn't do anything she might regret.

All he wanted to do was hold her. He didn't even know why. Normally, he extracted himself from a woman's bed as quickly and painlessly as possible. But not with Isabelle. With her it was different. Maybe it was because they were friends. He wasn't sure, but he didn't question it. For once, he just let himself enjoy the feeling of holding a woman close without the intent of seducing her.

He moved his body so he was tucked behind her, the blanket and all their clothing between them. It wasn't as nice as it would have been with both of them naked, but it was nice enough that he wasn't complaining. His hand found a comfortable resting place on the curve of her hip, and he buried his nose in her hair, breathing in the floral scent of her shampoo.

This was it, he decided. This was what both David and Caleb had found that he hadn't. There was always a slow burn of attraction when he was near Isabelle, but there was more, too. He wasn't here for the sex. In fact, he'd come here knowing that there would be no sex involved whatsoever. But still he'd come. For Isabelle.

Maybe he loved her. He couldn't be sure, because he'd never really felt it before. Sure, he'd loved his mom, and he'd lay down his life for his buddies any day of the week, but romantic love? He'd never felt it.

But he'd seen it. He'd seen it every time David looked at Noelle and every time Caleb touched Lana. What they had was real. Lasting. The kind of thing that fairy tales were built on.

And that was the real problem. He wasn't a fairy-tale kind of guy. He was broken. Warped. More than a little tarnished. His dad had fucked with his mind and crippled him for anything even resembling a normal family. He could never be what Isabelle wanted. What she deserved. So even if he did love her, he couldn't stay. In fact, if he really loved her, he'd make sure the idea of him staying never even crossed her mind.

He couldn't be her Prince Charming, so he had to be a man and step aside so she could find the man who could be.

Isabelle shifted in her sleep, and Grant realized he'd been gripping her too hard. He eased off but couldn't bring himself to move away. Not yet.

She didn't even know he was here, so it couldn't possibly hurt her if he stayed. He might pay for his weakness later, but she wouldn't, and that's what really mattered.

Grant set his internal alarm clock for two hours and

let himself drift off to sleep holding Isabelle. It was the one and only time he'd allow himself the pleasure, so he soaked it up, let it fill up the empty places inside him that had been hollow for so long.

Right before he drifted off, he realized that he'd never be full. He could hold Isabelle for a lifetime and still not get enough of her. He never should have come here and gotten a taste of what he couldn't have, but it was too late for that. He might as well enjoy it while he could.

CHAPTER TWENTY

———— ❦ ————

Amanda pulled into Vicky's neighborhood around five a.m. Her body ached with exhaustion, which had forced her to pull over at a rest stop for a few hours last night. Beside her, Rachel was sleeping.

The neighborhood was filled with homes that all looked the same in the dark. They weren't very big, but they were all new, with neat, clean lines and manicured landscaping. Even with all the leaves gone, the neighborhood looked fresh and full of hope.

Vicky was a lucky woman.

Amanda found the right house and parked on the street out front. She didn't want to ring the doorbell yet and wake Vicky up, so she'd just wait until she saw a light go on in the dark house.

Her car was almost out of gas, so she turned it off and tucked the blanket more tightly around Rachel, praying the engine would start again if they needed more heat.

She leaned her heavy head back against the seat and closed her eyes. She must have fallen asleep, because she woke up when she heard a car door slam shut nearby. One of the neighbors was getting into his truck.

The sky had started to lighten, and a quick glance at

Vicky's house, now lit up from inside, told her it was time to see if their friendship was still there, or whether she'd burned all her bridges with Vicky.

"Time to wake up and go inside, baby."

Rachel opened her eyes and nodded. Amanda bundled her up in the blanket and led her to the door.

If Vicky turned them away, she wasn't sure what she'd do next. She had nowhere else to go.

With a quick prayer for luck, Amanda rang the doorbell.

The chime seemed loud in the quiet stillness of morning. A few seconds later, the door opened and Vicky stood there in her bathrobe, her bright red hair mussed from sleep and her eyes wide with shock. "Amanda? What are you doing here?"

"I'm in trouble, Vicky. I was hoping I could come in and talk to you about it."

Vicky's hand fluttered to her throat. "Now isn't a great time."

"I know it's early, but this is important."

"You don't understand," said Vicky, shooting a quick glance at Rachel. "You really should go."

A cold, bleak despair washed over Amanda. "Please, Vicky. I know I wasn't always a good friend to you, but I really need your help."

"Princess?" came a man's deep voice from somewhere behind Vicky. "Who is it?"

Amanda knew that voice. She knew that deceptively gentle tone. *Princess.* It's what Bobby had called her, too.

He was here.

His blond head appeared over Vicky's shoulder, looking as handsome as ever. When he saw them, a cocky grin lifted one side of his mouth. "Well, looky who's here."

Rachel's small body went still and a pained, strangling noise came out of her.

Amanda didn't understand. She stood there in shock for an awkward moment before the gears in her head started to spin again.

"What is he doing here?" asked Amanda.

"I live here now," said Bobby. "Nice place, isn't it?" He looped an arm over Vicky's shoulders. "We're getting married this spring."

Married. Vicky and Bobby were getting married. Amanda knew he'd cheated on her with Vicky, not to mention all the others, but she'd never thought it was serious. Apparently, she'd been wrong.

Not that she cared who he married, other than the fact that whoever it was would suffer. No one deserved Bobby, especially not Vicky.

Rachel started to shake. "You promised," she whispered so low Amanda didn't think anyone but her could hear it.

She'd promised not to send Rachel back to her daddy, and here he was.

"This was a mistake," Amanda managed to choke out. "I'm sorry." She took Rachel's hand and pulled her back toward the car.

Before she managed to get the door unlocked and get Rachel inside, Vicky was there, her eyes pleading for forgiveness. "Don't go, Amanda. Come inside. You drove all this way for a reason—you might as well tell me what it was."

"Never mind. It was clearly a mistake."

"If I'd known you were coming, I would have met you somewhere else. Why didn't you call?"

Amanda buckled Rachel's seat belt and spared a quick glance into her daughter's face. It was pale. Her eyes were distant and haunted, and a slow, steady stream of tears slid down her smooth cheeks in silent agony.

It was happening again. Rachel was retreating in on herself, fading away.

"We need to go. It's a long drive back home." Amanda shut the car door.

Vicky grabbed hold of Amanda's arm. "Please, let me explain about Bobby."

"No need. I really don't care what he does or who he's with. I just hope you know what you're getting into."

"He's changed," said Vicky.

Amanda laughed. It was a bleak, hollow sound. "Weren't you the one who told me men never change?"

"He's different now. I swear it. You should give him a chance."

Amanda pulled her arm free and hurried around to the driver's side. "No, thank you. And for your sake, I hope you're right."

"Wait. Just stay a few minutes."

Amanda didn't answer. She was too tired to argue about this, too devastated to try. It had clearly been a mistake to come here—one she wasn't going to repeat.

She slid the key into the ignition, and thankfully, her car started on the first try.

It was the best thing that had happened to her since the night Rachel was born.

⤙❧⤚

Isabelle woke up reaching for Grant. It wasn't until the sleep had faded from her mind that she realized he wouldn't be there.

Her hand fell back to the covers, and she let out a low groan of regret. She never should have let him in her bed. In her body.

And now, not only did she have to figure out how to best take care of Everett today, she had to do it alone. If Grant came anywhere near her, she was afraid she'd be weak again and let him work his way deeper into her life—so deep she'd never find a way to get by when he left.

He was here to protect her from a killer, but she had to be the one to protect her heart from him.

The best thing to do was just get moving. Get through the pain today would bring.

She had to start planning Everett's funeral, deal with getting his body released for burial. There was no one else to do it.

She had no idea what kind of funeral he'd want. Something simple, nothing flashy, and certainly nothing expensive. He hated wasting money. Not that he needed to worry about that anymore.

The weight of her grief pressed down on her, holding her to the bed and driving the breath from her lungs.

Everett was really gone. He wasn't coming back.

Her bedroom door opened quietly, and Grant slipped in.

Isabelle wiped away the sheen of tears wetting her cheeks before he could see.

She pushed herself to a sitting position, stifling a wince when her sore muscles protested the movement. Getting tossed around in the car yesterday hadn't done her poor body much good, although she was pretty sure the soreness of the muscles along her inner thighs had a lot more to do with Grant than with her accident.

"I brought you some tea and ibuprofen. Thought you might need it this morning."

"Thanks." She took the pills and sipped her tea, keeping her head down, hoping he couldn't see that she'd been crying in the dimness of the room. Pity was the last thing she wanted from Grant.

He sat on the edge of the bed, watching her. "How are you feeling?"

"A little stiff, but I'll be fine. I should probably get moving," she said, hoping he'd leave.

"It's Saturday. You should rest and let your body recover."

"I'm just a little sore. Besides, I have to find out what to do for Everett today."

"I'll help you."

He reached for her hand, but she wrapped it around her tea before he could touch her. "No, thanks. I'd rather do it on my own."

"You don't have a car."

"I'll borrow Dale's."

"He's at his study group."

"So, I'll go when he gets back."

"You'd be safer if I went with you."

Maybe her body, but not her peace of mind. "I'll be fine."

Grant shifted his weight, leaning closer to her. Isabelle glanced up and wished she hadn't. His golden eyes glittered with frustration and his mouth was a flat, grim line. "Why are you pushing me away?"

"I'm not. I'd just rather do this alone."

He slid his thumb beneath her eye, wiping away tears from her wet lashes. "It's okay to let me see you cry. You get to cry when you lose a friend. It's in the manual."

"What manual?"

"The Top Ten Reasons Chicks Get to Cry manual."

He was trying to make her smile, which only made things worse. Every time he was sweet to her, it made it that much harder to think about him walking away.

She needed to put some distance between them. Sex had been a big mistake.

"I'm going to get a shower," she said as she tried to scoot past him.

He didn't let her go. He wrapped his long fingers around her arm and held on tight. His tone was light and flirtatious, but his eyes told her it was a lie. "Want some company?"

"No, thanks."

"Oh, come on. I know you've got to be sore. I could rub some of that soreness out of your muscles for you. All that hot water and slippery soap would feel good."

"I'm fine."

She slid her legs off the bed and tugged her arm. Grant didn't let go. He gave her a hard look. "I warned you I wouldn't let you do this."

"I'm not doing anything."

"You're pushing me away because we had sex."

"I am not," she lied.

"I won't let you do it. Our friendship is too important."

"What friendship?" she shot back, jerking her arm free of his grasp. "I sent you a birthday and Christmas card every year. So what? I sent them to everyone. That doesn't make us close."

He flinched as if she'd slapped him. His voice was a flat monotone of masked pain. "My mistake. I guess I read more into it than I should have. It won't happen again."

He turned to leave, and Isabelle could see the ache coursing through him, pain she'd caused with her careless need to protect herself.

As much as she wanted to hold her heart safe, she couldn't do it at Grant's expense. She couldn't drive him away like that.

"Grant, wait."

"I have work to do," he said. "I'll try not to get in your way."

He shut the door with a soft, final click.

Isabelle didn't know what to do, what to say. She'd never thought in a million years that she could hurt him. He seemed invincible.

But she was wrong. Inside that invincible shell somewhere lurked the angry, insecure boy he'd once been, and Isabelle had just stabbed him in the heart.

Damn it. How could she have been so careless? So selfish?

She had to fix it, or at least try.

Isabelle raced from her room to find Grant, only to see him pull out of her driveway in an angry screech of tires. She ran out the front door to stop him, but it was too late. He was already gone.

❧

It was too early for Grant to find an open bar, but it was never too early to find a willing woman. A grocery store, a library, even a gas station would work. He'd find his target, give her a smile, and in no time, he'd be fucking too hard to think about Isabelle and the fact that he'd made a complete ass of himself.

He'd read too much into her kindness over the years. They were just fucking greeting cards. Bits of paper and ink. She sent them to everyone. He wasn't special. He should have known better than to think he was.

Grant pulled in to the nearest grocery store, hurried inside because he'd forgotten his coat, and grabbed a plastic shopping basket. The place was crawling with women, though most of them had kids tagging along and rings on their fingers.

He hit the produce section and spotted his prey. She was perfect. Blond, short, and nothing at all like Isabelle.

Grant put his best panty-dropping smile on and moved in for the kill.

Keith pulled up to Wyatt's motel and parked with his trunk close to the door so no one would see him carry Trina inside.

Now that the police were involved, things were going to be a lot harder for Keith. Luckily, no one would believe Wyatt was innocent, which made him perfect to take any suspicion off of Keith.

He snapped on a pair of rubber gloves before he even got out of his car. After so much practice, being careful to leave behind nothing to link him to the deaths was now second nature to him.

He knocked on the door of the motel room Wyatt had rented. No one answered, which didn't surprise him. Who would want to hang around in a dump like this if there was anywhere else they could be? It was positively depressing with its faded paint and winter-dead, weed-riddled landscape. He had no idea how the motel stayed in business. Likely local prostitute traffic.

It was easy enough to break in with the tools Keith had acquired from one of his clients years ago. It took him only a few seconds to bypass the lock and enter the squalid room.

He carried his supplies and the duffel bag containing Trina's limp body inside. He hung the cracked "do not disturb" card on the doorknob and locked the door behind him.

The stench of mildew nearly made him gag, so he covered his mouth and breathed through his shirt. Hopefully, his work wouldn't take long.

There wasn't much sitting around, just some fast-food wrappers and a couple of empty beer cans. Wyatt had apparently already moved out, though he'd used a good chunk of his bouncer's paycheck to pay for the week. Keith had checked. He didn't want any mistakes. Isabelle was too important to him. Even if he saved no one else, he had to save her.

He loved her.

Keith shoved aside enough trash to make room for his supplies: a coffee mug, a disposable box knife, a bag of fancy tea flowers, Super Glue, some cellophane, and a pretty red ribbon—all wiped clean of fingerprints. That and a pouch of shredded jimsonweed leaves was all he would need to free Isabelle.

He doctored the tea, leaving behind no trace that the package had ever been slit open along the bottom. The Super Glue sealed the cut closed so it was barely visible—and then only if someone knew what they were looking for. Isabelle wasn't suspicious enough to look for evidence of tampering. He only hoped that the same could be said of Grant.

Keith made sure to leave enough of a mess behind to prove to the police that Wyatt had been the one who poisoned Isabelle. A couple of leaf bits on the floor. Another one that didn't quite make it down the sink. Another sliver of jimsonweed trapped inside a clear drop of glue on the table's surface.

Once Trina's body was found, this place would be crawling with cops, and they'd find everything he left behind. Wyatt would be arrested, and the rest of Keith's siblings would let their guard down.

He packaged up the World's Best Teacher coffee mug stuffed with poisoned tea in cellophane and tied it with the pretty ribbon. Monday morning he'd intercept one of Isabelle's students on her way to school and have the special delivery hand carried to Isabelle's desk.

Isabelle was little Melissa Norton's favorite teacher. Keith had heard her say so on one of the days he'd followed her and her friend home from school. The chatty girls had paid him no attention as he'd followed behind them in jogging clothes. The mini amplifier he'd carried looked like an MP3 player and had picked up their whole conversation. The things he'd heard Melissa spew told him just how gullible she was, just how easy it would be to get her to play her role in helping free her favorite teacher.

Now all he had to do was take care of Trina, and everything else would fall in line.

Keith pulled the painter's disposable coveralls on over his clothes, making sure he was covered from head to toe. Freeing Trina was going to be messy.

It was late afternoon before Isabelle heard the rumble of Grant's Mustang in the driveway again. She put down the cap she'd been crocheting in an effort to distract herself and keep her fingers from dialing his cell phone. He'd left because he wanted to be alone, or at least not with her. He'd left because she'd hurt him. She'd driven him away. The least she could do was give him some time to himself.

She opened the back door for him, relieved that he'd actually come back, that he wasn't gone for good.

His sun-streaked hair was a tousled mess, damp as if he'd just showered, and she was pretty sure the red smudge on his shirt was lipstick.

He'd been with another woman.

Jealousy and sense of betrayal filled her, and Isabelle locked her knees to keep from crumpling to the floor under the weight of it. She knew she had no claim on him, but the idea that he'd sleep with her one night and find another woman the next day was beyond painful. She wanted to crawl into herself and disappear.

When she stood frozen, blocking his path, Grant took her by the arms and moved her back. He didn't just come inside, shut the door, and stop there. He walked forward and kept walking. Isabelle backed up fast to keep him from running her over.

"What have you done to me?" he demanded. Angry desperation glittered in his eyes, making them glow in contrast to his tanned skin.

She bumped into the kitchen counter and grabbed it to steady herself. "What are you talking about?"

"It's not supposed to be like this," he snarled. "I like women. Lots and lots of women. And Susan was really nice. Pretty. Busty as hell."

Susan. Knowing her name made it real.

A little piece of Isabelle's heart shriveled as he'd confirmed her suspicions. She couldn't get enough air to speak, even if she would have had something to say.

Grant pressed his hands to the counter on either side of her body, caging her in place. "And she wanted me. What the hell have you done to me that keeps me from fucking a pretty, available woman who wants me?"

He didn't have sex with her? The tightness in her chest eased enough so she could say, "I didn't do anything."

"You sure as hell did. You pushed me away."

"So you went to find another woman?"

"Why not? You didn't want me. You made that abundantly clear. We're not even friends, right?"

"Grant, I'm sorry. I didn't mean what I said. We are friends. I care about you."

Some of the tension drawing his face tight faded away. "Then why did you turn cold like that?"

How could she explain it to him when she didn't even understand herself? "You scare me."

"I'd never hurt you."

"No, not like that. The way I feel about you scares me. The way I want you scares me."

His eyes brightened with interest. "You want me?"

"Of course I do. What sane woman wouldn't?"

"Susan wanted me, too. I couldn't keep her hands off me."

Isabelle closed her eyes, and all she could see was some busty blonde with her red, red lips on Grant. "I really don't want to hear about this."

But he kept on telling her anyway. "And the whole time, while she's kissing my neck and feeling me up, I kept thinking about you. About how she wasn't you and how it just felt . . . wrong." He leaned down until his mouth was at her temple and his breath was caressing her skin. "I kicked her out of the hotel room, and before she was even gone, I had to wash her off of me. I couldn't stand the feel of her mouth on my skin." He pulled in a shuddering breath. "What the fuck have you done to me, Isabelle? And how do I make it go away?"

Grant breathed in Isabelle's scent, letting it calm his frayed nerves. He knew she didn't have an answer to his questions. No one did. He was messed up. That was the only explanation he could find.

Or maybe it was just this place. The home of bad memories. It brought out too many emotions in him. Made him feel things he shouldn't, think of things best left in the past.

But he couldn't leave. Not with a killer still on the loose.

He'd never be able to live with himself if he left Isabelle and Dale alone to fend for themselves.

His hands slid over her back, tracing the delicate bones of her spine. He liked the way she felt against him, how she was so warm and soft. And he didn't have to break his neck bending down to kiss her, either. She was tall enough that her mouth was in easy reach, tempting him to steal another taste. He just knew that if he did, she'd soften for him and make those faint sighing noises of pleasure that drove him wild.

And just like that, he went hard, his cock swelling under his fly.

Thank God. For a while there, he'd been afraid his dick was broken, 'cause it sure as hell hadn't responded to the blonde, and that had never happened before in his life. His dick always responded. Always. Until today.

Some of his panic faded away as his body became familiar territory once again, working the way it was supposed to when he had a woman in his arms.

Isabelle sucked in a breath and her hands gripped his biceps as if to steady herself.

Oh, yeah. She'd felt his erection, too, not that he could exactly hide it when he was pressed up against her so close.

"Grant," she started in a worried tone.

"Shh. Don't worry. I'm not going to push."

Her hands slid up to his face, and she held him between her palms. Those exotic eyes flickered across his features, and Grant felt her gaze all the way to his toes.

"This is a mistake," she whispered.

"No mistakes." He wasn't going to do anything she'd regret. He was going to be good. Honorable. Then he and his grounded dick were going to go back to his room and get off so he'd have enough control left around her to keep his word.

"But it's my mistake. Dale is out with Angela for the evening, and there's no one here I can hurt. No one but myself."

Grant had no clue what she meant, but when she pulled him down and covered his mouth with her own, he no longer cared.

Her tongue played along his lips, and her silken sigh slid inside him, heating him hard and fast. Sweat broke out along his spine, and his hands clenched against her back. He locked their bodies together tight, and through the thin fabrics between them, he felt her nipples tighten against his chest.

A deep moan rumbled out of him. He needed to get her naked and feel her nipples harden against his tongue. Right. Now.

Isabelle's lips parted, and her sharp teeth nibbled at his mouth before she deepened the kiss and gave him what he wanted. The taste of her filled his senses, making his head spin. She was such a great kisser, never holding anything back. She speared her fingers through his damp hair and held on while she drank her fill.

Grant lifted her until she was straddling his hips and pulled his mouth away long enough that he could carry her back to her bed. He wasn't going to give her any time to change her mind. Not now, not when she was fire in his arms and kissing him like she was starving for him.

He kicked the bedroom door shut in case they were still occupied when Dale came back, and he set her down on the mattress.

She hadn't made her bed, which was just as well, because Grant was planning to make a mess of it, anyway. This might be the last time he ever got to enjoy naked Isabelle, and he planned on doing all those dirty things he'd spent the past few days fantasizing about. Assuming he could think clearly enough to even remember what they were.

Grant pulled his shirt over his head and tossed it aside. His boots were next, while he still had the sense left to remember how to get them off. The whole time, he watched Isabelle, searching for signs of hesitation.

She'd said something about making a mistake, and Grant sure as hell didn't want to be a part of that. He wanted to make her feel good, so good she'd let him do it again any time he wanted.

Isabelle glided off the bed and knelt in front of him in a move so graceful he couldn't believe it had really happened. She was all sinuous curves and sleek lines, moving like some kind of cat as she came to him.

She stared up at him with dark green eyes as she opened his jeans and freed his erection. Her long, slender fingers closed around him, stroking and sliding over his cock until his knees threatened to give out. And then she took him in her mouth, and Grant found the strength to stay standing. No way was he going to buckle when it might make her stop.

The heat of her mouth scalded him and sent streamers of warmth spiraling outward. He grabbed her head to help steady himself, but it did no good. His world was spinning, shrinking down to the suckling heat of her mouth and his battle to make it last longer than ten seconds.

He knew he couldn't hold out much longer, and he gave

her hair a little tug to warn her, but Isabelle let out a wicked little snarl and slid his cock deeper in her mouth.

Spots of flickering light filled his vision, and he gritted his teeth to hold out just a little longer.

He wanted to do so many things to her, and he wasn't going to have the strength left to do them if she blew the top of his head off with that sweet, hot mouth.

"Enough," he gasped and jerked out of her reach. His dick throbbed in anger, but he ignored it.

Isabelle licked her lips. "I wasn't done."

"You are now. My turn."

He saw her open her mouth to argue and knew if she said anything else, anything about wanting his cock in her mouth again, he wasn't going to survive. So before she could sway him with her shiny, hot mouth, he pounced.

Grant took her down to the mattress and pinned her with his body. He covered her mouth in a kiss meant to distract while he used every skill he'd learned over the years to rid her of her clothes as fast as he knew how. Something ripped, but he didn't give a fuck. Whatever it was, he'd get her a new one. Then he'd find a way to get her to let him rip that one off, too.

In seconds, she was staring up at him, completely naked and a little shocked. "Not fair."

He stared down at her sleek body, all bare and laid out for his enjoyment. The lights were on, and he could see every inch of smooth skin, every swath of flushed heat he'd caused.

Grant liked making her glow like that. In fact, he was wondering just how far down her body he could make her turn such a pretty, hot pink.

"I'd say it's more than fair. Or at least it will be in a minute."

Challenge blazed bright in Isabelle's eyes. "I wanted to make you come."

"And you will. Just not yet."

"Why not?"

"Ladies first."

She moved as if to slip out from under him, but Grant was faster. He pinned her, straddling her thighs as he gathered her hands and held them to his chest. His erection bobbed, thrusting out obscenely in front of him from his open jeans, but there wasn't much he could do about that right now.

"I should make you stop," she said, though the threat would have had more teeth had it not been issued on a breathless sigh.

"All it takes is one word. Two letters. Starts with N."

He held his breath, praying she wouldn't say it. Seconds ticked by, and slowly, her body relaxed.

Grant let out a breathless sigh of his own. He let go of her hands and scooted down her body, being careful not to abrade her skin on his jeans. The rasp of denim on flesh made her shiver, but not nearly as much as his tongue did as it slid over her collarbone.

He spaced kisses between licks and soft bites as he worked his way down her body. He wasn't normally the kind of guy who left a mark, but with Isabelle, he couldn't help himself. He sucked her skin against his teeth, leaving behind little love bites wherever he passed.

She took hold of his hair and guided him where she wanted him to go. A dark grin stretched his mouth as he gave in to her wishes and suckled her breasts as she demanded.

Fingernails bit into his scalp, and her whole body shuddered beneath him.

Grant lingered only long enough to sate her before he pressed her thighs wide and settled between them. The scent of her arousal filled the air and made his teeth ache with the need to taste her. He knew firsthand just how sweet she was and how her sexy whimpers made his head swell. Both of them.

She hadn't let go of his hair, but Grant didn't mind. He knew just where to go and what to do. He kissed a path to her hip, in the hollow between her hip bone and her stomach. With a light touch, he ran his tongue along the area until he found just the right spot, the one that made her twitch and gasp every time he touched it.

Isabelle hissed and her grip tightened, telling Grant he'd hit gold. He sucked her skin as he slid two fingers along her slick labia, teasing her just a moment before he eased his way right inside, nice and easy. Her muscles tightened around his fingers and he sucked harder, tightening his teeth against her skin just a bit. Just enough to let her feel it.

A rush of wetness drenched his fingers, and a long, slow cry bubbled up out of her throat. Her body contracted, then shuddered, and the grip around his fingers tightened as an orgasm shook her body.

Grant smiled in victory, but he wasn't done yet. Not even close. While the climax was still shimmering through her, he found her clit and flicked his tongue over the distended little button. His fingers filled her while his knuckles grazed against her sweet spot with every stroke.

She hadn't even caught her breath from the last orgasm before he was driving her toward the next. He'd never get enough of hearing her like this, never get enough of feeling her clench around his fingers, or his cock.

As he forced the second climax from her body, Isabelle nearly ripped Grant's hair out. She was panting and tugging hard at his hair to get him to take her.

That was more than fine with him. He found a condom in his pocket, shed his jeans, and covered himself before Isabelle came to her senses. He flipped her onto her stomach and slid into her from behind, just like he'd been aching to do since the moment he saw the idea darken her eyes with lust.

She was soft and wet from her orgasm, and he slid in so easy it was like breathing. Her body was hot against his, hot around his, and so tight it had him panting.

He buried his nose in her hair and breathed deep. She smelled so fucking good, tasted even better. He nudged her hair aside and kissed her neck as he started moving inside her. Long, slow thrusts that wouldn't irritate her sensitized tissues but would keep her nice and hot and aching for more.

Soon, Isabelle was shaking again, struggling to pull in a full breath. Grant rolled them to their sides and stroked her hip, finding that spot he knew made her crazy. His fingertip hit the place Grant had marked with his teeth, and she twitched as if he'd applied an electric current.

"Too much," she told him.

"Just go with it. I promise you'll like it." And to prove his point, he pressed his hips forward and locked hers in place so she had no choice but to accept his deep thrust.

She moaned, and her hand fisted in the sheets.

She was close, which was good, because Grant wasn't going to be able to hold out much longer and he needed to hear her come for him just one more time.

Sweat dripped down his back as he worked to bring her pleasure while staving off his own impending orgasm. That telltale shudder shook her body, and Grant knew she was close. He reached around and cupped her breast, catching her nipple between his fingers. She went tense, and her toes curled against his shins as the first wave of her climax washed over her.

The sound she let out was a clear, shimmering cry of pleasure, and it sent Grant right over the edge. Her body rippled around him, squeezing his cock so hard he lost control. He thrust into her, rolling her onto her stomach so he could ride her harder, deeper. Sizzling currents raced through his blood and sent shockwave after shockwave of release through him.

Minutes later, he regained enough sense to realize he was crushing Isabelle. He rolled off, regretting the need to leave the sweet clinging heat of her body. He wrapped the spent condom in tissue and tossed it in the trash. Even that much effort made his arms shake.

Sweat cooled on his chest and thighs as Isabelle rolled over and curled against his side.

Grant held her close and refused to let himself think about anything more than the pounding of his heart. Every time he started thinking, he got himself into trouble, and he wasn't willing to sacrifice even a second of this time with her, right here, right now.

Much later, as the sun set, Isabelle rose up over him with that wicked smile back in place.

"My turn," she told him as she moved down his body and slid her lips over his cock.

Grant didn't think he had any starch left in him, but Isabelle proved him wrong. One swipe of her tongue and he was hard again, throbbing with need and ready to let her do as she pleased.

She did, and although he wasn't sure he was going to live through it, he didn't really mind.

Trina woke up in a strange place. Her eyes were blurry and took a moment to adjust, but when they did, she saw the rundown walls of a cheap motel room. Water stains wept down one corner, and the graying edges of dated wallpaper curled up to collect dust.

She tried to lift her head to look around, but she was dizzy. Her whole body felt heavy, weak. A whimper of fear slid out of her, and a second later, the face of her husband's killer appeared.

"You're awake. That's good. I wasn't sure you'd wake up in time." He gave her a gentle smile that made his blue eyes crinkle and her skin crawl.

There was something so familiar about his eyes, but no matter how hard she tried, no matter whether or not he wore a mask, she couldn't remember who he was or why she felt she should know him.

He stroked her cheek and she felt the cling of latex gloves over her skin. "Are you comfortable?"

Comfortable? She almost laughed but stopped herself before making the mistake. Her head throbbed where she'd hit the wall. She didn't need another lesson in how the killer dealt with anger.

"What am I doing here?"

He was wearing a white suit of some kind over his clothes. "It's not your turn, but I'm changing the rules. The police know too much, so now it's your turn."

The police were looking for her? A fragile thread of hope grew inside her, driving away some of the fear she'd been living with for weeks. "My turn for what?"

"Freedom."

"You're going to let me go?" she asked, letting that thread of hope swell.

"I'm sorry I made you wait so long. I know how hard it must have been for you. At least you had the medicine to help you sleep through it."

Trina had no idea what he was talking about. Had he done something to her in her sleep? Raped her?

She didn't think so. Surely she would have felt sore if he had—there would have been some sign.

Unless he'd been gentle, like he was being now.

Her stomach heaved, and she found the strength to lean over the side of the bed before she vomited onto the floor.

The killer stroked her hair and spoke soft, comforting words. "It'll all be better soon. Just lie back down. I'm going to make it all better."

She was shaking by the time she flopped back onto the pillow. Whatever he'd injected her with was still clinging to her, sapping her strength, exhausting her. She tried to fight it, but she was already feeling the tug of sleep. Maybe he'd given her too much this time. "Please, I need help."

"I know. Just hang on. I just need one more thing before I free you."

Trina felt a sharp sting in her scalp and saw him tuck a few strands of her hair into a plastic bag. He sealed it and moved out of sight for a moment.

When he came back, he had a long knife in one gloved hand and a can of hairspray or something in the other. He smiled down at her and said, "It's time."

In that instant, Trina realized he was going to kill her. He wasn't going to let her go.

She screamed, but only a squeak came out before her mouth filled with a sharp medicinal stench. A second later, her body fell away and she couldn't drag in enough air to fill her lungs, much less scream.

"Don't be afraid," he told her. "I'll be right here with you."

Tears of panicked fear leaked from Trina's eyes as he propped her limp body against the headboard.

"It'll be faster this way."

Her mind reeled at the thought of what was going to be faster, stumbling over the terrifying possibilities.

He positioned her arms and legs to his liking, then took the knife and jammed it into her body.

Disbelief seized her mind until he lifted the bloody blade and plunged it down again. Blood sprayed across his white clothes. Her blood.

Trina tried to move but couldn't. She was frozen in place. Helpless. He was killing her, and all she could do was lie there and watch in horror as blood leaked out, soaking the cheap bedspread.

"I'm sorry it has to be this way," he explained as he plunged the knife in over and over, "but Wyatt is a cruel man. The police have to believe this is his handiwork."

Trina's body shook with each blow, but she was unable to move.

His face came into view, and it was spattered with her blood. He gave her a gentle smile. "I'm going to find an artery now so it will be over fast."

Fast. The small part of her mind that accepted her fate decided that was a good thing. She only wished she knew why he was doing this. Why had he killed her husband? Why was he killing her?

Her eyes fell shut, and she could no longer keep them open. There was an odd fluttering in her chest, and she thought it was strange to feel that when she couldn't feel anything else.

Her body shook again, and she felt the pressure of his blow deep in her gut. "No more nightmares for you, Trina. You're safe now."

Safe. Such bullshit.

"Sleep now," he whispered. She could hear his voice close to her ear but couldn't find the strength to open her eyes and look at him, much less flinch away from him. "It's safe to sleep now."

Trina didn't have a choice. She couldn't stay awake any longer.

At least she was going to see Henry again. At least her nightmare was over.

CHAPTER TWENTY-ONE

———— ❧ ————

By the time Monday morning rolled around, Isabelle regretted that she had to go back to her real life. The weekend had been a fantasyland where she, Dale, and Grant were all safe and cozy at home, enjoying each other's company.

Sunday, while she was cooking lunch, Grant and Dale finished installing the security system, and the sound of their deep voices chatting and laughing made her heart swell until she thought it would break open.

And at night, after Dale had gone to sleep, Grant came to her. He made her feel cherished and showed her things about her body she'd never known. The pleasure he wrung from her was almost too intense to be real, adding to the fantasy-like quality of those two short days.

It was easy to forget her friends had died, which only made Monday morning that much more difficult to face. She had an appointment at the funeral home today.

Thankfully, the principal had given her the day off to take care of the arrangements. All she had to do was drop off her lesson plan for the sub.

She'd just gotten dressed and walked into the kitchen when the phone rang. She answered it, and Detective

Mathews's deep voice filled the line. Without preamble, he said, "We have a suspect."

"Who?"

"We started looking into Lavine's life more deeply, looking for people who might have wanted revenge for his death. Wyatt's name was on a list of family members. He's Lavine's nephew."

Shock ripped through Isabelle, and she gripped the phone tighter. "How can that be? How could I not have known Wyatt and Lavine were related?"

"They didn't share a name. We only found out because we have access to the right databases."

Isabelle stood there, glued to the spot, shaking and unable to process the news. She didn't want Wyatt to be the killer. She didn't want Dale's father connected to this in any way, because it connected Dale, too. Thanks to Wyatt, Dale had enough of a horrible legacy to live down without adding murder into the mix. "Are you sure he's the killer?"

"Everything points to him. I had your car checked for prints as Grant suggested. Wyatt's were found all over it, especially in the areas where the car had been tampered with. And it *had* been tampered with, Isabelle. We found enough tool marks to prove that without a doubt. Between that and the family connection to Lavine, it's a pretty safe bet that Wyatt's our guy."

"He sabotaged my car? How could he have done that knowing his own son might have been in there with me?"

"We'll know more after we question him, but first, we have to find him."

"You don't know where he is?" asked Isabelle with a squeak of panic in her voice.

"I've got men watching his motel room, but he hasn't come back yet. We're working on getting a warrant to search it right now, and I've got officers out visiting the homes of friends he was known to hang out with before his arrest. I'll let you know when we find him, but in the meantime, be careful. If he's our guy, I don't want you going anywhere near him."

"I won't." Her hands were shaking as she hung up the phone.

Dale's father was a killer. She didn't know how Dale would handle that news, not after everything he'd been through.

Grant and Dale came into the kitchen, talking about breathing exercises. She had no idea what for, but it hardly mattered. When Grant saw her face, his smile fell and he crossed to her. "What's wrong?"

Dale didn't know about the murders, and she couldn't bring herself to tell him. Not yet. Not until the police were sure it was Wyatt.

Isabelle forced her expression into a neutral mask. "That was the police. Wyatt's gone missing. They said we should keep our distance if we see him."

Dale snorted in disgust. "Like we needed anyone to tell us that. No one wants to be around a jerk like him."

Grant gave her a hard stare, like he knew there was more to the story she wasn't telling him. She shook her head a tiny bit, hoping Dale didn't see the motion.

Grant did. He shed his suspicious look with ease, taking her lead. "If he shows up, what are you going to do, Dale?"

"Steer clear. Don't worry. I have nothing to say to him."

"If you get close, he might hurt you."

An angry flush rose up the back of Dale's neck as he put his jacket on. "You don't have to tell me that. I know just what he can do. I've seen it all."

But he hadn't. Isabelle wept inside for the pain she knew would come to him if Wyatt was responsible for all those murders. She prayed the police were wrong, even if it meant the killer was still out there on the loose.

She grabbed Dale's arm and made him look at her. "Promise me you'll be careful."

"I will. Things are good now. I'm not going to do anything to mess that up." He leaned down and kissed her head in a bumbling, awkward move, then rushed out the door.

She watched him through the window as he got in his car and drove away.

Grant's hands settled on her shoulders, his warm comfort sinking into her. He turned her around to face him. "Tell me the rest, what you didn't want Dale to hear."

"Wyatt is Lavine's nephew."

Grant's brows lifted in surprise. "Seriously?"

Isabelle nodded. "Detective Mathews thinks he's the killer. They're looking for him now."

"Do they have any hard evidence against him?"

"Wyatt's fingerprints were on the underside of my car."

His eyes narrowed to menacing slits. "I should have kept Wyatt from running the night Dale climbed out his window. You never would have been in that accident, and Everett would still be alive."

"You can't blame yourself. It's not like any of us knew what he was going to do."

"Why didn't you tell Dale?" asked Grant.

"Because I'm hoping the police are wrong."

"Wrong? Wyatt is the nephew of the only man who connects all the people that have been murdered. He sabotaged your car, which could have easily killed you. He probably sent those thugs after us outside the restaurant, too. How much more evidence do you need that he's the killer?"

"You're right." She let out a heartsick sigh of regret. "I'm denying the truth, wishing Dale didn't have to be touched by this sickness. He's already been through so much. I just want to protect him."

"You should tell him. He's stronger than you think."

Grant had been right about Dale before. He was probably right now, too. "I will. After school, I'll tell him everything. For now, he knows to stay away from Wyatt, which will keep him safe enough to live one more relatively normal day."

One more day to be a kid before she shattered his world and told him his father was a killer. He was the son of a murderer, the great-nephew of a child molester and rapist.

Isabelle laid her head on Grant's chest and breathed in his clean scent to help calm her worry. He was so strong and solid, so comforting in the face of all this ugliness. She was going to miss having him here, feeling his touch bring her to life.

If Wyatt was found today, Grant would likely leave tomorrow.

Her fingers curled against his back, gripping him tight. She wanted to hold on to him. Keep him forever. Instead, she pulled away and drew a deep breath into her lungs.

"We should go. I want to make sure the sub has time to look this lesson plan over before class starts."

❧

Grant dropped Isabelle off at the front doors of her school so she wouldn't have to walk in the cold. He had just pulled into one of the visitor slots when his cell phone rang. It was David's number on the caller ID, and Grant wished he was more of a coward so he wouldn't have to deal with this call.

He was already cringing when he answered the phone. "Hello."

"Where the hell are you?" asked David.

"Springfield."

"Still? Please tell me you're on your way out of town right now."

"Sorry, man. I really am, but I can't leave yet."

A grinding sound that could only mean expensive dentist bills filled the line. "I need you. Now. As in yesterday. If I lose this contract, I won't be able to employ you. Not to mention I won't be able to pay Caleb, either."

Well, shit. Grant had been aware there was a big contract David was working on, but he hadn't realized just how pivotal it was to his business. Maybe he should have asked better questions. Not that anything would have changed his mind about staying to help Isabelle. "I don't want to lose my job, and I sure as hell don't want Caleb to lose his, but I can't leave Isabelle until this mess is sorted out. It's too risky."

"Then bring her with you. Do whatever it takes, but get your ass to Denver."

"I'll try. I swear I will, but in the meantime, can't Caleb step in?"

David's long pause was not a good sign. "You don't know?"

"Know what?" asked Grant, already dreading the answer.

"Lana was admitted into the hospital last night."

A sick sense of dread squeezed Grant. "Hospital? I thought she had the flu."

"She does, but apparently, it got bad enough that she couldn't quit puking. They admitted her for dehydration, but there's no way Caleb will leave her, and I'd never ask."

Poor, sweet Lana. She'd been through so much it hardly seemed fair she'd have to deal with this, too. "Oh, man. I didn't know. Caleb's got to be a wreck."

"That doesn't even come close to describing him. Don't try to call. He nearly reached through the line and strangled me for waking her up this morning with my call. I'm sure he's turned his phone off by now."

"He's only three or four hours away. I wish I could go sit with him. Keep him company," said Grant.

"If you have time for that, you sure as hell had better make time to get your ass out here."

"It's not an issue of time. I can't leave. There are people in danger here."

David let out a long sigh of regret. "I really hate to say this, but if you can't come today, I'm going to have to find someone who can. This contract is too important to screw up."

Grant felt his future plans slipping away and his chance for something resembling a normal life along with them. Finding another job as good as the one David offered him just wasn't going to happen. There were things he could do—plenty of ways to make money—but none of them would be the same as working with his old buddies. They were the closest thing to family he had, and the idea of letting go of that made him sick.

Still, David had a company to build, and Grant couldn't be there to help make it happen. Not when Dale's and Isabelle's safety was at stake. There was no choice. So what if his plans didn't pan out like he wanted? He was tough. He'd suck it up and move on. Some people were never meant to be part of a family, anyway. He was probably one of them.

Grant forced his voice to come out steady and even, showing no signs that his world and all his bright, shining plans for his future were falling apart. "I understand. I'll call Mad for you. He left the service two days before me. He's probably done getting drunk and laid by now. Maybe he's bored and ready to work again."

"Madison Parker?" asked David.

"You remember him?"

"I worked with him once. Quiet guy, but he got the job done, right?"

"Every single time." In fact, he was probably a better man for the job, anyway. Mad was a freaking machine. He would have found a way to keep everyone here safe and still make it to Denver by sunset.

"Can I trust him?" asked David.

"With Noelle's and your son's life."

"Okay. Call him. I'm desperate enough to give him a shot."

He ended the call and tried not to pay attention to the searing pain of loss ripping him apart. His dream of days spent working side by side with David and Caleb, and his evenings hanging out with his almost-nephew, crumbled.

The bitter taste of loss coated his mouth until he thought he might throw up.

It had been so long since he'd dared to dream about anything more than his next conquest in bed. Pursuing this dream had demanded more courage than any mission he'd ever undertaken. And where did it get him? Right back where he'd started, with nothing in his future but the bleak knowledge that no matter how hard he tried, how long he worked, he would never truly belong.

He'd always be the one on the outside looking in, wishing for something others took for granted—something he could never have.

The hot tear hitting the back of his hand surprised him. He hadn't cried in years, and he sure as hell wasn't going to start now.

Grant shoved away his regret at losing his job. No sense in throwing a fit over something that was already a done deal. David had a family to think about, and Grant wasn't going to get in the way of something like that, no matter what it cost him. His happiness was expendable.

He scrolled through his contacts until he found Mad's number. Before Grant had even hung up the phone, Mad had agreed to help and was out of his hotel room and heading for the highway. With luck, he'd hit Denver by sundown. Knowing Mad, he'd work though the night and keep working for the next ten days straight if that's what it took to help David.

So much for Grant's dream of being a part of David's business—part of his family. He'd have to find his future elsewhere, which was one bleak fucking prospect.

It made him wish more than ever that he could be the

kind of man who could find it with Isabelle. Too bad he cared about her too much to risk trying.

Wyatt was pissed. Isabelle walked into her school like nothing had happened. He'd seen the wreck on the news. He'd seen her car. How the hell had she walked away from something like that?

Fucking airbags.

Wyatt's time was running out. He'd ditched his motel room and was sleeping on an old girlfriend's couch, but sooner or later, the cops would track him down if he stayed in town. He needed to get out, but not without his son.

Maybe the plan to get Isabelle out of the picture was flawed, anyway. Who knew what those nosy social service fucks would do even if she was gone? Chances were they might find another Isabelle to put Dale with and he'd be stuck finding him all over again.

What Wyatt needed to do was convince Dale to leave with him. Make it look like he ran away. But how was he going to do that? Dale had been brainwashed and wasn't likely to trust him. What he needed was leverage—a way of convincing Dale to come peacefully.

Isabelle was an obvious choice, but she had that goon living with her now. No way was Wyatt going to mess with that guy. He wasn't made of hulking muscle, but there was something about the way he moved, some kind of confidence that told Wyatt he was dangerous. He'd learned to spot men like that in prison and keep his distance. He wasn't about to fuck things up by getting stupid now.

So if he couldn't use Isabelle, who could he use? That

blond piece of fluff Dale drove to school this morning? It wasn't the first time he'd seen them together. Maybe there was something going on between them.

Hell, maybe Wyatt would bring her along with them. He hadn't had a piece of ass that fine in years. He was due.

A plan started forming in Wyatt's head, and he laughed at how simple it was. All he really had to do was grab the girl. If Dale cared about her, he'd come along without a fuss. If not, then Wyatt still had himself a sweet little thing to fuck. It was a win–win situation, just the kind he liked.

CHAPTER TWENTY-TWO

———— ❧ ————

The visit to the funeral home to plan Everett's service was harder than Isabelle had expected. Thank God Grant was there to hold her hand and help her get through it.

The coroner still hadn't released his body yet, and they had no way of knowing how long it might be until they did. Hopefully not too long. She needed this to be over—to know Everett was resting in peace and that she'd done everything she could to give him the kind of respect and love a real family would have.

Grant hit the drive-thru at a burger joint, but Isabelle wasn't sure she could eat right now. She was too upset. Too heartsick over realizing that she'd really never see Everett again—never see him blush because she caught him looking at her, never hear him lecture her about putting more money into her retirement account.

"We'll get you through this," said Grant in a steady, confident voice.

Isabelle wondered if he'd ever been unsure of anything in his life. If so, she'd never seen it. He was rock solid, and she couldn't imagine having to deal with all of this without him.

When he left, she would probably grieve for him

as much as she was for Everett. What a lovely thought that was.

"I'm going to be fine," she assured him. "It's just hard right now, you know?"

Grant nodded, sparing her a quick glance away from the road. "The funeral will be tough, but so are you. And I'll be there by your side."

"Don't say that, Grant. We don't know how long it will be until they release the body, and if the police find Wyatt and prove he's the killer before then, you'll already be gone. I don't want you making promises just because I'm upset."

"I'm going to be here for Everett's funeral," he stated in a hard tone.

"You have your job to think about. I doubt your boss is going to appreciate you taking time off so soon after starting."

His hands tightened on the wheel, and his voice took on an unnaturally neutral cadence. "Don't worry about my job. I've got it covered."

Isabelle let it drop. He was a grown man and could make up his own mind. Besides, she really wanted him by her side when they stood at Everett's grave. She didn't want to face that alone.

Grant pulled into her driveway and killed the engine. Before she could open her door, he turned in his seat and took her hand in his. Bright shards of clear amber shone in his eyes, and he had a fiercely determined set to his hard jaw. "We're going to get through this. The police will find Wyatt, Amanda, and Keith will be safe, and you won't have to worry about any of us anymore. All you'll have to worry about is figuring out how you're going to keep up with all those kids you're going to bring into your home."

That was a happy thought, and she so desperately needed one of those right now. "How do you know? How do you know that's the way it will end?"

"Because you didn't stop fighting when the police didn't believe the suicides were murders. You didn't give up. We have the police on our side now, working on the case, and as much as I think that Detective Mathews is a dickhead for thinking I could kill those people, he's smart and determined. He's not going to let us down."

Isabelle clung to that notion and let it make her feel better. She still wasn't as confident as Grant was, but she'd never met anyone who was.

"Will you do something for me?" she asked.

"Anything in my power, honey."

"If something happens to me—"

"It won't."

She covered his mouth so she could finish. "If something happens to me, will you take care of Dale until he graduates?"

Under her hand, Grant's face went white. His pupils contracted down to tiny black points, and a fine sweat broke out along his forehead. "I can't, Isabelle. I'm sorry."

"But he doesn't have anyone else. His dad will try to get him back, and I know you'd be able to keep him safe. He's almost done with school, and he's no trouble at all."

"It's not that. Dale's a great kid. But I can't be his dad."

"Why? You're great with him. He listens to you. Looks up to you."

"Only because he sees me as some random guy who

will be gone in a few days. If he actually *had* to listen to me, it would be different."

"Why?"

Grant got out of the car, slamming the door hard. His sack of fast food was still sitting between the seats. Isabelle grabbed it, along with the coffee mug full of fancy tea one of her students had given her, and followed him inside.

He'd made quick work of unlocking the door and was no longer in the kitchen by the time Isabelle walked in. She threw the bag of food and tea on the counter, along with her purse and jacket, and went to find him. She was not going to let him leave her hanging like this, not for something this important to her, and not when he was obviously in pain.

He was already up the stairs when she caught up with him. She followed him into his room without asking permission. She didn't even care she was invading his private space.

He kept his back to her, and she could see tension vibrating his frame. "I don't really want company right now."

"Fine, then answer my question and I'll get out of your hair. Why can't you be Dale's father? Is it something he did?"

He turned around and looked at her like she was insane. "God, no. He hasn't done anything wrong."

"Then what is it? You're a good man. You like him. I trust you. Why won't you take care of him for a few months? Is it your job?"

"I don't have—" He ran his hands through his hair, making a mess of it. "It has nothing to do with the job."

"Then what, Grant?"

"I just can't be anyone's dad. At least not yet."

Isabelle had no idea what he meant by that. "Why not yet? Is something happening I don't know about? Are you going back into the military again?" The thought that she'd have to worry about him day after day and go for months without hearing from him scared her silly. She wasn't sure how she'd deal with it if he said he was going back to that life again.

Not that she had any say in the matter.

"There's nothing you need to know," he said.

It was an evasive answer, but she let it go in favor of pursuing what she really wanted to know. "Then what's going on? If you're not ready to be a dad now, when will you?"

He whirled around. His face was angry red, and his lips were pressed together so hard they were a bloodless white. Pain glowed in his eyes—a kind of pain she hadn't seen since the day he'd been arrested for killing Lavine and hauled off to jail in handcuffs. "Never, okay! I'm never going to be worthy of that kind of responsibility. I'm great at keeping people alive. You want me to kill someone? I can take them out from so far away they'll never hear the sound of the bullet that ripped their brains out. But I can't be responsible for raising anything resembling a normal adult." His voice grew softer, regretful. "It's just not in me, no matter how much I wish it was. I know that now."

Isabelle was stunned silent. She'd had no idea he felt that way. How could one man be so wrong about himself? She had to make him see reason—see the truth. "I've never known a man who will make a better father than you."

"Bullshit," he snapped.

"Hardly. Do you really think I'd put Dale with someone I thought would be bad for him?"

"You're desperate," he said as if that explained everything.

"Asking you was not an act of desperation. Who better to raise Dale than someone who knows where he's been? What he's going through?"

"The blind leading the blind?" scoffed Grant. "Is that your idea of good parenting?"

"You're not blind. You're experienced. You know the price a child pays when his parents don't care. You've lived it."

His gaze went to the carpet, and his shoulders hunched in shame. "Which means I'll make the same mistakes."

"No. It means you'll know better than to make them."

Grant shook his head. "I can't talk about this anymore. Just let it go, Isabelle. Find someone else."

He was hurting, and she was causing it. She had to stop pushing, at least for now. She'd give him time to think about what she'd said, but there was one more thing he needed to know. "Taking care of Dale is not something I would ever coerce you into doing, but whoever I'd find to care for him will be my second choice."

Grant let out a heavy sigh of regret. "I can't be the man you want."

"You already are."

"I don't mean sex."

"Neither do I."

She couldn't stand seeing him hurt any longer without trying to comfort him. She had to touch him, had to try to ease him. She didn't want him to feel like he was alone. He'd been alone for too long.

Isabelle went to him and ran her fingers through his hair to straighten it. The smooth strands slid between her fingers, and Grant stood statue still, letting her fuss over him.

"Maybe you were only a good time in bed to a lot of the other women you've encountered, but you're a lot more than that to me. You always will be," she told him. "You know that, right? You know what a great man you are, don't you?"

The tightness around his mouth softened. If she hadn't known better, she would have thought she saw the hint of tears welling in his eyes. Sometimes it was easy to forget Grant was human like the rest of the world. He was so capable and confident, like he could carry the weight of the world on his shoulders and still have room for more.

He closed his eyes and swallowed hard. "You shouldn't have so much faith. People will just let you down."

"Not you," she assured him. "You've never once let me down."

"If you hang out with me long enough, I will."

"Is that an invitation?"

His jaw tensed, though she couldn't tell if it was anger or frustration that caused it. "Isabelle, I can't—"

She covered his mouth with her fingers. The smooth warmth of his lips made her shiver. "I know. I shouldn't have said that. I understand the rules between us."

He pulled her hand away. "Damn it. There aren't any rules."

"Yes, there are. For both of us." She couldn't give up her dreams, not even for Grant. She'd learned the hard way that a man who didn't want what she wanted out of life would never make her happy. Nor would she make him happy. And she wanted Grant to be happy, even if it was with someone else.

She'd be smart if she just learned to enjoy him now, get over her feelings for him, and move on with her life. Let him do the same. It wasn't fair of her to try to make him something he didn't want to be, no matter how good at it she thought he'd be.

She'd stop pushing so she didn't mess up what little time they had left. She had now, and for now, she was the luckiest woman alive, and would be until the day he left.

Maybe today if the police found Wyatt.

She wouldn't think about that now. She couldn't. Letting him go was going to rip her apart. She loved him. She couldn't pretend it was something else any longer. Her childhood hero worship had turned into something deeper, something more permanent.

Something she was going to have to learn to live with when he was gone.

Isabelle stepped back, separating herself from him even though it was the last thing she wanted to do. "I'll leave you alone."

He grabbed her hand before she moved out of reach. "No. Don't leave."

She turned toward him again and saw something in his face she'd never seen before. Uncertainty. He was frowning, and his eyes were darting around the room.

"Grant? Are you okay?"

"No. I just . . . don't leave me." The words came out strangled, like he couldn't get enough air.

"Okay. I'll stay."

He didn't act like he heard her, he just kept talking. He

pulled her against his body and caged her with his arms. "I'll make you feel good if you stay, Isabelle. I swear it."

Instantly, her body responded to his offer and his nearness. Her skin grew warm and her stomach tightened. She couldn't seem to look away from his mouth. She wanted to kiss him, but not because he was worried she'd leave him. She had to convince him that she'd stay with him even if he didn't make promises that heated her blood.

"You don't have to do that to make me stay," she told him.

He tightened his grip as if he thought she might be jerked away from him if he didn't hold on tight enough. She'd never heard Grant beg, but he was getting frighteningly close. "I need you. Please."

She opened her mouth to reassure him she wouldn't go anywhere, but before she could speak, he kissed her. It was a hot, desperate kiss that made her toes curl inside her shoes and her lungs work overtime. His tongue slid inside her mouth to find hers, and all her thoughts scattered. All she knew was that the man she loved was kissing her—needing her—and she couldn't bring herself to push aside something she wanted so much.

Her body relaxed against his, melting into his tight embrace. She didn't even have to worry about standing up under her own power. Grant would keep her steady.

His kisses moved over her chin and down her throat, nipping and licking as he went. "That's right, honey. Just let me make you feel good."

And he was. Already her body was humming along, eager for whatever he did. Her fingers dug into his back, and she loved the feel of his hard, powerful muscles bunching whenever he moved. He was so strong, but it didn't make her feel weak by comparison. Instead it made her feel safe, protected.

His quick, elegant fingers unhooked her bra and slid around front to tease her breasts. Without touching her nipples, where she wanted him most, he traced a spiral path over her skin, making her arch her back.

"I want to see you," he told her as he tugged her shirt and bra off over her head. She was sure her flyaway hair was a static-y mess, but she couldn't bring herself to care.

The room was bright, with sunlight streaming in through the window, but she didn't care about that, either. She wanted him to look at her if that excited him, and it had last night. She'd never forget the way his eyes darkened to bronze when he looked at her naked body. Just like they were right now as he stared at her naked breasts.

His half-lidded eyes, heavy with arousal, fixed on her chest. He drew one long finger over the swell of her breasts in a touch so light she wanted to scream for more. "I love how you blush here for me. Such a turn-on to know you can't hide how much you want me."

Isabelle hadn't realized her flushed chest turned him on, but she was glad it did, because there was nothing she could have done to stop it. "It's only fair," she told him as she pressed her palm against his erection. "You'd never be able to hide this, either."

Grant groaned, and his head fell back. Isabelle was filled with a rush of womanly power knowing she'd done that to him with just a touch. It made her feel bold and more than a little aggressive to wield such power over a man as strong as Grant.

She wanted him naked so she could feel his erection filling her hands as she stroked him. She wanted to hear the sounds he made when she touched him just right and see the way his body tensed as he held back from the brink of orgasm.

Isabelle managed to get his fly open, but his jeans were too tight for her to push them down. Grant obliged her by stripping, flinging his clothes to the floor.

She watched, fascinated by the way he moved. Sleek, powerful muscles shifted under his skin, making her mouth water. He didn't try to hide from her but stood there and let her look her fill.

He was blindingly beautiful in the bright light of day. His skin was smooth and tan, though there were a few pale scars here and there that marked the risks he'd taken and sacrifices he'd made in the line of duty.

She found one near his left shoulder and pressed an open-mouthed kiss to the mark.

Grant shivered. "Take off your pants, Isabelle."

She ignored his order and found another small scar on his ribs. She kissed it, as well, and watched in awe as the muscles in his stomach rippled.

She spied another scar on his right hip and knelt so she could reach it, too. She lingered over the kiss, swirling her tongue over the mark, making him shiver.

His erection bobbed in front of her, impossible to miss. She gave him a wicked smile, then ran the tip of her tongue up the length.

Grant hissed out a vivid curse and fisted his hands in her hair. Since he'd come into her life, she finally understood all those women who enjoyed performing oral sex on men. It was a thrill to see his reaction, to wield the tremendous power to make him feel so good he shook with the force of it.

She took him into her mouth, and she could feel his body quiver with barely controlled passion. Oh, yeah. She could get used to this.

He didn't give her much time to enjoy herself before he pulled away and lifted her to the bed. "Pants. Off," he said in words so thick with need they were nearly unintelligible.

Isabelle grinned and obliged him by stripping out of her slacks. She lay back on the wide bottom bunk bed, wearing only a pair of green satin panties.

Grant's eyes zeroed in on those panties and his cheeks darkened. "Tease," he accused.

"They match my eyes."

This time, it was his turn to smile, though his was so dark and knowing she was almost afraid of what he was thinking. "Yes. They do."

He covered her body with his and took her mouth in a deep kiss. Isabelle groaned as goose bumps rose up along her limbs. The man knew how to kiss, and she was pretty sure that every time he did that swirling thing with his tongue, she lost another pile of brain cells to overheating.

His big hand cupped her breast. Her nipple hardened against his palm. She felt him smile against her mouth in response.

Grant shoved a hard thigh between her legs, pressing it against her mound. Shocks of sensation rioted through her belly. She made a desperate noise and dug her fingernails into his back.

"Like that?" he asked her.

Speech was impossible, so she didn't try. Instead, she moved her hips, grinding herself against him because it felt too good not to.

He toyed with one nipple while moving down to take the other into his mouth. Heat and sensation jolted through her, meeting up with all of the hot pleasure pulsing low in her abdomen.

Her panties were slick and wet as she rubbed up against Grant's thigh, but it wasn't enough. She wanted to feel him inside her, filling her up.

With clumsy hands, Isabelle pushed him away enough that she could grasp his erection. As hot as she was, his skin was even hotter, smooth and slick from her mouth and his own excitement. She spread her legs wide and pulled the gusset of her panties aside while using her other hand to guide his penis where she needed it.

The tip of him slid along her slick folds, and she pressed her hips forward to join them together.

"This feels too good. So hot." Grant went still, then pulled away from her, out of reach. He was panting, staring down at her exposed flesh while he licked his lips. "Need a rubber."

Right. She'd forgotten in the midst of the haze of pleasure engulfing her, but thankfully, Grant had more sense.

He took care of the problem while Isabelle shed her panties. When he came back to the bed, she expected him to take up where they left off, but instead, he gave her a dark, hungry look and knelt between her knees. He spread her thighs wide and lowered his head between them. His tongue grazed over her in a hot, wet caress.

Her whole body tightened with something too intense to be called pleasure, and her hips rose up off the bed toward his mouth. Grant pushed her back to the bed and held her hips in place while he licked and kissed her as he pleased. His tongue did that exquisite swirling thing and she was lost. The world spun away, and her body exploded in the most awesome, devastating climax she'd ever had.

Grant was with her the whole way, using his tongue to keep her spiraling out of control.

She hadn't even regained the ability to see when she felt the weight of his body settle over her and his erection slide inside her slick body. His movements were gentle, but she could sense his desperation in the way his body shook with tension.

He plucked at her nipple, which sent shockwaves of sensation to her womb and made her abdomen tighten. He must have felt it, too, because he sucked in a breath and his hips bucked forward as if he couldn't control them. His movement hit a sweet spot inside her, and all of the relief her climax had given her was swept away. That achy need was back, gnawing at her insides for relief, and Grant was being too gentle. Too careful with her.

"Roll over," she ordered him in a near snarl. She'd never sounded so forceful during sex before, but Grant didn't seem to mind.

He easily shifted them, rolling her body along with his until she was on top. The movement pressed him deeper and made Isabelle gasp. No way was she going to last long like this. She felt so full she could barely breathe.

Isabelle pressed her hands to his chest for leverage and lifted her body off of his. The ride back down was long and slow and had Grant gripping her thighs hard enough to leave white marks around his fingers. He made a sharp, guttural sound of pleasure that thrilled her down to her toes. She wanted to make him feel good, and now she knew just how to do it.

She set a teasingly slow pace that pressed him as deep

inside her as she could stand on every stroke. His body had been made just to fit hers, hitting the right spots without her even having to try.

It didn't take long for Isabelle to be hovering at the edge of orgasm again, but she didn't want to go alone this time. She wanted to feel Grant coming inside her when she let go—to know she was giving him as much pleasure as he was giving her.

His hands moved to her waist, making her speed up the pace. Beneath her, his body was coiled tight. She leaned down so she could kiss this neck, and the movement ground her clitoris against him. An electric current streaked through her core, and she couldn't hold back any longer. Her climax crashed over her, making her gasp and tighten around Grant's erection.

A hoarse cry rippled out of her as her body flew apart.

Grant's hands clenched on her waist, and his hips lifted up off the bed, shoving hard inside Isabelle. From the depths of her own release, she heard him let out a rough roar. Then she felt him throb inside her as he came in time with the dwindling pulses of her own orgasm.

Isabelle collapsed on top of him, breathing hard. Her body felt heavy and boneless, and a faint buzzing sensation made her skin tingle.

"You okay?" asked Grant in a rough, sexy voice.

"I thought you were an expert on women."

"You're not just any woman."

And if that wasn't the perfect thing to say, she didn't know what was. She turned her head enough to kiss his jaw.

Grant gave her a tight hug, then shifted her body so they

were no longer joined. "After that, I bet you're hungry," he said.

"I probably will be in a minute. Right now I'm just thirsty. All that hard breathing made my throat dry."

He rolled her over so she was on the bed and kissed her nose. "Stay right here and I'll make you some tea."

"You need to eat your food, assuming it's still edible. I can make my own tea."

Grant shook his head and gave her a sultry smile that melted her will into a puddle. "I want you to stay right here. Completely naked. I'm nowhere near done with you."

Chapter Twenty-three

———— ❖ ————

Grant had done a lot of things for a lot of women over the years, but he couldn't remember ever making tea for one of them while wearing nothing but his underwear. Maybe that was because he never stuck around afterward long enough for it to be an issue. Or maybe it was because he'd never cared about any of the women he'd slept with as much as he cared for Isabelle. The thought of leaving her to fend for herself, even for something as simple as a drink, bothered him.

He was so fucked. He'd really dug himself a hole this time, getting involved with her like this. She wasn't just some woman that he could smile at and wave good-bye to when it was all said and done. She was part of his life, and no matter how complicated things got, he wasn't giving her up.

At least he'd gotten out of enough situations that appeared to be hopeless to give him faith that he might also find a way out of this one. He wasn't sure how, but he'd find a way. Isabelle was too important to him not to find one.

Grant opened the bag of fast food and eyed the contents. The hamburgers might be salvageable, but no way was he eating those cold, greasy fries.

Isabelle's refrigerator was nearly bare, thanks to Dale's bottomless stomach, but there were still a few oranges and some celery sticks. Between that and the bag of chips he'd spied in the cabinet, there'd be plenty for a light lunch for both of them.

The microwave beeped and Grant pulled Isabelle's tea out. A pretty flower of tea leaves with a pink center floated in the top of the cup. He'd never seen anything like it before, but knowing Isabelle, she'd get a kick out of it. Even if one of her students hadn't been thoughtful enough to give her the gift, she probably would have enjoyed the frivolous bit of fluff.

Maybe he'd get her some more of the tea flower things when these were gone, just to see her smile.

Then again, maybe he'd be gone before they were.

What a fucking bleak thought that was.

Dale felt Angela's fingers slip between his as they walked out to his car after school. She didn't need a ride. She had her own car. But he'd been a dork and asked her if she wanted a ride anyway, just because he wanted to be with her every moment he could. The fact that she'd said yes still made him grin like an idiot.

Holding her hand made him grin even wider.

She was so pretty today with her blond hair pulled up in a loose ponytail. On other girls, it would have looked sloppy, but on Angela, it was just messy enough to be sexy. It looked like she'd been messed up a little by rolling around in his bed.

And it was *his* bed. No way was Dale going to ruin his fantasies by having it be some other guy who'd made her hair look like that.

She leaned close to him as they walked, and he was sure he could feel the soft curve of her breast against his arm.

Instant boner.

Dale shifted his books to hide it and slowed their pace so he didn't pinch himself. She looked up at him with those pale blue eyes, and he knew that no matter how much he wanted to do her, he'd hold back and be cool. He wouldn't so much as try to feel her up, because he didn't think he could stand it if she dumped him.

Not that they were really dating. Neither one of them had said anything like that. But she had kissed him. Saturday night when he dropped her off at her doorstep. She'd gone up on her tiptoes and kissed his cheek. He'd been so thrilled he hadn't even cared she'd left a shiny patch of lip gloss on him. Hell, he hadn't even cared if he ever breathed again.

Thankfully, she'd slipped inside her house before he could screw things up with her. He'd had a full day to think about how to hold on to Angela, and he'd decided to let her take the lead. He wouldn't push her to do anything, no matter how hard it got.

And it was pretty freaking hard right now.

"Do you want to go back to my house for a little while?" she asked him.

His mind filled with all the things he could do to her there, and blood loss to the brain struck him speechless for a moment. "Um."

"I mean, my mom will be there, but she won't mind if we watch TV or something."

A chaperone was a good thing. He kept telling himself that over and over in the hopes he'd believe it. "Yeah, sure. That sounds good."

Angela smiled and leaned her head on his shoulder.

Dale felt like a raging stud. He had the prettiest girl in town on his arm, asking him to her house. No guy had ever been luckier.

He was so wrapped up in the feel of her against his arm that he didn't notice his dad parked next to his car until it was too late. Wyatt got out of his car and stepped in their path.

"Introduce me to your girlfriend, son," said Wyatt.

"Is this your dad?" asked Angela, smiling.

She held out her hand for him to shake, but Dale shifted his body, pushing her behind him.

Angela gasped in shock or pain. Dale couldn't be sure, but either way, it made him feel like garbage to know it was his fault.

"Don't touch her," groaned Dale.

"Just trying to make nice, son."

"Stop calling me that."

"Like hell I will. You're my goddamn son, and you'll show me respect."

Dale felt shame and anger bubble up inside him. This was the ugly side of his life he never wanted Angela to see. When he was with Isabelle, he could pretend that he was a normal kid with a decent family, but now she'd know better. She'd never want him around again. The best thing he could do was get her out of harm's way.

"Go inside, Angela."

"I'm not going to leave you," she said.

Wyatt leered at her. "Don't send the pretty little thing away. I want to get to know her."

Dale saw the lust in his dad's eyes, and it made him sick. He tried to shield her more with his body and said, "Please, Angela. Just go. I'll be fine. You won't."

He heard Angela's feet pounding on the pavement across the emptying parking lot. He didn't stop to see if she'd drawn attention by running. He didn't want to take his eyes off of Wyatt.

"She's a fine piece of ass, son."

Dale's fists bunched, and he longed to slam one into his dad's face—a face that looked so much like his own he hated looking in the mirror.

"What do you want?" Dale demanded.

"You and I are going to take a little trip."

"Like hell we are."

Wyatt rolled his shoulders like he used to do before beating Mom, so he wouldn't pull a muscle. "You've gotten uppity, son. We're going to have to fix that, you and I."

"The courts are never going to give me back to you. Why don't you just give up and go fuck yourself?"

"Don't push me, boy."

"Why not? What are you going to do? Beat me up on school grounds like some kind of bully? There are cameras all over this parking lot."

Wyatt's eyes widened and he scanned the rooftop. "Get in the car, boy."

"Fuck you."

"Get in the car, or I'll make a late-night visit to your

pretty little friend. I ain't making this trip alone. Would you rather she came with me?"

He'd do it, too. Dale was sure of it. That predatory light in Wyatt's eyes when he looked at Angela was proof enough for him. He knew exactly what his father was capable of.

Dale swallowed hard. All he had to do was get back into the school and call the police.

He took a small step back so he could turn and run, but Wyatt was fast and grabbed the back of his jacket. Dale jerked to a halt. He flung the stack of books he carried at Wyatt's head. One of them hit the mark.

Wyatt reeled back but hadn't let go of Dale's jacket, so he went right with him. Dale landed on top and tried to scramble away.

By now, kids all around them were staring, but none of them moved to help.

Dale had just made it to his feet when something hard slammed into the side of his head. Bright lights flashed in Dale's eyes, and a consuming dizziness swept over him.

A second later, he was shoved headfirst into his dad's car. Wyatt climbed in after him, pushing him hard into the passenger's seat.

Instincts took over, and Dale scurried away from his dad, curling into as small a space as possible, protecting his head.

The car pulled out, jolting over the speed bumps as Wyatt raced from the lot.

❧

Isabelle let the answering machine pick up the call that threatened to interrupt her bliss. She was too busy enjoying the feel of Grant's mouth feathering light kisses over her stomach.

She felt like she was floating just above the bed, drowsy and content from the slow, lazy loving he'd given her after they finished their lunch.

He'd fed her slices of orange, and she'd licked the juice from his fingertips. That's all it had taken to put that hungry look back on his face, a look that made her feel like the sexiest woman alive.

Sweat cooled on her body as Grant kissed his way up to her neck. She tried to stay awake and enjoy him enjoying her, but her eyes kept drifting closed.

"I think you nearly killed me," she told him.

"Only nearly? Guess you've still got some life left in you, then." His hand smoothed over her hip and up to cup her breast.

Isabelle gave him a weak smile. The man had loved her so good it made her head spin. "Too tired."

"Later, then." He kissed her mouth briefly and pulled the blankets up over her body. "You get some sleep. You're going to need your rest for later tonight after Dale goes to bed."

Oh, baby, that sounded good. Even as tired as she was, she couldn't stop the little spike of longing that slid through. Just thinking about having him again made her body quiver.

"Can I have a drink before you go?"

"Sure, honey. Your tea's all gone, but you can have some of my Coke."

She tried to sit up, but her body was too weak.

Grant chuckled, and it was the sexiest sound ever. "I guess I really did wear you out. Here."

He lifted her head enough that she could sip through the straw, but the cool liquid did little to ease her burning throat. Maybe it wasn't just the heavy breathing that had dried her out. Maybe she was coming down with something. Heaven knew she was subjected to tons of germs at work with all the little munchkins running around.

Grant smoothed her hair back from her face. "You sleep. I'll see who called and be downstairs if you need me."

She opened her eyes for the thrill of watching him walk away, but everything was fuzzy and dim.

An uneasy sense of worry slid under her skin. This wasn't right. None of what she was feeling was right. "Grant?"

"Yeah, honey?"

She tried to sit up and couldn't. Her stomach rolled, and she thought she might throw up. Her head lolled to the side like an infant's. "I think something's wrong with me."

"Isabelle?" Grant's voice was panicked, and she heard dishes crash to the floor but couldn't see anything.

He pressed a hand to her head, then lifted her eyelids one at a time. "Oh, God," he breathed out. "Did you take something?" he demanded.

She tried to shake her head but couldn't. "No."

"Any medicine?"

"No."

His voice was normal again. Eerily neutral. "Okay, honey. I want you to listen carefully. Can you do that?"

She made a sound that vaguely resembled an answer.

"I need you to stay awake."

She couldn't. She wanted to, but she was too tired, and that couldn't be good. She knew that much.

Her body jerked, every muscle locking down hard. It hurt. She'd never known pain like that could even exist. It had to be killing her.

Tears of fright leaked from her eyes, and she heard Grant's muffled curse.

She couldn't die without him knowing how she felt. How much he meant to her.

Isabelle struggled through the pain to pull in enough breath to speak. "Love you," she whispered. Then another convulsion hit, harder this time, and she wasn't strong enough to keep it from dragging her down into the black.

CHAPTER TWENTY-FOUR

Wyatt hadn't said a word to Dale, and it was beginning to worry him. Whatever his dad had planned, Dale wasn't going to like it. All he could do was keep his eyes open for the first chance he could get away.

Dale wasn't going to be happy until Wyatt was back in prison where he belonged. Only then could he be sure Angela was safe.

"I've got us a place all picked out," said Wyatt.

"Where?"

"Don't worry about it. You'll see when we get there."

"How much farther is it?"

Wyatt's hand shot out faster than Dale remembered and slapped the back of his head. Dale bit his tongue hard enough to draw blood.

"You sound like some fucking kid. Grow up and shut up. We'll be there when we're there," said Wyatt.

Dale refused to let his dickhead father intimidate him further. "Why did you even bother to bring me along?"

"You're my son," he said as if that explained everything. "You belong with me."

"I don't want to have anything to do with you. Why can't you get that through your head?"

"That's just that goody two-shoes you've been shacking up with talking."

"First, I'm not 'shacking up' with her. She's my foster mom. Second, what the hell is that supposed to mean? She has nothing to do with me choosing not to be a part of your life. I chose that all on my own."

Wyatt grunted. "You even sound like her, all high and mighty. I can tell I've got my work cut out for me."

Dale did not want to know what that meant. Whatever Wyatt had planned, it couldn't be good. He needed to get the hell away from Wyatt while he still could.

The hard edges of Dale's cell phone in his pants pocket pressed against his thigh, comforting him. He'd turned it off for school and hadn't had a chance to turn it back on again, so at least it wouldn't ring and give away the fact that he had a way to contact the police. All he needed now was a little privacy and the police would be hot on Wyatt's tail.

Dale kept a close eye on the signs so he'd know where to tell the police to find them.

He wondered if Angela was okay and if she'd ever speak to him again after seeing how ugly his roots were. Maybe it was better if she didn't. The thought made his stomach hurt, but he knew better than to fool himself into thinking it wouldn't matter to her. It would. How could it not matter to her? She'd seen what an asshole his father was. She had to know that the apple never fell far from the tree. She was certain to move on to a better guy. That was the cold, hard truth, and there was no escaping it. Might as well suck it up and move on.

Story of his life.

Grant was normally really good at keeping a level head. It was one of the things that made him a kick-ass sniper. But this was not normal. Isabelle was sick, and he was pretty sure he knew why.

The tea. It was the only thing she'd had eaten or drunk that he hadn't.

He'd seen a poisoning only once before, and it hadn't been nearly as ugly as this was. That had been a quick, quiet death. There was nothing quiet about the way Isabelle was thrashing around, like she was having a seizure.

Grant scrambled to get his cell phone out of his discarded jeans and dialed 911. He didn't even wait for the operator to finish his intro before he started talking. "My girlfriend's been poisoned."

"Poisoned? Do you know how?"

"She drank some tea. There must have been something in it."

"I'm calling an ambulance for you now, sir. Please stay on the line."

"What should I do? Should I make her throw up?"

"No, sir. That can cause more harm than good. The ambulance will be—"

Isabelle started seizing again, and Grant let the phone drop so he could keep her from hurting herself. He held her body tight against his and whispered into her ear, "You're going to be fine, Isabelle. Help is on the way."

She let out a low, pained moan that nearly stopped Grant's heart. She was hurting, and there wasn't a fucking thing he could do about it.

Rage fountained up inside him, making him shake with the force of it. Someone had hurt his Isabelle, and they were going to pay.

The paramedics arrived, and Grant sprinted downstairs to let them in. They hauled in their equipment and knelt beside Isabelle.

"Tell us what happened here," said one of the paramedics. He was in his midthirties and had an air of calm competence about him that made Grant move aside and put Isabelle into his seemingly capable hands.

"She's a teacher. One of the kids at school gave her some tea. It was these flower ball things that opened up when you put them in hot water. We shared lunch, and that was the only thing she had that I didn't."

He swabbed Isabelle's arm for an IV. "Is she on any medication?" he asked.

"I don't know." Admitting it made him sick. He didn't know her at all. Why hadn't he taken the time to get to know her better? Why hadn't he insisted on finding out more about her?

Because he never did. That's why. No ties, no commitments. Just sex.

He was such a fucking shallow asshole for not caring more.

"Would she have any reason to want to hurt herself?" asked the female paramedic, giving Grant a mistrustful scowl. She was younger than her partner, with a cynical bitterness about her that came only from learning the hard way not to trust people.

"Hurt herself?" asked Grant, not understanding what she meant.

"Kill herself," said the woman in a flat, indifferent tone.

"God, no. Isabelle would never do anything like that."

"Kathy, I can't get a line in. You try."

Kathy moved around Isabelle just as another seizure wracked her body. "Hold her down," she ordered.

Grant helped them hold her still while he tried not to let himself think about what could happen.

He couldn't lose her. Not Isabelle.

Finally, Kathy managed to get an IV started. He only hoped that it would help flush the shit out of her system.

"Her pulse is getting weaker," said the man. "We need to move."

"Where's the stuff you think poisoned her?" asked Kathy. "We'll need to bring it with us."

"In the kitchen. I'll get it."

He raced downstairs and grabbed the bag of tea. The paramedics were already on their way down with her, so Grant followed in their wake.

Kathy stopped him from getting into the back of the ambulance. "I'll take that, sir." She held her hand out for the tea.

"I'll carry it." He started to step up into the back of the ambulance when Kathy grabbed his arm and stopped him while snatching the bag of tea from his hand.

"I think it would be best if you followed us in your own car."

"I want to be with her."

"I understand that, sir, but we need the room to work." It was a lie. Grant could hear it in her tone. But why would she lie about that? Why wouldn't she want him to ride along?

Oh, God. "You think I poisoned her?"

"I'm not saying that, sir. I just think it would be best if

you followed behind us. Besides, you're still not wearing any clothes."

Grant looked down and realized he was wearing only his underwear, standing out on the street. Not that he gave a fuck what Isabelle's neighbors thought of him, as long as he was with her and she was safe. "Please. I'd never do anything to hurt her. Just let me come with you."

"They won't let you in the hospital like that. Go get dressed and follow us. We're wasting time arguing." With that, Kathy shut the doors and the ambulance drove off with the wail of sirens floating behind them.

Grant stood there in shock. He should have been cold, but instead, he was just numb. Isabelle might be dying, and he was at least partially responsible.

He'd fed her poisoned tea.

She said she loved him.

His brain couldn't wrap around any of it. For the first time in his life, he had no idea what to do. This was all too much, and he had no one to turn to. His friends were busy dealing with their own problems, the police had already thought he might be the killer, and the only person in this whole town who gave a shit about him might be dying.

He was alone and powerless to do anything to help Isabelle.

Grant didn't know how long he stood there, but he was shivering when he finally pulled himself together enough to go back in the house. Two minutes later, he was in his car, dressed, and screeching down the quiet neighborhood street toward the hospital.

One thing was for sure, he was no longer waiting around for the police to find the fucking killer. He was

going to hunt the bastard down himself and take him
out. Head shot. Nice and clean and guaranteed to work
every time.

If he was going to be in this alone, he was going to do
it his way. No matter what it cost him.

CHAPTER TWENTY-FIVE

———◆———

Detective Mathews was waiting for Grant at the hospital. As Grant came through the doors, Mathews stepped in front of him, blocking his path.

Grant barely resisted hitting the man just to make himself feel better.

He shoved his way past the detective and went straight to the emergency room desk. "I don't have time to deal with you right now. I need to check on Isabelle."

"They're still working on her. You have a while before they'll let you see her."

"They'll let me see her now," said Grant, knowing he sounded threatening to the young woman behind the desk. If he had to scare a few people to get in to see Isabelle, then that's what he'd do.

"She's only been here a few minutes. Let them do their job."

"If she's only been here a few minutes, how did you get here so fast?"

Mathews's face went blank. "I was already here visiting someone."

The woman behind the desk spoke with a harried-looking man in scrubs and pointed to Grant. He walked over and asked, "Are you with Isabelle Carson?"

"Yes. Is she okay?" *Dear God, please let her be okay.*

"We've stopped the seizures, but it will be a while until the lab can figure out what she ingested. Do you have any idea what was in the tea?"

"No."

"How long ago did she drink it?"

Grant looked at the clock on the wall. "I don't know exactly. About two hours ago."

The man nodded and wrote something on a chart.

"When can I see her?" asked Grant.

"As soon as she's stable. She's not out of the woods yet, so if you think of anything that might help us, please don't wait to let us know."

The man walked off, and suddenly, Grant wasn't sure he could stay standing. His legs were weak and shaking, and he thought he might throw up.

Isabelle wasn't safe yet. Grant would have given anything to take her place right now. This helplessness was killing him.

Detective Mathews shoved a chair under Grant and eased him into it. "Are you sure you didn't get any of that stuff into you?"

"I'm sure."

"Did you bring it with you?"

"The paramedic took it with her in the ambulance."

"Hold on. I need to take a look at it. I'll be right back."

Grant sat there in a plastic chair with his head in his hands, trying not to throw up. Isabelle had been poisoned. He'd been right there and he hadn't seen the danger. He'd handed her the cup himself and smiled at her while she drank it down.

He didn't think he'd ever be able to forgive himself for that. He should have known something was wrong. His instincts should have been better.

Mathews came back a couple of minutes later with a paper cup of water. "Drink this."

Grant eyed the cup. "You think that's going to make me feel better?"

"If you feel like I think you feel, you'll try anything."

He was right, but Grant wasn't going to ask him how he knew. He didn't need to know anything about Detective Mathews other than how good he was at his job. Based on where Isabelle was right now, the answer was not fucking good enough.

Grant slugged the water back, but it didn't help him feel better. He still wanted to physically fight his way back to Isabelle's side if that's what it took. Her being in danger again hurled him back to that night when he was willing to kill to keep her safe. He didn't know what it was about her that triggered his caveman instincts, but they were rampaging through him, growling at him to take Isabelle and hide her away where no one could ever get to her again.

"The best thing you can do for her now is to let the doctors work."

"I want to be with her."

"I understand how you feel, but you'd just get in the way. They'll come get you if she takes a turn for the worse."

"How do you know?" demanded Grant.

Mathews stared at him for a moment as if studying him. Whatever he saw seemed to satisfy him. "Experience," he said. "Let me buy you a cup of coffee in the cafeteria and we can talk."

"I don't want any fucking coffee!"

Several heads turned toward Grant. One of them was a small boy with wide, frightened eyes. He stared at Grant while he clung to his mother's arm.

Grant felt like a total shit for scaring the kid. "Fine. Coffee." He told the nurse at the desk where he'd be, gave her his cell number, and followed Mathews down a long hall.

The man knew exactly where they were going without even needing to read the signs, which made Grant wonder just how much time he'd been spending here lately.

Not that he cared.

"I'm sorry I jumped to the conclusion that you were guilty. I shouldn't have done that."

"I really don't give a shit about that anymore. I'm too worried about Isabelle to care how much of a prick you are."

Mathews nodded. "Fair enough."

"Daddy!" came a high-pitched, excited voice from behind them.

Grant turned and saw a little girl, maybe four years old, running toward Mathews. He bent down, scooped her up, and kissed the top of her head. "Heya, pumpkin. Aren't you supposed to be with Aunt Janet?"

"I saw you go by Mommy's room. You should come back and sit with her. She likes it when you hold her hand."

"I will really soon, but I have to work now."

The little girl pouted and looked up at her father with giant brown eyes. "You always gotta work."

Grant said, "Go ahead. I can get my own coffee."

"No. We need to talk. There's been a development in the case. Just give me a minute."

Mathews carried his daughter into one of the rooms, and Grant followed him. He stood in the doorway and watched as Mathews handed his girl to a woman sitting beside another woman's bed. "You be good for Aunt Janet," he told her. "I'll meet you at home for dinner."

"Pizza?" asked the little girl.

"If you're good."

Mathews kissed his daughter, then went to the bed and did the same to the woman lying there. She couldn't have been thirty yet, but she was dying. Grant was no doctor, but it was impossible to mistake. She was bone thin, and her skin had an ugly yellow cast to it. She had dark hollows under her eyes and they barely fluttered when Mathews smoothed patchy wisps of hair back over her balding head. His wedding ring flashed in the bright fluorescent lighting, and Grant realized that this had to be his wife.

"Love you, sweetheart. Be back soon," he whispered, but Grant heard it. His heart ached for the man, but like with Isabelle, he was helpless to do a damn thing to make it better.

Mathews shut the door behind him as he left his wife's room. Nothing in his face showed he was suffering. If Grant hadn't seen what the man was going through for himself, he never would have believed it.

"You should go spend time with your family," said Grant.

"I've got to do my job. The bill collectors don't care that my wife is sick."

"I'm so sorry."

"Forget it," said Mathews. "And I mean that. This is none of your business, and I expect you to respect that."

"Sure," he said, though he knew it was a lie. That was not the kind of thing a man forgot easily.

They went to the cafeteria and got coffee. Whatever pain Mathews was suffering, he somehow managed to push it aside long enough to do his job. "Where did Isabelle get the tea?"

"At school. She said one of her students gave it to her."

"Today?"

"Yes."

"We got that warrant to search Wyatt's motel room this morning. There were bits of plant matter in there."

"Plant matter?"

"I assumed it was pot, but after seeing the tea, I think it's a pretty safe bet those plant bits are what he used to poison Isabelle."

That fucking bastard. Grant was going to kill him. He was going to force-feed him a gallon of that tea and see how he liked it.

Mathews kept talking while the seething rage swelled inside Grant, taking over.

"I'll have a sample sent to a lab, but the results could take weeks," said Mathews.

"You can't wait that long to charge him with the murders."

"We won't have to. The poison wasn't the only thing we found in his room. Trina Skinner's body was on his bed."

"The woman who went missing?" Another victim. Another innocent woman dead. "How?"

"She was stabbed twenty-seven times."

The paper cup in Grant's hand collapsed in his grip and coffee sloshed onto the table.

Wyatt really needed to die, and Grant was more than ready to be the one to make that happen.

Mathews nodded. "She hadn't been dead long. Wyatt must have been holding her all this time. We're not sure where."

Grant did not allow himself to think about the horror Trina must have faced since she was abducted two months ago. He was already teetering on the edge of going hunting for Wyatt right now. His rifle was in his trunk. All he had to do was find the man and it would all be over.

If it weren't for his need to be near Isabelle, his need to know she was going to make it, he'd already be gone. "Why keep her so long and risk getting caught?"

"To kill her in the right order would be my guess."

"That means he skipped Amanda, killed Trina, and moved on to Isabelle."

Mathews shook his head. "Amanda wasn't around, so maybe he decided to move on without her. Either that, or he already got to her and we haven't found the body yet."

"No. Amanda's fine. She called us this weekend and told us not to worry." Grant's tone was clipped and cold with denial. Amanda and her little girl were safe. He refused to believe anything else.

Mathews's mouth flattened like he didn't quite buy it. "If you talk to her again, tell her to stay put until we've caught Wyatt."

"How long will that take?"

"I wish I knew. You could pack up and leave town if it would make you feel safer."

"I'm not going to feel safe until he's back behind bars." Or dead. Dead would be better.

The harried-looking young man in scrubs came into the cafeteria and scanned the room. Grant's heart gave a hard thump of anxiety as he rose to his feet.

The man saw him and headed his direction. Grant met him halfway.

"Isabelle's stable now," said the man. "You can see her in a few minutes once they get her settled in a room."

"Is she awake?"

"Not yet. It may take a while."

"But she'll be fine, right?"

"We can't know for sure if there will be any lasting effects from the poison until after she's conscious."

"What the hell is that supposed to mean?" demanded Grant.

Mathews put a restraining hand on his arm. "One step at a time, Grant. She's going to live. Count your blessings."

Grant jerked away from the detective and gave the intern a hard stare. "Tell me what that means."

"It means that we don't know. I'm sorry. Toxins are difficult to treat when we don't know what they are. We treated her symptoms, and she seems to be recovering."

"Seems to be?"

"We'll just have to wait and see."

The man's vague answers were threatening Grant's tenuous control. He wanted to lash out and pound the answers out of this guy, even though he knew it wouldn't help.

Mathews stepped between them before Grant could do anything he'd regret. "Take us to her. He needs to see for himself she's okay."

The man in scrubs looked nervously from Mathews to

Grant, apparently catching on to how close he was to see-ing violence up close and personal. "Uh. Right this way."

❧

Isabelle felt like she'd spent the night tumbling inside a dryer. Her skin was hot and parched, her stomach was spinning almost as much as her head, and every muscle in her body ached. Even her eyelids.

It took her a minute to convince them to work, but fi-nally, she cracked an eye open. Grant was the first thing she saw, though he was a bit fuzzy around the edges. He was sitting beside her, watching her with bloodshot eyes. When he saw her move, he jumped out of his chair and hovered over her.

"Hey, beautiful. How are you feeling?"

Her throat was raw, and when she spoke, only a hoarse whisper came out. "Like crap."

Grant smiled a little. "Sure beats the alternative."

"Feeling good?"

"No. Feeling nothing. You scared ten years off my life."

Isabelle frowned in confusion and looked around. She wasn't at home. She was in a hospital.

Slowly, bits and pieces of memories came back to her, though they were vague and fuzzy, as if she'd seen every-thing through a heavy fog. "What happened?"

"I'll fill you in in a minute. Do you hurt anywhere?"

Her vision cleared enough that she could make out his face better. He looked horrible—like he'd been through the wringer himself. "Grant, what happened?"

He looked at the wall behind her. "You ate something bad."

Isabelle remembered the pain. That was not food poisoning. She'd had that before, and as horrible as it was, this was much worse. "You're lying. Why are you lying to me?"

"I don't want to scare you."

"Then tell me what's going on. You're freaking me out."

He pulled in a deep breath and let it out. "The tea you brought home was poisoned."

Poisoned? Isabelle's mind struggled to make sense of that and couldn't. "That can't be true. None of my students would do anything to hurt me."

"Did one of the students actually give you the tea?"

"Melissa Norton."

"I need to tell Mathews." He stood up as if preparing to leave.

"Grant, wait. Don't leave me. I don't understand what's going on. I need you."

Grant halted midstride, turned around, and came back to her bed. Some of the tension had left his body, but there was still a feral light in his golden eyes that worried her.

He stroked her cheek, and his cool hand felt good against her hot skin. "I'm just going to get you a doctor and make a quick phone call. I'll be back in two minutes, okay?"

Isabelle nodded and closed her eyes. She was so tired, even though the clock in the room said it was just barely five. When she opened them again, an hour had passed and Grant was gone.

Keith sat beside her, holding her hand, looking so worried it broke her heart.

"Hi," she said.

Keith's head jerked up. "Hi, yourself."

"Where's Grant?"

"He asked me to come sit with you for a little while. He ran home to get you some clothes and to check on Dale. They should be back any minute. How are you feeling?"

"Honestly, not so good, but I'll live."

Keith's blue eyes filled up with tears, and he gripped her hand so hard it hurt. "I'm so sorry, Isabelle. You shouldn't have to suffer like this."

"I'm just tired."

"Try to sleep, then. You'll feel better if you sleep."

CHAPTER TWENTY-SIX

Grant had one foot out the door on his way back to the hospital when Isabelle's home phone rang. He picked it up, hoping it was Dale.

"Hello."

"Grant?" It was a girl's voice, tight with panic.

"Yeah."

"Thank God. I've been trying to reach you for hours. Dale's dad was at the school, and he was acting so mean. I ran inside to get help, but I was too late." Finally, he recognized the voice as Angela's.

"Slow down. What about Dale?"

"His dad took him."

"What? When? Where?" He shouted the questions into the phone like a barrage of gunfire.

She started crying, and Grant reeled in his temper. "Take a deep breath, Angela, and tell me what happened."

"We were walking out of school. Dale's dad was waiting for him."

"And Dale left with him?"

"Yes."

"In his dad's car, or his own?"

"His dad's."

"Where did they go?"

Angela hiccoughed. "I don't know. Dale told me to go inside."

"And you did?"

"Yeah."

"Good girl. Did you tell someone at school?"

"Yes. They called the police."

"How long ago?"

"Over two hours ago. They've been trying to call Isabelle, but no one answered."

Grant glanced at Isabelle's answering machine. The thing was blinking like crazy. The police had probably tried to call her cell phone, too. He dug through her purse and found it. Ten new messages.

Shit. This was so not good.

"Okay. Did you tell the police what happened? What you saw?"

"Yes."

"Did any of the policemen give you a phone number to call?"

"Yes."

"Give it to me."

It took Angela three tries to speak clearly enough for Grant to get the number down.

"Are you at home?"

"Yes."

"I want you to stay there, got it?"

"What about Dale?" she asked.

"I'll take care of Dale. You need to stay home and stay out of this. Wyatt is a dangerous man, and I don't want you getting hurt. Understand?"

"Yes. When you find Dale, will you have him call me to tell me he's safe? Even if it's late. I don't care."

"I promise."

Grant hung up and dialed Dale's cell phone. It went straight to voice mail. "Dale, if you get this, call my cell. I'm coming to find you. Just hold on."

Next, he called the number Angela had given him on his way to the car. There was no way he could let Isabelle know that Dale was missing. Not in her current condition. She was too weak to stay awake for more than five minutes. He was going to have to find a way to deal with this as best he could and pray the police didn't mess up her recovery by letting her know what was going on.

The doctors had said she'd probably sleep through the night, so he had that long to find Dale and bring him home safe and sound.

At least Keith was up there with her and he didn't have to worry about her safety while she was in the hospital.

Grant had seen the horrified look on Keith's face when he showed up and saw her lying there so weak and pale. In that moment, Grant realized Keith loved her. He didn't like it, but he could hardly blame the man.

Keith would watch over her until Grant could get back to her side.

"What exactly is it you want from me?" Dale asked his father.

The highway was nearly empty this far out of town. The sun was setting, and the idea of being alone in the dark with Wyatt was bringing back all kinds of bad memories. It didn't matter how quietly he hid in the closet, Wyatt would always find him and drag him out.

"I want to teach you how to be a real man before it's too late and that bitch turns you into a weakling."

Dale felt like lashing out at Wyatt for insulting the only person in the world who actually gave a shit about him and what he wanted. She didn't even laugh when he told her he wanted to be a marine biologist. Instead, she went out and bought him a fish tank.

"What the hell are you talking about? Isabelle was taking care of me, not that you'd know what that looked like if you sat on it."

Wyatt pulled back his hand as if to strike Dale, but he refused to flinch. He was tired of being afraid of his father. He was nearly a man himself now and needed to grow some balls. "The next time you hit me, I'm gonna hit back. Got it?"

Wyatt grinned and wrapped his arm around Dale's neck, pulling him over for a hug. "That's my boy. Don't let no one push you around."

Dale's stomach clenched. If his father approved of him, he had to be doing something wrong. He needed to get away. He needed to escape before he lost every opportunity he might have.

"I've got to use the bathroom," he told Wyatt.

"Hold on and I'll pull over where you can piss."

Dale needed civilization, not just some tree along the side of the road. "I need to take a dump, and I'm not doing it outside. Find a bathroom."

Wyatt grunted his disapproval but said, "Fine. I saw a sign for a gas station a few miles up in Rolla. We'll stop there." He reached under the seat and pulled out a gun.

"But let me be clear, son. You give me any shit at all or try to run, and I'll end you. I'd rather have no son than one who betrayed me."

Grant hated lying to Isabelle about Dale, but he didn't know what else to do. There was nothing she could do to help him, and worrying wasn't going to help her recovery. As it was, she looked like she was barely able to keep her eyes open.

She was speaking quietly with Keith, who stroked the back of her hand as naturally as if he'd been doing it for years. Grant suffered through a kick of jealousy. Even though they'd slept together, that didn't give him any claim on her. He was leaving. She was entitled to her own life without him. Even if it included Keith.

Grant plastered a smile on his face as he made his presence known. "I brought you some clothes in case you want to put on something that doesn't leave your ass hanging out."

"Now, why would she want to do that?" said Keith. "She'll spoil the view."

The paper sack crunched inside Grant's tightening fist. "I also threw in some of the stuff you had sitting by your sink. Don't ask me what it all is, but it's in there. So is your toothbrush."

Isabelle gave him a weak smile. "Thanks, Grant. I'll feel a lot better in my own pajamas, even if they won't let me go home and sleep in my own bed tonight."

"The doc said you could go home tomorrow if everything looked good."

"Where's Dale? I thought he was coming with you."

Grant wasn't a natural liar, but he'd learned how to do it just in case he needed to in his job. He made his voice casual and kept looking at her right in the eye as he lied. "He's studying with Angela tonight for some big test tomorrow, and I didn't think you'd want him to mess that up."

Isabelle frowned. "No, of course not. He needs to study and not worry about me. I'll see him tomorrow."

"I'll take care of him for you, Isabelle. I swear it." At least that wasn't a lie.

She reached out a hand toward him, and Grant couldn't help but take it. He'd wanted to touch her so bad—pull her tight against him and never let go—but she looked fragile. Breakable.

Her skin felt dry and still too hot, but it wasn't as bad as it had been before. Whatever they'd done to treat the poison was working. Thank God.

"I know you'll take care of him. It's nice not having to worry about him. You're handy to have around."

Handy? He was a fucking liar. He had to get out of here before she saw it in his face. He had to find Dale and bring him home safely. The boy had no one else right now.

Grant knew how awful that felt.

"I've got to go, honey."

"Go?"

"I'm meeting with Detective Mathews in a few minutes. We've got to figure out how to track Wyatt down before he hurts someone else."

A look of disappointment strained her features for a moment before she gave him a brave smile. "Okay. Will I see you tomorrow?"

"Yes. Bright and early. Dale and I will be coming to

take you home." He kissed her head and silently begged for her forgiveness.

Grant set the clothes on the bed. "Keith, can I talk to you for a minute?"

"Sure." He winked at Isabelle. "Be right back."

Grant closed the door, leaving him and Keith standing in the hall where Isabelle couldn't hear them. He didn't bother with small talk—not with the guy who would likely take his place in Isabelle's bed once he was gone. "Wyatt kidnapped Dale."

"Oh, God, no. That man's a killer. We've got to find him."

"I'm on it, but I don't want Isabelle to know. She's dealing with enough right now. I'm not sure she could also deal with knowing her son is being held by a fucking psycho."

Keith's mouth tightened in anger. "No, you're right. She shouldn't have to worry."

"Can you stay with her? Keep her safe in case Wyatt comes back to finish the job? I'd ask for police protection, but one of them might spill the news about Dale."

"Of course I can stay. No problem," said Keith. "I won't leave her side."

Grant clapped a hand on his shoulder. "Thanks, man. I owe you."

"No you don't. We're practically family. There's nothing I want more than to take care of Isabelle."

That punch of jealousy was back, making Grant wish he could hate the guy. But he couldn't. Not when he was so devoted to Isabelle. "You care for her, don't you?"

Keith's blue eyes brightened, and an almost ferocious expression tightened his mouth. "I love her. I'd do anything for her."

"I'm glad she has you in her life." It was another lie, but one he knew he had to come to accept. That didn't mean he had to like it.

"Me, too."

Grant was going to punch the guy if he stayed any longer, so he said, "Gotta run. Call me if you need anything."

Keith went back into Isabelle's room and shut the door behind him.

Keith reached into his pocket for the syringe he'd brought with him. As weak as Isabelle was, it wouldn't take long for the drug to take effect. She'd drift off peacefully this time. He wouldn't mess up and hurt her again.

He slipped back inside her room quietly. She hadn't been able to stay awake for more than a minute or two since he'd arrived, and her eyes were closed again, her face relaxed in sleep.

Good. He could do it now and hold her hand until the end.

Keith kept his steps quiet as he moved to her side. It took him only a moment to get the drug into the saline bag dripping into her vein. He didn't even have to touch her and risk waking her to do it.

His prints were on the bag, but he doubted anyone would bother looking for them. And even if they did, it wouldn't matter. Keith was nearly done with his work. It was almost time for him to sleep, too.

He sat beside her, took her slender hand in his, and waited for her to drift away.

Isabelle forced herself to wake up again out of sheer will-power.

Grant was hiding something. Something bad.

Keith stroked the back of her hand, but even that much contact made her skin itch. She pulled her hand away and sat up in the bed.

Keith frowned at her. "You should sleep."

"Later. Right now I want you to tell me what the big secret is."

His blue eyes widened with a flash of panic. "Secret? I don't know what you're talking about."

"What did Grant tell you in the hall?" she asked. "If it has something to do with my health, I have a right to know."

For a second, he looked almost relieved that she'd caught him in the act. His body sagged a bit, and he let out a deep breath. "Grant asked me to watch out for you. He's worried."

"If he's worried, why isn't he watching over me himself? It's not like Grant to pass off his responsibilities to someone else." Unless something bigger was happening.

That had to be it. Something big was going down, and he didn't want her to know about it.

"Maybe you don't know him as well as you think."

"I know him well enough to know that he's trying to protect me because I'm sick. Did they find Wyatt?" she asked.

"No." Keith's tone was clipped, as if he was angry with her.

"Then what? What could possibly be so important he couldn't even stay five minutes?"

Keith grabbed the remote. "Don't worry about it. Let's see what's on."

"I don't want to watch any stupid TV. I want you to stop lying to me. Where is Grant?"

"I don't know. Maybe he's got a date," snapped Keith.

Isabelle sat there in shock. Not because she thought Grant was out with another woman. She knew he wasn't so cold he'd leave her sitting in a hospital while he went and had a good time. She was shocked because of the hateful way Keith was acting. That wasn't at all like him. "You don't like Grant, do you?"

"He's a user. A womanizer. You never should have slept with him."

"That's none of your business."

"He's not good enough for you, Isabelle. He never has been. I don't know why you've carried a torch for him so long."

"He's a good man. Caring. Selfless. Honest."

"Apparently not so honest if he's lying to you about where he is."

"The only reason Grant would ever lie to me would be to protect me." Which begged the question what was he protecting her from that kept him away.

A greasy sense of unease crept up her spine. Something was wrong. Grant would have been here by her side otherwise.

So would Dale.

Grant's evasiveness finally made sense, and Isabelle felt herself start to shake with panic. "Where is my phone? I need to call Dale."

"You heard Grant. Dale is studying. You shouldn't interrupt him. Let's watch TV."

"Give me the damn phone!"

Keith blinked in shock. "Dale is fine. Don't worry."

He knew something. Isabelle could see it in the way he wouldn't meet her gaze. "You know what's going on. Tell me."

"There's nothing to tell."

"You're lying."

Keith closed his eyes in frustration, then finally said, "Grant went to find Dale."

"What do you mean 'find' him?"

"Please, Isabelle. You shouldn't become stressed right now. Your body can't handle it. I don't want you to suffer."

Isabelle grabbed Keith's shirt and jerked him hard toward her so they were eye to eye. "Tell me where my son is. Now."

Keith gently pried her hand away from his shirt. She was too weak to stop him. "I'm sorry. Wyatt has him."

Panic took over her body, making it hard to breathe. Her vision receded until everything looked far away, gray and fuzzy. "God, no."

Keith eased her back on the bed with gentle, insistent hands. "It's going to be okay, Isabelle. The police are looking for him. So is Grant. Dale will be fine."

"Dale is far from fine. Wyatt is a murderer."

"And now that he's kidnapped Dale, he will be put back behind bars where he belongs. This will all be over soon."

She had to do something to find him. She couldn't just lie there. She had to find her son.

Isabelle threw back the covers and slid out of bed. Her

head spun, but she ignored it, keeping a hand on the bed to steady herself.

Keith grabbed her shoulders. "Get back in bed. You're going to hurt yourself."

"No, I'm going to hurt *you* if you don't let me go." She jerked her arm away and grabbed the bag of clothes Grant had brought her. Thankfully, he'd not only brought pajamas, but also something to wear home tomorrow.

Isabelle slid the panties and jeans on under her hospital gown, heedless of Keith there watching her dress. The IV was going to have to come out before she could put her top on, so she started to pull at the tape holding it in place.

"At least let me get a nurse to take that out so you don't damage your vein and bleed all over the place."

She wasn't worried about a little blood. She was terrified of what would happen to Dale. He was so angry at his father that he might do or say something that would set Wyatt off. What if Wyatt hurt him? Beat him and left him for dead in some deserted area? What if Dale was too weak to get help? Or worse, what if Wyatt didn't bother to hold back and killed Dale outright, like he had the others? He could do it. Isabelle was sure he was both physically and emotionally capable of murdering his own son.

Isabelle couldn't let any of that happen. She needed to find Dale. Help him. She couldn't sit by and do nothing, not when she was the one who was supposed to protect him and keep him safe.

"Fine," she told him just to get him to leave the room.

The moment he was gone, she pulled the IV out of her arm and used the tape to hold a wad of tissue against the wound. She was already dressed and out of the room before Keith came back.

CHAPTER TWENTY-SEVEN

Dale thanked God that the men's room at the little convenience store they stopped at was for one person at a time. He flipped on the light and locked the grimy door behind him.

With shaking hands, Dale powered on his cell phone—which seemed to take forever—and dialed Grant. Maybe he should have called the police, but he didn't have time to explain his parental situation before Wyatt would become suspicious. Grant already knew what was going on. He could call the police.

"Dale. Are you safe?" asked Grant.

Dale kept his voice low so it wouldn't carry through the flimsy door. "Yeah. I'm at Donny's Gas Up, right outside of Rolla."

"Donny's Gas Up. Outside of Rolla," repeated Grant, as if for the benefit of someone nearby. "Stay there. Police are on the way."

"I don't know how long I can stall. I'll try."

Grant's voice was calm and sure, and it somehow helped Dale to find his own confidence. "You do what you can. We'll do the rest. I want you to stay on the line so we can track your cell phone, okay?"

"He might hear it."

"I'll mute it on my end so he can't hear anything we say. All you need to do is hang on."

Dale could do that. Help was on the way. Isabelle trusted Grant, and that was good enough for him to do the same. "Okay. I gotta get back out there or he's going to start getting suspicious."

He put the phone in the pocket of his letter jacket to keep it close at hand. If he wasn't able to stall long enough for the police to show up, at least he'd be able to drop clues about which way they were going. The police would be able to follow them.

This was almost over. Within hours, his dad would be back in jail and out of his life for good.

Wyatt pounded on the door. "Hurry up in there."

"I'm coming. Just a sec," said Dale. He flushed the toilet and ran water in the sink just in case Wyatt was listening.

Dale opened the door, and Wyatt handed him an armload of bottled soda and snacks and a wad of small bills. "Pay for this while I go. Meet me by the car."

"Do you mind if I get a cup of coffee?"

"Yeah. Whatever. Just be quick."

Dale turned to go, but Wyatt stopped him, grabbing his arm hard enough that it hurt. Dale took the pain without letting it show on his face. He didn't want to give his old man the satisfaction of seeing his pain.

"Don't do anything stupid, son." Wyatt lifted up the front of his shirt enough that Dale could see the metallic gleam of the handgun shoved in his waistband. "I'm sure you wouldn't want anyone getting hurt."

Dale's vision narrowed until there was nothing else but

that gun. There was no question in his mind that Wyatt would use it. He would. He'd probably enjoy it, too.

Dale swallowed hard, trying to make room to speak so Grant could hear Wyatt was armed. "I'll do whatever you want. Just don't shoot anyone."

Wyatt clamped a hand hard over his mouth. "Keep your voice down, boy, and get your ass back to the car."

Dale nodded, and Wyatt shoved him away hard enough that he stumbled. A bottle of soda fell to the floor and rolled away. Dale scrambled after it, making note of which one it was. Who knew when a spewing bottle of soda might come in handy as a distraction.

The bathroom door slammed shut, and Dale carried his food to the front counter. "I want a cup of coffee added to this," he told the woman at the register.

Her nametag read "Liz," and she looked like he pictured a grandma should. She had short gray hair that she probably had styled once a week by a woman she called a beauty operator. The lines on her face were deeper around her mouth, telling him she'd shared a lot of smiles in her lifetime, and she wore a sweatshirt inviting people to ask her about her grandkids.

Dale didn't. He simply went to make himself a cup of coffee and prayed she'd live long enough to tell the next customer about them.

"Oh, sweetie," she said, "that coffee is old. Let me make you a new pot."

Dale was torn between wanting to stall like Grant had told him to and wanting to get Granny Liz out of harm's way. In the end, it wasn't really a choice. "No, thanks. I like the old stuff better."

She wrinkled her nose in distaste but shrugged. "You

young kids sure have your own way of doing things. My grandson, Trent, is the same way—eating things I wouldn't feed to a skunk."

Through the window, Dale saw a Missouri highway patrol car pull into the parking lot. Two policemen got out.

From the back of the store, Dale heard the bathroom door open.

"You go ahead and get your coffee," said Granny Liz. "I'll ring you up."

Dale didn't know what to do, so he tried to pretend everything was fine. He wasn't being held against his will by his gun-toting ex-con father. He was just picking up some snacks for the ride home.

The sweat drenching his palms proved him a liar, but he ignored it. He knew if he so much as looked toward Wyatt, he'd be able to tell that Dale was working against him.

The electronic doorbell chimed as the cops walked in. "Evening, Liz," greeted one of the officers.

"Hi, Sid, Anton. I was just about to fix a fresh pot of coffee. Interested?"

"Yes, ma'am."

They sounded so casual that it had to be a coincidence they were here. Surely these couldn't be the police Grant said were coming. No sirens. No lights. These men didn't even have their guns drawn.

Granny Liz came over to where Dale was adding sugar packets to his coffee one at a time. He'd lost count of how many he'd used, but it didn't really matter. His nervous stomach would never settle down enough for him to actually drink the stuff.

"Excuse me," said Granny Liz. "Mind if I scoot in here and make some fresh coffee?"

Dale's mouth was too dry to speak, but he nodded and shuffled to one side.

"That's enough sugar, son," came Wyatt's warning voice from behind him. "We gotta get back on the road if we're going to make it home in time for your sister's birthday party."

That lie jarred him just enough that he actually flinched. Hot coffee sloshed over the side of his cup, burning his hand.

Dale gasped and jumped back, shaking drops of coffee from his skin.

"Oh, sweetie! Let me get you some ice," said Granny Liz.

Wyatt grabbed Dale by the back of his jacket and shoved him toward the door. "He'll be fine. Let's go, son."

Dale's hand screamed with pain, but he ignored it. All he wanted to do was get out of here before someone got hurt. The police could catch up with Wyatt farther up the road, where there was no Granny Liz around to become a target.

"It will only take me a second," said Granny Liz.

Wyatt wasn't waiting. He grabbed Dale's arm and pulled him toward the door.

"Don't do anything stupid," growled Wyatt in Dale's ear.

The radios the patrolmen were wearing squawked to life. Dale couldn't understand the codes the dispatcher used, but he did catch his father's name come over the static-y line.

Wyatt came to a dead stop. It lasted only a second. Maybe the cops hadn't even seen it.

"Excuse me, sir," said one of the cops. "Can you please hold on a minute?"

"We're in a hurry, officer," said Wyatt.

"This will just take a moment."

Dale looked over his shoulder. One of the policemen was speaking into the radio. The only word Dale caught was "backup."

This was going to end badly, and from the tension quivering through Wyatt's body, he knew it, too.

"Sir," said the cop, this time more firmly. "I need you to put your hands where I can see them and turn around slowly."

Wyatt let go of Dale's arm long enough to spin him so he was facing the cops and loop a thick arm around his neck. Dale was too shocked to react. He'd known for a long time that his father was a worthless waste of oxygen. Dale had been beaten and smacked around more times than he could count, but never in his most disgusted imaginings had he thought that Wyatt would use his only son as a human shield.

Dale staggered under the betrayal. It ran so deep he was sure his very soul bled out the last hope he had that his Dad cared for him even a little. He only wanted Dale back because he was Wyatt's possession. His property.

"We're leaving," said Wyatt to the police. "Get out of the way and no one will get hurt."

"I'm sorry, sir. We can't let you leave with the boy."

Liz came back out from the storage room carrying a dish towel for the ice pack she was going to make him. She froze in place when she saw what was going on.

Neither one of the patrolmen so much as glanced her way. Their eyes were fixed on the threat.

Dale felt Wyatt reach for his weapon with his free hand.

There were three targets in the room, and Wyatt wouldn't hesitate to take out all of them. Even Granny Liz.

No way was Dale going to let that happen.

"He's got a gun!" shouted Dale.

Wyatt's grip on his neck tightened until Dale could no longer breathe. Out of the corner of his eye, he saw the gun in Wyatt's hand shining in the fluorescent lighting.

Both officers pulled their weapons. They'd spread out enough that Wyatt couldn't possibly keep his eye on both of them.

Liz cowered on the floor near the donut display, repeating a low, terrified mantra of "God, no."

Wyatt pulled his gun free and alternated pointing it at the two men. "I'm going to walk out that door. If you try to follow me, I'll kill the boy."

Another slice of Dale's soul shriveled and died. He was amazed by how much it hurt. Even more amazed that he was still alive and breathing after suffering a blow like that from his own father.

"That's not going to happen," said one of the officers. "Put the gun down. There's nowhere for you to go. Every road is blocked."

"He's *my* son. He belongs to me. You have no right to take him away," growled Wyatt.

Dale clawed at his arm, struggling to get enough air into his lungs to breathe.

"You're hurting the boy," said the second officer in a calm tone.

"I'll do a hell of a lot more than hurt him if you don't get the fuck out of my way." Even as he said it, Wyatt's arm tightened.

Dale's vision filled with spots, and he tried not to panic.

Maybe he should just give in and pass out. Wyatt wouldn't be able to hold him up and keep an eye on both policemen. It was worth a shot. At this point, he didn't have a lot to lose.

Dale went limp, and Wyatt staggered under the sudden shift of weight.

His gun went off. Dale's vision gave out, and the deafening noise combined with his sudden blindness was enough to send Dale headlong into panic. He forgot all about his plan and started fighting like his life depended on it. He landed one or two solid blows before all he was hitting was air.

Somewhere to his right, he heard a frantic scrambling sound, a sickening thud, then another, and finally, the sound of something hard crunching.

Slowly, as Dale gasped for air, his vision started to come back. He sat up and surveyed the scene.

Granny Liz was crouched over one of the policemen, whose skull was grotesquely sunken on one side. He wasn't moving.

The second officer lay twitching in a puddle of his own blood. He struggled to operate the radio at his shoulder, but his body wasn't cooperating. His bloody fingers slipped on the plastic.

Wyatt stood there, the butt of his gun smeared with blood and bits of skin. He was breathing hard and looked pale and terrified. "We gotta go, boy."

Dale wasn't about to leave that policeman here to bleed to death. Even if the whole mess hadn't been his fault, he still couldn't have left him. "I'm staying."

Wyatt grabbed a fistful of Dale's hair and jerked him up to his feet. "You're coming with me."

Dale felt a blind rage take hold of him, and he let it. He was tired of being afraid. Tired of being pushed around by the one man who should have been willing to do anything to take care of him. He balled up his fist and slammed it hard against the side of Wyatt's head, knocking him down.

Pain shot through his hand and up his arm, but he ignored it.

Wyatt pushed himself to his feet and aimed the gun at Dale's chest. "Get in the fucking car, boy. This is your last warning."

No. Dale was not going to be pushed around any longer. He was nearly a man himself. It was time he started acting like one.

He planted his feet and gave his dad a hard stare. "Shoot me if you want, but I'm staying here."

Sirens wailed in the distance, getting closer.

"You might as well stay, too. There's no way you'll be able to outrun the police in that crappy car of yours."

"Fuck!" shouted Wyatt.

"It would be best if you turned yourself in."

Wyatt's face darkened to an angry red. "I'm not going back to jail."

Dale shrugged. "We'll see." He truly didn't care. Either way, Wyatt was out of his life for good. He wouldn't let it be any other way. All the fear he'd carried around for seventeen years evaporated. Wyatt no longer held any power over him.

"You're no fucking son of mine."

Dale nodded slowly and allowed himself a little smile. "That's the only good thing you've ever said to me."

Wyatt sneered, then raced out of the store and fled across

the parking lot, toward a neighborhood. Dale wanted to watch him so he could tell the police where he'd gone, but the bleeding man needed his help more.

Dale scrambled to his side. The bullet Wyatt fired had gone into the man's neck. Blood seemed to be gushing out of the wound with every beat of his heart. He pressed a hand to the wound, praying he could slow the bleeding enough to keep him alive until help arrived.

"Dale!" he heard Grant's voice faintly, as if coming from a long distance.

It took Dale a moment to remember the phone in his pocket. He pulled it out with one bloody hand. "Grant, two policemen have been hurt. Bad. Send help."

"It's already on the way. Just hang on."

Blood was still pooling on the floor despite Dale's efforts. Liz was breathing into the body of the second man, but with a head wound like that, Dale was pretty sure he was already gone. "Tell them to hurry. He doesn't have long."

CHAPTER TWENTY-EIGHT

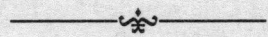

Grant felt helpless as he listened to Detective Mathews give orders over the phone. The state troopers and local police in Rolla were all closing in on Dale's location.

At least Wyatt had left Dale alive. Grant would never have been able to live with himself if anything had happened to Dale.

For the first time in his life, he had an idea of what it must have been like for David to lose his wife and why he'd chosen to go into isolation. The pain of almost losing Dale on top of Isabelle's close call was enough to make Grant want to crawl away and lick his wounds. He felt sore inside, like his organs had all taken a beating. But it wasn't a physical kind of soreness. It was deeper than that. Much worse.

And it wasn't over yet. He still had to face Isabelle and tell her what had happened to Dale. Tell her that he'd hidden the danger to her son from her.

He was pretty sure she'd never forgive him, but he'd done what he thought was right. He couldn't help himself when it came to protecting her. It was like it was part of his genetic code or something, and no matter what he did, he couldn't change it, any more than he could grow taller or make his eyes turn blue.

"The ambulance is here, and police are looking for Wyatt," said Dale over the phone. "I'm gonna clean all this ... blood off."

Grant gripped the phone so hard his hand cramped. "Blood? Are you hurt?"

"Not my blood." Dale sounded like he was trying not to throw up or cry or both. "I'll call you back later."

"Can I come get you?"

"No. The police said they'd bring me home after they take my statement."

"Stay safe. See you home soon."

Grant hung up the phone and looked to where Mathews was on one of the hospital phones. There hadn't been time to go back to his office, so they'd taken over an empty room. Mathews was still speaking with dispatch or whoever it was he'd used to convey information to the officers on the scene. After another couple of minutes, he, too, hung up the phone.

"They've secured the scene," he said. "Wyatt's still missing, but Dale's fine. A little shaken, but they'll bring him back soon."

"I need to go to him."

"You're not legally connected to him. After tonight, I don't think they'd let a strange man anywhere near him."

"Isabelle can't go."

"They're not going to charge Dale with anything. He's not in any kind of trouble. They know he was an innocent victim."

"Someone should still be with him," said Grant.

"They'll have him home in about the same amount of time you could drive there and get him. Just let them bring him back. I promise you that since he tried to stop that cop's bleeding, no one will mistreat him in any way."

"How are the patrolmen?"

Mathews's jaw clenched. "One of them died on the scene. The other is in bad shape, but he could still pull through."

Grant couldn't help but grieve for the man who'd died in the line of duty. If it weren't for him, Dale might still be out there with Wyatt. "I wish I'd have let them know sooner about Wyatt's weapon."

Mathews rubbed his eyes in a gesture slow with fatigue. "They were both wearing a vest, but it doesn't do a bit of good against a skull fracture. Or a lucky shot to the neck."

"Wish that made me feel better," said Grant.

"You and I both know that's not the way it works. The only thing that will make you feel better is to get your family home, safely tucked in their own beds, and watch them sleep every night until you start to believe that they really are safe."

Man, that sounded good. Too bad that wasn't part of his reality. As soon as everyone was truly safe, he had no reason to stay. He couldn't be the man Isabelle needed, and he sure as hell wasn't going to stick around and watch while she found one.

"They're not my family," said Grant, feeling a jolt of painful loss he didn't understand.

"Maybe not on paper, but you treat them like their your own. They probably feel like that, too."

Grant had no idea. It had been so long since he'd been part of a family that he wasn't sure if he even remembered what it was like. All he knew that whatever he was feeling right now sucked, and if that's what it meant to have a real family, he wasn't sure he was a strong enough man for the job.

"I've got to go see Isabelle. Let her know what's going on."

Mathews lifted a dark brow. "Are you sure about that? I mean, wouldn't it be better to wait until Dale is home safe and sound?"

"The longer I wait to tell her, the worse it will be for both of us."

"Good luck. You're going to need it," said Mathews. "And when you see her, will you tell her that I questioned Melissa Norton and she told me she got the tea from a delivery man. He asked her to give it to Isabelle. The kid had no idea it was poisoned."

Grant's phone rang. Caller ID showed the number was private, but he didn't dare not answer it, in case it had something to do with Dale. "Hello."

Keith's voice wavered nervously in Grant's ear. "Isabelle found out about Dale and left."

Panic slammed down hard on Grant. "Left?" he shouted. "What the hell do you mean she left? Where is she?"

"She was so upset I went to get a nurse to see if they could sedate her. She was gone when I got back. I have no idea where she might be." He sounded frantic, but not half as frantic as Grant felt.

"How long ago?"

"I was only gone a few minutes."

Grant was sincerely regretting his decision to take her clothes. A woman in a hospital gown would have drawn a lot more attention, making it harder for her to get away. "She won't get far without her car. I'll have them seal the hospital."

"I'm on it," said Mathews, picking up the phone.

CHAPTER TWENTY-NINE

———— ❧ ————

Wyatt needed a place to hide so he could clean the blood off. He hated being on foot, but he'd be harder to find this way than in his car, especially with the highway patrol on his trail. At least he hoped that was the case.

The nearest neighborhood wasn't going to work. The houses here were new. They'd have decent locks, maybe even security systems, not enough trees to hide him. He needed an old neighborhood—one with old locks and loose windows. Maybe he could even find something abandoned or vacant.

He figured he had only a few minutes before the police were crawling all over this development. A few construction workers were still hammering away. One of them had left his ancient truck unlocked with an open toolbox in the back. That's all Wyatt needed to make his escape.

A minute later, the truck rattled to life and he rolled away as casually as his racing heart would allow. The noise of the work going on must have masked the sound of his getaway, because no one followed him out of the development.

Wyatt wasn't going to give up on his son. What Dale had done today proved he had a backbone. He wasn't a lost cause. Wyatt would have to punish him for his defiance, but after that, they could move on and be a family again. But for that to happen, he had to get Dale back.

Kidnapping him again wasn't going to work. He needed to find a way to make Isabelle give Dale to him willingly. If Dale knew she didn't really want him, maybe he'd decide life was better with his old man.

There was only one thing he could think of that would make Isabelle decide to give him Dale. He needed an even trade—some other kid she'd be willing to bargain for—and he was pretty sure he knew exactly who to pick. He'd been watching her house long enough to know there was one little girl she was close to, one little girl whose mother was hot enough to get Wyatt's attention and timid enough to tell him she knew her place in the world.

He'd followed her home a couple of times before, thinking he might be able to use her to get closer to his son.

His instincts had been almost right. It wasn't the mom he needed. It was her daughter.

Isabelle made it as far as the door to the hospital when she realized she had no car. Hers was in a crumpled heap somewhere. She didn't even know where.

Grant had been thoughtful enough to bring her purse. She checked her wallet for cash so she could call a cab, but all she had was a five. The ATM by the gift shop was out of order. She had no clue if cabs took plastic and didn't want to ask any of the hospital staff for help, because they'd see the ID band around her wrist and try to stop her from leaving. No matter how hard she pulled, she couldn't get the stupid thing off.

She thought about calling one of her friends to come get her, but she didn't have her cell phone and couldn't for the life of her remember even one of their phone numbers.

Helpless frustration made her fatigue worse. As it was, she was having trouble walking around without using the wall to keep her steady. Her head was spinning, and her legs shook.

And Dale was out there somewhere, needing her.

Isabelle pushed herself toward the pay phone. Maybe by the time she got there, she'd remember a number she could call.

The single pay phone was tucked into a shallow alcove. Isabelle tried to prop herself up on the wall, but her legs wouldn't cooperate. She slid to the floor, unable to reach the phone and too weak to stand up again.

Not that it mattered. The only number that came to mind was Grant's. Of course she'd remember his and no one else's. She remembered everything about him, just like she'd always remember how he hid from her that Dale was in trouble.

"What the hell are you doing?" came Grant's angry voice from a few feet away.

He came toward her, as smooth and graceful as ever. At that moment, she hated his boundless strength simply because she didn't have it. "Where is Dale?" she demanded. Grant crouched beside her, pressed a hand to her head and felt her pulse. She tried to swat him away, but even that was too much work. "Answer me, damn it!"

His pale eyes widened in shock at her language. "Dale is fine. He's on his way home."

"Why should I believe you? You lied to me before."

Grant's nostrils flared with anger. He handed her his cell phone. "Call him."

She did. He answered on the third ring. "Hello?"

"Dale, are you okay?"

"Isabelle? Yeah, I'm fine. Didn't Grant tell you?"

Isabelle sagged with relief, unable to even keep her eyes open. "Thank God. Where are you?"

"I'm at a police station in Rolla. They'll probably keep me here for another few minutes before they take me home. Don't worry. I'm fine."

"Police station?" That sounded bad. She needed Keith's skills as a lawyer to tell her how to handle the situation, but there was one thing she knew just from talking to him.

Before she could say it, Grant snatched the phone away and held it against his chest.

Isabelle stifled her outrage long enough to tell Grant, "Tell him not to say anything. I'll be there as soon as I can."

Instead, Grant told Dale, "I'll be waiting for you at home when you get there. See you soon." He hung up.

Isabelle tried to grab the phone away. "Why didn't you tell him what I told you to?"

"Because he's not being accused of anything. He's at the police station because he's a witness. That's all. Hell, he may have even saved a man's life tonight. I wasn't going to let him think you thought he was guilty of something just because you don't know the whole story."

"I'd have known all of that if you'd have told me my son was missing."

"You were in no shape to handle the news. I was taking care of it."

"You don't get to decide what I'm able to handle. That's my job. Not yours."

"Wrong. You needed me to help, so I'm helping."

"I don't need your help with my son."

Grant flinched so slightly she wasn't even sure it had really happened. "You'll be pleased to know, then, that Mathews did most of the work. He was the one with the right connections. He was the one who called in police from all over the area where Dale was, making it possible for them to find him and bring him home safe."

She'd hurt him. Then again, part of her had meant to. He had no right to take the decisions about her son out of her hands. Dale was her responsibility. Not his.

Isabelle was too tired and fuzzy-headed to make any sense out of this mess. The only thing she was sure of was that there was no way she was staying here tonight rather than with her son. She was going to be waiting for him at home, too.

She tried to stand up but couldn't. Her legs were too weak to support her.

"Let's get you back into bed," said Grant. Whatever anger or hurt he felt, it was hidden now. His tone was neutral and his face blank. He slid his hands under her, and she couldn't find the energy to push him away. No matter what he'd done tonight, his arms still felt good around her.

He held her close to his body and carried her back toward her room.

"I'm going home now," she warned him.

"You don't need to. You can trust me to take care of Dale long enough for you to recover."

"I'm going home. My son was kidnapped, and I didn't even know it. The least I can do is be there when he gets back."

Grant stepped into the elevator. "He doesn't know you were poisoned. I didn't think he needed anything more to worry about, either."

Isabelle agreed with his decision, which made her wonder if his decision to keep Dale's problem from her might also make more sense to someone looking at it objectively. Maybe when she wasn't so angry, she'd think about that. Right now, she just didn't have the strength to focus on anything but getting home. Even that seemed like a monumental task.

Keith was pacing in her room when they got back. "Where was she?"

"*She* was looking for a ride home," said Isabelle.

Keith had the good sense to blush at his faux pas of talking about her like she wasn't there. "Are you okay?"

"Fine."

Grant laid her on the bed, and she could see the way his jaw was bunching with frustration. "Get a nurse, Keith. Isabelle wants to go home."

"That's ridiculous. You nearly died today. You can't leave. She needs to have that IV put back in."

"Get a nurse," repeated Grant, more firmly this time. "I'm not chasing her around the hospital again. If she wants to go home, I'm going to be the one to take her."

Keith shook his head and muttered something rude as he left the room.

❧

Keith wanted to slam Grant's head into a wall. How could he support Isabelle going home? She needed to be here in the hospital, where he could finish the job she'd botched.

Poor thing. She'd suffered so much because he hadn't planned carefully enough. He'd never meant to hurt her. She didn't deserve any more pain in her life than she already had.

He wanted to take care of her. She was more important to him than the others. He loved her, and he couldn't mess this up again, which was why he'd planned everything so that he could finish freeing her tonight.

But that wasn't going to happen now. Isabelle was going home, thanks to Grant.

The arrogant prick.

Grant was a man who didn't deserve a painless death. Keith wasn't so cruel that he'd let him continue to suffer the nightmares and constant, grinding shame. He wouldn't make Grant live the bleak isolation of being alone in his suffering, day after day. Keith would still help him. But maybe he wouldn't worry so much about it being easy on Grant.

A quick survey of his knowledge of poisons told him just the one to use. It was tasteless, odorless, and completely lethal, even in small, bite-sized doses.

CHAPTER THIRTY

———⌘———

Grant watched Dale sleep for the better part of an hour, then went to do the same with Isabelle.

Mathews was right. It helped knowing they were safe. Maybe in a few days, after they found Wyatt and put him behind bars, he'd start to believe it.

The police were scouring Rolla for signs of Wyatt. So far, no luck.

"How long do you plan to stand there?" asked Isabelle in a sleepy voice.

"Sorry. I didn't mean to wake you."

"You didn't. My body is exhausted, but my mind is wide awake."

Grant wanted to go to her, to hold her in his arms, but he didn't dare. Not after the way he'd lied to her about Dale. Their time together was probably over now, and as much as he wished it to be otherwise, he could hardly blame her for not wanting to be with him any longer.

It was best if he just played it cool. It might hurt less when she turned away from him that way. "I hate it when that happens."

"You've got to be tired, too," she said. "It's been a long day."

"One of the longest ever," he agreed. "But I'm not ready to sleep."

"Okay, then at least come lie down."

Grant stood still. Not "go lie down" but "come lie down." Was that an invitation to join her? It couldn't be. Not after what he'd done. "Aren't you still mad at me?"

"I hated what you did, but I understand why you did it. I still haven't told Dale the whole truth, so it'd be a bit hypocritical of me to hold it against you. Besides, I'm too tired to be mad." She pulled back the covers, and this time, there was no mistaking the invitation.

Grant pulled off his boots, but he didn't risk taking anything else off. No matter how mad she was at him, she still lit his blood on fire, and he didn't trust himself not to push her for more than she was physically and emotionally ready to give. It made him an ass, but at least he knew his flaws.

He slid under the blankets with her and moved until his body was cradling hers. It felt like heaven to have her so close—to be able to smell her hair and feel her skin and know she was safe because he could feel her pulse thrumming through her body.

He probably should have insisted she stay in the hospital for overnight observation, but he had to admit this was much better. Not to mention the fact that she was an adult and fully capable of making her own decisions, even if he thought they were bad ones.

She settled against him and let out a resigned sigh. "I think we should leave town until Wyatt's found. I can't put Dale at risk again."

"We can go to David's if Dale's caseworker will let you take him out of state."

"I'll tell her it's a vacation. She'll argue that he should be in school, but I'll get his work from his teachers or something."

"If she doesn't agree, you could let me take him. That way you wouldn't be responsible."

"You mean kidnap him?"

"Yeah."

"So you'd go to jail for it?"

Grant shrugged. "Better me than you."

"How do you figure?"

"I'm expendable."

"Expendable? What's that supposed to mean?"

"Just like it sounds. If one of us has to go to jail to keep Dale safe, it should be me. Besides, if they wanted to arrest me, they'd have to catch me first. I'm pretty good at hiding."

"No one is going to jail. I'll get permission for a short trip. His caseworker wants Dale safe as much as we do."

"Not likely, but we'll try it your way first."

Maybe it wasn't too late for him to work with David. He didn't even really care if he got paid. He just wanted to be useful. Included.

"What about Keith?" she asked.

"He's a big boy. He can leave town, too, if he wants."

"With us?" she asked.

Grant didn't like the idea of having another man tag along, but if Keith helped her feel safe, or she felt the need to protect him, who was he to argue? "If you want. We'll talk to him about it tomorrow."

"Maybe they'll find Wyatt tonight and we won't have to go anywhere."

She'd stay here. He'd leave. It didn't sound that great

to him. Not anymore. "Try not to worry about it now, okay?"

He felt her hair slide over his cheek with her nod.

Grant stopped talking, and after a few minutes, he felt her drift off to sleep. He didn't think he'd be able to join her, but apparently he was wrong. Just after two in the morning, Isabelle's cell phone woke him with its jaunty little jingle.

She stirred but didn't wake. Grant grabbed the phone and answered it. "Hello?"

"Help me." It was a little girl's voice shaking with fear, and instantly Grant was wide awake, his body ready to fly into action.

He slid from the bed and headed for the bathroom as he asked, "Who is this?"

Her response was a small, terrified whisper. "Rachel."

Amanda's daughter. Calling in the middle of the night.

Grant forced his voice to sound calm when everything inside him was screaming that something was wrong with the child. Why else would she be calling at two in the morning? "What's wrong, honey?"

All he heard for a moment was a harsh panting sound, like she couldn't get enough air.

"Rachel? What's wrong?"

"There's a bad man in the house, and he's hurting Momma."

Thank God for all those years of training in Delta Force. If it hadn't been for them, Grant was pretty sure he would have panicked. Instead, his mind was already spinning toward how to save the girl and her mom. "Where are you?"

"Under my bed." There was a crash, like the sound of wood splintering, then Rachel yelped in fear.

"What bed? Where did your mom take you?"

"Home."

Amanda was supposed to be out of town. Why would she be at home? He wasn't about to waste precious time asking her about it now. "Can you get out?"

"No. I'm upstairs."

Grant opened his mouth to tell her he was calling for help when he heard a woman's terrified scream. A gunshot followed a moment later. Then silence.

"Rachel?" shouted Grant. "Rachel, are you okay?"

The line went dead.

CHAPTER THIRTY-ONE

Grant called Mathews on his cell while he dialed 911 on Isabelle's phone.

Isabelle sat up in bed, bleary-eyed, but as she listened to him telling them what was happening, he saw her face go pale.

"Rachel," she whispered.

"Sir, do you know the address?" asked the 911 operator.

"Isabelle, what's Amanda's address?" asked Grant, still struggling to sound calm.

Isabelle pushed her weak body from the bed and hurried into the kitchen. Grant followed her. She pointed to an address in her book, and Grant read it off to both of them.

"Units are on the way," said Mathews.

"Police will be there shortly, sir," said the dispatcher.

Grant looked at Isabelle and moved the phones away from his mouth. "Do you want to drive or handle the phones?"

"Phones. You drive. Use every trick you know to get us there. We can't let anything happen to Rachel."

Dale poked his messy head over the railing. "What's going on?"

"Go back to bed," said Isabelle.

Dale's mouth hardened. "It's my dad, isn't it? He's hurt someone else."

"I hope not," said Grant.

Isabelle was sliding her coat on over her pajamas and shoving her feet into a pair of shoes by the door.

"I'm going with you," said Dale.

Grant knew that look on his face. He'd seen it time after time during his special forces training. It was the one men wore when they'd decided nothing was going to stop them from reaching their goal. It was the look of a man who didn't take no for an answer.

Arguing with him would only waste time. "We're leaving now."

Dale didn't even bother finding shoes. He was the first one out the door.

Wyatt heard the little girl's whimpering cries. He doubted she even knew she was making them.

He reached under the bed until he felt the girl's arm. He pulled her out, ignoring her ineffective struggles. She slapped at him, even clawed at his fingers, but she was too scrawny for it to be of any use.

He jerked her hard, so she'd understand who was in charge. The girl gasped, and a cordless phone skidded across the worn wood floor.

Wyatt pulled her to her feet and shook her by the shoulders. "Did you call someone?" he demanded.

Her eyes were huge and red from crying. She made pitiful sobbing noises that shook her thin frame and made him want to shake her harder. Snot leaked from her nose, making Wyatt's stomach turn. He hoped he didn't have to keep her long before he could trade her for Dale. He wasn't sure how long he could stand dealing with the whimpering mess.

God, he hated little kids. Maybe it was a blessing that he'd been in prison while Dale was growing out of this disgusting phase.

"Answer me, damn it!"

The girl looked at the floor and hunched her shoulders as if trying to make herself look smaller.

Wyatt slapped her face, just hard enough to get her attention.

She gasped and covered her face with her hands.

"Who did you call? The police?" When she didn't answer again, he raised his hand. "Don't make me hit you again," he told her.

"Isabelle."

Wyatt smiled. "Good girl. I was going to call her anyway."

Then he heard the sirens and realized that Isabelle had probably called the police. He hadn't had the chance to warn her not to.

Fuck!

Wyatt dragged the girl out of the room, picking up the phone on his way. He needed to get out before the police came.

She tripped on the stairs and would have fallen down if he hadn't been holding on to her. He picked her up with one arm and tossed her over his shoulder.

By the time he'd gotten downstairs, he could already see the glow of flashing lights winking through the blinds.

A frustrated roar burst out of him, making the windows shake. This was not supposed to happen. It was supposed to be a clean trade. He'd get his son and get out of the country without the police being the wiser. But no, the soft little girl who couldn't stop crying long enough to wipe her nose had ruined everything.

Wyatt tossed her on the floor, next to her mother's bleeding body. "See what happens when you try to fuck up my plans?" he asked her.

She was sobbing, holding the arm she'd landed on close to her body. "Momma?"

"Momma didn't listen to me," said Wyatt. "The same thing will happen to you, too, if you don't listen."

The girl shook her mom's shoulder, but the woman didn't move. Blood oozed out of a hole in her chest, but apparently, the girl hadn't figured out what that meant. "Momma, wake up. Please, Momma."

Police cars started flooding the street out front. There was no way Wyatt was going to get out of here without being caught. His plans had to change.

At least he had a hostage.

Grant made the fifteen-minute drive to Amanda's in less than half that. Isabelle's stomach rebelled at the sudden turns and dangerous speed even as she admired the skill it took to get them there safely.

Amanda's street was blocked off by police cars, and they couldn't get closer than a hundred yards. They got out and headed down the cracked sidewalk.

Light flashed everywhere, and neighbors poked their

heads out to see what was going on. Some of the police had their weapons drawn and all of them kept careful watch on the house. In the deep shadows behind the run-down home, Isabelle thought she saw movement.

"There's someone back there," she told Grant.

He took her arm to steady her over the broken concrete, which was good, because her legs still weren't working like they were supposed to.

"It's SWAT," he said.

"How can you tell?"

"They're moving in standard two-by-two formation."

An officer in uniform stopped them in front of Amanda's neighbor's house. "You can't come any closer."

"Is Detective Mathews here?" asked Grant.

More than a hint of sarcasm tinted the young man's tone. "Yeah, but he's a little busy."

"I'm the one who called it in. Where is he?"

The officer hesitated for a moment as if deciding whether or not to cooperate, then pointed to a clump of men near one of the patrol cars.

Grant told the policeman, "I'm going to him."

"I can't let you do that. The man inside is armed."

"I know. I heard him fire a round when the little girl in there was talking to me on the phone. I'm not trying to interfere, we just want to know what's going on. These people are friends."

"Can you please find out if they're okay?" She didn't realize until Grant petted her hand that she was squeezing his arm hard enough to leave bruises. She relaxed her grip and took a deep breath. She had to stay calm so she'd be able to help if they needed her.

The officer gave him a brief nod. "Stay here. I'll go get him."

Isabelle's phone rang. It was Amanda's number. A jolt of panic shot through her, and she nearly dropped the phone before she could push the talk button. "Rachel?"

Grant leaned close to the phone, and she angled it so he could hear, too.

"No," came Wyatt's angry voice. "But she's right here. If you want her back, then get these fucking cops out of here."

"Not going to happen," said Grant. "You might as well give up now. It beats being taken out in a body bag."

"Do they make those in kids' size?" asked Wyatt. "'Cause that's what they're gonna need for the little girl here if they don't back off. I already took out her mom. Don't think for a second I won't do the same to her if I have to."

In the background, Isabelle heard Rachel's pitiful whimper of terror. She was still alive. They weren't too late.

Isabelle nearly crumpled with relief.

"Let me talk to Rachel. Please," she begged. "She's just a little girl."

"You want her. I want Dale. The only way you're getting her is if Dale agrees to come with me."

Isabelle's throat clamped down so hard she couldn't talk. She felt Dale's presence at her back and prayed that he hadn't heard that.

"Sure," said Grant, sounding totally casual. "Whatever you want. Just don't hurt the girl, or the deal's off."

Isabelle stared at him in shock. "You can't—"

Grant's hand clamped down over her words, cutting them off. He mouthed the words "Trust me."

She did. He'd never do anything to jeopardize a child.

Isabelle nodded and Grant removed his hand.

"What can't I do?" demanded Wyatt.

Mathews arrived then, and Grant held up a finger for silence. "How do you want this to go down?" he asked.

"Get the cops to leave. Then we'll talk." Wyatt broke the connection.

Isabelle felt hot tears slide down her cheeks. She could only imagine how frightened Rachel must be. "We've got to do what he asks."

"What does he want?" asked Mathews.

Isabelle made the mistake of looking at Dale. She saw the moment he realized what was going on—the way his bright blue eyes dulled with shock and anger.

"He wants me," said Dale. It wasn't a question. He knew. "Fine. I'll go to him."

Grant clasped the boy's shoulder. "That's not going to happen. We're just playing along to keep him from hurting Rachel."

Mathews's jaw clenched. "What about the woman who lives here?"

Instead of responding to Mathews's question, Grant looked at Isabelle. "I'm sorry, honey."

Isabelle started to shake. Her knees felt wobbly. This couldn't be happening. Amanda was working so hard to build a better life for her daughter. It couldn't end like this. It couldn't. "She might be okay. Maybe he just injured her."

"Maybe," said Grant, though he didn't sound convinced.

He looked to Mathews. "You need to have your men back off. He's twitchy."

"We can pull the units back some. But no way will we let SWAT back off. Not as long as there's a chance one of them could take him out."

"I could take him out," stated Grant. There was no bravado in his voice, just simple, lethal fact.

"I don't doubt it. I've seen your records, but you're a civilian now. You need to let us handle this."

Grant's fists clenched tight.

"I'll go talk to him," offered Dale.

"No," said all three adults at the same time.

"It's me he wants. If he's going to have a hostage, better me than some scared little girl."

"He's already killed at least eight people," said Mathews.

Dale's body went still. "What do you mean eight people?"

"He doesn't know," said Isabelle, feeling the weight of her decision to hide the truth bearing down on her. "I didn't want him to know."

"Know what? Don't treat me like a child," Dale ground out. "I deserve to know what's going on."

Grant's fingers slid over Isabelle's hand in a soothing caress. "He's right, Isabelle. He's nearly a man now. He can handle it."

Isabelle's eyes closed in regret. Things would have been so much easier if Dale had been a child who needed to be protected. But he wasn't. He was already being forced to face his father's mistakes, and coddling him would only make her feel better. Not him.

"Go ahead," she told Mathews. "Tell him what you know."

"Wyatt has been killing people since he got out of

prison. He's tried to kill Isabelle twice now. He sabotaged her car, then poisoned her."

Dale's face went white, his eyes flat as he looked at her. "Poison? That's why you were sick tonight. He tried to kill you to get me back."

"No. This wasn't about you," she said. "All of the people he's killed lived in the same foster home years ago."

"It's my fault," said Grant. "I'm the one who killed his uncle. He may be getting revenge on all of us, but I was the one who caused it."

"No, my father caused it," said Dale, looking a little sick.

The detective's lips pressed together.

"Dale . . ." Isabelle reached for him, but he jerked away from her touch. She wanted so badly to comfort him, but she had no idea what to say or do to make any of this better.

He closed his eyes, pain tightening his face. "If I don't go in there, he's going to kill Rachel, too."

"You can't stop him. Let the police handle this."

"She's right, son," said Mathews.

Dale glared at him. "I'm not your son. I'm his. I can't let him hurt a little girl."

"We won't let that happen," said Grant.

Dale glared at Grant. "You can't stop him, either, I don't care how big and tough you think you are. I'm the only one who can stop him. *I'm* the one he wants."

Grant gave Isabelle a guilty look before he said to Mathews, "Maybe he can help. Maybe if he pretends to go along with Wyatt's plan, he'll let Rachel go."

Mathews shook his head. "It's too risky."

"I'm not taking any risk at all talking to him on the phone," said Dale.

"We've got a hostage crisis specialist already on the way," said Mathews. "We just need to keep things quiet until then. She'll know the best way to handle this."

Grant muttered a low curse. "You think Wyatt's going to wait until some specialist gets here? He's getting twitchier by the minute. You have to do something now."

"You're not in charge here, Grant. Either shut up and let us do our job, or leave. I won't have you making things worse."

Grant pointed to the chaos around them. "How much worse do you think this can get? Does Rachel have to die before you'll move in?"

"SWAT is on standby. We know what we're doing."

"Tell that to Rachel," shouted Grant. "She's in there, scared to death, and we're standing around out here waiting for some specialist to arrive. Fuck that."

Grant turned and stalked away back toward his Mustang. Isabelle turned to follow him, but Mathews stopped her by taking hold of her arm. "Let him go."

"Are you going to let me talk to Wyatt?" asked Dale.

"Not yet. The longer we stall, the better. Phillips—the negotiator—is good. If anyone can find a way out of this mess, it's her. All we have to do is stall until she gets here."

"How long will that be?" asked Isabelle. All she could think about was little Rachel in there, alone and afraid. Something like this would be hard on the strongest child, but Rachel didn't even have that going for her. She was emotionally frail. Something like this might destroy her.

For all Isabelle knew, it might already be too late.

CHAPTER THIRTY-TWO

———❧———

Grant was good at not being seen, and with all the excitement and people milling around, no one noticed him carrying his duffel bag away from the scene. He slipped silently over a fence, being careful to avoid the yards with dogs in them. The last thing he wanted was to have any attention called to him now.

Wyatt wasn't going to stop, so Grant was going to stop him. The life of a little girl was at stake, not to mention Isabelle's and Dale's lives. He was willing to take the risk in exchange for being sure the job was done right, because although the police had procedures and protocol to follow, Grant didn't. He might go down for killing the bastard, but prison would be easier than trying to live with himself if he stood by and did nothing.

He found a vantage point in a rotting tree house that had probably gone so long without use it had been forgotten. The structure was sound enough to support his weight and had the added advantage of a straight line of sight into Amanda's back windows.

Grant loaded his rifle and peered through the scope. Six armed men in black stood waiting outside the back door for the signal to move in. One more was stationed farther back—a sharpshooter. He figured there was at least one more sniper out there, but he couldn't see him. That was a good sign.

The blinds were mostly shut, but Grant could see movement behind the windows, too big to be Rachel. He settled himself and let the world fall away. Nothing mattered but his target. There was no rush. No pressure. Just the feel of the rifle in his capable hands and his breath moving in and out of his lungs.

Sooner or later, he'd get a clean shot. And when he did, he was taking it.

Wyatt paced the room. This was so messed up. They said they'd send Dale in five minutes ago, but he still hadn't come. What was taking so long?

He hit redial. The man who called himself Detective Mathews answered. "Everything okay in there?" he asked.

"Fucking great. Where's Dale?"

"We're getting him into a vest right now."

"I'm not going to shoot him."

"It's just a precaution. Standard procedure."

Sweat rolled down Wyatt's back. They were stalling. He could feel it in his bones. The question was, what for?

A sick, greasy dread filled him up. They were moving in to take him down. He had to get out of here. Now.

Wyatt hung up the phone and grabbed the little girl from where she was huddled over her mother's corpse, bawling. He picked her up and held her in front of his chest to keep the cops from shooting him.

But where to go?

The phone rang, but he ignored it. The time for talk was over. His only chance now was to get out of here and try to make the trade later.

His car was parked a block over, behind the house. He'd sneaked in through the yard, thinking he'd be less visible that way. Maybe he could get out the same way.

Wyatt peered through the blinds. The brat kicked and fought against his grip, so he squeezed her until she yelped with pain and settled down.

Outside, he could see at least two or three guys. They were waiting for him to come out. Even so, it still beat facing the twenty or thirty cops out front.

And he did have the girl to shield him. No way would the cops fire at him while he was holding a little girl.

As far as he could tell, it was his only chance, and he'd better take it while he could. He had no idea of what they were planning to do with him, but he doubted it would be good.

With his pistol in one hand and Rachel plastered against his chest, he kicked open the back door and eased out into the dark.

Grant saw Wyatt peer through the slats in the blinds, but Grant couldn't see Rachel, and he wasn't taking any chances.

There was plenty of time to think. No rush.

The cold sweat sliding over his ribs proved him a liar. This was not the same as taking out a target—killing a man he'd been ordered to kill, or one who was prepared to shoot back at him and his buddies.

This was his call. His decision.

"You can't do it, Grant," came Isabelle's gentle voice from below the tree house.

Surprise rippled through him, making his muscles tense.

"You shouldn't be here. Go back to Dale."

"You *can't* do this," said Isabelle.

"I have to. Rachel isn't safe."

"Let the police deal with it."

"Because they've done such a great job so far? No. I know what I'm doing."

Her voice was pitched high with desperation. "Do you?"

He heard a scraping sound as she climbed up to the tree house and peered over the edge. "So you're okay with killing a man?"

"Won't be the first time. You know that."

"This is different. You're playing judge, jury, and executioner, and you have no right."

"No, I'm killing a man before he can hurt the people I care about."

"What about Dale? Do you care about him?"

Grant's jaw ached from clenching it too hard. "You know I do."

"How do you think he'll feel when you tell him you killed his father?"

Grant hadn't stopped to think about it. He was reacting to a threat with the most effective means he knew how.

"Or were you just planning on not telling him anything? Pretend it didn't happen? Do you think you could ever look him in the eye again without thinking about how you killed his father?"

Grant hesitated. His finger vibrated against the trigger. "Wyatt deserves to die."

"Yes, but you don't deserve having to tell a boy you murdered his father. You don't deserve to spend the rest of your life in prison."

Grant hated it that she was right. Prison he could probably learn to handle, but Dale looking at him with hatred in his eyes? That he'd never survive.

Grant pulled in a breath and flicked on the weapon's safety.

A gunshot rang out, and Grant located Wyatt through the rifle's scope. The back of Wyatt's head exploded at the same instant a hole appeared in his skull. Two more shots rang out—likely one from each sniper. Wyatt fell to the ground, landing on top of Rachel.

Armed men swarmed over the body, but Grant didn't stick around long enough to watch.

"Time to go," he told Isabelle.

"Did you . . . ?"

"No. It wasn't me, and I don't want them to think it was. Come on."

A few quick, efficient movements later, Grant had his rifle back in the duffel bag. He eased out of the tree house and walked casually toward Amanda's place with Isabelle at his side. Nearly everyone was behind the house where all the action was. He veered well around them, keeping out of sight.

There wasn't a single policeman near his car when he stowed his weapon, and he and Isabelle went to find Rachel.

❦

Isabelle held Rachel's hand while the paramedics read-
ied her for transport. She was listless and unresponsive.
The only sign she gave that she was still with them was a
constant stream of tears down her cheeks. Isabelle gently
wiped them away, but Rachel didn't flinch, even though
the bruise on her face had to hurt.

"Can I come with her?" she asked the paramedic.

"Are you family?"

"No."

"I'm sorry. An officer will ride with her, though."

"But her mother was killed. She doesn't have anyone
else."

"No, ma'am. The woman inside isn't dead. They're
working on her now."

Isabelle's heart gave a hard kick. "Are you sure? We
were told she died."

"She's alive, though just barely."

Isabelle clutched Rachel's hand, trying to convey to her
some sense of hope. "You hear that, sweetie? Your mom is
alive. They're helping her right now." If she heard it, she
didn't acknowledge it.

The paramedic checked his watch and made a notation.
"You should go now. We're ready to transport her."

"I'll meet you at the hospital, Rachel. Don't worry. I'll
be there." Isabelle didn't know what else to say. It's not
like she could tell the girl everything was going to be okay.
She knew better than to offer an empty promise like that.
Rachel's life had been irrevocably altered tonight, and it
was going to be a long, slow recovery process—and that

was assuming Amanda would live through this to offer her support.

Amanda. Isabelle needed to go to her, too. She needed to see for herself that her friend was alive and do whatever she could to help her stay that way.

"Be strong," she told Rachel as she leaned down to kiss her forehead. "I'll see you soon."

Isabelle climbed down from the ambulance on weak legs. She felt like her whole world had been ripped apart and she couldn't find the pieces to put it back together. Everything was too big. Too heavy. Even standing was a chore.

How was she going to find the strength to support Rachel through this? And poor Amanda. If she lived, God willing, her life would be turned upside-down. She'd have even more to face, and the woman was barely holding it together as it was.

Isabelle stood there as the ambulance rolled away. She felt like a total failure. She should have found a way to prevent this from happening. She should have made sure Amanda had really left town. She knew what a strain that was going to be on her finances not to be able to work. Why hadn't she predicted something like this could happen?

She didn't have time to dwell on her mistakes now. She had to focus on not making any more. She had to check on Amanda, then get to the hospital and be there for Rachel.

Isabelle turned to take a step toward the car, and her body wouldn't move. She was frozen on the spot, trembling with fatigue.

That stupid poison was still mucking up her system,

making her weak. And she couldn't be weak right now. She had too much to do.

Warm, strong hands settled on her shoulders, and she flinched before realizing it was Grant. He didn't say anything, just pulled her against his body and held her for a moment.

Police scurried around them. Lights flashed. Sirens screamed as more police arrived on the scene and the ambulance left. Paramedics wheeled Amanda's motionless body out of the house and raced her toward a second ambulance. Dale spoke to Mathews, standing a few feet away, his body tight with rage and grief. He'd just lost his father, found out the man was a killer. She needed to be there for him, too.

All of this had happened because Isabelle hadn't done the right thing. She hadn't steered the police toward Wyatt. She hadn't even thought he was that much of a threat. She'd never imagined he'd try to hurt the people she grew up with.

"It doesn't make any sense," she said.

"Something like this never does," said Grant.

"It's over now, though. Right?"

Grant was quiet for a too-long moment before responding. "The rest won't be easy, but at least the killing is over."

It sounded almost like he was talking about something else, but she had no idea what it might be. Nothing even came close to being as big as the events they'd gone through in the past twenty-four hours.

She couldn't just stand here. People needed her. And yet she wasn't sure she was physically strong enough to walk across the street to where they were loading Amanda.

Isabelle forced herself to leave Grant's embrace and take a shaky step. Then another. Grant's arm came around her, supporting her. "You should be in bed yourself," he told her.

"Don't," she said. "Either help me or leave me be. I can't fight you, too."

Grant sighed but did as she asked and took her arm. The paramedic was just closing the back door of the ambulance when they got there.

"Is she going to be okay?" asked Isabelle.

"We don't know yet." The older man shut the door, and the rig sped off much faster than Rachel's had.

"I'll drive you to the hospital," offered Grant. "I'd rather you be there than anywhere else right now."

"I'm fine," she assured him. "Just a little weak. I need to be with Dale."

Grant spared a quick glance Dale's way. "Let me do that. He's going to be angry, and that will only hurt you."

"I deserve it. I should have seen this coming."

"Bullshit," snapped Grant. "This isn't the kind of thing you can predict. There's no use in sparing what little strength you have left on guilt. You need to be strong for him. Let him know that you're not going away, too."

"I'd never leave him."

"It's going to take him a while to believe that." It was the voice of experience talking, and her heart broke for the boy he used to be. Alone, abandoned, and afraid.

She pressed her hand to his chest and nodded. He felt so strong under her fingers. Invincible. She could only hope that Dale would grow up to be as good and strong a man as Grant.

"I'm going to start convincing him now," she said. "He needs to know I'm here for him."

Isabelle went to Dale, not caring that she was interrupting his conversation with Detective Mathews. She pulled him into her arms, reaching up to hug him. She held on tight and whispered in his ear, "You and I are going to get through this together, okay?"

"I'm fine," Dale told her, anger ringing in his voice. "I'm glad he's dead."

Grant pulled Mathews aside and gave them a moment of privacy.

She didn't chastise him for his statement. How could she when she was also glad Wyatt was dead? He was bad for Dale. He'd terrorized and killed people she cared about. She was relieved he was no longer able to hurt them.

"It's just you and me now."

Dale's arms tightened slightly around her. His voice was small, uncertain. "And Grant, right?"

Isabelle stifled a sob of heartbreak so Dale wouldn't feel it. She had to be strong for him and not think about herself. "For a while. He'll have to leave soon to start his job."

Dale nodded. "Sure. Whatever."

He didn't want Grant to leave. Maybe he was already seeing Grant as a father figure—someone to replace Wyatt.

Isabelle realized in that moment that she could give him every ounce of strength she had, every sliver of patience and understanding, every second of her free time, and it would never be enough. No matter what she did or how hard she tried, she could never fill that gaping hole losing his father had caused. No one could.

The future stretched out ahead of her, ugly and bleak, like the gaping maw of some demonic monster. She couldn't keep doing this—couldn't face the pain of more children like Dale. It was tearing her apart to see him hurt. How could she ever have thought she was strong enough to do this?

Her plans for a happy home filled with smiling faces crumbled. The future she'd hoped for didn't exist. She'd been a fool to think it did. Everything she'd dreamed of was hopeless. Every sacrifice she'd made a foolish, vain waste of time. Happy endings weren't real.

Isabelle was going to break down into a soggy mass of tears. She needed to get away from Dale before she did it. He didn't need to see her break down, too.

She pulled away and turned so he couldn't see her face. "Grant's driving me to the hospital. I'm going to wait for him in the car."

"Give me a minute to finish up with the detective and I'll go with you." His voice was calm. Too steady for a boy who'd just lost his father. That wasn't a good sign. Dale had a long, rough road ahead of him.

She nodded and walked away as fast as she could.

CHAPTER THIRTY-THREE

———— ❧ ————

Isabelle spent two exhausting days at the hospital, and Grant was by her side the whole time. She wasn't sure what she would have done without his quiet strength and support to keep her going.

She was going to miss him so much.

Amanda was going to make a full recovery, though it would take a while. Isabelle had assured her that she'd keep Rachel safe with her and come visit every day until Amanda was released, which would probably be tomorrow or the day after.

Dale was quiet, throwing himself into his schoolwork in an effort to help distract himself from his grief. Angela called every day, but so far, Dale had refused to speak to her.

But of all the people who had been affected by Wyatt's actions, Rachel was the one Isabelle worried about most. She hadn't said more than a few words since that night, and she hardly ate or slept. Her doctor recommended a good therapist who specialized in dealing with traumatized children.

Rachel's first appointment was tomorrow.

Grant had given Rachel his room and filled it with things

he'd gathered from her home. He'd spent a lot of time with her, just sitting and watching TV. He'd tried to do the same with Dale, but he wasn't interested. Dale preferred to stay closed up in his room.

Isabelle figured he'd come out when he was ready to talk. He needed a little time and space to figure out how he felt about his father's death. A little therapy for him wouldn't hurt, either. Too bad he'd refused. She'd keep working on him in a day or two, after he'd had time to process the reality of what had happened.

It was getting late. Isabelle sipped hot cocoa she'd made for everyone and watched Grant as he sprawled on the carpet, coloring pictures of fish with Rachel.

"I think we need more green over here. Fish like green plants, like in Dale's fish tank. What do you think?" he asked her.

Rachel didn't answer, but she handed him a green crayon.

"What's that?" he asked, pointing to her page.

"It's a house for the fish."

"It looks great. I love the flowers on the wall."

"They're daisies."

"Beautiful ones," he agreed. "Wish I had some of those for my house."

"Where is your house?"

Grant's coloring stalled for a moment. "I don't have one yet."

"Oh."

"Do you think I could take this drawing with me to put up when I do get one?"

"Okay," said Rachel with a hint of pride in her voice.

"We should take some of these to your mom to put in her room."

At the mention of Amanda, Rachel went still.

"Don't you think she'd like that?" asked Grant, his voice gently coaxing.

Rachel was quiet for a long time, but Grant didn't pressure her. He continued coloring.

Slowly, Rachel picked through the pile of crayons and found all of the blue ones. "Momma likes blue," she said.

"Right, then. Blue it is. We'll make one all blue just for her."

"My daddy never colored with me."

"No?"

Rachel shook her head.

"He probably didn't know how fun it was."

"Daddy doesn't like fun. He likes quiet."

Grant's jaw tightened, but that was the only outward sign he gave toward Rachel's heartbreaking conclusion.

"I bet he misses you," said Grant.

It was more charitable than Isabelle could have ever been, but then again, Grant hadn't been around to watch the bruises on Rachel's body fade. He had no idea what the little girl had been through. It was probably better that way. Knowing Grant's protective streak, he'd hunt Rachel's father down and end up in jail before dawn.

"Do you miss your kids?" Rachel asked him.

"I don't have any kids."

Rachel turned to him and looked up at him with hopeful speculation in her eyes. "Are you married?"

"No."

"My Momma is pretty."

"Yes she is," agreed Grant. "Just like you."

"She's not married anymore, either. You could date her."

Grant glanced up at Isabelle, his eyes pleading with her to rescue him.

Isabelle took pity on him. "Grant can't stay here, Rachel. But I'll be here. And Dale. We can color with you whenever you like."

"Is Dale old enough to be a dad?"

"Not for a long time." Hopefully.

"Oh."

Rachel went back to coloring, and Grant stood up in an unnaturally clumsy motion for him. He asked Rachel, "I'm going to get a drink. Want anything?"

She shook her head.

Grant went into the kitchen, and Isabelle followed him. Her muscles felt rusty and out of practice. Everything about her felt off, like she was just borrowing someone else's body for a while. She hadn't slept much, and although the poison was completely out of her system, she still felt weak sometimes—probably because she wasn't eating or sleeping right.

It was time to get this over with. She'd waited too long already, and she was starting to depend on Grant. So was Rachel. It was best to do it fast, like ripping off a bandage. Let it hurt all at once rather than feeling the pain slowly over the course of days.

As much as Isabelle wanted Grant to stay, she knew he wouldn't. And when he left, he'd feel guilty for walking away from the kids and the problems they had yet to face. She didn't want that for him. She loved him and wanted him to move on with his life and be happy. She loved him enough to respect his choices. Because of that, she had to ask him to leave. Now, before she no longer could.

CHAPTER THIRTY-FOUR

Grant heard Isabelle's light footsteps behind him. He pulled a glass from the cupboard and asked her, "Want one?"

"Sure."

He filled glasses with ice and poured them both a soda.

"We need to talk," she told him.

Conversations that started with that phrase never went well. He let out a small, resigned sigh and sat down at the table. "I'm sorry about that. I didn't mean to make things harder on Rachel."

"She's talking now, which is better than before. It will make things easier on her when she sees the therapist tomorrow."

He pushed her soda across the table, being careful not to touch her hand. He wanted to touch her so badly—to pull her into his arms and hold her. If he touched her even a little and felt her soft skin against his, his resolve would snap. He'd pull her against him, and although he'd only mean to comfort her, he'd want more.

Grant didn't want to be selfish. Not with Isabelle. He'd be a good boy and keep his distance.

"Okay, then why do I feel like I'm in trouble, being asked to stay after class?" he asked.

Isabelle gripped her glass hard and stared at the table. "I think it's time for you to go."

Shocked outrage rocked him, making his body tense up. She wanted him to leave? He'd tried so hard to do everything right, and she still wanted him to leave?

Grant's jaw clenched until he could swear he heard teeth crack. It took him a moment to speak, but when he did, his words were clipped. "You still need me. You can't do this all by yourself."

"I can take care of two kids by myself. Women do it every day."

"Amanda will be coming to stay here soon. Then you'll have two kids—both of whom are messed up right now—and a woman who needs lots of care. Are you going to try to work and do all that, too?"

"I'm going to take some time off work to take care of her. And Keith offered to come every day for a few hours and help out."

Grant bit back a scathing comment about just how he thought Keith wanted to help her. That was just his jealousy talking, and no matter how much Isabelle hurt him, she didn't deserve to see that ugly side of him.

"Why?" he demanded. "Why get rid of me now?"

"I'm not getting rid of you at all."

"Yes, you are, and I think I have a right to know why."

Isabelle rubbed her eyes, suddenly looking more tired than she had since the poison had hit her. Grant had to clench his hands together to keep from reaching out to her.

She clearly didn't want that from him anymore.

"Rachel is getting attached to you," she said.

"So? Don't you think she deserves a little adult comfort right now? If she feels safe with me, what harm could there be in that?"

"The harm will happen when you leave."

"I'll stay as long as I need to."

Why not? He had no place else to go now. He didn't want to go back into the army, and he no longer had a job waiting for him. He could go hang around with David or Caleb, but he'd just be in the way. They had their wives now. They didn't need him.

Isabelle's eyes brightened with frustration. "You'll stay until she's eighteen? Until she's through college? Are you going to be the one to walk her down the aisle when she marries? She needs permanence right now. Stability."

"And I'm not stable?"

"Your life is in Colorado. Why are you acting like it's not?"

He looked at the table. She didn't know he'd lost his job, and that's the way he wanted it. He didn't want her to know he was just another unemployed, homeless loser. He wanted her to remember him as a better man than that. "You're right. My life isn't here. I should just move on before I make things harder."

Isabelle laid her hand on his wrist. Grant flinched and barely restrained himself from turning his hand over so he could feel the slide of her fingers over more sensitive skin. That would be the same thing as torturing himself, and he didn't need to help any in that department.

"You'll always be welcome back," she told him in a voice so sweet it made his throat tighten. "Any time you want to come for a visit."

He gave a harsh bark of mocking laughter. No sense

in letting her believe in some fairy tale between them. He knew once he was gone, she'd move on with her life, even if she didn't know it yet. "Yeah. I can just see it now. Me sleeping on the couch while you and whatever man you end up with lie in bed together down the hall. Thanks, but no thanks. If you want me to leave now, I will, but I think it's best if we just cut our ties."

She squeezed his wrist. "I won't ever do that, Grant. You're part of my life."

"Not a big enough one to matter." He jerked away from her and pushed away from the table, making the chair legs scrape loudly against the floor.

"Please don't do this, Grant."

"Do what? I'm just doing what you asked me to—leaving."

"Tonight?"

"Why not? It's better for everyone this way. You said so yourself."

Isabelle grabbed his arm before he could leave the kitchen. She wasn't strong enough to stop him, but he took the hint and stopped himself.

She stepped around him so she could look him in the eye. His body was rigid, vibrating with hurt and anger.

"I've known from the moment you stepped through my front door that you would eventually leave again. It was just a visit. Was I wrong? Do you want to stay?" she asked him.

"Not if I'm not wanted."

She cupped his face in her warm hands, and it took everything Grant had not to kiss her. He loved her so much. He'd never thought he'd love anyone again after his mom died. But Isabelle had done something to him to bring that part of him back to life. It hurt so much he wasn't sure he could be grateful.

She'd said she loved him, but she'd also been out of her mind at the time, afraid and in pain. And she hadn't said it since.

"You're wanted," she whispered. "More than you know. But I've been through this before. Twice. We want different things out of life. It will never work for us, and I'd rather see you happy with someone else than miserable with me."

She'd given him a chance, and Grant pounced on it. "What do you want that's so different from me?"

"A family. You said yourself you didn't want to be a father. Those two things can never mix."

He'd never said he didn't want to be a father. He'd said he *couldn't* be one—not unless he was sure he could be a good one. There was a big difference between those two things, but he wasn't strong enough to explain the details to her without crying like a baby. She saw him as a hero, and he liked that. Heroes didn't cry, so Grant kept his mouth shut.

Besides, she was right. The two of them could never mix long-term. He'd want her to have everything she wanted, and when he couldn't give it to her, it would kill something inside of him. He'd become bitter and resentful. He'd ruin her life.

It had happened to his parents, so Grant wasn't foolish enough to believe it couldn't happen to him. History had a way of repeating itself. There was no escaping it.

"I'm going to go pack."

"Please don't leave tonight. You're upset, and I'd worry

about you being out on the roads so late. You've been taking care of us, and I know you've hardly slept at all."

"I'm fine. I've been trained to go without sleep," he said.

"Maybe, but I haven't been trained not to worry." She leaned against him and laid her, head on his shoulder. "Please. Wait until morning."

This time Grant failed to stop himself. It might be the last time he ever got to hold her, and he wasn't going to let it slip by. He wrapped his arms around her waist and pulled her close.

The scent of her hair would be with him until the day he died, haunting his dreams, taunting him with what could have been.

"I'll wait." Because she'd asked him, and Isabelle Carson might never ask him for anything ever again.

Dale's stomach finally forced him out of his room. At least it was late and he wasn't likely to run into anyone. He couldn't stand the looks of pity he kept getting, or hearing how sorry people were that his father had been killed.

He wasn't sorry. He was glad the bastard was dead. Maybe if he said it loud enough, often enough, people would start to believe him.

Maybe he would believe it himself.

The stairs creaked under his feet like they always did, and he saw Grant sit straight up on the couch where he'd been sleeping.

"I'm just getting a snack," said Dale. "I didn't mean to wake you up."

Grant shrugged and tossed off the blanket. "I wasn't really sleeping anyway."

Dale eyed the duffel bag sitting at the foot of the couch. A razor, a toothbrush, and a change of clothes sat on top of it. Isabelle had told him that Grant was leaving in the morning, but until now, Dale wasn't really sure it would happen. Seeing him all packed and ready to go made it seem more real.

He'd gotten used to having Grant around. It was kinda nice having another guy in the house—made him feel less conspicuous somehow, like less of an intruder.

"Mind if I sit with you?" asked Grant.

"Whatever."

Grant poured himself a big glass of milk while Dale nuked some leftover lasagna.

"Isabelle would insist on you having some kind of veggies with that," said Grant.

"Yeah, she would. Good thing she's asleep."

"I suppose I should insist on her behalf."

"Don't bother. You're leaving in a few hours, anyway. No point in sucking up to her now."

"It's not about sucking up," said Grant.

He got up, fetched a couple of apples out of the fridge, and washed them off. He set one on the table beside Dale. "Eat it. It's good for you."

Dale rolled his eyes. "The last thing I need is another wannabe parent. Just back off."

"Nope. Not going to happen. You're pissed off at the world right now, and that's fine, but you don't get to make Isabelle's life hard because of it. She doesn't deserve that."

"A lot of people get crappy things they don't deserve. They should learn to suck it up."

"Is that what you're telling yourself? To suck it up?" asked Grant.

"Don't try to psychoanalyze me. And don't pretend like you give a crap."

"I'm not pretending. I do care."

"You care so much that you're leaving? What a guy."

Grant's face darkened to an angry red. "I never planned to stay. Besides, why should you care if I go? You don't need another wannabe parent hanging around anyway."

"Damn right."

Grant slugged back the rest of his milk, and when he was done, all his anger was gone, like he'd just pushed it away.

Dale wished he knew how to do the same. He'd always thought he'd wanted his dad out of his life, but now that he was gone and there was no hope of him ever coming back, he wasn't so sure. At least when Wyatt was in prison, there was a chance he'd become a good man—a chance that someday things would be different between them. But not now. All those chances were over.

Grant stood and laid a strong hand on Dale's shoulder. He should have jerked away or shaken it off, but something in him reveled in the comfort Grant's hand offered. "I know you hurt right now, but I want you to know something I wished someone had told me when my mom died."

"What's that, oh expert?"

His mocking tone didn't even make Grant blink. His gaze was steady, confident. "It will get better. Maybe not much and maybe not right away, but you won't always feel like this."

Dale prayed he was right. He wasn't sure how long he was going to be able to stand feeling the way he did now—suffering through this constant, searing pain, like someone had scooped out a big chunk of him and poured in acid in its place. Nothing mattered but finding a way to escape this reality. He didn't give a fuck about school or his SATs. He couldn't even bring himself to talk to Angela. It's not like they had any future together, anyway. Why bother?

He just wanted to crawl back into bed and try to sleep. It was the only thing that worked. Thank God he had a bottle of sleeping pills to help him get there.

CHAPTER THIRTY-FIVE

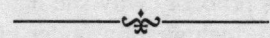

Grant lay on the couch, unable to sleep. Thoughts of what he'd do and where he'd go now that he was leaving Isabelle filled his head. It should have been an easy decision for him. He'd spent years dreaming about what he'd do after he left the army. And now he could do anything he wanted. Except stay here.

Sunlight filtered through the living-room curtains. It wasn't even six, but Caleb had always been an early riser.

It was selfish of him to make the call, but he couldn't seem to stop himself. He felt too alone not to reach out to his friends.

Caleb answered on the second ring. "Hey, Grant. Hold on a sec," he said in a whisper.

Grant heard Lana make a sleepy, contented sound in the background, then the click of a door closing. "What's up?" asked Caleb.

"I was calling to see how Lana was." It was only partly the truth, but it made him feel like less of a jerk for interrupting his friends' rest.

"David didn't tell you our good news?"

"No, but I could sure use some of that right now."

"Lana's pregnant." Grant could hear the proud smile in Caleb's voice.

"Congratulations, man. That's fantastic. Is she feeling better?"

"The flu is gone, thank God. Morning sickness made it worse, which is probably why she had a tough time of it, but they got the dehydration under control and she's home now. If I'd known she was pregnant, I wouldn't have freaked out quite so much."

"You didn't know? I thought you were going through fertility treatments."

"We'd saved up for them but hadn't actually started the process. Now we can use that money to get a house. Fix up a nursery."

"I'm so happy for you." And he was. The tension in his body had started to ease at the sound of his buddy's happiness.

"I just wish you were going to be around, man. Have you got a job lined up yet?"

"Not yet."

"I'm sure you'll find something. Hell, you could be a recruiter from the way David tells it. Mad is working out great. I don't think the man ever sleeps for all the work he gets done."

Grant's hand tightened against a stab of jealousy. "Good to hear. Think David will need any more help?"

"Not with Mad around. That man does the job of three people."

A gaping hole opened up in Grant's chest, and his last shred of hope flew out of it. "Sounds like it's really working out, then."

"I've never seen David happier."

"He deserves it. You do, too."

"How are things on your end?" asked Caleb. "How's it working with your lady?"

Grant forced his voice to a careless tone. "Didn't work out."

"Sorry, man. I bet the rest of the single female population is thrilled, though. Think of all those women you'll get to enjoy now that you're a free man."

Somehow, the prospect of hanging out with women he cared nothing about wasn't as appealing as it had always been. Maybe it was just a passing thing. He sure as hell hoped so.

"I was thinking I'd come for a visit," said Grant.

"I'd love to see you, but can we hold off for a few weeks? Lana's still feeling sick, and whatever time I'm not taking care of her, I'm working. There wouldn't be any time to spare right now, and I don't want to have you come out just to ignore you."

"Oh, sure. No problem. We'll do it another time." He had nothing but time.

"Sounds great."

Grant heard Lana say something in the background he couldn't quite make out.

Caleb said, "Gotta go, man. Lana pukes if she sits up before eating some crackers, and she's all out."

"Take care," said Grant.

"You, too."

Caleb hung up, leaving Grant in the same place he'd been before he'd bothered his friend. No sense in bothering David, too. It was only five there, anyway.

Grant was just going to have to suck it up and move on. He'd find something to do. His military background would help him land a decent job, even if it wasn't near anyone he cared about. It wasn't like they needed him, anyway. All his friends were doing great, and that was what really mattered.

When Isabelle got up the next morning, Grant's things were already in his car. He was really leaving.

She knew sending him away now was the right thing to do. Better now than when they could no longer live without him—when everyone around her loved him as much as she did.

The heavy weight of grief settled in her chest. This was worse than losing Everett, though she thought that feeling that way somehow made her a smaller person. She couldn't bring herself to care. The man she loved was walking out of her life, and he was never coming back. He'd said he meant to cut their ties, and she knew Grant was a man of his word. This was the last time she'd ever see him.

Isabelle wiped her tears on her sleeve before she went into the kitchen. She could hear Grant's deep voice speaking to Rachel, though she couldn't hear if the girl responded. With a bright smile plastered on her face, she pushed through the kitchen door.

"Morning," she greeted them.

"Morning," said Grant. "There's more French toast if you want some."

"Thanks."

Isabelle would eat because it was the right thing to do, even though she already felt sick knowing what she had to face today. How could she smile and wish Grant farewell?

How was she going to stay strong knowing she'd no longer wake up to his gorgeous smile and teasing banter? How was she going to sleep without reaching out for him?

Keith was bringing Amanda here soon, and she had to pull herself together. There was too much to do, and everyone was depending on her. She had to be strong. Later, she promised herself, she'd mourn Grant. Later. Not today.

Isabelle had barely slept last night, and the need for caffeine pulled at her. She poured herself a cup of coffee and filled it up to the brim with milk so she could stand to drink it. She sat at the table.

Rachel's French toast was dotted with melted chocolate chips in the shape of a happy face. Grant's doing, no doubt.

The girl lifted her mug. "Grant gave me coffee, too."

Isabelle peered into the mug and saw only milk. She gave Grant a questioning look.

"Just a teaspoon," he explained.

"I want to be wide awake when Momma gets here. When is she coming?"

"As soon as the doctors check her out, they'll let her come home. It shouldn't be too long."

"Keith called," said Grant. "They're actually on their way now."

Isabelle gulped her coffee down. "I've got to get clean sheets on my bed before she gets here."

"You're giving her your bed?" he asked.

"Stairs will be hard for her for a few more days. I'll sleep upstairs, and Rachel can sleep with her mom."

"Yay!" shouted Rachel.

Isabelle's mouth curved in a real smile. Making Rachel happy again was going to be therapeutic.

"Can I help you with the bed?" Rachel asked.

"Sure. Go brush your teeth and get dressed. I'll wait for you."

Rachel raced off, leaving Isabelle alone in the kitchen with Grant. An uncomfortable silence clogged the air between them.

Isabelle cleared her throat, hoping to break the awkward quiet. "When you get settled, will you send me your new address? I'd hate to miss sending you a birthday card."

"I don't know if that's a good idea."

"Why not?"

He reached up and smoothed a hand over her hair. Isabelle couldn't stop herself from leaning into his touch.

"Because I don't want to be reminded of how I feel right now on my birthday. I know you and I can never work, but that doesn't mean this is any fun. Leaving you hurts."

She wanted to tell him to stay if it hurt so bad, even if his leaving had been her idea. The words pounded at her heart, trying to get out, but she held them back. She was an adult. Sometimes the hardest decision was the right one. She knew that. All she had to do now was accept it—hold out just a little longer until he drove away.

"I understand," was all she said.

"I'll send you my contact information so if you need me again, you'll know where to reach me. But please, don't call just to catch up on old times. Don't write to ask how I'm doing. Just let this be a clean break. Please."

Isabelle nodded. Tears burned her eyes, and she had to get out. She didn't want him to see her cry.

She jumped up from the table and left him sitting there alone.

CHAPTER THIRTY-SIX

❧

Grant carried Amanda into the house and got her settled in Isabelle's bed while Keith went over the various medications she was supposed to take with Isabelle. The poor woman was exhausted and white with pain by the time he tucked her in.

"Are you sure they shouldn't have kept you a couple more days?" he asked her.

Amanda shook her head. "No insurance. I'll be fine once I take the pain pills."

"I'll get them," said Grant.

He left the room and found Isabelle in the living room with Keith, who held a white paper sack.

"Amanda could use some of her pain meds," he said.

Isabelle nodded. "I'll take care of her. You can go now. I don't want to hold you up."

Grant felt a little more of the ground under his feet slip away. He was stalling. First, he'd told himself he needed to fix Rachel breakfast. Then he wanted to help get Amanda taken care of. Now he was telling himself he needed to make sure she got her pills.

They didn't need him for that. He was looking for reasons to stay. Time to suck it up and act like a grown man.

"You're right. I should get going. Long drive." To where, he had no idea. There was no place for him to go anymore. All he knew was that he couldn't be anywhere near Isabelle or he'd end up right back here like some kind of deranged stalker.

"I brought you a snack for the road. Cookies," said Keith. He held the sack out to Grant.

"Thanks," said Grant, taking the sack.

Isabelle walked to the door and opened it—a clear sign she was asking him to leave now.

Grant could take a hint. He walked to the door, paper sack in hand, but got only as far as the threshold. Isabelle was only a few inches away—so close he could smell her. His stomach tightened as if preparing to take a punch. He took a deep breath, and knowing he would later regret it, he leaned over and kissed her.

She went stiff, but only for an instant. Her mouth melted under his, opening for him. His body trembled with the force of his need to pull her against him one more time. He barely resisted but managed to hold back at least that much.

He pulled away, and her cheeks were wet with tears. This was as hard on her as it was on him. That was the thought that finally got him moving. He didn't want her to suffer. He loved her too much for that.

"Good-bye," he whispered.

Her exotic eyes were a luminous green, and he knew he'd never forget exactly how they looked right at this moment. "Take care of yourself, Grant."

"I will." What choice did he have? There was no one else to do it for him.

Keith's hard slap on his back jarred Grant's gaze away

from Isabelle's. "Thanks for all your help." He stood next to Isabelle and put an arm around her. Grant wanted to break it off and use the bloody end to wipe the smug smile from the man's mouth.

"Don't worry," said Keith. "I'll take good care of her when you're gone."

Isabelle took a quick shower while Keith was still here to watch over everyone for her. Besides, it was the only place in the house that would muffle the sounds of her crying. She thought she'd be stronger—hold it all in until Amanda was well and Dale and Rachel had started to heal—but she'd been wrong. The pain of losing Grant was overwhelming. Too much to bear wearing a smile on her face.

Five minutes of tears left her tired but better able to focus on what she needed to do. People needed her now, so she would throw herself into that. Thank God she had the distraction to keep her from dwelling too long on how lonely she was, or how it felt when Grant's Mustang had slid down her street, carrying him out of her life for good.

She dried her hair with a towel, not wanting to take the time to blow it dry. It didn't matter how she looked, anyway. There was no one around for her to try to impress anymore.

When she came out of her bathroom, Amanda wasn't in bed. With those pain pills running through her system, she should have been out like a light. Maybe she'd had to use the bathroom and gone upstairs because Isabelle had been in this one.

Isabelle felt guilty for taking so long in the shower.

She went down the hall, into the living room, and stopped dead in her tracks. Amanda was tied to one of her kitchen chairs, as were Dale and Rachel. They were all gagged with duct tape. Amanda's head fell limply from her shoulders at an awkward angle. Rachel was white and trembling. Dale's skin was red with rage, and his eyes darted from her to the kitchen door over and over.

He was trying to tell her something. Whoever had done this was in there.

Panic jolted through her, making it hard to breathe. Hard to think.

She had to get to a phone. Call the police before she gave away the fact that she was also home.

Isabelle turned around to go back to her bedroom to use the phone and ran right into Keith. He steadied her, keeping her from falling.

"Someone's here," she whispered to him. "I've got to call the police."

"No need, Isabelle. We won't need them for a while yet." His voice was soothing, gentle, and way too loud.

She covered his mouth. "Shh. Quiet. They'll hear you."

His grip on her arms tightened. "They? You mean the bad guys who broke in here and tied everyone up?"

A sick sense of understanding slithered around inside Isabelle's stomach. Keith was smiling. Relaxed.

Why wasn't he afraid? Why didn't he . . . Oh, God. He was the one who'd done this. Tied everyone up.

Isabelle nearly doubled over under the pain of betrayal. It didn't make any sense. "Why?" she asked him, unable to think of anything else to say. "Why are you doing this?"

He gathered her hands behind her back, and she felt the cold metal of handcuffs bite into her wrists. She was so shocked that Keith would harm the people she cared about, it hadn't dawned on her to fight back until just now. Too late.

Whatever Keith meant to do, it wasn't good. She had to escape.

Isabelle shoved her knee up into his groin as hard as she could. He twisted and caught most of her attack against his thigh.

Keith grabbed a handful of her damp hair and wrenched her head back so far she could hardly breathe. "Don't make this harder on yourself than it has to be. I know how much you're hurting. I'm going to make it all better."

He carried her toward a chair facing the rest. Isabelle kicked but couldn't find a target. Her toe slammed into the wall, making pain shoot up her leg. He dropped her into the chair and she popped right back up, trying to run away. Her balance was off because her hands were locked behind her, and she hadn't made it more than three steps before Keith caught her and put her back in the chair.

He sat on her, pinning her in place while he wrapped ropes around her body. Isabelle leaned forward and bit his shoulder, tasting blood. She wasn't sure what happened next, but when she woke up a few seconds later, she was staring at the ceiling. Her head pounded and her arms throbbed.

From somewhere nearby, Isabelle heard Rachel's muffled sobs of terror and Dale's furious grunts.

Keith picked her and the chair up together and put them back in place. A few quick tugs of the rope and she was locked against the chair. Isabelle screamed. Her legs were still free, and she kicked out blindly, hoping to hit something, anything, to make him stop.

Behind her, she heard the sound of tape ripping from the roll. He grabbed an ankle and taped it to the leg of the chair, then did the same with the other. All that kicking and she hadn't landed a single blow.

Isabelle screamed louder.

"Now," said Keith. "I know you're scared, but you don't need to be. It's almost over."

Fear chilled her to the bone. That mockingly gentle tone he used was more frightening than if he'd been raging at her. "Let me go, Keith."

He shook a bottle of pills in front of her. She couldn't read the label, but she was pretty sure that whatever was in there wasn't going to be good for her.

"You're going to be good and do exactly what I say."

"Screw you!" she shouted.

Keith frowned his displeasure. "That's no way for a teacher to talk. I expected more from you."

"Prepare to be disappointed, then, *you demented fuck.*"

Keith walked to where Amanda slumped. He grabbed a handful of her hair, pulled her head up, then let it fall back to that awkward position. "She has the right idea. Don't fight it. Just let go."

Isabelle couldn't tell if she was still alive. She couldn't focus long enough to tell if Amanda was still breathing. *Please, God, don't let her be dead.*

"Why would you hurt her? What has she ever done to you?"

"I didn't hurt her. I freed her."

Freed her? He wasn't making any sense. How was she going to reason with him if she didn't even know what he wanted? "You're insane. What are you talking about?"

Keith's mouth tightened, and his eyes glittered with unshed tears of sympathy. "The pain. Poor, sweet, Isabelle. I know you're hurting. I can see it in your eyes. They're all red and puffy from crying, so don't try to deny it."

"Why do you care if I cry?"

"Because I love you. I loved all of them. That's why I had to help them."

All of them? "Who?"

He frowned like she was stupid. "Our brothers and sisters."

It took her a moment to untangle his meaning, and when she did, a cold lump of dread swelled up in her gut. He'd killed their friends, not Wyatt. He'd killed the children they'd grown up with. He'd staged the suicides while pretending to be her friend the whole time. "I trusted you."

"I know. That's why it was so hard to wait to free you. But you had to let Grant stay here and make yourself unavailable. He was the only one who had a prayer of trying to stop me, but he's no longer an issue."

Grant. Thank God he got away free. At least she'd managed to save him by driving him away. It made the pain of losing him insignificant. "When he finds out about this, he'll hunt you down."

Keith knelt before her. His blue eyes blazed with a ferocious, insane light. He was mad. Completely bonkers.

He put a comforting hand on her knee, and Isabelle strained to get rid of his touch, but she couldn't move.

"Grant's already gone, honey. I don't know if I believe in an afterlife, but if it comforts you to think you'll see him again, then by all means, do. I want to make this easy on you."

Grant gone? No. It couldn't be. Surely she'd know somehow, deep down, if he'd died. "He's not dead."

"If he's not yet, he will be any moment now. One bite of those cookies is all he needed to help him escape."

Grant's cookies were poisoned. Just like her tea. It hadn't been Wyatt who'd done that, either.

"You're wrong. Grant's stronger than I am, and I survived that tea you poisoned."

Keith gave her a condescending smile. "I never make the same mistake twice. I assure you I was more careful in choosing my poison this time. And the dose."

Isabelle refused to believe it. If she did, her world would implode and she wouldn't be able to get them all out of this mess. Grant was alive. Safe. He had to be.

"You're not going to get away with this. I saw you touch the sack. Your fingerprints will be all over it."

"I don't plan to *get away* with anything. After I've helped you, I'm finally going to be free myself."

He meant he was going to kill himself.

The whole situation shifted into something darker. It was bad enough that they were all tied up, worse that he wanted them dead, but now Isabelle had no way to reason with him. He was a man with nothing to lose, and there was nothing more dangerous than that.

She had to save the kids. "Please, let Dale and Rachel go. They have nothing to do with this."

"I admit I hadn't intended to include them at first, but now that I have a better idea of what their lives have been like, I don't see any other option. I could never forgive myself if I left them here to suffer—orphans alone in the world."

"What do you care if they go free? You'll be dead."

"What kind of man would I be if I used that as an excuse not to do what I know is right? Those children are suffering the same way that you and I have suffered for years. Dale would probably end up a suicide before the year was out, anyway. Why should he have to endure all that time when the end result is the same? And Rachel. Once Amanda is gone, she'll end up back with her father."

"No. The courts would never grant him custody. Amanda had his parental rights terminated."

"It won't matter. I've seen decisions like that reversed before. It might happen again." He went to Rachel and stroked her cheek. "You'd rather go to sleep forever than go live with your daddy again, wouldn't you, sweetheart?"

Rachel trembled, and her eyes were huge with fear. Isabelle saw her look grow vacant as she retreated into herself.

"Leave her alone! I'm the one you want to kill. Not her."

Keith stood and an angry snarl twisted his face. "I'm not *killing* anyone. I'm helping them. Do you think planning all of this has been easy for me? I've sacrificed so much to help all of you. You have no idea."

"Please, Keith. Please let them go. They'll be fine. They'll take care of each other the way we did." She nearly gagged but managed to say the words, "The way you're helping me now. Give them a chance."

"I'm glad to see your protective instincts are as strong as ever. It'll make things easier on both of us. The others were easy, but I don't think I could bring myself to hurt you again. I love you too much."

"If you're not going to hurt me, then let me go now. I can take care of the kids. You know I'd never let them suffer."

"That's not what I mean. I just mean that in your case, it won't be an act. It really will be suicide."

"I've got too much to live for to ever kill myself. You're insane if you think otherwise."

He gave her a sad smile. "Don't worry. I'll help you do the right thing." He took a glass of water from the table nearby. "You're going to swallow this entire bottle of pills."

"No. I'm not."

A look of disappointment crossed Keith's face. He took a pillow from the couch, calmly walked to Dale, covered his face with it, and began to suffocate him.

Shock froze Isabelle in place for a moment. She couldn't believe this was really happening. The man she'd thought her friend since she was a child was killing her son.

The beaded fringe on the pillow shook as Dale thrashed against it, trying to breathe.

"Keith, no!" She struggled against her bonds until she heard a loud pop in her shoulder followed by blinding pain. Blackness inched over her vision, but she fought it. She had to stay awake for the kids. Had to save them.

She didn't want to die, but she'd do anything to protect Dale. Anything.

"Stop!" she shouted.

"Are you going to cooperate?"

"Yes. Just let him live. Let him go."

Keith nodded and set the pillow in Dale's lap, keeping it handy in case he needed it again, she was sure. Dale's face was blood red, and he sucked air in through his nose, making a horrible, sickening sound.

Isabelle ached to go to him. To help him.

Keith opened the bottle of pills and poured three into his palm. "Open wide," he said.

"You promise to let him go?" she asked.

Keith shrugged. "Like I said, he's not going to need me to help him."

He was wrong. Dale wasn't going to kill himself. He was stronger than that. He was a survivor.

Isabelle swallowed hard, trying not to throw up. Her shoulder throbbed, but at least the pain wasn't going to make her pass out any longer.

Enraged, frightened tears streamed over the tape covering Dale's face. His eyes were pleading with hers not to do this, but she had no choice. "I love you, Dale. None of this is your fault. You stay strong for me. You hold on."

Dale shook his head, telling her not to do it, but she knew it was the only way.

Isabelle opened her mouth.

Hard, bitter pills hit her tongue, then Keith held the glass for her to drink. She swallowed them, hoping she'd just drift off rather than suffering like she had the last time Keith had poisoned her.

"Only seventy-two more to go," said Keith in an almost cheerful tone.

Another handful of pills went into her mouth. Isabelle swallowed those, too. She had no choice. She was trapped. No escape.

Chapter Thirty-seven

———— ❧ ————

Grant felt sick. Every inch he put between him and Isabelle made him feel worse.

He eyed the bag of cookies in the front seat and cringed. He hadn't been able to eat this morning, but he still wasn't hungry. Walking away from Isabelle had killed his appetite, along with other, more vital parts of him he had no name for.

Another mile marker flew by. Grant swallowed and gripped the steering wheel harder. He couldn't do this. He wasn't a strong enough man to do this again—to go out into the world on his own, utterly alone, with no home, no family, no future.

He loved Isabelle. He needed her. How was he going to live without her?

How was he going to wake up every morning and not know how she was, what she was feeling, what she was doing? And what about Dale and Rachel? He'd grown attached to them, too. He didn't want to disappear from their lives. He wanted to be a part of them—to color with Rachel and make her feel safe, to help Dale ace his test, be there when he graduated from high school. College.

Dale and Rachel both deserved a father figure, and Grant wanted it to be him.

But if he truly cared about them, wouldn't he just keep driving? He wasn't father material. That's why he had to keep away from Isabelle, too. She deserved someone who shared her dreams—someone who would be as good a father to her kids as she was a mother—and that wasn't Grant. He could never be that man.

Could he?

A sliver of hope expanded in his chest, burning so hot he had to pull over to the side of the highway to keep from crashing his car. Traffic sped by him, rocking his car slightly as it passed.

Maybe he wasn't good father material now, but maybe he could be one day. His entire military career had been a series of impossible challenges. He'd met every one without flinching. Maybe he could do this, too.

He wasn't afraid of hard work. He wasn't the kind of man who saw failure as an option. He'd never given up on anything in his life. Why would he give up on the single most important challenge he'd ever faced?

Sure, his dad had been a raging asshole, but he'd also been a drunk. Grant wasn't either of those. He'd made sure that he didn't follow in his father's footsteps that way. Why, then, was he so afraid he'd be the same kind of father?

The stakes. That was why. They were high when kids were involved. As long as he was alone, he couldn't fuck up anyone else's life but his own. If he became a husband, a father, that changed everything. It would no longer be a training op, but the real thing. Real people could be hurt.

Tiny, defenseless people. And Isabelle, whom he loved more than anyone or anything in his life.

Then again, weren't those the very people he'd be willing to risk everything to help? People he loved?

Grant's heart slowed. Time stretched out, giving him time to make his decision. This only happened whenever he had an important shot to make. It was how his mind allowed him to deal with life-or-death decisions, and this was definitely in that category.

Could he escape his past, his heritage? Could he overcome all his flaws and weaknesses to deserve the things he wanted most out of life? A home. A family.

Did he dare to take that risk?

If that was the cost of having forever with Isabelle, then hell, yes. He'd risk anything for her and her children. And he'd succeed. He always did when the stakes were high. He would now, too.

The fact that he couldn't walk away from Dale, Rachel, and Isabelle now had to be worth something. It had to prove that he wasn't a quitter and that he didn't just walk away when things got hard, like his old man had.

Grant wasn't like him. He was better than that. He deserved a chance to prove to Isabelle that he could be the man she wanted. Be the man *he* wanted to be.

Excitement made him shake as he merged back onto the highway and took the next exit ramp. He had to get back to Isabelle. Right now. He couldn't wait to ask her to give him a chance. She wouldn't have to give up any of her dreams for him.

He'd make them all come true.

❧

Isabelle thought she imagined the knock on the front door. Then Keith set down the half-empty bottle of pills and she knew that it had really happened.

A flash of hope filled her, and she pulled in a deep breath so she could scream loud enough to be heard.

Keith's hand clamped hard over her mouth and he gave her a stern look. "Scream and you'll be sorry. Or should I say, Rachel will be."

Isabelle nodded her head just to get him to move his hand. Whoever was out there was her only chance of getting Dale and Rachel out of this alive. She'd stay quiet until he was far enough away he couldn't stop her scream.

Keith moved his hand, but rather than going to see who was at the door, like she expected, he ripped off a length of tape and sealed her mouth shut.

Isabelle screamed anyway, but it wasn't loud enough to be heard through the heavy wooden door.

The knock came again, more insistent this time. "Isabelle, I need to talk to you."

Grant! He was alive. And he'd come back to her.

Relief swept through her, so sharp it stung. She shifted her weight, trying to rock her chair so he'd hear the thud. She screamed behind the tape until her throat burned. Dale did the same.

Keith's face went white and his blue eyes widened in disbelief. "No. It wasn't supposed to happen like this. I planned so carefully."

"Isabelle, I know you're in there. All the cars are here. Please let me in." Grant sounded almost desperate.

"He can't hear you," said Keith in a whisper right by her ear. "He'll go away in a minute, thinking you've rejected him. He'll go back to his car, drive away, and it will all be over." He sounded nervous, like he was trying to convince himself more than her.

"I'm not going to let you shut me out," said Grant. "I love you. Do you hear me?" His voice got loud enough even her neighbors would hear. "I love you, Isabelle. I'm not leaving until you let me in."

"Damn it!" seethed Keith. "Why is doing the right thing always so complicated?" He stomped away, behind her where she couldn't see. When he came back, he was wielding a gun.

Isabelle's blood ran cold. He was going to kill Grant right now. Right here.

She had to warn him. She screamed louder, begging Dale with her eyes to help her, too.

Keith went to the door. She couldn't see him around the corner, but she could hear him turn the lock.

"Hey, Grant," said Keith, sounding like nothing was wrong.

"I need to talk to Isabelle."

"She doesn't want to see you. I'm sorry. It's best if you just go."

No! Isabelle rocked her chair, scooting it the last few inches until she was near the wall. Her head was the only thing she could move, so she slammed it against the wall. Pain exploded in her head. She shook it off and did it again. This time, her vision filled with flickering lights. She couldn't let herself pass out, and she blinked hard to clear her vision.

"What was that?" asked Grant.

"What?"

"That pounding?"

"Dale's music," said Keith, smooth and calm.

"That didn't sound like—"

Dale tipped his chair over, and it broke apart under his weight. The sound of splintering wood filled the room.

"What the hell?"

There was a harsh grunt, then Grant appeared around the corner and took in the situation in one sweeping glance. Behind him, Keith approached, gun in one hand, what looked like a can of Mace in the other.

Isabelle screamed and jerked her head, trying to tell Grant Keith was behind him. He spun around and saw the gun. Grant reacted in a brutally fast attack. One second, the gun was in Keith's hand, the next, it was skidding across the floor.

Grant pinned Keith to the wall by the throat. Keith lifted the can of Mace and sprayed. Grant knocked the can aside, deflecting most of the spray away from his face, but some of it went into his right eye.

Grant's body went limp and crumpled to the floor. His eyes were still open, staring without blinking. He lay there limp, like a puppet with cut strings.

Keith retrieved the gun and stood over him. That feral glow of insanity was back in his eyes. He was going to kill Grant while Isabelle watched, both of them helpless to stop it.

CHAPTER THIRTY-EIGHT

Grant was seething, boiling over with the kind of rage and desperation he'd felt the night he'd killed Lavine, but it didn't do him any good. He couldn't move. Couldn't even blink.

Whatever Keith had sprayed him with was fast, potent stuff. If he didn't find a way to throw off the effects, they were all dead.

He heard Isabelle's muffled scream from across the room. Keith had her tied to a chair. Blood ran down the side of her face, mixing with panicked tears. And her eyes, they were wide with terror and anguish.

Keith had hurt her, and Grant was going to kill him for it.

Grant tamped down the urge and tried to concentrate on what he needed to do to save her and the others. He took a quick survey of his body, trying to move anything. All he got was a tiny wiggle in his toes. Not much, but something. He had no idea how long this stuff lasted, or if it was permanent.

Panic made his heart pound. What if he wasn't able to help them? What if he had to watch them die?

Get a grip. Focus.

At least his heart was still working. Whatever had paralyzed him could have done so to his heart muscle and diaphragm, as well. He could still breathe. That was something.

Keith grabbed him by the arm and dragged him over the floor. "Why do you have to make things so hard on me?"

Grant's foot twitched. He moved it again, just to be sure it wasn't an accident. It moved.

Excitement raced through him. He was metabolizing the paralytic quickly. Maybe if he revved up his heart rate to speed his metabolism it would help. He could slow his heart when he needed to take a shot. Maybe he could do the opposite now.

Keith arranged Grant's body so he could see the room. "Stay right here. I'll be back for you in a minute as soon as Isabelle finishes taking her medicine."

Dale struggled to rid himself of the ropes and bits of broken chair that were taped to his legs. Keith was hardly paying him any attention. He walked by, backhanded Dale in the face, and the boy went down hard without so much as a twitch.

A splinter of wood cut Dale's face, and blood oozed into the carpet.

Rage took over. Grant let it. He gave in to the feeling and let it consume him. His heart hammered in his chest, and sweat beaded up on his skin. He was going to kill Keith. He'd spilled a child's blood. He'd hurt Isabelle. No one hurt his Isabelle.

Keith set the spray can down, picked up her chair, and moved it away from the wall. He inspected her head with gentle fingers. "You shouldn't have done that. I hate seeing you bleed."

He ripped the tape from Isabelle's mouth, and she screamed loud enough to wake the dead. "Help!"

Keith clamped a hand hard over her mouth. "Shut up, or I'll shoot Dale in the head right now. Understand?"

Isabelle went silent.

A buzzing sensation lightened Grant's limbs. He could move his arms now, though he was careful not to let Keith see. Another minute or two and maybe he'd be able to sit up.

Keith poured pills into his hand and pressed them into Isabelle's mouth. "We're running out of time. Swallow faster."

"Please don't make me do this," begged Isabelle around the pills.

Keith smoothed her hair away from her sweaty face. "It'll be okay. You'll see. Just a few more and everything will be okay."

"You're crazy. I don't want to die," she sobbed.

"You're just afraid." Keith's soothing caress over her hair made Grant want to break his fingers one by one.

"Of course I'm afraid. You're killing the people I love."

Keith's face twisted, and his blue eyes glowed bright. He grabbed her hair in his fist and leaned down close to her face. His voice was harsh and biting. "Not killing. Helping. I would never kill anyone. Say it."

Isabelle clamped her lips together.

Keith jerked her head back. "Say it!"

She said nothing.

Keith let her go, walked over to Rachel, and put the gun against her temple. "Say it."

Grant couldn't wait any longer. He felt heavy and weak, but at least he could move. He surged up from the floor and tackled Keith. They went down in a clumsy sprawl of arms and legs, but at least the weapon was no longer pointed at Rachel.

A gunshot blasted through the room. Grant felt no pain, which didn't mean anything, but he also didn't feel the force of the bullet, which meant he either hadn't been hit or had just been grazed. Either way, he was still moving, and he shoved forward, slamming Keith to the ground.

Keith punched Grant in the jaw, making his head snap to the side. He was a strong motherfucker. Stronger than Grant had guessed.

Grant grabbed the hand with the weapon, keeping it pointed away from the others. Keith hit him in the head again, and this time, he didn't bounce back so well. His body still wasn't working right, and every move was slower and weaker than normal. Keith twisted his body and pinned Grant to the ground. Grant had to use both hands to keep Keith from shooting him. Unfortunately, that left Keith a free hand to lock around Grant's throat.

Keith squeezed, blocking off his air.

Grant twisted his arm, trying to pry the gun away. He was getting weaker by the second without any oxygen. He felt like a fish out of water, clumsy and flopping around on the ground.

Behind Keith, Dale's fish tank bubbled merrily, its occupants blissfully unaware that if the gun went off, their world would be shattered. Literally.

Which was a good idea. Fifty gallons of water was freaking heavy.

Grant lifted his leg and caught his foot in a decorative curl of the iron stand. He pulled, but it was too heavy. Nothing happened. He pulled harder.

Fireworks went off inside his eyeballs. He was running out of air and time. If he didn't do this, Keith would live and Isabelle and the kids would be murdered.

No fucking way was Grant going to let that happen.

He let his rage fuel his strength and pulled, using every bit of power he had left. The aquarium tilted. He pulled more. It tilted farther, then fell in slow motion, crashing over Keith's back.

The weight was staggering—glass shattered and water spewed everywhere, drenching them.

Keith let go of Grant's neck. Grant shook his head so he could get a breath of air and not water. As soon as he sucked in his first breath, he shoved Keith's groaning body off of his and looked for the gun. It had been washed away and lay on the floor near Rachel's chair.

Grant's body felt heavy and weak, but he pushed to his feet. He had to take care of securing Keith before he could go to Isabelle.

Dale was already up and working on freeing Isabelle. Grant held out his hand to Dale. "Tape."

Isabelle's voice was shaky. Strained. "Help Rachel and Amanda first. Please."

Dale grabbed the roll of duct tape and tossed it to Grant. He made quick work of securing Keith so the fucker had no chance of getting free. He had plenty of nasty cuts over his back, but Grant couldn't bring himself to care enough to stop the bleeding.

"You okay?" he asked Dale.

He cut one of the ropes holding Rachel to her chair. "Yeah."

"Thought he knocked you out."

"I'm good at faking it. I wasn't any fun for Wyatt to hit

once I went down," said Dale. "Guess it was good I had the practice, huh?"

Grant had no idea what to say to that. Poor kid. But he'd be here for them to talk about it later. He'd help Dale work through things. Grant wasn't going anywhere.

He picked up the gun as he passed it, checked the safety, and shoved it into his jeans.

Now, finally, he could go to Isabelle.

"How are you, honey?" he asked her.

"Just get me loose."

Dale had cut away the remaining ropes and tape but didn't have a key for the handcuffs. "Did you see a key?" he asked her.

Isabelle shook her head. She didn't look good. "I need to throw up. Help me to the bathroom."

"Keith fed her a bunch of pills," said Dale. "Like fifty."

"Less than that," she said. "I counted thirty-eight."

Grant had to make a conscious effort not to panic at that news. No time for a bathroom. There were dying fish all over the floor, anyway. It's not like the carpet was going to be saved.

Her hands were bound, so he used his fingers to gag her and made her throw up. The pills were all still mostly intact, which had to be a good thing. He counted thirty-five.

Isabelle shook in his arms, and he couldn't stand to let her go. He pulled his cell phone out of his pocket, but the fight or the water had killed it. "I'm going to call for help. Just hold on, okay?"

"I'll do it," offered Dale.

"Is Amanda alive?" asked Isabelle.

Grant glanced at her. She was lying on the floor, but she was breathing. "Yes."

"How's Rachel?"

She hadn't moved. Dale had freed her, but she still sat there, staring into space. "She's not hurt. How are you?" asked Grant.

"I'm fine. Just scared," said Isabelle. "I'd really like to be out of these handcuffs, though. Think you can find a key?"

"Anything for you, honey." Grant went to Keith and found his keys in his pants pocket. A handcuff key dangled there next to his car keys.

Grant unlocked them, but one of her arms didn't move.

She sucked in a sharp breath. "I think I dislocated my shoulder or something."

That hurt like hell, he knew for a fact. "Just sit tight and the ambulance will be here in a minute."

"I'm really sick of ambulances," she said.

"This is the very last one. Promise."

"God willing." She sounded so tired. That wasn't good.

"I'm going to make sure of it," he said. "I'm sticking around, Isabelle."

"I admit I could probably use the help for a few days. Besides, you broke that fish tank. The least you can do is clean it up." She gave him a weak smile.

Grant kissed her head, being careful not to hurt her. "I mean I'm *staying*. For good. I want a chance to make things work between us. I love you too much to walk away."

She looked up at him. Her eyes were red and puffy and the most beautiful green he'd ever seen. He'd never get tired of looking at her. "You love me?"

"I do."

"I love you, too," she said.

Grant's soul sang out the Hallelujah Chorus. A sappy smile filled his face, and all his strength came flooding back. He felt invincible. "Enough to take a risk I might screw things up?"

"At least that much."

"I want to do this right. Give you what you want. Be a good husband. A good father. I don't know if I'll be good enough, but I want to try."

Isabelle gave him a disbelieving stare. "The police are on their way. Again. You were nearly killed today. Twice. We have a catatonic child and a mourning teen to deal with, not to mention an unconscious woman with a bullet wound. Oh, and let's not forget the raving, murderous lunatic who wanted to help us all by killing us. You're sitting in a room full of dead fish and vomit and you haven't run away yet. I'd say you pass."

"But I did leave," he reminded her.

"Only because I asked you to. I shouldn't have done that. I'm sorry."

Grant shook his head. "I'm glad you did. It helped me realize I wasn't like my dad. I don't run away when things get tough."

Isabelle looked around the destroyed room. "No. You don't. Hopefully in the future, we won't ever have to deal with anything so exciting."

"Boring would be nice, wouldn't it?"

"Heaven," sighed Isabelle.

EPILOGUE

❧

Grant shoveled the last of the snow from the sidewalk and stretched his back. The last ten months had been good. Not easy, but good.

The only shadow that had passed over their lives was Keith's suicide shortly after his arrest. Grant hadn't realized just how insane he'd become over the years. At least he was no longer suffering.

"Watch, Uncle Grant," yelled Rachel.

"I'm watching."

She slid down the gently sloping lawn on her sled, squealing as she zoomed past him. Grant smiled and wished he'd remembered the camera this time. That was one of those dad things he hadn't quite gotten the hang of—knowing which moments were going to be the kind he wanted to preserve.

Maybe he should just keep one with him all the time. Seemed like lately, every moment was a good one, worthy of saving.

The home of bad memories had earned a new name. Now it was just home.

"Cocoa's done," called Isabelle from the kitchen.

Rachel brushed off the snow and ran inside.

Dale and Angela were holding hands, cute as ever. He'd been accepted at Texas A&M, thanks to his hard work and kick-ass SAT scores. He was leaving next fall, and apparently, he and Angela were getting in all the time together they could before he went off to become a marine biologist.

Amanda was in school, too, working on her nursing degree, which was great for Grant and Isabelle, because they got to see Rachel more often than ever.

Grant had never thought babysitting could be so much fun.

Isabelle set steaming mugs of cocoa in front of them. Her wedding ring sparkled, filling Grant with a sense of pride. She was his wife. His family. He could hardly believe how lucky he was to have her in his life permanently.

"You got more marshmallows," said Rachel.

He gave her an indulgent grin and switched the cups. "Better?"

"Yep."

Isabelle sat down beside him, close enough to touch. So he did. How could he possibly resist touching a woman as warm and beautiful and sexy as Isabelle? He didn't waste effort trying anymore.

"We got a letter today," she said.

Grant slid his hand along her thigh. He wouldn't have a chance to be alone with her until after Amanda came to pick up Rachel, but that just gave him more time to plan what he wanted to do to her tonight. Something special.

The idea made his blood heat.

"Oh, yeah?" he asked, a little distracted by thoughts of getting her naked.

Isabelle gave him a knowing grin. "Katy will be coming to live with us next week."

Grant's heart stopped for a second. This was it. His first foster child with Isabelle. Part of him wasn't sure it would ever really happen.

He should have been scared, but he wasn't. He was excited. Thrilled.

He was a father. David had given him a great job designing security plans that let him work from home a lot. He had Isabelle and Dale. He had Rachel a lot of the time. Now he was going to have another little girl to love, too. He was the luckiest man alive.

"Really?" asked Rachel, her face glowing with anticipation. "Is she the girl you told me about? The one who's my age?"

"She sure is," said Isabelle.

"We'll get to play together all the time, won't we?"

"All the time," said Grant. "When she gets here, maybe you can help us paint her room."

"Purple," declared Rachel.

"We'll let Katy pick the color, okay?"

"But I get to help?"

"You do."

"Because I'm part of the family?" asked Rachel.

"That's right," said Grant, but he was looking at Isabelle. "We're all family now."

Dear Reader,

I really hope you enjoyed reading NO ESCAPE. If you did, you may want to check out the first two books in the series, which feature Grant's buddies David in NO REGRETS and Caleb in NO CONTROL.

I'm currently working on my next romantic suspense as well as some other fun projects. If you'd like to find out more, come by my Web site (www.shannonkbutcher.com) and check it out.

Best wishes,

THE DISH

Where authors give you the inside scoop!

From the desk of Andrea Pickens

Dear Reader,

As you can imagine, swashbuckling secret agents cannot be distracted by trifling matters, such as the state of their wardrobe. They have much more important things to think about—like swordplay, spying, and seduction. (It goes without saying that they are *lady* spies. Men would have no interest in discussing the cut of their trousers, would they?) However, there are exceptions to the rules of engagement, especially when the spies in question have known each other since childhood. So, when three best friends got together to discuss a recent mission—as documented in THE SCARLET SPY (on sale now)—the conversation went as follows:

Siena *(to her friend Sofia)*: "Nice dress."

Shannon *(sounding a little jealous)*: "I had to wear pink, rather than that luscious shade of scarlet." A *sigh.* "Pink is not my best shade."

Sofia *(with a sardonic smile)*: "Well, it didn't matter overly much, seeing as how it seemed to come off you rather quickly. Mr. Orlov has very clever hands."

Shannon (*her face turning red*): Expletive deleted.

Siena (*tactfully changing the subject*): "Nice pistol. Is it one of the new turnoff Italian pocket models?"

Sofia (*flashing up the weapon*): "Yes, isn't it cute? And it matches the trim on my reticule."

Shannon (*to Siena*): "How come we only got daggers?"

Sofia (*with an airy wave of her hand*): "You two are dangerous enough without gunpowder. Lord Lynsley knew he could trust my ladylike restraint."

Shannon and Siena (*chortling in unison*): "You, a lady?" *The sounds of mirth grow louder.* "Ha, don't make us laugh."

Sofia (*arching a brow*): "I might surprise you."

Shannon (*narrowing her eyes*): "What's that supposed to mean? We are sisters-in-arms and have been for years. There are no secrets between us."

Siena (*after a slight pause*): "Are there, Fifi?"

Sofia (*fluttering her lashes*): "Sorry, girls, you will just have to read my story . . ."

No matter how hard they tried, her friends could pry out no further information. I, on the other hand, managed to learn a few more tidbits about Sofia's scarlet secrets. They involve a trip to London, where she encounters the sinfully sexy

Lord Osborne as well as a devilishly dangerous adversary, who . . .

Well, it's a long story, and I'm running out of space here. You will just have to visit www.andrea pickensonline.com for a more tantalizing peek at THE SCARLET SPY and her adventures.

Happy reading!

Andrea Pickens

♥ ♥ ♥ ♥ ♥ ♥ ♥ ♥ ♥ ♥ ♥ ♥ ♥

From the desk of Shannon K. Butcher

Dear Reader,

I'm a planner. I like to schedule things, make lists, and keep my life in nice, neat, organized bundles so I know what I'm going to be doing for the next two years or eighteen months, if I'm getting sloppy.

Needless to say, it doesn't always work.

For instance, as careful a planner as I am, I never planned for Grant, my hero in NO ESCAPE (on sale now). I never even saw him coming until he was there on the page, making me grin.

When I wrote NO REGRETS, Grant was just a buddy—a sidekick created to add a bit of comic relief. By the time I'd finished NO CONTROL, I knew Grant was destined for his very own book. He kept popping up in my head, demanding a happy ending of his own.

Even though I didn't realize it at the time, Grant was born years before I'd even decided to give writing a shot. It was the day my husband taught our then five-year-old son a lesson he called "drive-thru justice." The two of them had picked up fast food on the way home, and when they got back with our feast, the toy was missing from the kid's meal. It didn't matter that our son didn't really need the toy or that there were likely five more like it in his room. What mattered was that he'd been looking forward to that toy all day, he'd been really good in school, they'd ordered and paid for it, and it wasn't in the sack. That toy was important to our son, so my husband declared they would get drive-thru justice. They drove all the way back to the restaurant and demanded the toy. And got it.

In the end, I think my husband spent more time playing with the toy than our son, but that lesson of justice—of righting even a small wrong on the behalf of someone who couldn't—always stuck in my head. It came out in the form of Grant—a man who refused to let people smaller and more helpless than him be mistreated in any way.

That trait nearly landed Grant in prison when he was a teen. Now, years later, Grant is back in the last place on earth he wants to be—his hometown—to check on an old friend who left him an odd phone message he couldn't ignore. But he finds out that Isabelle is not okay. She's afraid, and Grant has never been able to ignore her fear. Not fourteen years ago when he killed the man who tried to rape her, and not now. It doesn't matter that she's a grown woman and perfectly capable of taking care of herself or that she never really intended for Grant to get caught up in this mess.

Of course, fixing it isn't going to be easy. Someone is killing people from their past and staging the deaths as suicides, and bodies are piling up fast. Grant and Isabelle must work together to convince the police that Isabelle's suspicion of murder is right before the next person falls victim.

This book was without question the hardest one I've ever written. Not only does it deal with some really tough issues, but also when I was outlining the story, it was nearly impossible to create a woman who was able to make Grant give up his womanizing ways. I mean, the man has it all—looks, brains, courage . . . stamina. Luckily, Isabelle is more than up to the task of taming Grant and giving him the life he so richly deserves.

Enjoy!

Shannon K Butcher

www.shannonkbutcher.com

♥ ♥ ♥ ♥ ♥ ♥ ♥ ♥ ♥ ♥ ♥ ♥ ♥ ♥ ♥ ♥

From the desk of Lori Wilde

Dear Reader,

Starry-eyed Rachael Henderson from ADDICTED
TO LOVE (on sale now) is mad as heck, and
she's not going to take it anymore. After being
stood up at the altar—*twice!*—on the very same
day, she learns her parents are getting divorced
after thirty years, and it's the last straw. Born on
Valentine's Day in Valentine, Texas, she's convinced she's been fed a line of bull about love.
She's a romanceaholic, but no more! She's drawing
a line in the sand. Determined to stomp out unre-
alistic ideas about love, she starts Romanceaholics
Anonymous.

Except she never counted on one very sexy
sheriff with a heart as big as Texas.

Take Rachael's test to see if you, too, might be
a romanceaholic. And visit Rachael's Web site at
www.romanceaholicsanonymous.com.

You might be a romanceaholic if:

- You replace the heroine's name with yours
  when reading a romance novel;
- You knock down bridesmaids to catch the bou-
  quet;
- You go to the rodeo just to watch the wranglers
  in their Wranglers;

- You wear nothing but a black silk teddy and stilettos while cooking dinner;
- You have a wedding planner on speed dial;
- Your everyday dishes are Royal Doulton's Allure bone china;
- You purchase rose-colored prescription eyeglasses;
- Your voice mail says, "Leave a message, hug, hug, kiss, kiss";
- You've placed your phone number inside fortune cookies and passed them out to handsome single men;
- And, last, but not least, you spray lavender on your sheets at night.

Hope you enjoy ADDICTED TO LOVE!

Lori Wilde

www.loriwilde.com